Final Care

Don Stratton

To Pauline

Any man could, if he were so inclined, be the sculptor of his own brain

Santiago Ramon y Cajal

Final Care

Prologue

THE WOMAN TOOK A DEEP BREATH, steadied herself at the piano, and began playing the complex piece. At that precise moment millions of specialized brain cells—cells reawakened from their dormancy—began infiltrating her cerebral cortex. They weren't her own cells; instead they'd come from a donor.

During early embryonic development these very cells once coordinated the assembly of complex circuits in the donor's brain—circuits that equipped the donor with an exceptional capacity for developing precision hand and finger coordination. Once they'd completed this task, sometime during early childhood, the cells had gone dormant.

Years later, after the donor had gone on to become a world-renowned concert pianist, some of these dormant cells were carefully removed during an outpatient procedure without the donor's knowledge. The cells were cloned, mixed with an ingeniously crafted cocktail of molecules reawakening their genetic machinery—allowing them to once again generate and guide circuit development—this time in the woman's brain.

But something had gone wrong. Something had changed within the cloned donor cells. Something deep in the workings of their internal machinery wasn't stable. An internal clock had started ticking, and time began to run out for the woman.

Chapter 1

JENNY LAHTI SAT BACK AT THE BREAKFAST TABLE on their balcony overlooking the harbor of Naples and watched her husband Charlie reading the guidebook, *Naples: Things To See And Do.* The twisted olive tree beyond the white-washed stone wall that separated their hotel balcony from the sharply dropping hillside to the tranquil sea below provided just enough shade to prevent them from squinting in the bright morning sun.

As she gazed contentedly across the harbor to Mount Vesuvius in the distant background, Charlie suddenly plopped the guidebook on the table with dramatic flourish.

"I have it, I've figured it out. We're going to see the Roman ruins at Pompeii and Herculaneum."

"Really?"

"Right, we catch a motor coach at the Piazza Garibaldi—about twenty minutes from here. It leaves in two hours. It's an all-day guided trip and includes lunch. We'll be back here at the hotel by six."

Charlie clasped his hands behind his head with a smug, satisfied smile. "What do you think of that incredible planning?"

"Awesome, Charlie, truly awesome. The way you were able to sift through all that material and find the *very* one I'd carefully circled with my bright red felt-tip pen only adds proof to your amazing planning ability."

Charlie scowled and leaned forward, adjusting his glasses. He examined the brochure more closely. With mock humility he said, "Why honey, you're right, it is circled in red. I hadn't even noticed."

Jenny rolled her eyes heavenward and grinned, "Why me, Lord?"

They laughed at the old joke and finished their breakfast while eagerly anticipating the day's adventure.

An attractive diminutive woman with light blond hair reflecting her Nordic heritage, Jenny was proud of how she'd maintained her looks since their last trip to Italy, thirty years earlier. Charlie had decided that a honeymoon in Naples would be the perfect way to start their lives together. She'd just graduated from the nursing program at Michigan Tech in Houghton and Charlie was a newly minted electrical engineer. They'd combined the joys of low airfares and Arthur Frommer's gift to American travelers on a budget, *Europe On $10 A Day*, and planned their honeymoon. Frommer was right. They actually did it on ten dollars a day and had the time of their lives.

As she looked at Charlie now she knew it had all been worth it. With two lovely daughters, both happily married and gainfully employed, they were eagerly awaiting the birth of their first grandchild.

The ride to the famous volcano that had erupted in 79 A.D., burying the homes of Roman patricians in the seaside cities of Pompeii and Herculaneum, offered Jenny and Charlie a chance to absorb the history of the area presented by an enthusiastic tour guide named Angelina. After lunch they began the climb to the crater where they were promised a spectacular view of the lava flows and the Bay of Naples. Both Jenny and Charlie had taken care of themselves, staying fit with regular exercise and healthy diets. Neither was worried in the slightest about the climb.

Jenny first noticed something was wrong about ten minutes into the ascent; Charlie wasn't keeping up with the rest of the group. For some reason, he was lagging behind. She slowed down so he could catch up with her.

"What is it? Are you okay?"

"Yeah, yeah. It's just my fingers feel funny, you know, kind of tingly. But I'm fine."

"Are you sure? You know we don't have to do this climb. We can wait until the others return from the crater and just tour the ruins instead."

"No, no. I'll be okay," Charlie said, hiking up his pants and throwing his shoulders back.

They continued for a little longer, until Charlie said, "I can't move my arm. I don't know what's wrong."

Fully alarmed now, Jenny's nursing training took over. She flagged down the tour guide and told her they were going back, Charlie needed medical help—now. The guide's response was professional and caring. She called the tour office on her cell phone and after a moment told Jenny they were arranging for an ambulance to meet them at the bus park where they'd started the climb. They'd be taken immediately to the hospital.

Three hours later, the staff at the Clinica Mediterranea Hospital confirmed that Charlie had suffered a stroke and he needed to stay overnight so they could evaluate the extent of damage.

The next morning, the young doctor who'd examined Charlie took Jenny aside. "Mrs. Lahti, a blood clot lodged in a small artery on the right side of your husband's brain, the part that controls the left arm and hand."

"What does that mean?"

"First of all, he was lucky the damage wasn't more extensive. We've started treatment to dissolve the clot, but he's not out of the woods yet. He'll need therapy to help him recover his normal movements."

"What do you recommend?"

"Well, if he were my father, I'd transfer him to the Caravaggio Neurological Institute in Sorrento for further evaluation and therapy."

Jenny frowned with concern, "I've never heard of it."
"They're respected worldwide for their work with stroke patients," the doctor told her. "They do a remarkable job. I'd be happy to arrange for the transfer if you like."

CHARLIE'S RECOVERY AT THE INSTITUTE was remarkable. Jenny made a mental note to thank the young doctor who'd referred them. The Institute and its staff were wonderful. It had been two and a half weeks since his admission and today had been a good day in therapy. Tony Pompa, the physical therapist assigned to him, seemed genuinely excited about his progress. Earlier that morning, Charlie had proudly shown Jenny that he could juggle five small balls in the air in an amazing routine. He'd never juggled anything before in his life. Tony had told him that learning to juggle was an excellent way to regain the control he'd lost. Charlie had always prided himself on his ability to overcome all obstacles and had been determined to succeed.

Two days later, when the second stroke hit, it was massive and hemorrhagic, meaning a blood vessel had ruptured in his brain. It occurred in a critical location called the Circle of Willis, a strategic arterial arrangement that supplies fresh arterial blood to both hemispheres. The result was catastrophic and Charlie was dead within minutes.

Jenny had only now begun to come out of the fog of the first stroke. Somehow she'd managed to call the girls and tell them what had happened. The people at the Institute had been very kind and put her in contact with Mr. Minnelli, the local representative of Final Care in Naples.

"Mrs. Lahti, Final Care understands the uncertainty and fear you must be experiencing," Mr. Minnelli said in a warm soothing tone. "I'm truly sorry for your loss. Please know that our only business is helping people in your exact circumstance cope with the difficult logistics of transporting a deceased loved one from one country to another. I assure you we'll handle all the necessary local and international paperwork, preparation of your husband's remains and transportation and delivery to a funeral home of your choice."

Charlie had been a vigorous man of sixty, still very much running his avionics software company, SkySoft, Inc., in Sarasota, Florida. Their home was just twenty-five minutes south in the lovely Gulf Coast city of Venice.

"For a flat fee of $8,500," Mr. Minnelli continued, "we'll take possession of your husband's remains and make all arrangements for preparation and air transport back to the States. All we'll need from you is the name of the funeral home you'd like to use. If you're not sure, we can even make inquiries for you. Again, the fee is fixed, and our contract will assure you that no hidden charges will show up later. I'm sure the American Consulate verified the integrity of our company."

"Thank you, Mr. Minnelli," Jenny responded, beginning to feel better now that she seemed to be getting things under control. "The Consulate did highly recommend you, and you've been most kind. I'll be using the Bremmer Funeral Home in Venice. My husband and I made arrangements with them a few years ago. All you need to do is contact them."

"Very good, Mrs. Lahti. Again, we're sorry for your loss, and you can rest assured we'll take care of all arrangements from this point on."

Jenny moved through the next four days in a blur. Final Care helped her arrange for a commercial flight back to Florida. She flew from Rome to Tampa, where her younger daughter, Fran, and her husband picked her up at the airport for the sixty-mile drive south to Venice. Her other daughter, Carol, and her husband were scheduled to arrive the next day for the viewing at 4:00 p.m. The funeral would follow one day later.

Jenny found the presence of her daughters a great comfort. The two girls and their husbands shared memories and stories of Charlie, helping her understand that life would still go on. They laughed and cried together and took some small comfort in the fact that Charlie's death was quick and he apparently didn't suffer.

THE NEXT AFTERNOON they arrived early at Bremmer's Funeral Home so they could be in place when guests began arriving. The owner, Willard Bremmer, greeted the family and invited them into the viewing room. Out of respect for their mother's privacy, the daughters stayed back and allowed Jenny to walk alone up to the coffin. As she did so, Jenny hesitated, realizing that she hadn't seen Charlie since the stroke that had killed him instantly five days earlier.

Approaching the open coffin, she gazed upward, delaying as long as possible the inevitable sight she knew would confirm once and for always that her beloved husband Charlie was really dead.

As her gaze dropped to the casket, the room began turning in circles. Beginning to feel faint, she gripped the side of the coffin, and just before collapsing to the floor her brain registered a confusing and horrifying reality. The body in the coffin wasn't Charlie.

Chapter 2

HUNTER MCCOY WAS JUST CLEANING UP after spending the day doing caulking and chinking repairs on his log cabin on the shore of Lake Superior, just north of Marquette in Michigan's Upper Peninsula, when his dad stepped out onto the back porch.

"Something's wrong, Hunter. I just got a strange call from Henry."

"What do you mean, strange? He's in Florida, isn't he, at his brother's funeral?" Hunter put down his caulking tool and wiped his hands on a rag sticking out of his back pocket.

"Yeah, he is, he's there, but his dead brother isn't."

Not sure he heard that right, Hunter looked sharply at his dad, "What?"

"Just what I said. They went to the funeral home for the viewing, and when his sister-in-law, Jenny, looked in the coffin, it wasn't her husband, Charlie, it was some other dead guy."

Hunter ran both hands through his short salt and pepper gray hair and exhaled. "So where is he?"

"That's just it. They don't know. The funeral guy is just as confused as they are. The company that shipped his body from Europe, where he died, says they don't make mistakes like that."

Giving up completely now on his repair work, Hunter followed his dad into the cabin, ducking slightly to get his six-foot-two frame under the door beam, and began to wash his hands in the kitchen sink.

Ed McCoy put his hand on his son's shoulder. "Here's the thing. Henry wants you to go down there and find Charlie."

Hunter dried his hands, sat down at the kitchen table with his dad, and thought about it. It made sense. Both Henry and his dad knew about the "find-and-correct" jobs he did off-and-on for people, when his work schedule allowed it. And since all three of his current post-docs were doing residencies this summer—two in surgery and one in internal medicine—he'd already decided to shut down the lab and spend the time with his dad at Anue.

"Here's what Henry told me," his dad went on. "Jenny and Charlie were in Italy on a vacation when Charlie had a stroke. He was making great progress toward a recovery in some clinic, and then, out of nowhere, he had a second stroke and died. So they shipped his body back to Venice— Florida, not Italy. Only it wasn't him."

"And they don't know where the right body is?" Hunter asked, shaking his head in amazement.

"That's what they said. The local funeral home guy is trying to get answers and getting nowhere. Henry said he didn't want to ask you, but we both know how good you are at this kind of stuff."

Hunter didn't relish the idea of leaving his dad alone right now. This was the first time they'd spent together since the previous summer—almost a year. Hunter hadn't made it back at Christmas or even spring break, and he knew his dad was having some problems and had been lonelier than ever over the winter.

He headed back out to clean his tools and put them away, thinking about Henry Lahti. Henry was a lifelong friend of his dad's, and was a true "Yooper," born and raised in the Upper Peninsula, just like Hunter and his father. He was a game warden working for the Department of Natural Resources in Marquette County. Hunter had gotten to know him just three years ago, after buying the log cabin, locally known as the "Niemi place," off county road 550, halfway between Marquette and Big Bay. He'd renamed it Anue—"black bear" in the Wyandot Indian language.

Hunter had been away from the UP for quite a while by then, having given up the secretive work he'd been doing as an intelligence agent with the Department of Defense. He'd replaced that life for the pursuit and completion of a Ph.D. in physiology, something he'd always wanted to do from his undergraduate days as a biology major.

Almost immediately after getting his degree he'd accepted a position as assistant professor of medicine in the Department of Physiology at the University of Virginia School of Medicine in Charlottesville.

Shortly after settling in at the medical school, he'd decided to buy Anue, which had worked out beautifully. His dad lived there year round and took care of the place, and Hunter would come up in the summers to fish and spend time with him. His mother had died when Hunter was ten, and Ed McCoy had raised him and his brother Gary alone after that. Since Gary's death, his dad was the only family Hunter had and vice versa.

Everything had been working out great, Hunter thought, at least until a month ago, when Henry Lahti called him in Virginia.

Hunter recalled his initial anxiety as he thought about that phone call now.

"Hunter, It's Henry Lahti."
"Hi, Henry, what's up?"
"It's your dad. I'm worried about him."

Hunter remembered the chill he experienced with this announcement.

"Worried? What are you talking about? What's wrong with him?"

"That's just it. I don't know. We'd scheduled a trip into Marquette a little over a week ago, and when I went to pick him up he was wandering in the snow between the house and the lake. He didn't recognize me when I found him. He seemed confused, as if he didn't know where he was. I got him in the house, and then it was like he slowly came out of it and we made our trip to town. I called him a few times after that and everything seemed okay again. Then yesterday we were playing gin rummy at the Laughing Whitefish in Big Bay and he made some elementary mistakes—totally unlike him. He got mad and cursed me out as if it were my fault. He stormed out and went home. I don't know what to do."

Hunter's duties at the med school had bound him there until the end of the semester, so he'd asked Henry to keep an eye on him until then. Henry had, and while there didn't appear to be any more incidents during that time, he'd reported that his dad seemed depressed.

Now, with this call for help from Henry in Florida, Hunter felt conflicted. He'd just returned from Virginia three days before to spend the summer with his dad and he'd been waiting for just the right moment to talk with him about the episodes. He didn't want to leave him until he had.

Still, he rationalized, a mix-up of bodies shouldn't take long to sort out and they'd have the rest of the summer together to deal with it.

As if he'd been reading Hunter's mind, Ed McCoy emerged on the porch and said, "He really needs you, Son. I'll be fine here until you get back."

Hunter paused a little longer before answering. "Call Henry and tell him I'll catch the first flight in the morning."

Chapter 3

SAWYER INTERNATIONAL AIRPORT HADN'T always been called that. From 1958 until 1993 it had been known as K.I. Sawyer Air Force Base. Located southeast of Marquette, it was home to several fighter squadrons and a B-52 wing of the Strategic Air Command. With the end of the Cold War, the base was decommissioned and turned over to Marquette County.

As far as Hunter could tell it was now the only county airport in the country with a twelve-thousand-foot runway big enough to land the space shuttle.

After changing planes in Detroit he landed at Tampa shortly before noon. Henry spotted him first as he exited the secured area.

"Hunter, good to see you," Henry said, as the two men shook hands. "Thanks for coming."

Hunter towered over the smaller man. "Come on, Henry. You didn't really have any doubt now, did you?"

Henry smiled and shook his head. "I know you're worried about your dad," he said. "Have you had a chance to talk with him about—you know?"

"Not yet, but I will—soon. He insisted you needed my help more than he did."

Henry nodded. "He would."

As they were crossing the Sunshine Skyway Bridge over Tampa Bay on the eighty-minute drive south to

Venice, Henry said, "My sister-in-law, Jenny, wants to hire you."

Surprised at this, Hunter said, "Are you sure she can afford to pay me? I know you can't, so don't worry about it. I'll just help her out as a freebee for a good friend—you."

"No, no, don't give up your pay so quickly. Believe me, she can afford it."

"How's that?"

"I never told you about my brother, did I? After graduating from Michigan Tech in electrical engineering, he became a software engineer. Started his own company, SkySoft, Incorporated, in Sarasota. He turned out to be an expert at developing avionics software for the aircraft industry. Those big planes are full of computers and somebody has to write programs for them. That was Charlie.

"Eventually his company began building hardware and software exclusively for military aircraft. Today his stuff is in virtually every new piece of flying military equipment. His company is worth hundreds of millions."

Hunter whistled softly. "Wow." He gazed out the window at the turquoise waters of Tampa Bay. "So what do the local funeral home people say about losing a body?"

"They're as confused as we are, since they didn't do the preparation work. A company in Brussels that specializes in that sort of thing shipped the body to them, or rather they were supposed to. They came highly recommended, and assured Jenny they'd take care of everything—preparing the body, all the paperwork, everything."

When they finally reached Venice, Henry said, "We're going right to Charlie's house on the island."

"He lives—lived—on an island?"

"Well, sort of. Apparently the island of Venice isn't a natural island, but was created."

"Created?" Hunter chuckled, his green eyes sparkling. "How do you create an island?"

"It seems the Intracoastal Waterway, which extends south from Tampa to Fort Myers, didn't have the consideration to include Venice, so the town fathers dug a channel just east of the city to connect the north and south waterways. This technically turned the charming city of Venice into an island."

JENNY'S HOME WAS A BEAUTIFUL three-story house about twenty years old, situated conveniently three blocks from Venice's picturesque downtown shopping street. The house faced the Gulf of Mexico, with a sand beach for a front yard.

Jenny Lahti appeared to be in her late fifties or early sixties, with light blond hair cut short in an attractive style, framing a beautiful high-cheekboned face. Dressed in white slacks and a pale green cardigan sweater over a white blouse, she smiled at Hunter and firmly shook his outstretched hand.

"It's a pleasure to meet you, Hunter. Henry's told me all about you. He seems to think you can do anything. Can you find my Charlie for me?"

Hunter liked her directness and sincerity. He decided to be equally direct. "Yes, I'm sure I can."

She invited them all to sit, and Hunter, choosing the sofa, began. "Mrs. Lahti—"

"Oh please, call me Jenny. A little less formality is in order, don't you think, given the circumstances?"

"Jenny it is then," said Hunter. "Did the funeral director know your husband?"

"No, not really. We both went to see him a few years ago to get our arrangements in order ahead of time. You know, so we wouldn't have to deal with all that at a time when it might be too hard. When one of us would be gone, so to speak." Her soft pale eyes turned misty as she said this.

Hunter could imagine.

"He only saw Charlie that one time, and only for a half hour or so. So no, Mr. Bremmer didn't know him, and I'm sure the poor man didn't have any idea the body he received wasn't Charlie."

"About that, I understand he called Final Care to find out what happened. Did he learn anything?"

"They told him they don't make mistakes like that, but they'd look into it."

Hunter nodded, thinking it sounded like they were covering their butts and circling the wagons. "I see. Well, I'll start with Mr. Bremmer."

Henry stood up. "Take my rental car; I'll stay here with Jenny."

Following Hunter to the door, Jenny said, "And come back here later. I'll make dinner for us. And before you say no, I need the diversion. I'll enjoy doing it. My daughters and their husbands will be here too. You can meet them all."

Hunter found his way to Bremmer's Funeral Home. It was just off Business 41, also known as the Tamiami Trail, or just "the Trail" to locals. It resembled funeral homes throughout the country, a large two-story, white frame house, with a drive-through portico and a one-story flat extension on the back where, Hunter assumed, the work with the bodies was done.

He found Willard Bremmer in his office near the front entrance to the main building. He was tall and thin and had a kindly smile that softened his otherwise classic undertaker look. Dressed impeccably in a dark suit and tie, he invited Hunter in and asked him to take a chair.

"Mr. Bremmer, I'm a friend of the Lahti family. I want to ask you about the missing man, Charlie Lahti."

"Yes, yes, it's terrible. I'm afraid I still don't have an answer. Final Care said they were looking into it. Can you believe that? Looking into it? They lost a body and they're looking into it? I've never heard of such a thing, and my family has been in this business, right here, over fifty years."

Suddenly cautious, as if Hunter might be bringing news of a lawsuit, he paused, "I'm sorry, what did you say your interest was in this business?"

"Relax, Mr. Bremmer, I'm on your side here. I am a friend of the late Mr. Lahti's brother. Mrs. Lahti asked me to help find her husband's body. I've got considerable skills in finding missing people—and things—and I'll help you solve this problem. She fully understands it's not your fault."

Hunter could see the man begin to relax a little. "Call me Hunter. May I call you Willard?"

Still cautious, Bremmer said, "Certainly, Willard it is."

"All right, Willard, can you tell me what you know about Final Care? Have you worked with them before? Are they reputable?"

"Yes, they've been in business a long time. Americans regularly die abroad and with so many retirees here in southwest Florida who have the time and money to travel to Europe, I'm sure Florida has more than her share. I've dealt with them twice in the past. Each time it went perfectly. There were no problems."

"What did they tell you when you called and told them they'd shipped you the wrong body?"

Bremmer exhaled in righteous indignation. "Can you believe this? The man said, 'That's not possible.' I told him maybe he'd like to try explaining that to the dead man's wife and the family of whoever they sent me."

Hunter chuckled. "A real bureaucrat, eh?"

"I've got another word for it," grumbled Bremmer just as his phone rang.

"Excuse me," he said, picking it up. "This is Willard Bremmer." During the call Hunter watched as a procession of emotions played out over Bremmer's face. Whatever the caller was saying took some time. Finally, Willard spoke. "No, I don't understand. Is the body in Tampa or isn't it?" Bremmer listened, shaking his head in disbelief. "No, I don't understand at all. You're telling me the deceased, Mr. Charles Lahti, was sent to Johnson's Funeral Home in Tampa by mistake instead of to me in Venice. Is that right? Bremmer looked at Hunter and rolled his eyes in disbelief. "Yes, yes. Certainly, I can drive Mr. Cole's body to Tampa, and then I'll drive Mr. Lahti's body back here. That'll straighten this mess out."

Bremmer listened to a lengthy one-sided conversation on the phone. Finally, he sighed deeply and looked up at the ceiling in seeming despair. Then suddenly he sat straight up. "Miami?" What are you talking about? What's it doing in Miami?"

After a pause Bremmer practically shouted, "You're not at liberty to say? What the hell does that mean?"

After another pause while Bremmer listened with growing exasperation on his face, he nearly shouted, "What do you mean you don't know when the body will be released?"

After another two or three minutes during which Bremmer became even more agitated, he finally slammed the phone back in its cradle and stood up. He stomped around the room and then sat back down and faced Hunter, exhaling loudly.

"I don't believe this. I just don't believe it."

Hunter waited for Bremmer to calm himself.

After another extended exhale, Bremmer explained. "This is just crazy. All right, okay, here's the story. Two men died, Charles Lahti and Richard Cole—that's the name of the body they sent me by mistake. Both were embalmed at the same time at Final Care's European facility in Brussels. Mr. Lahti's body was mistakenly linked with Mr. Cole's papers and sent to Johnson's Funeral Home in Tampa, while Mr. Cole's body, accompanied by Mr. Lahti's papers, was sent here.

"Sounds like that explains the mix-up. So what's the bit with Miami?" Hunter asked, unwrapping a piece of spearmint gum and popping it in his mouth.

"I don't understand it, something about the screw-up and preventing it from happening again. Somebody from the Caravaggio Neurological Institute will be flying into Miami from Italy the day after tomorrow. Apparently Final Care has a US staging facility at the International Airport in Miami."

Hunter sat bolt upright. "Wait a minute, that Institute— that's the place that was treating Charlie Lahti after his stroke. According to Jenny, he was making great progress there when he died of a second stroke."

Willard held his palms up imploringly. "Why would someone from a medical institute have to fly to Miami if Final Care was responsible for the mistake?"

"Exactly what I'm wondering," answered Hunter. "And why would Final Care even cooperate with the Caravaggio Institute? Why would they send the body to the facility in Miami? It seems to me their obligation is to the two families they have contracts with and not some medical institute in Italy."

That evening over dinner, Hunter met Jenny's family and explained what Bremmer had learned about the mix up and that Charlie's body was in Miami. He told them that someone from the Institute where Charlie had died was coming to Miami to prevent it from occurring again.

"What would the Institute have to do with it, Mr. McCoy?" Jenny's daughter Carol asked.

"That, Carol, is what I'm going to Miami to find out."

Chapter 4

HUNTER RENTED A CAR AT TWO the next afternoon and drove to Miami where he checked into the Courtyard Miami Airport hotel planning to go to the Final Care facility first thing in the morning. He grabbed a surprisingly good dinner in the hotel restaurant, went up to his room on the fifth floor, opened his laptop, logged into the hotel's Wi-Fi system, and got to work.

He began with Final Care's website. They were big. The company had been founded in 1987 in Brussels, when an official at the American Consulate had died suddenly and it fell to the Consul General to have the body shipped home for burial. He'd phoned a local funeral home called Flanders and arranged for them to prepare and ship the body back to the States. Even though Flanders Funeral Home was a new young company, they did such a thorough and professional job that the Consulate continued to recommend them whenever American citizens died in Belgium.

Flanders quickly become expert at handling the voluminous and complicated legal paperwork necessary for repatriating deceased Americans—either their bodies or cremains — from Belgium. All the embalming and prep-aration work was done at their facility in Brussels. And they were savvy enough to recognize the need for their unique product among distressed Americans when someone died elsewhere abroad.

As he read on, even Hunter could see the potential for expansion throughout Europe. As their business grew, American consulates in the neighboring countries of Germany and France began referring inquiries from Americans to Flanders. Apparently each of the European Union countries had its own unique laws and statutes governing the handling of deceased foreigners within their borders. Flanders—later renamed Final Care—mastered them all, expanding over the next decade to cover the entire continent. Now, Final Care had offices in all major and minor European cities and most Middle Eastern and North African tourist areas as well.

Hunter followed multiple links from the Final Care homepage and learned that unless the death was questioned in some way by the local authorities, Final Care could have a representative meet with loved ones of the deceased within hours of the death and arrange for transport of the body to the Final Care facility in Brussels for pre-flight preparation, including embalming or cremation. They would also arrange for transport to the funeral home of choice in the deceased's home city.

The Final Care facility at Miami International Airport was mostly used for temporary storage when a time lag occurred between connecting flights from Europe to their final destinations in the United States. They also used the Miami facility to embalm and prep bodies in cases where the family wanted it done in the States rather than Europe.

To Hunter's eye, they looked like a well-run outfit. Their fees were clear and up front and seemed reasonable. The list of testimonials from satisfied customers was long and impressive.

He sat back and pushed the laptop away from him. *Why would an outfit like this give Bremmer such a hard time? It doesn't make any sense.*

He looked up the Caravaggio Neurological Institute in Sorrento, Italy, where Charlie had died. Their homepage featured a beautiful medical campus set in the mountainous hillside of Sorrento, overlooking the Bay of Naples with Mount Vesuvius in the background. There were photos of medical staff in crisp white coats walking purposefully across beautifully manicured lawns.

Hunter clicked on the Staff link and saw they had forty-two permanent staff physicians. Several were Americans. He was impressed to recognize a Nobel laureate in physiology and medicine on the staff. Because physiology was Hunter's own field, he even knew the man. They'd met professionally several times at international research meetings.

Next he opened the link to Services performed at the Institute. It appeared to Hunter they were a fully functioning hospital with rehab facilities and a medical research center specializing in neurological disease. They had clinical programs in epilepsy, Alzheimer's disease, multiple sclerosis, neuromuscular disease, stroke, and sleep disorders.

Nero Caravaggio, an Italian neuroscientist, had founded the Institute in 2004. He was internationally recognized for his research in neuroplasticity. His early work focused on the mechanism by which nerve cells develop highly efficient connections with other neurons and muscle cells as motor skills develop.

Nothing unusual here. They look like an outstanding operation. Why would the Institute send someone to Miami to see Charlie's body because of a mistake made by a funeral business?

Chapter 5

SIX O'CLOCK IN THE MORNING was Doctor Nero Caravaggio's favorite time in the laboratory. He liked to arrive early, before his two research assistants, so he could plan the day's experiments without the interference of their well-meaning but distracting suggestions. It wasn't that they weren't brilliant, they were, and he valued their input—but only after explaining his own thinking first.

He'd had no idea when he'd begun his studies on neuroplasticity over twenty-five years earlier, that he'd have so much success. His groundbreaking work speeding up and promoting nerve plasticity, the ability of nerve cells to grow and develop new sprouts, was legendary. When a nerve to a muscle is cut or damaged, the neurons—nerve cells in the nerve—no longer send impulses and the muscle is paralyzed. Nero developed a procedure for promoting growth in the damaged neurons so they'd grow new extensions that would re-innervate the muscle cells. In this way the paralysis could be overcome.

A major part of the process entailed applying a mixture of nerve growth factors and gene stimulants he'd ingeniously developed to the damaged nerve along with sufficient stimulation to cause its neurons to begin the repair process. The medical community had come to refer to this mixture as *Enhancement*.

The potential for this technique to enhance nerve cell growth and development, and thus treat neurological paralytic disorders, brought Caravaggio international prominence, leading in turn to the vast sums of money that allowed him to create the Caravaggio Neurological Institute.

Already, his early work promoted new discoveries in laboratories around the world. Researchers were now using this core information to make significant headway in the treatment of spinal cord injuries, even getting new growth in spinal neurons that were thought to be beyond help when damaged.

Nero was proud to have attracted so many highly qualified physicians and scientists to work at the Institute, allowing it to grow far beyond his wildest dreams. Their patient records listed prominent people from around the world who could afford the very best treatment. He was frequently in the running for the Nobel Prize in Physiology and Medicine himself, and someday he'd probably get it.

But enough reminiscing, Nero thought; time to get on with the day's work. He would have the lab to himself, since his two research assistants were in London at a research conference, a conference he'd sent them to. They'd be gone for a week.

Although Nero would turn sixty-two in a week, his dark black hair, which he wore combed straight back close to his head, showed no hint of gray. He stood only five foot six, but his rather round face featured intelligent blue eyes and an expression that said to anyone talking to him, "I'm paying attention to what you're saying, and it'd better make sense or don't waste my time."

Today he'd perform a ritual he'd started sixteen months ago, right after he'd first tried a new version of *Enhancement* he'd called *Enhancement II* and saw its incredibly promising results in a program he'd been conducting on a secret experimental basis, a program only a few other members of his professional staff knew about.

It was almost as if his lab had two faces, a public one that showcased the research he and the two research assistants conducted and published for the scientific community at large, and the secret one operating below the radar.

Nero removed a small vial of *Enhancement II* from his white lab coat pocket and took it to a large instrument against the back wall of the laboratory. Earlier he'd taken the vial from a locked refrigerator in his office that only he had access to.

He unwrapped a new syringe and needle from a drawer in a desk next to the instrument, then pierced the vial's rubber top, removed a small amount of the liquid within, and injected it into a tube specially designed to fit into a compartment of the instrument. Next, just as he had every thirty days for the past sixteen months, he activated the instrument and eagerly watched the data unfold on the screen.

When he was satisfied, he printed out the results and placed them in a folder he'd take home and securely store in his personal wall safe. He also carefully wrapped the used syringe and vials in a paper cup he'd take back to his office for secure disposal.

Walking back to his office with a satisfied smile on his face, he thought back to the breakthrough moment when he'd finally figured out the ingredient that was missing in *Enhancement* — the ingredient needed to convert it to *Enhancement II*.

The realization of what was missing came to him, oddly enough, while he was taking his young nephew on a tour of the ruins at Pompeii almost two years earlier. An appreciative smile spread across his face as he recalled the story told by the young tour guide, Nikko.

NIKKO HAD TOLD THE GROUP THAT THE ONLY real account of what had happened during the eruption of Vesuvius was to be found in two letters written by Pliny the Younger to his friend Tacitus, a historian, in which he described, among other things, the rescue work undertaken by his uncle, Pliny the Elder.

Nikko went on to tell them that those two letters had been preserved and known for hundreds of years—nothing new there. Remarkably however, historians had recently uncovered a third letter from Pliny the Younger to Tacitus, a letter just published in the prestigious *Journal of Archeological Research.*

This third letter told the story of a young slave boy, Felix, and his sister, Livia, the only survivors of a noble family of four who were racing for the seashore during the eruption with plans to take the family boat across the bay to Misenum and safety.

Livia and Felix accompanied the twin brothers of the family, Lucius and Manius, both of whom were skilled archers. Felix, an extremely clumsy boy, was forced to carry the twins' valuables—in this case their archery equipment, bows, arrows, and quivers.

Apparently Felix stumbled on a rock, fell forward, and lost his grip on one of the quivers, and its arrows fell out. One of them lodged between the rocks with its arrowhead pointing up. As Felix stumbled he accidentally tripped Lucius, who fell forward onto the upturned arrow, which penetrated his skull, killing him instantly. His twin, Manius, enraged at Felix, pulled the arrow from Lucius and stabbed the slave boy in the head—in exactly the same spot.

Then, in what must have been a remarkably brave move, Livia grabbed Lucius's knife and killed Manius. Seeing that now both Lucius and Manius were dead, and that Felix was still breathing, Livia pulled the arrow from his head and tried to save him. She dragged him to the beach, now only twenty yards away, where she managed to find a family who took them aboard their boat, and they set off for Misenum. The family knew Livia and Felix were slaves, but given that their master and his family had apparently perished at Pompeii, formally granted them their freedom. They looked after the siblings, and amazingly Felix, who didn't die, recovered remarkably well over the course of the next year. Livia told Pliny her brother had always been clumsy and uncoordinated. Nevertheless, after his recovery, a remarkable thing happened. His clumsiness began to disappear, and he developed a coordination he'd never had before. He was suddenly able to toss rocks and hit a target. He no longer threw like a girl, in his sister's words. He could climb a ladder and not fall. Moreover, most amazing of all, Felix developed incredible skills as an archer.

"GOOD MORNING DR. CARAVAGGIO," said Nero's secretary as he approached his office, the young woman's jubilance, startling him out of his reverie.

"Good morning, Nina."

In his office, gazing out over the Bay of Naples, Nero remembered that hearing the story of the slave boy and the arrow was like having a veil lifted from his eyes. Suddenly, with an incredible clarity, he realized what had been missing from the secret project he'd been working on—the factor that would allow his research to reach its maximum potential. It was buried in that story, and he was sure he knew how to find it.

Chapter 6

HUNTER SLEPT THROUGH THE NIGHT with no dreams—an unusual occurrence for him—and awoke to a gray concrete sky and a light but persistent rain. The waitress in the hotel's breakfast room told him it wasn't unusual in the summer but usually happened in the afternoon. *So much for sunny Florida*, he thought.

The Final Care facility turned out to be a warehouse on the periphery of Miami International Airport, much like the freight and hangar buildings seen around all major airports. He parked outside the building and looked around to find a front entrance.

The single story structure was clearly not designed for walk-in customers. It featured several large garage-type doors through which, presumably, trucks or other large vehicles could enter. Hunter finally spotted a small doorway with a sign over it that read Final Care. Two cement blocks, a pail, and a pile of rags were standing guard to one side.

Opening the door he walked into a small entrance-like area with a water cooler, a desk, a chair, and a file cabinet. If there'd been a receptionist, Hunter assumed she'd be here at this desk. Off this room he could see a small office fronted by a large glass window. Looking in, he saw it too was empty.

Where is everybody?

He noticed a closed door at the back of the room with a sign that said NO ADMITTANCE. Seeing no bell on the desk to ring for service, he opened the NO ADMITTANCE door and stepped into a long hallway with multiple doors leading off it.

"Hey, what are you doing back there?" a man's voice shouted behind him.

Hunter turned to see a large man entering the outer office through the same door he'd just used. He must have been outside the building, Hunter thought.

"You're not allowed back there. Who the hell are you?"

Hunter walked back into the office area and ignoring the man's rudeness put his hand out. "Hunter McCoy. I came in a minute ago and no one was around. I stepped in here to find somebody."

The man ignored his outstretched hand. "Jim Dyson, manager. Whaddya want?"

"How about we sit down and I'll explain it to you? That your office there?" Hunter pointed at the glass window.

"Right here'll do just fine," Dyson grumbled, making no attempt to be civil.

Hunter decided to play this like any concerned citizen. "I've been hired to find out why Final Care shipped the body of Mr. Charles Lahti to Tampa instead of Venice, where it should have gone. Further, I want to know precisely why it wasn't driven directly to Venice, a one-hour trip."

The man groaned. "Not that again. I've already told that funeral home guy why it had to come here."

Hunter could see the man was going to be defensive and not helpful. He decided to ratchet up the pressure a bit.

"You the head man here, Dyson? If you're not, I don't want to waste another minute of your apparently very valuable time." The sarcasm hung in the air between the two men.

"Oh for crying out loud." Dyson slumped behind the reception desk while Hunter took the only other chair and stared at him, unsmiling.

"Look, what did you say your name was—McCoy? This is what we do here. My guys meet the big airliners coming from Europe with our sealer casket transport equipment. We offload the caskets and bring them here to store until their next scheduled relay flight, usually to the home city, or town, or whatever. Sometimes it's just a few hours but it can be up to three days; depends on flight availability and the sense of urgency of the family. Basically we act as a temporary warehouse for these bodies."

"That's all you do?"

Dyson stared at him, clearly impatient to get him out of here. "No. We also have a small embalming and body preparation operation, one part-time embalmer. That's it."

"All right. So why did Charlie Lahti's body have to come here instead of going straight to Venice? By the way, it is here, right?"

"Yes. It's here," growled Dyson. "And the dead guy's been nothing but a pain in the ass. Some big-shot doctor from Italy gets here tomorrow and checks something, I don't know what, and then, if we're all lucky, he'll let me ship the damn thing to Venice."

Hunter, starting to get irritated, let the man's insensitivity go for the moment. "I'd like to see the body, verify it's here and talk with the embalmer."

Dyson lit a cigarette and blew smoke directly in Hunter's face. "Oh, you'd like to see the body and verify it's here, would you. I've just told you it's here, and that's good enough for you, mister—and for his damned loved ones." He sneered. "And for that nosy funeral parlor guy too."

Dyson was a big man, almost as big as Hunter, but he'd crossed the line with that last remark about "damned loved ones." Hunter stood up, reached across the table and grabbed the man's shirt collar with one hand, and began to squeeze. As the man tried to stand up and shake off

Hunter's grip, McCoy applied even more pressure freezing him in place. Then, dragging Dyson further out of his chair, Hunter brought the man's face to within inches of his own, his unblinking green eyes boring into him.

"Now listen to me. I'm going to tell you this once. You're going to walk me back and show me that body, and you're going to do it now."

Dyson, apparently not a complete idiot, immediately and accurately sensed the danger in refusing. Shaken, and with considerably less arrogance, he said, "What the hell, okay. What do I care if those fucking Italians said not to let anybody near it? What difference does it make, anyway? He's just another stiff." Immediately regretting his words, he stammered out, "I—I mean—just another deceased—person."

Hunter kept him up close for another moment and let him stare into his green eyes, cold as ice, just to make sure the man got the message. Then he let go of his shirt. "Let's go."

Dyson went into his office and grabbed a clipboard, examined it, and led Hunter back through the "No Admittance" door into the long hallway. As they walked down the hall all the way to the end, Hunter saw rooms with smoked glass windows and lettering indicating the purpose of each room. The door at the end of the hallway opened into a large room with maybe ten metal caskets on gurneys. The room was much cooler than the rest of the building, and he presumed the caskets contained bodies waiting for further shipment.

Dyson stopped at a casket toward the back of the room. He checked its number with his clipboard. "Here it is."

Unsmiling, Hunter said, "Open it."

"Come on, man," whined Dyson. "I could lose my job for this."

Hunter fixed him with a level stare, said nothing, and waited.

Licking his dry lips, thinking it over, and correctly sensing he had no choice, Dyson sighed and went to work on the casket. Once opened, Hunter could see the inside had been packed sufficiently to prevent the body from moving in flight. Most of the packing was dry ice. Hunter exposed the face and looked at the late Charlie Lahti. He knew it was Charlie from the pictures Jenny had shown him. Hunter reached in and exposed his right hand.

"No, you can't touch anything. I won't—

"You won't what? I'm looking for this ring," he said, holding the man's right hand, "to complete my identification." Hunter saw the gold coin ring on his finger, just as Jenny had described.

Satisfied, Hunter told Dyson he could close it up.

Back in the manager's office, Hunter wondered about the comment the man had made about the Italians. "Why'd they tell you not to let anybody touch the body?"

"How the heck do I know? I just work here."

"Who's coming from Italy tomorrow?"

"Don't know. Some doctor, I was told."

"A doctor? Why a doctor? If they're just checking on a mix-up, what do they need a doctor for? What does he need to do?"

"Look, McCoy, like I said, I just work here. I take orders. I do my job."

"When does he arrive? Is he coming alone?"

"Yeah, they just said one guy, he gets here around noon. They told me not to let anyone near the body. They were insistent about this."

What could be so important the Institute would send a doctor all the way to the States, so important they'd even delay delivery to a widow who had a contract and already had a funeral planned?

Hunter got up to leave. "I'll be back in the morning to see the man from Italy."

AFTER HUNTER LEFT, DYSON IMMEDIATELY made a phone call. "Jesus, what do you know about this dead guy, Charlie Lahti?" he said into the phone. "Some goon named Hunter McCoy was here and showed a lot of interest in him, forced me to show him the body."

Dyson was quiet for a minute listening to whoever was on the other end of the line. "What do you mean where did he look? He looked at the body. I could get in big trouble over this if something's going on and I don't know about it." Another pause. "Yeah, he's coming back tomorrow."

Dyson ended the call.

Chapter 7

THE NIGHT AFTER HIS VISIT to the Final Care warehouse, Hunter had dreams about death. He'd always associated death with cold. Charlie Lahti's body was packed in dry ice. The large room with the caskets was cold. Charlie's hand was cold when he checked for the coin ring. Even when he used to have the nightmares about his brother Gary's death in Pakistan, he'd wake up covered in sweat but always felt cold.

Gary had been a Marine, assigned to Hunter's squad carrying out a cross-border operation into the mountains of Pakistan to track down and extract a terrorist leader called Mahmud e Raq. They succeeded, but Gary was killed. Hunter had seen him in the center of a large explosion outside the cave where Mahmud e Raq was hiding. It was probably a land mine.

They couldn't find his body, and operational orders were to get Mahmud e Raq back to the authorities for interrogation. Hunter never forgave himself for leaving Gary behind. Now, many years later, the nightmares were less frequent, but even when he thought about it during the day, a chill came over him and he still fought back the rage.

After a fitful night spent dreaming about death, he'd awakened wondering why Charlie's body had to be evaluated by a doctor. Hunter, a medical scientist himself, couldn't imagine a reason. As far as he knew they hadn't done an autopsy. They surely wouldn't do one now. Did they think he was contagious with something? He'd find out soon. He looked at the bedside clock—3:05 a.m.—and groaned.

WHEN HUNTER ARRIVED AT THE FINAL CARE building at
9:00 a.m. he was two hours too late. The man from the
Institute had arrived on an earlier flight and had already
done his "evaluation" of Charlie's body. He was just
finishing up in the embalming room and washing his hands
when Hunter came through the door with Dyson.

A big man, as tall as Hunter, with hairy arms and dark
hair sticking out the neck of his short-sleeve scrubs, looked
up from the sink and dried his hands. He was young, maybe
in his mid-thirties. "Who is this?" he demanded of Dyson,
in Italian-accented English.

Not waiting for Dyson, Hunter extended his hand.
"Hunter McCoy, and you are?"

Ignoring Hunter's outstretched hand, the man narrowed
his eyes at Dyson and then looked back at Hunter. "Do you
work here, with him?" he asked, nodding his head at the
manager.

Funny, no one seems to want to shake my hand.

Withdrawing his outstretched hand, Hunter paused,
sizing up the man before replying, "I work for this man's
widow." He pointed at the body in the opened travel casket.
"She asked me to find out why he was sent here—
presumably so you could see him—rather than to Venice,
Florida, where she had a funeral scheduled."

The man stared at Hunter, apparently trying to
formulate what he was going to say next. Hunter suspected
he was concocting a lie. But then why would he?

"What are you a detective of some kind?" the man
asked with a sneer.

"A medical scientist, actually, professor, University of
Virginia School of Medicine."

"You look for missing bodies?" the man asked,
incredulous.

"Sometimes."

"Sometimes?"

"Sometimes."

The two men eyed each other, again for a long moment. Finally, seemingly having reached a decision, the man responded.

"Look, it's quite simple. At the Institute we take our patient's privacy and security seriously. Instead of the traditional wrist bracelet with the patients' name, date of birth, his doctor, and other information, we utilize a more secure and private system. We use a one-inch square adhesive patch with an imbedded microchip containing all the patient's records and information, and apply it to the back of the wrist. That way, a small hand-held scanner can easily identify the patient and all pertinent information concerning his condition, treatment, therapy, etc. Our doctors, nurses, therapists, lab people, and others, use these scanners to access patient information."

"They all carry scanners with them?"

"Of course. Everybody who interacts with our patients has one."

"So how can the patient's privacy be protected if everyone can access the information?"

The man sighed, as if resenting he had to explain something so obvious. "Not everyone's scanner is programmed the same way. For example, the scanner of a phlebotomist drawing blood at the bedside would only reveal the name and date of birth of a patient. It would not reveal medical records or other information.

"A nurse's scanner would also reveal the patient's diagnosis, any meds he's taking, and other information necessary for his care. Any information not germane to good nursing care would be unavailable. The patient's principal physician would, of course, have access to everything. So you see—"

Hunter interrupted. "What does this have to do with the mix-up of the two bodies?"

"That's Final Care's issue to deal with, not mine. But before we could release it to them, I needed to know if this body really is Mr. Charles Lahti. Our records showed the patch applied to Mr. Lahti when he first entered the Institute for therapy was not removed after his death. Our policy requires the patch be removed and returned to our record files if the patient leaves or dies while in our care. We had no record of it being returned."

He reached for an envelope on the table and opened it. "Of course, now I see why." Lifting out a small transparent and colorless patch, he showed it to Hunter. "This is the patch. I just removed from Mr. Lahti's wrist."

"How do you know it's him?" Hunter asked.

Rolling his eyes as if he were getting bored with Hunter's questions, he answered, "That's why I'm here. I was Mr. Lahti's principal physician when he was with us. I recognize him."

The man showed Hunter a small device about the size of a cell phone. "I used my scanner to read the chip to further confirm this was indeed Mr. Lahti and he had the correct patch on him. You see, McCoy, even in death we take the patient's privacy seriously. I was sent because I was the only one authorized to read all of his records.

"After we heard about the mix-up between the two bodies we had to be sure who was who. If this weren't Mr. Lahti, I'd be flying to Venice or Tampa—wherever the other body is—right now to examine it."

The hirsute physician turned back to his work.

"Now, if you'll excuse me, I need to finish up here." Then, nodding to Dyson, he added, "I'm authorizing you to ship the remains to the family so they can get on with the burial. Is there anything else, McCoy?"

Hunter had to admit it made a certain kind of sense. And the body was now presumably going to be flown to Bremmer's and Jenny. "I didn't catch your name."

"I am Dr. Giovanni Phillippi."

"And your specialty, Doctor?"

"My specialty?"

"Yes, what's your medical specialty?"

The man straightened his shoulders before answering, obviously suspicious of the probing question, "Neurosurgery."

Neurosurgery? Come on, they sent a neurosurgeon all the way from Italy to remove a patch that didn't even require instruments; you just peel it off with your fingers? I don't buy it. And why would Charlie have a neurosurgeon as his principal physician? A neurologist would make more sense.

As if reading Hunter's thoughts, Phillippi said, "It's not so unusual. All of our patients actually have a team of specialists looking after them. I'm just one of them, and I was free to travel. Now, if you'll both excuse me, I have to pack up and get ready to return to Sorrento."

Wait, first he was the man's principal physician and now he's just one of the team? Something doesn't add up here.

Dr. Phillippi picked up the envelope and the small handheld scanner he'd presumably used to read the patch. Then, realizing too late that his surgical pouch with its full set of tools was still open and seeing the recognition on Hunter's face, he snapped it shut and with considerably less civility, asked them both to leave.

Dyson left immediately, while Hunter stayed where he was momentarily and stared evenly at Phillippi. Both men knew there were questions left unanswered.

Finally, Phillippi said, "Look, McCoy, you have what you came for. Mr. Lahti's body is being released and will be flown back to Venice today. Final Care has made all the arrangements, and you're free to return with it on the same charter flight if you'd like. Now I really must go." He snatched up the pouch and showed Hunter the door.

Hunter began walking down the corridor toward the exit through the front office until he heard Phillippi close the door behind him. He doubled back toward the preparation room. At the door he listened for a few moments and when he heard nothing, he slowly opened it and entered. Phillippi wasn't there but Hunter could hear his voice coming from behind a door on the other side of the room. Carefully he moved along the wall to within a few feet of the door, where he put his ear to the wall and could just make out what was apparently a one-sided phone conversation.

"—No, it's okay, I've got it. Don't worry. And I have the patch too. But we may have a problem, some med-school professor, Hunter McCoy, hired by the widow. No, I don't know that. How would I know that? Christ, man, it's your job. I've done my part and I'm getting out of here, now."

Hunter scanned the room for somewhere to hide in the event Phillippi suddenly came through the door. He spotted a large counter just to his left that he could reach quickly.

"Why am I suspicious?" Phillippi asked, his voice rising. "He saw my instruments and I could read the recognition on his face. He'd know those tools wouldn't be necessary to remove a patch. You'd better get your people on this."

Hunter determined the conversation was over and crouched momentarily behind the counter. When Phillippi didn't return, Hunter hurriedly left the building and walked to his car in the parking lot.

What's going on here? What did he say? 'I've got it— and the patch too'? What did he get from Charlie's body that required surgical tools and a neurosurgeon?

Chapter 8

THE MAN—CURRENTLY USING THE NAME RACHE—gazed out over the rail that circled the wide veranda on the third floor of the twenty-million-dollar mansion on the Atlantic Ocean just north of Miami. He'd rented it for a month but actually lived in a much more modest apartment in the suburbs under a different name. Still, he could easily afford the rent.

He was middle-aged, of medium height and weight, with sandy hair turning gray, combed downward in all directions in the style of a medieval monk. Still, he was an altogether ordinary-looking man who wouldn't earn a second glance by a passerby on the street. But those who'd been unfortunate enough to cross him knew he was anything but ordinary.

He stood looking east, over the vast expanse of blue water. A warm ocean breeze off the Gulf Stream drifted in through the open sliders. He formed a steeple with the fingers of his hands, touching the tips to his lips, wondering about the man at the airport.

Who is Hunter McCoy?

Rache pondered the options and didn't like any of them. Could McCoy in any way upset the plan he'd carefully set in motion? He dismissed this almost as soon as he thought it. Of course not, how could he?

No, Rache's decades-old plan for retribution would most definitely succeed. It was carefully planned, it was justified, and justification meant everything to him. Justification would set things right. It would remove his shame, a shame that consumed him with its voracious appetite for vengeance. He continued to stare out at the ocean.

It's all about pain, really. Pain is everything. Without it nothing would have been accomplished. Without it the thief would have won. All that's been taken from me would have stayed lost and had no meaning, then or now. But that won't happen. I've seen to it. It's taken years, and the pain has strangely been its own reward. It offered satisfaction when nothing else would. It encouraged me to go on when nothing else could.

My success has been monumental, global, celebrated, even envied—envied by those who work for me, though I'm unknown to most of them. They believe they've done it all on their own, that their success is theirs and not mine. It's been perfect, all part of the plan, the grand plan put into effect so many years ago, and it's worked perfectly. All the pieces are falling into place. The endgame is almost here.

In the beginning, Rache had actually tried to get help. He'd seen a psychiatrist who'd listened to his story of betrayal and then told him he had it all wrong. *He* was the problem and not those who'd worked against him. *He* was the one who was sick and needed help and if he didn't change the plans he'd unfortunately confessed to the psychiatrist, the esteemed doctor would have to inform the police.

That evening when the psychiatrist didn't return home, his wife reported him missing. He turned up two days later on the front steps of a police station, dead, with his tongue cut out and serving as a bookmark for the page in one of his textbooks that described the concept of patient confidentiality. The book was nailed to his chest with a steel spike.

The experience with the psychiatrist only reinforced Rache's justification for vengeance. He didn't doubt for an instant the correctness of what he'd done to the man. The act of vengeance was a proper response. It set right the unprofessional conduct of the man and his threat to go to the police. The psychiatrist wouldn't do it again to someone else, and that thought gave him immense pleasure.

In the same way, he knew he would take tremendous satisfaction in the righteousness of his long-planned scheme for vengeance for the wrong done to him by those he thought had loved him. They hadn't loved him, they'd betrayed him, and his suffering was made all the worse by their actions since. The deep and ever-growing agony in his soul over their betrayal was only mitigated by his absolute certainty of the correctness of the plan he'd come to call the endgame. This thought brought him back to the issue of McCoy. *I have too much time and pain involved in the endgame to suffer interference now. It's unthinkable. It can't happen.*

Earlier, Rache had instructed Traveler on how he wanted McCoy handled. Traveler, forty-four years old, six feet tall, extremely fit from daily rigorous workouts had worked for Rache for many years. He seemed to have a perpetual slight smile on his face that masked the dark uses to which Rache frequently put him. He was an extremely skilled killing machine with an incredible variety of weapons. Completely hairless due to a genetic defect, his evenly featured face might still have been handsome except for the eyes. His perpetual smile couldn't overshadow those soulless eyes.

In a quiet even tone, frightening by its deceptive softness, Rache told the man that he needed to know what McCoy knew or suspected and if he was working with anyone else. Traveler, as he always did, got the message loud and clear. If he didn't get this information, he, himself would be killed. Over the years, he'd seen the consequences of failing this man in any way, no matter how small. Still, with a confidence that came from years of successfully serving him, Traveler said, "Consider it done."

This gave Rache comfort as he stepped away from the rail and sat in one of the large cushioned wicker chairs adorning the deck. The smile that evolved slowly across his face derived from menace rather than joy. He picked up the glass from an end table and sipped his twenty-five-year-old scotch, his determination deepening with each sip.

Nothing and no one can stop me—I have become Rache.

Chapter 9

THE *EMERALD SEA* WAS ANCHORED in the fabled yacht harbor of the Principality of Monaco for a long night of refueling. She was showing minimal lights as befitted her current docked and mostly vacant status. The owner of the ninety-meter Benetti, billionaire Umberto Carlucci, and his guests were ashore, dining at the exclusive Le Louis XV Alain Ducasse at the Hotel de Paris, one of Monaco's prestige eating-places.

The vessel would take all night to fuel. The crew had been granted shore leave. Only the captain and a single crewmember remained on board.

The slim figure dressed completely in black stepped out from the darkened doorway in the ship stores building at the end of the dock and easily boarded the yacht after spotting no visible security. The intruder quickly made for the master stateroom, being careful to stay in the shadows as much as possible.

Knowing exactly where to go, having been there once before, the black-clad figure entered the stateroom and went immediately to the safe behind the painting of the owner's wife that dominated the wall behind a small sitting area.

The thief keyed in the combination—surreptitiously observed on a previous visit while watching over the shoulder of the surprisingly unconcerned Carlucci as he'd opened it. The safe, satisfactorily, silently opened again, as it had earlier. Reaching in, the thief removed a black velvet jewelry wrap and opened it.

Exquisite. What a shame.

After closing the safe and replacing the painting, the thief quietly and unnoticed left the ship and slipped back into the famous playground of the rich and famous.

Chapter 10

"TOMORROW AFTERNOON? THREE-THIRTY? Wonderful. Mrs. Lahti will be greatly relieved."

Bremmer stood up and walked to the window, heaving a huge sigh of relief, himself, reflecting on what he'd just heard. The guy from the Caravaggio Institute apparently had done whatever he'd needed to do with Mr. Lahti's body and it was being flown by charter jet directly to Venice. McCoy would be on the same flight. Final Care said they were taking full responsibility for the mix-up and wanted the funeral director to tell Mrs. Lahti they were extremely sorry for the affair and she'd be charged nothing for the whole business. In fact, they'd send her a three-thousand-dollar check for her inconvenience and—not incidentally, he smiled—they were going to double his regular fee for any inconvenience he'd been caused.

The woman, Margot Janssen, calling from their Brussels Headquarters, said the mix-up had occurred at their facility there. She said it had never happened before but they'd identified the glitch in their system that allowed it and it'd been fixed. They'd also severely reprimanded the representative who'd been so uncaring and thoughtless to him on the phone.

Delighted the affair was coming to a satisfactory conclusion Bremmer dialed Mrs. Lahti.

HUNTER WAS IN HIS HOTEL ROOM at the airport getting ready to return to Venice on the charter flight with Charlie's body. With no time or opportunity to further examine it himself, he fully intended to have Bremmer do it once they were back in Venice.

After making a decision, he dialed a number on his secure phone known only to a few people. A woman's voice answered, "McMurtle Manufacturing. How may I help you?"

"I need seventeen front-end loaders by noon tomorrow. Can you help?"

"Just a moment, sir."

After a wait of several minutes, a strong male voice said, "What's up, Hunter?"

Hunter immediately recognized the voice of his former boss, Colonel Deacon Wogen, Assistant Director of the Defense Intelligence Agency of the United States Department of Defense.

A little over a year ago, Deacon had taken the extraordinary step of reinstating Hunter on an ad hoc basis. The idea was, whenever the DIA's inquiries involved higher education he'd be temporarily reactivated to advise them. Such reinstatement would also include Interpol and the Virginia State Police. That's what Hunter was seeking now.

"Deacon, this is going to seem a little premature and maybe out of line."

After a short laugh, the Assistant Director said, "You don't say. In other words, standard operating procedure for you."

"Guilty as charged. But here's the thing. I'm asking you to reactivate my Interpol status. I think I might be on to an international crime of some kind involving the transport of American civilian bodies across international borders. I don't see any DOD connection just the possibility of a global operation."

"I take it this has grown out of one of your—what do you call them—find-and-correct jobs?"

"Exactly."

After a pause and an audible sigh, Deacon said, "So explain it to me."

Hunter did, giving him all the information he and Bremmer had gathered on Charlie Lahti, including what he'd learned in Miami and overheard from the neurosurgeon.

"Hold on." Deacon considered the situation for several minutes. Hunter was used to Deacon's long pauses while the man's incredible brain processed information like a computer. He'd learned to say nothing during these times. Just wait. Finally, Deacon came back on.

"Now listen, Hunter, this might be more important than you think. We know who Charlie Lahti is. DOD awarded his firm, SkySoft, a contract to encrypt communications between ground-control units and our military drone program.

"The software he developed is called RaptorCrypt. It's already been delivered to us, installed, and is proving highly successful. Since the incorporation of RaptorCrypt not a single downlink has been hacked by terrorists. Before that, our video reconnaissance data on targets and insurgent movements had been intercepted by the Iranians as well as insurgents in Pakistan, Afghanistan, and more recently Iraq and Syria."

Hunter waited.

"I'm going to activate you again—DIA, Interpol, and the Virginia State Police."

Hunter knew the civilian police connection was necessary for the Interpol activation.

"Since you're already on the trail of what happened to Charlie Lahti, you're involved. Just keep your eyes open for any military connection. You've got your credentials with you I assume?"

"Yup, I do, but Deacon—"

"Now listen, if you get any inkling of a link to RaptorCrypt, contact Connie Chang. She'll be your liaison to me. Otherwise make your requests for information through normal Interpol channels in Lyon and leave the DIA out of it. Contact Chang only if you find a link to the drone program."

"Understood. I'll use Eduard Gautier exclusively, sir."

Deacon chuckled. "Maybe you'll even meet him some day, Hunter. He's a great guy."

Hunter grinned. Over the years he had often used Gautier for information, but always over the phone, never in person. "Thank you, sir, I'll keep you informed."

DURING THE FLIGHT, HE TURNED HIS ATTENTION back to the situation with Charlie. What had Phillippi meant when he'd said, "I've got it"? He'd obviously taken something from Charlie besides the patch. He'd said, "I've got the patch, *too.*" Whatever it was must have required surgical tools and a neurosurgeon, but what? Charlie was at the institute for therapy. He hadn't had surgery. At least Hunter didn't think he had. He'd have to ask Jenny.

He tried to recall what else he'd heard. He remembered Phillippi saying something like "That's your job." Then "No, I don't know that. How would I know that? That's your job. I've done my part and I'm getting out of here, now."

When the flight landed at the Venice Airport Willard Bremmer was waiting.

"Mr. McCoy, Hunter, good to see you again."

"Same here. Charlie's on board and waiting for you."

"Any problems?"

Hunter hesitated, "No, not really, but I do want you to do something. When you get the body back to your facility, I want you to examine it carefully from head to toe. Look for anything unusual. Anything at all."

Confused, Willard said, "What am I looking for?"

"Just do it. I'll check with you later."

"Okay. Oh, and while you were in Miami, I got a call from Final Care. They've fixed the problem that allowed the mix-up to occur, apologized for the mistake, and won't charge Mrs. Lahti anything."

"Least they could do."

"Exactly," Bremmer agreed.

He said he had already called Jenny and given her the news. They set the funeral for the next day at 3:30 p.m., with a newly scheduled viewing from 1:00 to 2:30.

Jenny had already prepared a dinner for Hunter and Henry. She'd even planned it so they'd have time for a cocktail before sitting down to eat. Jenny had a glass of white wine and Hunter made himself his favorite drink, a perfect Canadian Club Manhattan on the rocks with a twist, from the stock in Charlie's bar. Henry had a beer.

In answer to their questions about what he'd found in Miami, Hunter told them he'd know more when Willard had a chance to examine Charlie's body. Jenny, still drawn from grief and worry, missed the hidden implication something was wrong. She just accepted that with Charlie back, everything had been resolved.

On the other hand, Henry shot him a look; he wasn't quite buying it. Hunter was on to something.

Chapter 11

AT 7:00 THE NEXT MORNING, six hours before the viewing, Hunter's room phone rang in The Inn At The Beach. It was Willard Bremmer.

"McCoy, can you come over here now? You've got to see this." The man sounded agitated. Hunter agreed immediately.

Bremmer met Hunter at the door and took him to the mortuary where what he assumed was Charlie's body was lying face up on a stainless steel table covered with a sheet.

"I'm not sure what you expected me to find when you asked me to examine the body but I've found two things that are strange."

Bremmer moved to the head of the stainless steel table. Making a "V" with his index and middle finger he pointed to two locations on the top of Charlie's head.

Hunter saw neatly combed grayish brown hair but nothing unusual. "What am I looking at?"

"Well, you can't see it without parting the hair, but look now"

Bremmer parted the hair in two locations over the top of the skull and then Hunter could see what he was getting at. There were two tiny holes through the scalp just to the right and left of the midline at the top of the skull.

"Do those penetrate through the skull?"

"I don't know."

"Could you find out?"

Bremmer hesitated. "I guess, but why?"

"The guy from the Caravaggio Institute who came from Italy to examine the body was a neurosurgeon. He gave me a cock-and-bull story about removing a patch from his wrist that wouldn't have required a neurosurgeon with surgical tools."

Bremmer used a narrow stainless steel probe and poked through one of the holes. After a little resistance where healing must have occurred, he went through the skull.

"He's had some brain surgery. This hole was drilled."

"Try the other one," Hunter asked.

Bremmer did, with the same result.

"So," Hunter said. "Two symmetrical holes were drilled through Charlie's skull, probably recently, given the weakness of the repair tissue. How did they think it wouldn't be noticed?"

"Oh, yes." Said Willard. "I didn't tell you this. Those holes weren't visible at first. They'd been carefully covered up with surgical putty. I only found them because you asked me to check the body thoroughly from head to toe. When I removed it, I found what you just saw."

"How recently would you say the putty was applied?"

"Very recently, if I had to guess."

Hunter thought back to the Phillippi's overhead phone conversation. *"I've got it and I've got the patch too."* What did he get? He must have retrieved it from Charlie's brain through these holes.

"You said you found two things."

"Yes, Mr. Lahti's body had already been embalmed just as the bodies had the other two times I've dealt with Final Care. The company was very efficient and the embalming was expertly done. However, something is weird. It may not mean anything, but I want to show you anyway. Look here."

Bremmer surprised Hunter by lifting the sheet and pointing to the cadaver's groin, were he could see a small neat incision that had been sutured up.

"What am I looking at?"

"You're looking at the site where the arterial embalming process occurred. There's absolutely nothing unusual about it at all."

"Then why are you pointing it out to me?"

"Because of where it's not."

"Excuse me?" said Hunter, confused.

"Let me explain," Bremmer continued. "When we embalm a body, part of the process is called arterial embalming. It involves locating a large artery and vein, usually side by side, and then injecting embalming fluid into the artery, having it circulate through the body's own vascular system, and then draining it out through the vein.

"In this case the embalmer used the femoral artery and the femoral vein. He accessed them through the small incision you see in the groin. We refer to this as the femoral route, or just 'femoral.' Most embalmers will choose the right common carotid artery and the right internal jugular vein in the neck, or just 'carotid' for short."

"And?" said Hunter. "Obviously this guy prefers the femoral technique over the carotid technique."

"Precisely," agreed Bremmer with a smile. "Embalmers are like anyone else. We find a technique we prefer and we stick with it. We don't flip from one technique to another unless there's a good reason, like damage or for cosmetic purposes."

"So what's your point?"

"This embalmer flipped, and there's no obvious reason for it. Come into my office, I'll show you."

In his office, Bremmer already had three identical folders spread out on his desk. Hunter walked around behind the desk with Bremmer so they could both read them. Hunter quickly saw they had Final Care typed on their front covers.

Bremmer waved his hand over them. "These are the documents that came with each of the three cadavers I received from Final Care over the past four years. Each contains all the information required by law when a body is shipped internationally."

He pointed to the first one. "This is the paperwork for the first time I dealt with Final Care four years ago. Look here, you can see the name of the embalmer—Johannes Donckers —typed below this line and his signature written over it." He turned the page and pointed to another line. "Over here you can see the method of arterial embalming that was used. In this particular case it was carotid, nothing unusual about that."

He tapped the next file with his index finger. "This one, from three years ago, same thing, carotid. Now here is where it gets weird. Both of these cases and the late Mr. Charlie Lahti were prepared by the same embalmer—Mr. Johannes Donckers. Why would he flip to the femoral route with Charlie?"

Hunter wasn't convinced. "Again, so what? Maybe he just likes the variety or he's trying to keep his skills intact."

Bremmer plopped down in his chair and sighed. "Well, if he is, he's the only embalmer I ever met who does. I have to tell you, I've been in this business a long time and this is unusual."

"So what are you getting at?"

"I don't know. But with the body missing for a few days, those holes in his head, and then that weird trip to Miami, it just doesn't feel right."

Hunter had an idea. "What about the other body, the one they sent you by mistake? What method was used on him?"

"Let me think now. Wait, it was carotid. Yes, I'm sure of it. I remember thinking he did a nice job with the sutures in the neck. I saw them when I prepped the body earlier for them to pick up."

"But you don't know if it was the same embalmer, do you? I mean you didn't get the paperwork for that body. You got Charlie's paperwork but the wrong body, right?"

Bremmer stroked his chin, "Yeah, that's right. I don't even know how many embalmers Final Care has. I just know I've had the same one each time."

Hunter was trying to find a simple explanation. "How about this? Maybe they had different embalmers but Johannes Donckers, signed off on all of them. Is that possible?"

"Possible, but highly illegal. A violation like that could cost them their license to operate."

Still not convinced they had anything here to worry about, Hunter nevertheless knew he shouldn't disregard Bremmer's gut feeling. "Willard, can you call Johnson's Funeral Home in Tampa and find out who signed off on the embalming of Mr. Cole's body, the one you were sent by mistake?"

While Willard made the call, Hunter couldn't help wondering if this irregularity and the holes in the skull were somehow related.

What had they done to Charlie?

Chapter 12

THE PEOPLE AT JOHNSON'S FUNERAL HOME in Tampa told Bremmer that Mr. Cole—the body mistakenly sent to Venice—had the same embalmer as Charlie Lahti; Johannes Donckers. In addition, Charlie's embalming had been femoral, while Mr. Cole's had been carotid.

"Willard, I'm starting to get an idea," Hunter told the funeral director. "Is there any way to find out which other funeral homes in Florida might have used Final Care in the past?"

"Not without calling them and asking. I suppose you could call Final Care and ask to see their records, although I don't know how you'd convince them you had a legitimate right to that information."

Hunter smiled, "I think I know a way. Can I borrow that directory of yours? As you said earlier, given the number of wealthy retirees in southwest Florida, it seems reasonable Final Care might have a larger business here than almost anywhere in the country."

Willard nodded and handed the book to Hunter, who got up to leave.

"Will you keep me informed of what you find out?"

"Sure."

Hunter planned to call the largest funeral homes in the region and ask if they'd ever done business with Final Care. He'd identify himself as an Interpol agent and bluff it with the funeral directors, leading them to believe his inquiries had something to do with an international criminal investigation.

As it turned out, three homes in Tampa, including Johnson's, one in Sarasota, and two in Fort Myers had had dealings with Final Care. Like true professionals, they refused to give any more details unless he showed up personally with credentials, which he promised to do as soon as possible.

After the funeral that afternoon, Hunter and Henry attended a reception for family and friends at the Lahti home, hosted by Jenny along with her two daughters and their husbands. Hunter was impressed by the number of people who attended and later came to the house to express their condolences to the widow.

Several high-ranking uniformed Air Force officers from MacDill Air Force Base in Tampa also attended. He assumed they were there because of the military connection with Charlie's company.

The next afternoon Hunter dropped Henry off at the Tampa airport for his return flight to Marquette. After returning Henry's rental car and checking one out in his own name, he planned to investigate the anomalies of the embalming techniques with the funeral homes in Tampa.

"There may be nothing to it," he told Henry, "but since I'll be in Tampa anyway, I'll check them out. And Henry?"

"Yeah?"

"Check on Dad, will you? Tell him I hope this business doesn't take much longer and I plan to be back soon."

"You got it."

"Tell him I'll call him, first chance I get."

Hunter started with the director of Franson's Funeral Home in Tampa.

"I don't understand. What does embalming have to do with police, and the international police at that?"

"I'm not at liberty to tell you that, sir," Hunter said, taking notes on a pad, because he assumed the director would expect him to.

"All I'm asking is for you to check your records and tell me the name of the embalmer and the arterial embalming site for the two remains you were sent from Final Care."

"Well, I guess there's no harm in giving you that. It's not like it's a secret or anything."

The director, Mr. Franson, a short friendly man wearing a black suit and purple tie expertly knotted, went to his file cabinet. He returned with two files. "Here we are; James Littleton, a little over two years ago, and Sylvia Johnson, this year."

Opening the Littleton file and adjusting his glasses, he said, "Let's see now, the embalmer was a Johannes Donckers and the route was carotid." Next he turned to the second file, Sylvia Johnson. "Okay, the embalmer was—how about that —Mr. Donckers again. Hmmm, the technique was femoral this time."

Hunter decided to verify Bremmer's analysis. "Is that common, Mr. Franson, I mean for an embalmer to flip back and forth from one technique to another?"

"Not really. Myself, I prefer the carotid artery and use it exclusively unless the body has been damaged in such a way as to make that route impossible. I'd say most embalmers use the carotid artery."

"So was the body damaged in this case?" Hunter asked.

"Let's see." The director checked his records, "No nothing unusual with the body."

"I see. I have one last question, Mr. Franson. Did you notice anything unusual about the remains Final Care sent you?"

"Unusual? What do you mean?"

"Just unusual. Did anything catch your attention, anything out of the ordinary?"

He carefully looked through the records and finally said, "No, nothing I see here or anything I remember. Sorry."

"That's all right. Thanks for your time."

"You mean that's all you wanted?"

"Yes sir, for now."

As Hunter drove across town to the other funeral home in Tampa, Harrington's, he did a mental tally for Johannes Donckers. Three times the embalmer used the carotid artery and two times he used the femoral artery. Either the guy liked variety, or he had some other reason for doing it.

"We've used Final Care four times over the last few years, Agent McCoy," answered Glen Harrington. "They've always treated us very well. The remains arrived on time, always in excellent condition, and the paperwork was complete. I'm sure you'll find that our records are thorough and above board," he added.

"I'm sure they are sir. I only have a few questions for you. Can you tell me who did the arterial embalming in each case, and the method they used?"

"Of course, I have it right here." He looked through the folders, and Hunter was not surprised when he told him the embalmer was Johannes Donckers in each of the four cases. Again, it was a mixed bag, one femoral and three carotid routes. The older files, three and four years ago, both reported carotid embalming, while the later two, both this year, were split, with one femoral and one carotid.

Hunter was running out of hope anything would show up. "Do you recall if there was anything unusual about the remains? Anything you might remember or anything you noted in your files?"

Harrington looked through his records. "No, there's nothing here that I noted. All four of them died abroad while on vacation. Three were in Europe and one, Mr. Rappaport, was on a tour in Egypt. He and two of the European vacationers were flown here directly from the Final Care facility in Brussels. The other one was flown from their facility in Brussels to their facility in Miami, and then on to us."

"Wait a minute, are you saying sometimes remains come directly from the European center in Brussels, but in other cases are flown from that facility to the Final Care facility in Miami first?"

"It looks that way."

"Why?"

"I don't know." He paused. "Now here's something, Agent McCoy. The deceased person with femoral artery embalming was the one flown to Miami before coming here."

"Mr. Harrington, is it possible the one sent to Miami wasn't embalmed in Brussels, even though the body was flown from there to the US? Instead the embalming occurred in Miami so a different embalmer did the work, and he prefers the femoral artery route?"

"I suppose it's possible, but in that case these records have been falsified, because the same embalmer's name and signature are on all four."

"Excuse me, I need to make a phone call," said Hunter, taking out his cell phone. He dialed Franson's Funeral Home. "Mr. Franson, this is Agent McCoy again. I wonder if you could re-check the records of the two remains we discussed earlier from Final Care. Specifically I want to know the transportation route from Europe to your facility."

"The transportation route?"

"Yes."

"All right. Give me a minute."

When Franson came back on the line he said, "Agent McCoy? Here it is. One was flown from Brussels to Miami and then on to us, while the other was shipped directly from Brussels to us. Does that mean anything?"

"Possibly. I have one more question. What was the arterial embalming route for the two?"

Hunter could hear the papers being shuffled in the background.

"Okay, here it is. The body sent directly to us had carotid embalming, while the other, the one that went to Miami, was embalmed via the femoral artery."

"Thank you." Hunter hung up and repeated what he'd found to Harrington.

"So what does it mean, Agent McCoy?"

"I don't know—yet. Maybe nothing."

RACHE WAITED PATIENTLY WHILE TRAVELER gave his report.

"Apparently Lahti's widow hired McCoy to find out why her husband's body didn't show up at his own funeral. Those idiots at Final Care shipped his body to Tampa directly from Brussels and it should have gone to Miami first. Instead they shipped another body directly from Brussels to Venice, the body she saw when she looked in the coffin expecting to see Lahti."

Rache put his hand up, indicating to Traveler that he should stop while he considered this. A moment later he signaled Traveler to continue.

"McCoy and Bremmer, the local funeral guy, have been checking with funeral homes that have used Final Care. McCoy has been asking about how they were embalmed, something about femoral or carotid routes, and who did the embalming."

Rache signaled him to stop again, got up and walked out onto his balcony overlooking the Atlantic coast. In the distance he spotted a freighter heading to the Port of Miami. He gripped the railing with both hands, a frown spreading across his face.

McCoy could be dangerous. Bremmer too.

He returned to the main room.

"Follow McCoy. Find a way to dissuade him from further investigation, but do not kill him. Find out what else he knows and if he's working for anyone else besides the widow."

Chapter 13

HUNTER'S FAVORABLE EXPERIENCE WITH the funeral directors in Tampa convinced him he could probably poll the Sarasota funeral homes and the three in Fort Myers over the telephone and save some time. It was apparent neither Franson nor Harrington considered the information he was seeking confidential.

It was noon when he reached Venice. His stomach reminded him he hadn't had breakfast. He found a restaurant called Robbi's Reef on the 41 Bypass, where he ordered the fish tacos, a delicious ice-cold Caesar salad, and a beer. The place was nearly empty, so he called Willard Bremmer and asked him to recheck his records on the flight routes of his three Final Care cases.

"What are you after?"

"It may be nothing. Can you check it out?"

"Sure, give me a minute." He returned to the phone. "Okay, I have it. All three were shipped directly from Brussels. The two earlier ones came here, while Charlie, of course, was accidentally shipped to Tampa first."

Still in the dark as to why Hunter wanted this information, Bremmer asked, "Are you on to something, Hunter?"

"Not sure yet. I hope to know more tonight."

Back in his hotel room, Hunter made his few remaining calls. The Sarasota funeral home and the three in Fort Myers revealed the same pattern. Combined, they had three cases in which carotid embalming was used, and in each case the body had been shipped directly from Brussels to Sarasota or Fort Myers, bypassing Miami. He also found one case in which the femoral artery was used and the remains were shipped from Brussels to the Miami facility first before being sent on to Fort Myers.

Taking a notepad from the desk in his room, he decided to chart it out—all the cases handled by Johannes Donckers for Final Care. That way, if there was a pattern he might see it.

On the left side of the page he tallied up the total number of cases in which carotid artery embalming was done—eight. Then he did the same for the femoral artery— five, for a total of thirteen cases in which Final Care had shipped bodies. Then, remembering the use of the femoral artery route had only started occurring recently, he redid the chart.

Prior to a year earlier, there were six cases. All embalmed via the carotid route, and all were shipped directly from the Brussels facility to their final destination. The other seven cases had all occurred within the past twelve months. Five of those seven were femoral, and had all been shipped to Miami first except Charlie, who went directly to Tampa. Of the other two cases, both carotid, one went direct to Tampa and the other, Richard Cole, went to Miami.

Now what did that mean?

Hunter wondered if the apparent difference in travel routes with the two types of embalming had anything to do with the mix-up in the bodies. Then it hit him.

Of course, why didn't I see this before? Charlie's remains were embalmed using the femoral artery. He should have gone through Miami to be consistent with the other femoral cases. But he didn't. On the other hand, Mr. Cole's remains had apparently been shipped to Miami first, but to be consistent with the pattern for carotids, there was no need for his body in Miami. It was a mix-up.

Once the mix-up was discovered, Charlie's remains were picked up in Tampa by Final Care and flown to Miami first, and then on to Bremmer's in Venice—but why? Then something else came back to him. It had bothered him ever since his trip to the Final Care facility at the airport in Miami. Something Dyson had said, something about it being already there. The Italians told him that as long as the body was in Miami, their guy would come there. In other words, the body already had to go to Miami for some other reason. The Institute sent Phillippi there because that's where the body was. It wasn't sent to Miami specifically for Phillippi. It was already going there for some other reason. It wasn't to be embalmed either, because Bremmer said that both Charlie and Cole had already been embalmed at the Brussels facility.

What do they do there?

Chapter 14

HUNTER CALLED JENNY AND SAID HE'D be over a little later to fill her in on what he'd learned so far. After he showered, he went to select a shirt from his suitcase—he hadn't had time to unpack or hang anything in the closet—he noticed something wrong. His socks were lying on top with his shirts below. He never packed that way and he knew he hadn't moved them from their customary location on the bottom with his underwear.

Someone's been in here. The housekeeper? Not likely, he thought. But then who else? No one knew he was working a case.

That's not exactly true, someone knew. Did it have anything to do with what I'd learned in Miami? Phillippi certainly had something to hide—the holes in Charlie's head. Dyson knew I was investigating. Maybe the break-in was linked to the suspicious embalming pattern, but that didn't seem likely, since the only ones who knew I was looking into it were the funeral directors, and they'd have no reason to search my room.

With no answers to these questions, he had no choice but to get on with his investigation, knowing he'd have to watch his back.

JENNY ASKED, "WOULD YOU LIKE SOME COFFEE? I just made a fresh pot."

"That'd be great."

She brought two steaming cups to the kitchen table, and they sat quietly for a moment while they sipped. Hunter began, "There are two issues that may or may not be related. Both are bothering me and both have to do with Charlie. Did he have surgery of any kind when he was being treated at the Caravaggio Institute?"

Startled, Jenny looked up. "Surgery? Good heavens, no. They did some brain scans and asked him to do things like talk and lift his arms, make fists, that kind of thing, while they looked at the images, but no surgery. I remember they'd attach a bunch of electrodes on his head during therapy sessions while he tried to juggle. I think they said it was to see if his brainwaves were working normally, or something like that. Why do you ask?"

"Do you remember a Dr. Phillippi? He was one of Charlie's physicians."

"Phillippi? No, I don't remember him. I remember the therapist — let's see — Mr. Pompa. He was very nice. He visited Charlie every day and assessed his improvement. I still remember how pleased he was when Charlie began to master the juggling. It was like a miracle. Then…"

Hunter could see her joy replaced by sadness as she fought back tears.

"Then the second stroke came and took him away from me forever."

Shaking herself from her reverie, she looked at Hunter again. "Why did you ask about surgery?"

Hunter explained everything he'd learned in Miami and the conversation he'd overheard between Phillippi and someone unknown. He told her his supposition that the neurosurgeon had flown all the way from the Institute to surgically remove something from Charlie's body. He concluded that something had been done to Charlie at the Institute, something they didn't want her to know about.

"There's another thing, something else that needs an explanation. Willard Bremmer was a big help in trying to clarify what happened in the case of the mix-up. Some of what I have to tell you may be a little disturbing. If you want me to stop just say so."

"Hunter, I've just lost the love of my life. Charlie will never be replaced in my heart. Somehow I'll go on. The girls will be a big help, and knowing Charlie would want me to, helps as well.

"Having said that, the one thing Charlie always told me was that I was tougher than he was. He had no doubts about my being able to carry on without him if it came to that. And you know what? I am tough. I want to know everything you've found out."

Hunter nodded respectfully." All right. I think something is going on with Final Care, something strange. There may be a perfectly rational explanation for it, but, at this point, I'm suspicious." Then he carefully explained the embalming differences he and Bremmer had discovered and the apparent different destinations depending on which type was used. Hunter also explained that they'd found evidence that Charlie may have had some kind of brain surgery.

"But here's the really strange thing. You would think that once Final Care discovered the mix-up it would have been a simple thing to drive the body that Bremmer got up to Tampa, where it should have gone in the first place, and similarly, to drive Charlie's body from Tampa directly to Venice to Mr. Bremmer. So—"

"Wait," Jenny said. "How was Charlie embalmed?"

Hunter paused before answering, "Charlie was embalmed via the femoral artery and, of course—"

"Should have gone through Miami after leaving Brussels," Jenny finished.

"Exactly."

Jenny sat silently for several minutes, thinking about the significance of these observations. Finally, she spoke. "So what *were* they doing with Charlie's body in Miami?

Why did he have to go there? What happens there, anyway?"

Hunter nodded, "That's really the question, isn't it? What do they do there? We have two mysteries involving Charlie that may or may not be related. Was something inappropriate done to him at the Institute? Moreover, if so, what and why? And if the pattern of embalming we've discovered dictated that Charlie's body had to be flown to the Final Care facility in Miami, what was the purpose? And since their cooperation is surprising, to say the least, is there a link between Final Care and the Caravaggio Institute?"

Hunter took a deep breath, "Jenny, there's something else you should know and it involves me."

"You?"

"Yes, I've been reactivated by the Department of Defense to be on the lookout in case I find a link between all of this and Charlie's military contracts with the drone program."

"What do you mean, you've been reactivated?"

"Before my medical school career, I was an intelligence agent with the Department of Defense and frequently worked with Interpol. From time to time they reactivate me to both positions when my inquiries show any potential for overlap with national defense or international crime. The mystery surrounding Charlie could potentially involve both."

Jenny got up and walked to the piano, and picked up a framed photo showing the two of them dancing. She pressed it to her breast and sighed. "Hunter, I know Henry called you down here to find Charlie. You've done that, and he's been properly buried, and I'm thankful.

"However, if something inappropriate was done to my husband at that Institute, I want to find out what it was. Henry told me a little about your background earlier and he seems to think you can do anything. If something is going on, I want you to find out what it is. I want to hire you to find out what happened to Charlie."

She turned to meet his eyes, her expression fierce. "Here's my proposition. I'll pay all your expenses plus—"

"Jenny?"

"Yes?"

"Let me tell you how I work. I'll find out what happened to Charlie. When I have, and it's over, you can pay me whatever you think it's worth, okay?"

Jenny nodded. "It's a deal. And Hunter?"

"Yes?"

"Don't quit until you find out what happened to my husband and why."

Chapter 15

BACK AT HIS HOTEL THE LATE AFTERNOON SUN was streaming in off the Gulf. Hunter pondered his next moves. Clearly he had to fly to Europe and check out Final Care in Brussels and the Institute in Sorrento personally. He made arrangements to fly to Brussels the next afternoon.

His cell phone rang. Recognizing the number he said, "Hello, Willard. What's up?"

An agitated female voice answered. "Mr. McCoy—you have to come here right away. It's Mr. Bremmer. It's terrible. The police are here. They want to talk to you."

Within ten minutes Hunter pulled into the lot at Bremmer's Funeral Home. Two Venice city police cruisers were already there with their lights flashing. *What the hell?* He thought. A female officer stopped him as he approached and asked who he was.

"The name's McCoy. I need to talk with whoever's in charge here."

She had him wait there while she went inside and returned with a large man wearing a rumpled shirt and tie under a sport jacket totally out of place in the summer heat of southwest Florida. He flashed his badge. "I'm Detective Ingham. Who are you?"

"Hunter McCoy. What's going on here?"

"Mr. McCoy, just the man I want to see. Where have you been today?"

"I've been in Tampa all morning, got back to Venice about two hours ago, had lunch at a restaurant on the bypass—Robbi's something or other—spent some time with Jenny Lahti and then returned to my hotel. Why? What's happened?"

"What's happened is that Willard Bremmer, the owner of this place," he indicated the funeral home, "was killed about two hours ago, according to the medical examiner."

"Killed?" Hunter was stunned. *What did I get the poor man into?*

Ingham said, "Come on over here; I have some questions for you." He led Hunter to a shaded group of outdoor table and chair sets, no doubt used by overflow mourners.

Once seated, Ingham looked at this notes. "The receptionist, Carol, says you and Bremmer were working together on something. She didn't know what." With that, Ingham put up his hand in a questioning way and raised his eyebrows. "So tell me."

Hunter explained about the missing body and his role in finding it. He told Ingham about the anomaly with the embalming techniques Willard had observed, which he'd been checking out. He also told him about the Miami trip and what he'd learned there.

"What are you? Some kind of investigator?"

Hunter knew it was time to fill him in, so he showed him his Virginia Highway Patrol detective shield and his Interpol credentials and explained he was investigating a potential international crime, and for added effect, he showed his DIA badge and suggested there might be a potential national security issue as well.

He had to hand it to Ingham. The man handled it well. Hunter compared his response to many he'd gotten over the years in similar situations where his credentials topped the local guy.

"I see. I suppose that puts a different light on things. Still, I have to deal with this homicide regardless of your mission. I don't get it McCoy, why is Interpol involved and what could any of this have to do with national security?" Hunter just looked at him saying nothing.

Sighing, Ingham said, "Okay, okay, I get it." He closed his notebook, "You're not at liberty to say. But given your background maybe you'd better see Mr. Bremmer's body."

Confused by this, Hunter followed Ingham into the main viewing room. Crime scene tape was up and the forensic people where hard at work around an open casket sitting on the viewing stand. At the casket Hunter looked in and saw Willard Bremmer with his hands crossed over his chest in the classic death pose. He would have looked like any other corpse except for the fact that he had been almost decapitated by what must have been a wire garrote. And then there was the large note pinned to his chest: Its message guaranteed that Hunter would do just the opposite.

LEAVE IT ALONE MCCOY

Chapter 16

SHORTLY AFTER NOON ON THE DAY AFTER Willard Bremmer's murder, Hunter was more determined than ever to fulfill his promise to Jenny that he'd find out what happened to Charlie. He waited at the gate for the 12:56 United Airlines flight out of Tampa to Brussels. They hadn't started boarding yet, so he called Anue.

"Dad, it's Hunter. How're you doing?"

"Okay, I guess."

Hunter thought he sounded a little distant. "Has Henry been by to let you know what we've been doing down here?"

"I don't..."

Hunter waited. "Dad, are you okay? You sound a little, I don't know, tired?"

"What did you ask me?"

"I asked if Henry had been by since he got back."

"Yeah, I think so."

"You're not sure?"

"I'm pretty sure. Yeah, I think...I mean, yeah, he was here."

This wasn't good. Hunter knew something wasn't right with his dad. He should get back up there now and get him in to see a doctor.

"United Flight 1583 will begin boarding at gate 26C in a few minutes," an amplified voice announced. "Check your boarding passes as we'll begin boarding by zones."

Shit

"Look, Dad, I'm going out of the country for a few days related to the missing body case, but I'll call you as soon as I can. Meanwhile, would you call Henry and have him over to the cabin for cards or something? You need the company, and I can't be there right now. Okay?"

"Sure, son, don't worry, I'll call him. What missing body case are you talking about?"

Oh boy. "You know, Henry's brother's funeral where the body didn't show up?"

"Oh, yeah, I remember something about that. I'll ask Henry about it."

"You do that, Dad. I have to go now. I'll call you later."

Hunter ended the call just as they called his zone. The flight was expected to get into Brussels the next morning at 7:15. It was hard not to fly back to Marquette instead, but he wanted to honor his promise to Jenny—and his silent promise to himself to find Willard Bremmer's killer.

Brussels was one of his favorite European capitals. He supposed it was because he'd never had a crime to deal within its city limits, something he couldn't say for many of the others. But then it might be he just found its Old World charm fit him like a warm sweater on a cold winter day.

During the twelve-hour flight he sat back in his aisle seat and thought about his dad. The man had been a rock all his life. He'd seen combat in the jungles of Viet Nam and had been a terrific father to both Gary and himself.

Following the death of their mother when the boys were young, Ed became both mother and father to them. Seeing him beginning to get confused and slip a little now was painful, and Hunter knew he should really be there to help. He made a mental note to call Henry and make sure he got over to see him, maybe even get him to a doctor if the case dragged on.

Deliberately setting the problem of his dad aside for the moment, he tried to put the past few days in perspective.

Final Care had said they'd found the glitch in their system that allowed the body mix-up to happen and corrected it. But that still didn't explain why a stop in Miami was seemingly required of those with femoral but not carotid embalming. Johannes Donckers, the embalmer who signed off on all of those cases had better have an explanation for that.

HUNTER HAD SCHEDULED AN APPOINTMENT with a Ms. Janssen at Final Care at 11:00 a.m. so he had time to check into the Holiday Inn at the airport, clean up, and have breakfast first.

Like the Final Care facility in Miami, the buildings in Brussels were also at the airport. He supposed this made sense, since virtually all the bodies were airlifted out.

During his breakfast of an omelet and croissant, he picked up a discarded copy of *USA Today* and saw a headline for a major jewel heist right here in Brussels. The bad guys had gotten away with some incredibly expensive pieces belonging to the wife of a Belgian tycoon in the international commodities market. It seemed there had been a number of high-stakes jewelry heists in Europe lately, more than usual, and the police supposedly had no clues.

After breakfast, Hunter headed out to the Final Care facility. Ever since the murder of Bremmer, he'd been on high alert, paying close attention to those around him. He hadn't made out anyone suspicious in the restaurant, yet he still had a feeling he was being observed. The feeling stayed with him as he took a cab to the Final Care building.

Chapter 17

WHEN HE ARRIVED AT THE BRUSSELS Final Care facility promptly at 11:00 a.m., Hunter was surprised at the warm reception he received in contrast to what he had experienced with Dyson in Miami or what Bremmer had experienced talking with their man on the phone.

"Mr. McCoy, please come in," said the smiling, pretty young receptionist who'd stepped out from behind her desk to greet him as soon as he came in the front entrance. "We've been expecting you."

Unlike the exterior of the huge building, which was airport outbuilding standard—a huge nondescript hanger—the large interior reception area was warm and inviting, like a beautifully furnished home. Paintings adorned the walls, and charming furniture and accessories gave the visitor the impression of a relaxed, comfortable, setting. Hunter even thought he recognized two hand-carved oak hutches.

"Flemish antiques?" he asked, pointing. "About 1880?"

"You have a good eye, Mr. McCoy. They are the most valuable pieces we have, 1881 to be exact. Are you an antique dealer?" she inquired.

"No, just an amateur admirer." Still, he marveled at how much he'd learned about antiques from his old girlfriend, Annie, when they'd been together in Charlottesville and she owned the antiques shop specializing in furniture and accessories.

"Is Ms. Janssen available?" he asked, changing the subject, to the apparent disappointment of the lovely receptionist, who was clearly enjoying her time with the tall handsome American.

"Yes, of course. I'll call her now." Returning to her desk, the receptionist punched a number on the phone.

A moment later, an attractive middle-aged woman, considerably more businesslike than the flirty receptionist, came forward from a hallway in the back.

"Good morning, Mr. McCoy, I'm Margot Janssen. Please, let's step back to my office." Then, addressing the receptionist, "Hetty, would you bring us some coffee?"

Her office was comfortable, like the reception area, and equally populated by paintings and antiques. While she had a desk, she gestured to two comfortable side chairs next to a coffee table on which Hetty instantly set a tray with a pot, two mugs, and an assortment of cookies and left them alone. Margot Janssen poured them both a cup and they sat back.

"Now, what can I do for you? I know you'd like information about the confusion of the two parcels. I'm here to answer all your questions."

"Parcels?"

"Sorry, that's a term we use in-house to describe the remains we ship. I know it sounds impersonal, but it really simplifies communication here in the plant."

"Maybe you could explain how the mix-up occurred."

"Certainly. In fact, I think a tour of the facilities would make it easier for you to understand how that happened and what we've done to ensure it won't ever happen again. But first let me tell you what we do here. Would that be all right?"

"Great," agreed Hunter.

"When a citizen of one country dies in another country in Europe, the Middle East, or North Africa, they generally contact their embassy or consulate, which then, in most cases, contacts our local representative. The representative then speaks with the family either by phone or in person and arranges to handle all aspects of preparing and sending the remains back to the deceased's home.

"We contact the local funeral home and work with them. We handle all necessary paperwork, embalming or cremation, and transport of the remains. Cremation or embalming is done here in this facility. No matter where the death occurred, the deceased is sent here for processing. We're, by far, the largest nonmilitary organization doing this kind of work."

"So are all the bodies either cremated or embalmed right here?" Hunter asked.

"Almost all. A few for various reasons are embalmed at our facility in Miami. These are usually cases in which the family insists on an American site for the embalming. Of course we respect their wishes."

"How many would that be?"

"It varies but probably averages about ten per year. Not many."

Hunter nodded. "That doesn't seem like enough work to keep an embalmer busy. Is he full time?"

"Oh no, part time. We contract a local man to come out to the plant at Miami when necessary. Of course we have to maintain a lab for him."

"I see." Hunter realized, too late, he should have talked with the part-time man in Miami when he was there.

Standing up and smoothing her skirt, Ms. Janssen said, "I think this would be a good time for the tour."

They started in the receiving area, where she introduced him to Mr. Keppler, the receiving agent who described what happens in his domain.

"Most of the parcels arrive here by air from the place where they died. Our people then retrieve them from the various airlines that we use and take them here to this receiving area. All parcels are accompanied by documentation prepared by the local Final Care representative. This includes a photo of the deceased, taken by the rep, the contract with the family, and all local and international paperwork required to get the parcel to us. Here, I'll show you."

They walked to a nearby silver metal container on a gurney that had one of the documentation folders securely taped to the cover.

"Wait," Hunter said. "If a photo accompanies the corpse how did they get mixed up?"

"Patience, Mr. McCoy," urged Ms. Janssen. "I'm coming to that. But you're right, that was part of the problem in this case."

"All right, go on, Mr. Keppler," Hunter said.

"At this point, I open the container and compare the photo to the deceased. When I've confirmed they agree, I roll the container to the preparation area, along with the accompanying documentation, I hand the documentation over to the embalmer along with the container.

"So at this point," said Hunter, "the deceased and his paperwork are always properly linked together."

"That's correct," Janssen replied, "except for one thing, and it's never happened before. Since the photos and the documentation are separate pieces, they got mixed up here in the receiving department. The photos still matched the bodies in the containers, so they appeared to be correct, but the documentation had somehow become switched, so while Mr. Lahti's photo matched Mr. Lahti's remains, the documentation said he was Mr. Cole and should go to Tampa. Mr. Cole's photo matched Mr. Cole's remains but the documentation said he was Mr. Lahti and should go to Venice."

She gave an apologetic smile. "The mix-up must have happened here, and we take full responsibility. But—and this is important—it won't happen again, because from now on all photos will be digital and printed out on the same documentation that has the deceased's name, information, and shipping destination. This should completely eliminate the possibility of a future mix-up."

Hunter had to admit the change they'd made, physically linking the photo to the documentation would no doubt solve the problem, and he told Ms. Janssen just that.

She smiled appreciatively and said, "Now let's go to the preparation area."

Hunter expected to be directed to a room he imagined to be filled with stainless steel tables and all the paraphernalia needed for embalming. Instead, he was directed to the office of Mr. Johannes Donckers, the embalmer.

Chapter 18

JOHANNES DONCKERS WAS OF AVERAGE height, a little overweight, appearing to be in his late forties or early fifties with a pattern baldness that gave him the look of a benevolent friar. His office, small but neat, featured a small bookcase filled with technical books and medical texts.

A young woman in her mid-twenties was leaning against the wall looking at Hunter. She appeared to be about five six, very attractive, with red hair and eyes even greener than his.

"Oh, I'm sorry, Johannes, I didn't know you had—company," Ms. Janssen said with a palpable disdain as she gave a curt nod toward the young woman.

Seemingly unaware of the tension between the women, Donckers said, "Margot, you know my daughter, Kat." Then he looked inquisitively at Hunter.

"Mr. McCoy is here to follow up on the mix-up of the two parcels last week," Ms. Janssen said. "He's representing the widow of Mr. Lahti."

Coming around the desk, the man extended his hand to Hunter. "A most unfortunate incident, Mr. McCoy. I'm sure Margot has described how it happened and that steps have been taken to ensure there won't be another such incident in the future."

"Yes it was and yes she has," answered Hunter. "And I believe I'll be able to report to the widow nothing was intentional. A mistake was made and her unfortunate experience will assure it won't happen again to anyone else."

Visibly relieved to hear this, Ms. Janssen said, "Mr. McCoy, I assure you, Final Care is happy to hear our efforts have been so kindly received. Now, if there is nothing else, I'll return you to the reception area, as I have a meeting I need to attend."

She started to leave, expecting him to follow. "Thanks," Hunter said, "but if Mr. Donckers doesn't mind, I'd like to visit with him for a few minutes."

Unsure what this meant, but still having her meeting to attend, Ms. Janssen simply nodded. "Well, all right then, Johannes, I'll leave Mr. McCoy with you."

When she'd gone, Mr. Donckers asked him to sit down. "What can I do for you, Mr. McCoy?"

Hunter wasn't sure how to broach this, nor was he sure he should with the man's daughter in the room.

Sensing his hesitance, Donckers said, "If you'd like to speak with me alone, my daughter can step outside for a while." He nodded at her.

She shrugged indifferently at Hunter and raised one eyebrow, smiling slightly, which he took as a challenge to ask her to leave, and waited for his answer.

"Not a problem for me. Just want to ask you about embalming technique."

"Oh, well then, it's all right. Kat's been okay with what I do since she was a little girl. Right, honey?"

"Yes," was the clipped answer.

She resumed leaning against the wall, crossed her arms, and waited, still flashing that challenging half smile.

"So what do you want to know about embalming?" asked Donckers.

Hunter sat in the offered chair and went right at it. "I want to know why you ship bodies with femoral artery embalming to the Miami facility first, before sending them on to their final destination."

Hunter made two observations in rapid order. Father and daughter quickly glanced at each other, apprehension unmistakable in both their faces. The daughter recovered faster, the slight smile quickly returning. Johannes Donckers was a little slower to resume his previous pleasant demeanor.

"Thank you for waiting until Ms. Janssen left before asking that question." He shifted uncomfortably.

"Why is that?" Hunter asked.

"I could get in a lot of trouble here."

The daughter looked at her dad again, this time with a genuine expression of confusion and concern, maybe even fear, on her face.

It was obvious the man was thinking fast and seriously troubled by Hunter's question.

"Mr. McCoy, are you in any way associated with Final Care?"

"I assure you I have nothing to do with Final Care. I'm only interested in the case of Mr. Lahti's temporarily missing body."

Donckers frowned. "Then what makes you think femoral artery embalming cases are sent to Miami first?"

Hunter explained how he and Bremmer had pieced together the information from funeral directors in Tampa, Sarasota, Venice, and Fort Myers. Then, staring straight at Donckers, he waited for the explanation.

Donckers sat back in his chair, looked at his daughter, took a deep breath and exhaled slowly, shaking his head. "It was dumb, I know. Let me tell you a story."

Kat stared at her father with undisguised fear, and Hunter watched her begin to fidget nervously with the gold chain around her neck, apparently not sure what her father was going to say.

Donckers cleared his throat and began. "It started with my cousin, Willie Hofmann. He lives in Miami. He's also an embalmer and works at one of the funeral homes in the city—Benson's. He and I went to mortuary science school together. When Final Care opened the facility at the airport and announced they needed a part-time embalmer, he asked me if I'd recommend him for the job. I did, and he got it. Willie prefers to use the carotid artery route whenever he can. But sometimes, particularly with females, who are viewed with exposed necks, the femoral route is better for cosmetic reasons."

Hunter wondered where this was going and caught a look at the daughter, who was visibly beginning to relax and had stopped fidgeting.

Donckers continued. "He knew my technique and had always admired it. And, well, I too prefer the carotid route, I decided to do several using the femoral artery and vein so he could see the results and learn from it."

"Sounds reasonable. Why are you glad Ms. Janssen left before I asked?"

The man looked down as if embarrassed. "Final Care incurs added expense when we route through the Miami facility—the company does, not the client. So my arranging for them to be shipped to Miami would be an unnecessary expense in the eyes of the company. They weren't going to be embalmed there. I'd already done it. It was only for the professional education of my cousin.

"Please, Mr. McCoy, I beg you not to tell. It won't happen again. He's learned what he needs to know, and it could cost me my job if they found out. I was only trying to be helpful to a fellow professional."

Hunter thought about it. The story made sense in way. And it explained the pattern he'd uncovered. It even explained the reason Charlie's body was shipped from Tampa back to Miami instead of directly to Venice. He glanced at the man's daughter. On a hunch, he decided to take a chance.

"Do you agree with that explanation, Miss Donckers?"

Momentarily startled by Hunter's question, she recovered. "Of course, why wouldn't I? What are you suggesting?" she snapped, the smile suddenly gone. Then softening her irritation, she continued. "Mr. McCoy, my dad needs this job. No harm was done to anyone. Can we— I mean, can he—count on your cooperation?"

Hunter wondered about the quickly corrected use of "we," but seeing no real reason not to cooperate, he nodded. "Sure, why not?" Turning his attention back to Donckers, he asked, "But would you answer a few more questions first?"

Donckers shuffled some papers on his desk and adjusted his glasses, and finally gave a hesitant "Okay."

"How long have you been with Final Care?"

Clearly pleased the question of the embalming irregularity had been disposed of, Johannes became almost chatty. "I was hired in January 2009. It was interesting, really, since I was already working at a successful funeral home in Antwerp at the time and wasn't even looking for another job. I got a letter from the top man at Final Care, in which he indicated they'd like me to come and work for them here in Brussels, and the salary would be more than double what I'd been making in Antwerp. Their top man claimed he'd been looking for just the right person, and his independent search suggested I was the man. So I took it."

"Who's the top man?" Hunter asked.

"I'm afraid I don't know. The offer was actually presented by their Human Resources department and they just said their top man was extending the offer."

Hunter stood up to leave. "I see. So it worked out for everybody then."

Donckers, visibly relaxed now, got up and reached across the desk to shake Hunter's hand.

Pushing herself away from the wall, Kat said, "You can stay, Dad. I'll walk Mr. McCoy to the reception area."

She walked with a catlike grace that reminded Hunter of a gymnast he'd once dated. Unsure of what to make of her earlier behavior and sensing there was more to the story, he said, "So Miss Donckers, I probably can't arrange a flight until tomorrow. Perhaps you could show me Brussels?" Then shading the truth, he added, "I've never been here before. How about I take you to dinner and you can give me a tour?"

She gave him smile that hinted of the challenge he'd seen earlier.

"All right, why not?"

Chapter 19

AFTER HUNTER AND KAT LEFT HIS OFFICE, Johannes Donckers sat back, breathing rapidly. He was hyperventilating and knew it. Feeling himself getting light-headed, he opened his desk drawer, took out a paper lunch bag, dumped the contents onto the desk, and began breathing into it. Within minutes his respiration began returning to normal.

He'd known it was all going to come crashing down on them some day. His past was coming back to haunt him, as he surely knew it would. He put the bag away, shut his office door, and sat in silence, closing his eyes.

Thirty years ago his name had been Gunter Hofmann not Johannes Donckers. He'd been only seventeen years old and he'd just killed the mayor of Cologne, Germany.

He and his fifteen-year-old sister, Lisa, had been guests for the day at the mayor's home when he heard Lisa screaming upstairs. He raced up to investigate and found the drunken mayor tearing at her clothes and forcing her onto his bed.

Grabbing a marble statuette from a nightstand, he swung it at the man, connecting solidly with the side of his head, sending him reeling, then crumbling to the floor. An enormous pool of blood spread out from his head. Checking to see if the man was dead, Gunter slipped in the blood and fell, drenching his white sweater in the warm crimson gore.

Panicking, he and his sister raced down the stairs and out to his car, but not before the maid saw him covered in blood. He drove his sister home but knew he had to get away. Fortunately he always kept his passport and some clothes in the boot of his Volkswagen. Discarding the bloody items, he changed and raced to the Belgian border. He crossed and drove to Brussels, where he knew his cousin, Willie Hofmann, was going to begin a program in mortuary science.

After spending the night in a youth hostel outside the city, Gunter read the next morning's news report of the Mayor's death. The German authorities were hunting him down. He was positively identified as the murderer, seen leaving the scene with bloodstained clothes.

The story his sister told of the Mayor's assault on her and how her brother had come to her rescue was dismissed as not credible and a feeble attempt to divert the authorities from the real crime—robbery. The Mayor's wallet and gold watch were missing, supplying all the proof the police needed to call this a robbery and murder.

Gunter knew that last bit about the watch and wallet had to be an attempt on the part of the mayor's family to cover up the truth. What chance did he have against such powerful people? The answer was painfully obvious— none, and he knew it.

With nowhere else to go he drove to his cousin's apartment, found him, and explained what he'd done.

Willie helped him get enrolled in the same mortuary science program—under a new name, Johannes Donckers. He and Willie went through the program together, and Gunter—now Johannes—stayed on as Willie's roommate, taking a job waiting tables in a local restaurant to supplement the money Willie's parents sent. The two boys got on well.

But then it all went wrong—terribly, horribly wrong.

Chapter 20

KAT TOLD HUNTER SHE'D PICK HIM UP outside his hotel at
8:00 p.m. Since he didn't have a car, she said it would be
more convenient this way and she'd give him a tour of the
city.

Hunter had taken a room at the Royal Windsor Hotel at
Grand Place in the city center, near the train terminal.
Wearing slacks, a dress shirt open at the collar, and a
lightweight sport jacket he stepped to the curb outside the
hotel at precisely 8:00 p.m. Looking for a car he was surprised to see a sleek black motorcycle pull up to the curb
next to him with a lone rider dressed completely in black
wearing a helmet and dark visor. The rider pulled off the
helmet and the full red hair, green eyes, and challenging
haughty air were unmistakable—Kat.

"Jump on, McCoy. Let's see Brussels at night."

He settled in behind her, wrapping his arms around her
surprisingly firm body. Hunter had long ago discovered he
preferred nighttime city tours: landmarks were always set
off by extraordinary lighting that cast shadows, giving them
a life and grandeur that was frequently diminished by
bright sunlight. Lights from vehicles, storefronts, street
lamps, even the occasional person lighting a cigarette,
added warmth and color to everything.

Of course he'd lied to Kat when he told her this was his
first trip to Brussels but it seemed like a good way to get
her to cooperate and to find out if there was anything

behind her earlier suspicious behavior. Besides, he quite enjoyed wrapping his arms around her.

With the two-way radio connection between their helmets, Kat surprised him by giving delightfully irreverent descriptions as she took them by the Grand Place, the Manneken Pis—the statue of the little boy peeing in the fountain—the Royal Palace, and the Art Nouveau district. UNESCO now recognized several of the Art Nouveau buildings as World Heritage Sites. As they drove through little streets, with centuries-old buildings, Kat's descriptions reflected a love for the city and its history that Hunter recognized as genuine.

An hour-and-a-half later, she pulled up outside a small restaurant on a single lane street, dark except for the lone ancient streetlamp on the corner. After locking the bike and taking their helmets with them, Kat led them into a small but charming bistro with perhaps ten tables, half of them already occupied by couples. The maître d' led them to one near the front, giving them a view of the other diners as well as the dimly lit street outside. Hunter deemed it perfect.

After they'd been seated and ordered wine, Kat politely challenged him. "So, what do you think of our city, McCoy? Too provincial for a big shot American like you?"

"I always say a tour is only as good as the guide." Then lifting his glass toward her, he added, "And tonight mine was exceptional."

She bowed a slight thank-you.

Over a dinner of mussels, a delicious potato soup and salad, they got to know each other a little.

"Tell me, McCoy, do you actually make a living finding missing dead bodies for widows?"

Hunter laughed. He liked her directness. "You'd be surprised. Things turn up missing all the time. I'm very good at finding them, and people do pay me for it."

"What I mean is, is that your full-time job?"

Hunter refilled their glasses from the excellent bottle of red wine the waiter had left. The both sipped a little before Hunter answered.

"No, I'm afraid my full-time job is a little less exciting. I teach medical students at the University of Virginia and I conduct research on blood vessels and circulation."

"You're a doctor?" she asked in surprise.

"I'm a Ph.D. physiologist—a medical scientist, not a physician. What do you do besides ride tourists around the city on your motorcycle?"

She gazed out the window at the street. It seemed to Hunter as if she was contemplating this for the first time. After a long moment she turned to look at Hunter, her usual challenging smile replaced by reflection.

Hunter thought she looked quite beautiful.

"My mother wanted me to be a pianist. She arranged for me to take lessons from the best teachers in Brussels when I was a little girl. I stayed with it for a while, but lacked the self-discipline to excel at it—unlike my mother. She was an immense talent, a concert pianist of incredible skill and flair. She played with all the leading orchestras in Europe and America. I'd marvel at how she'd memorize a piece then play it perfectly without any music in front of her. I suppose I knew I'd never be that good. Maybe that had something to do with my choosing another direction."

"What's her name? I've probably heard of her."

"Her name was Irena Rousseau."

Hunter lit up. "Sure, I know her. I even have some of her recordings. Wait, you said was?"

"Yes, she died almost six months ago."

"I'm sorry, Kat, that must have been hard."

"Yes, it was, but even harder on my father. They were very much in love. He was so devastated he was pretty much unable to work for several weeks afterward." She sighed. "Final Care was very good to him and allowed him to keep his job, while he made whatever recovery he could.

The only living relatives he has are me and that cousin in Miami he told you about earlier." He noticed she said this latter with considerably less warmth.

They were quiet for a few minutes, each sipping their wine and thinking their own thoughts. Finally Hunter asked, "So what do you do now? How do you pay the bills?"

Hunter sensed a kind of wariness, as she answered, "I'm a freelance gemologist. I appraise and purchase estate jewelry for many of the leading jewelers in Europe."

"That must be exciting."

"It is. Many of the pieces are incredibly expensive and their provenances have to be thoroughly checked out, so I travel a lot throughout the continent, both to appraise pieces that come available through estate sales and to advise the jewelers who hire me."

Hunter was surprised and impressed. "I see. So do you live in Brussels? Is this your home base?"

She looked at him for a moment before answering. "Right now I don't have a place, since I'm moving around so much. So while I'm here in Brussels, I'm staying with my father."

Abruptly changing the topic she asked, "Have you made flight arrangements yet? You said you were leaving tomorrow to fly back to the United States."

"Yup, I've made flight arrangements for tomorrow, but not to the United States. I'll be flying to Italy. Sorrento, actually."

"Are you on holiday then?"

"No, it's just another part of the mystery surrounding the late Mr. Lahti."

Furrowing her brows, Kat asked, "What do you mean?"

Hunter wasn't sure where he should go with this. On the one hand, Kat knew about his inquiry into the mix-up of the two bodies and he'd agreed to keep the information about her father's embalming activity from Final Care's administration, so a certain level of trust already existed between them. Still, his inquires at the Caravaggio Neurological Institute had nothing to do with her or her father. He decided to stick to the truth but keep it limited.

"Before he died, Mr. Lahti was on vacation with his wife in Italy and suffered a stroke. He was at the Caravaggio Neurological Institute in Sorrento for therapy when he had another stroke and died. The widow has a few questions concerning the care he was given while there. That's what I'll be doing."

It wasn't the full truth, but he thought it sufficient. Kat looked out the window again. Her smile was gone. *She certainly isn't going melancholy over my leaving. What's going on?*

When her thousand-mile stare continued for another minute, Hunter asked, "What's wrong?"

Turning to him, she shook her head. "You say Mr. Lahti had a stroke and went to the Institute for therapy. Then when he was there, he had another stroke and died."

Puzzled at this, Hunter replied, "Yeah, that's what happened. Why do you ask?"

"My mother died at the Caravaggio Institute of a stroke. She too had had an earlier one and was at the Institute for therapy when a second one killed her."

They both fell silent for a time. Hunter's background had taught him to be suspicious of coincidences. Suddenly he was even more anxious to investigate the Institute. *What's going on at that place?*

Hunter had a question he hadn't thought to ask Margot Janssen earlier. "Kat, do you know how Final Care learns when an American tourist has died and their services might be required?"

She shrugged. "I'm not sure, but I suppose they usually get recommended by the American Consulate nearest to where the death happens. That would probably be the first place an American family would turn in an emergency."

Yeah, that makes sense, thought Hunter.

"Of course," continued Kat, "in the case of your Mr. Lahti, it would have been automatic, and wouldn't have involved the consulate."

Confused, Hunter asked, "What do you mean?"

"The Institute would automatically use Final Care."

"Why is that?"

"Surely you know," said Kat

"Know what?"

"Nero Caravaggio, the founder and chief medical officer of the Caravaggio Neurological Institute, owns Final Care."

Chapter 21

KRIS HANSON WAS AT THE BABY GRAND piano in her living room, picking her way through a supposedly easy arrangement of a Chopin polonaise. She was embarrassed that her husband Carl, reading the paper in the other room had to listen to the multiple mistakes she was making. The dear man had to be a saint for not putting on earmuffs. Knowing the fault was her own and not the piano's, she gently closed the keyboard cover and walked to the kitchen, where she poured a cup of coffee and stared out the window at the lilac bush in the back yard.

Kris had been a real estate agent for most of her life, in Muncie, Indiana. She and Carl had met after college and were married after a two-month relationship they both knew was right. They'd never had children but it was okay, as they'd only needed each other. Carl bought a hardware store and through hard work and business savvy turned it into a respected chain of stores throughout the Midwest.

Kris had gotten her real estate license and was member of the "million dollar" club in sales almost every year until the Great Recession cut property values and sales drastically. Even then, however, she continued to thrive. All in all, they'd done very well over the years.

Now they were thinking of retiring. Carl had a buyer for the hardware chain, and they were looking forward to having more time to pursue their interests and for travel. Carl's hobby was American history and his home office was lined with books on the subject. He was looking forward to visiting sites he'd only read about.

For her part, Kris had always wanted to play the piano. And while she could read music very well, having taken piano lessons as a child, she could never really play well enough to perform in front of others. Then in January, on her sixty-fifth birthday on the Isle of Capri in Italy, a head injury changed everything.

As she and Carl were boarding the funicular for the ride to the top of the island, she slipped and fell backward hitting her head on the sharp edge of a concrete post. She was rushed to the local hospital and then airlifted to the Caravaggio Neurological Institute in Sorrento for surgery for a depressed skull fracture over the occipital lobe of the brain.

As Kris sipped her coffee, tears welled up in her eyes as she recalled how much her skills had deteriorated since the remarkable—really miraculous—improvement in her otherwise mediocre piano skills. During the three weeks of therapy following the surgery, they'd asked her to play specific piano pieces with electrodes attached to her head. They wanted to see if her brain waves were returning to normal as she carried out a skilled task. But to her amazement, she'd become an extraordinary pianist. The odd program, they'd devised for her therapy had not only returned her motor skills to normal, but her piano playing improved way beyond what she'd been able to do before. She couldn't explain it. It truly was like a miracle as her playing skills reached a professional performance level, something she'd always wanted to do. In fact, she'd become so good that when she got home she'd actually been asked to — and did — perform as a soloist with the Muncie Symphony Orchestra. She was still hardly able to believe it.

The thunderous applause as she'd stood to take her bow was the most beautiful music she'd ever heard. Kris remembered the wonderful prickly sensation on the back of her neck the next morning, as she'd read the review of her performance the night before in the *Muncie Star Press*.

She'd played the incredibly difficult Chopin Polonaise No. 6 in A flat OP. 53 to a packed house at Sursa Performance Hall on the campus of Ball State University, and her playing had been flawless. In fact, to use the language of professional musicians, it was the first time she'd ever played it "incident free." Her rehearsals had been extremely good but never perfect. But that night—that night was perfect. How had the *Star Press* music critic put it?

> *This reviewer is at a loss for words. Where did this marvel come from? Hanson's magnificent performance of the Chopin Polonaise was beyond criticism. Her touch, feeling, and oneness with the composer in this performance were inspired and flawless. And, on a personal note, it was totally unfair to this critic. If all performers were this good, I'd quickly find myself out of work. There was absolutely nothing in her playing to criticize. I can only fault her for being unfair to the musical public by waiting so long to display her enormous talent...*

The phone wouldn't stop ringing. Her husband had graciously agreed to answer it and respond to the many well-wishers who'd been calling, some who had been at the performance themselves, and others—old friends—who'd only read the reviews.

"How are you holding up to the adulation, honey?" her husband had asked as he joined her the morning after at the breakfast table.

"I couldn't be happier. It's what I've always wanted to do. You know that more than anyone. All my life I've wanted to play with the skill of a concert pianist. And now, apparently, I can," she remembered telling him.

KRIS WIPED AWAY A TEAR AS SHE RECALLED all of this. She supposed she should be happy though. She had achieved her dream, even if briefly. It's not as though she played worse than she had before Sorrento; she'd just lost all the incredible skill she'd developed.

As she got up to see if Carl wanted to go out for lunch, she stopped in the bathroom to get two aspirins. She felt a headache coming on.

Chapter 22

THE MORNING FOLLOWING THE CITY TOUR with Kat, Hunter caught the 9:20 Alitalia flight out of Brussels National Airport to Naples. During the flight he thought about Kat. After the restaurant she'd driven them to a lovely park where they'd locked her bike and walked arm-in-arm and talked for another hour. When he'd asked her if she had any work coming up, she'd said she had to go to Paris for an estate evaluation and would be gone only a day. Later, when she rode him to his hotel, he'd kissed her and thanked for the lovely evening. She'd returned the kiss and wished him well in Italy.

He'd planned to review his notes on the Caravaggio Institute, `but couldn't get the coincidences between Kat's mother and Charlie out of his mind. Both had a stroke that required therapy. Both had been transferred from a hospital to the Institute for that therapy. Both had apparently been making incredible progress when both suddenly suffered a second stroke and died.

On the other hand, was it so surprising? After all, people died in medical facilities all the time. You wouldn't go there if you were healthy. Still, with all the suspicions he was racking up about the place, it gnawed at him.

Speaking of coincidences, was it just a coincidence that Final Care is owned by the man who runs the Caravaggio Institute where Charlie Lahti died? Was it a coincidence Willard Bremmer was murdered after investigating the mix-up and the strange embalming pattern? Was any of this linked to Charlie's company, SkySoft, and the RaptorCrypt program? Had Johannes Donckers and Kat told him the whole truth about why the bodies were shipped to Miami? Too many puzzles and not enough answers, Hunter thought.

AFTER ARRIVING AT CAPODICHINO AIRPORT, Hunter rented a car for the drive to Sorrento, about forty miles away. The gorgeous scenic route, with a constant view of the bay of Naples on one side and the majestic background of Mount Vesuvius on the other, gave him even more time to contemplate his next move.

Should he begin with Phillippi, the neurosurgeon, and demand to know what was going on? Maybe go right to the boss and talk with Nero Caravaggio himself? Or would a less confrontational approach be best? He finally settled on the latter, knowing he could always get tough later if necessary.

Earlier, he'd noticed a green Audi that appeared to be staying with him. He couldn't make out whether the driver was a man or a woman, but there didn't appear to be anyone else in the car. Was he being followed or was he just getting jumpy?

Let's give it a test.

Up ahead on the left he saw a petrol station. He signaled for the turn and looked in the rearview mirror to see if the Audi would follow suit. As he pulled into the lot, the Audi continued down the road without even slowing.

Well that answers that question.

He was being overly cautious.

THE CARAVAGGIO NEUROLOGICAL INSTITUTE was a beautiful campus of modern buildings set in the wooded hills behind the city. Hunter found it easily using the GPS in his rental Fiat. The elegantly designed administration building was built like a pie with one wedge or piece missing at the front. A parking lot replaced the missing piece of pie.

"May I help you, sir?" asked a young woman in Italian-accented English, from behind a reception desk.

"Yes. My aunt quite recently suffered a small stroke while we were traveling in Italy, and her doctor suggested she come here for therapy. She asked me if I'd come first and look over the place, if that would be okay."

"Of course. How nice of you to care so much for your aunt. Let me call someone who can help you."

Hallways radiated outward in several directions from the reception area where he now stood. He saw people going about their business along most of them.

"Mister—? I'm sorry, I didn't get your name."

"Ashworth. Harry Ashworth, from Columbus, Ohio."

"Mr. Ashworth, if you'll just have a seat over there, someone will be with you in a few minutes."

Taking a seat on the indicated sofa, Hunter waited. Five minutes later a smiling woman who appeared to be in her late fifties came up to him and introduced herself.

"Mr. Ashworth, I'm Gina Lombardi. Perhaps you'd like a tour of the campus?"

"That'd be great."

She led him back out of the administration building to the small park out front.

"You may not have noticed when you drove up, but the campus is laid out in a circular fashion with the administration building we just left essentially at the center."

Hunter scanned the site and saw she was right. Just as the reception desk he'd just left was at the center of hallways in the building radiating outward in all directions, the administration building was itself at the center of multiple tree-lined walkways radiating outward toward groups of buildings in every direction.

"When Dr. Caravaggio started the Institute ten years ago, neurological care in this part of Italy was haphazard at best. Hospitals in the area might have had one or two doctors who could treat stroke, and that was about it. Neurological patients with degenerative diseases like Parkinson's, ALS, and Alzheimer's had no option but to head for Rome or be left essentially untreated."

"Very interesting."

As she led him down one of the walkways or "spokes" toward a large group of buildings at the end, she continued. "Did you know that Dr. Caravaggio, the founder of the Institute, is from Sorrento himself?"

"I didn't, no," Hunter responded.

Reaching the building at the end of the walk, Mrs. Lombardi didn't go inside, but instead led him along a beautifully landscaped winding path around the side to the back. There, he saw yet another example of the circle analogy. What he had taken for one building turned out to be five, neatly arranged in a circular pattern around a gazebo in a central courtyard where five paths radiated out toward them. Between the paths grassy areas with shade trees and flowerbeds, were occupied by patients sitting on benches or strolling along with white-coated staffers.

"This is the stroke campus, Mr. Ashworth. I thought you might like to see where your aunt would be if she comes here. These five buildings are all dedicated to stroke patients." Pointing to each in turn she described their functions. One was the housing building, where patients lived during their convalescence. Another was dedicated to physical therapy. Still another was the imaging facility, where brain scans and other evaluative work was done. The fourth was dedicated to surgery, and the final building was administrative specifically for the stroke campus.

"The medical staff here is without a doubt the best in Italy, perhaps in all of Europe, and even includes a Nobel laureate. Dr. Caravaggio himself has been nominated several times. We think it's only a matter of time until he gets the Prize too."

Hunter thanked Mrs. Lombardi for the tour and assured her he'd tell his aunt not to worry, she'd like it here. While they walked back to the main administration building and the parking lot where he'd left his rental, Hunter took careful notice of the grounds. He was particularly interested in the administration building on the stroke campus. Tonight, after hours, he planned on getting a much closer look.

Chapter 23

A SLENDER, BLACK-CLAD FEMININE FIGURE made her way through the woods toward a luxurious private villa with a spectacular view of the city of Paris below. The house was equipped with a sophisticated security system designed to protect it from intruders.

This intruder knew the occupants were away on a two-week cruise to the Greek Islands. Having previously dismantled the security system, her athleticism allowed her to easily scale the drainpipe on the white stucco wall to the second-floor balcony overlooking the pool below. Knowing exactly where to go, she swiftly found the door to the master suite and slipped inside. Moving straight to a painting of a pensive nude above a nightstand by the bed, she carefully reached up and removed it, laying it gently on the bedspread.

The next step wouldn't be so easy. The house security system might not include the wall safe she encountered next. Determining the combination of the safe wouldn't be a problem, as this intruder was a master safecracker. Six minutes later, taking a deep breath and holding it, she opened the door. Nothing. No loud alarm, but there could still be a silent one, so she moved rapidly, taking the contents and leaving the same way she'd come in.

Back on her motorcycle, Kat wrapped the goods in a felt sack and hid it in the secret compartment she'd engineered in the bike's saddlebag. Then she rode to the A1 highway and headed north to Brussels. Within three hours she was back in her room at her father's house, and with her cache safely under her pillow, she fell instantly asleep.

Chapter 24

TEN HOURS AFTER THE TOUR BY GINA Lombardi, Hunter approached the stroke campus again—this time in the dark and from the woods above the cluster of five buildings. Dressed completely in black, including black face paint, he moved silently and, he hoped, unseen. Constantly on alert for any sign of walking nighttime security, he stayed in the shadows cast by the lampposts and the inconvenient moonlight tonight's plan couldn't avoid.

Hidden behind a hedge about fifty feet from the back of the administration building, Hunter examined his target. From the gazebo and courtyard side, he saw only one door in the center of the two-story structure. Three windows to the left of the door and three to the right on the first floor, with an equal number on the second floor, probably indicated offices. Low-level security lighting illuminated the entrance, but aside from that, the interior appeared to be completely dark. He couldn't detect any movement inside or outside the building.

Keeping in the shadows he worked his way around to the side of the building. If he remembered correctly from his earlier walk with Mrs. Lombardi, a small wooden door was set back in a narrow entryway. When it came into view he saw no lighting, and this side of the building wasn't yet illuminated by the low-lying moonlight. This could be the way in.

He studied the door and saw no signs of a security system. The lock would present no problem at all. It was probably a custodian's entrance.

Retrieving his lock-picking tool and going to work, it only took a few seconds to overcome it. Carefully pulling on the handle, he opened the door a few inches. He heard nothing. Leaving the door slightly ajar, he stepped back into the nearby trees and waited. After ten minutes he determined no silent alarm had sounded.

Leaving the comforting nighttime sounds of crickets and tree frogs behind, he entered a quiet janitorial work area and pulled the door shut behind him. Using the red illumination feature on the flashlight app on his cell phone, he saw the room was a five-by-ten-foot rectangle littered with mops, pails, brooms, and all the paraphernalia of a custodian's closet. At the far end was what he was hoping for, a door, presumably to the working office area of the building.

Sure enough, it led to a hallway running the length of the structure with six offices on either side, accounting for the six windows he'd seen at the back of the building. He moved along the hall until he found a door with a smoked glass panel labeled PATIENT RECORDS. The lock presented little problem and he slipped inside. Alphabetically arranged file cabinets lined the room on two sides.

Hunter found the cabinet with the L's, easily popped the file cabinet lock, and thumbed through the files until he found what he was looking for—LAHTI, CHARLES J. Leafing through the papers, he saw it was mostly innocuous material, including admissions papers, reports from the doctor who recommended he be admitted to the Institute, authorization for treatment forms signed by Charlie and Jenny, and medical history supplied by what must have been Charlie's family doctor in Venice; nothing unusual so far.

Hunter continued and found a recommendation from the team of physicians and therapists who'd been assigned to Charlie's treatment—a pretty standard regimen for post-stroke therapy, walking, range of motion, speech-rehab, etc. No mention of any surgery.

Something was nagging him as odd about the paperwork; then it hit him, Dr. Phillippi wasn't listed as one of the physicians assigned to Charlie. He'd told Hunter he was Charlie's principal physician. Flipping through the remaining material in the folder, he found no mention of Phillippi at all. The only remaining papers dealt with the death and transportation of the body to Final Care in Brussels.

Ready to give up, Hunter almost missed it. Charlie had been admitted to the stroke campus on June 6 and housed in Building B. Then on June 8 he spent twenty hours in Building E and then returned to Building B. Five days later on June 13, he returned to Building E, this time for only two hours. He returned to building B the same day and stayed there for the remainder of his stay until he had his fatal stroke.

What were those buildings? Building B must be the Residential building Mrs. Lombardi had pointed out to him earlier. Were there letters on the five buildings in the stroke campus?

Hunter returned the folder to the file cabinet and left the building as quietly as he had entered. Still not finding anyone about, he made his way to the front of the building and looked for a letter of any kind that might identify the building.

Sure enough, above the front entry doors was a large A, the administration building. The next building was designated B. From his earlier tour, he remembered it was the residential building where the admitted patients lived during their stay on the stroke campus. When he got to Building E, he paused, confused, Charlie had apparently spent almost an entire day in the imaging building. *That is strange*, he thought, *why would they have patients stay that long in a building dedicated to imaging. Wouldn't patients just go there for the imaging and then return to the residence building?*

Deciding he wasn't done breaking-and-entering for the night, he searched for a safe entrance. Fortunately, the architecture of the five buildings was identical, and he quickly found the same side wooden door. This time when he emerged from the custodial closet, the set-up of the interior was completely different. He saw separate rooms labeled MAGNETIC RESONANCE IMAGING (MRI), COMPUTED TOMOGRAPHY (CT SCAN), even a Transcranial and Trans-carotid Doppler machine.

Hunter was impressed. Those babies were expensive. He thoroughly examined every square inch of the place, and apart from three offices he saw no indication that patients stayed overnight in this building. Only then did he recognize that each of the three offices had a small identifying sign on the wall to the left of each door. There it was: GIOVANNI PHILLIPPI, M.D.—NEUROSURGERY.

Hunter tried the door. It was locked. Hoping there was no alarm system here; he picked the lock and heard nothing. Apparently they didn't take security too seriously. The lone file cabinet next to the desk, also locked, again presented no problem. It took no time to find the LAHTI, CHARLES J. folder. This one was much fatter than the one he'd seen in the administration building.

Immediately Hunter saw the folder held several MRI images of Charlie's skull, with his name printed on each of them. Starting with the first, he examined the images and recognized standard sagittal and coronal sections showing Charlie's brain at various depths and locations. Hunter was no expert at reading brain images, but didn't see anything out of the ordinary until he came to the last three images.

What the — the images showed something had been implanted bilaterally in Charlie's brain, something very symmetrical and obviously manmade. The objects appeared to be about a half an inch long and maybe a tenth of an inch wide. They were near the surface of the frontal lobe just in front of the central sulcus. Apparently, Phillippi had inserted a small device into what Hunter recognized as the motor cortex on each side of Charlie's brain. Searching through the rest of the folder, he found nothing—no written surgical notes, just the images with Charlie's name, and Giovanni Phillippi, M.D.

What had Phillippi inserted into Charlie's brain? They appeared to be precisely placed into the primary motor cortex, also called areas 3, 2, and 1. Even though his specialty was vascular physiology, he knew enough neuro-science to recognize this was the region of the brain that controlled primary motor functions, such as moving the arms and legs, and working the fingers, etc. The primary motor cortex in the right hemisphere of the brain controlled such movements on the left side of the body while the primary motor cortex in the left hemisphere controlled such movements on the right side.

Hunter thought it might be some new surgical procedure for helping stroke victims recover lost motor capabilities. He went through Phillippi's desk and small bookcase looking for anything that might explain the odd objects. Aside from several standard textbooks on neurosurgery, he found nothing that helped.

He returned to the folder of brain images and studied the chronological sequence of the scans. Each of the images was printed on the bottom with the date, the time of day, Charlie's name and birth date, and Phillippi's name. There were three that didn't show the implants, all dated June 6, the day he arrived at the Institute. Another three, all showing the strange objects, were dated June 13, the day he came back for a second trip to this building. Had Phillippi inserted the strange objects on June 8, the day he spent twenty hours here?

As he was returning the images to the folder, the room lights suddenly blazed on.

"Chi diavolo sei?"

Hunter looked up and saw a security guard five feet away from him, crouched in a shooting stance with his pistol held steady on Hunter's chest.

Hunter put his index finger to his lips, suggesting the guard should be quiet, and then pointed to the file cabinet with both fingers as if to suggest something ominous was in there.

Momentarily confused and startled into doing just that, the guard took his eyes—and the gun—off Hunter for a fraction of a second and turned to gape at the cabinet.

That was all the time Hunter needed.

As the guard realized how stupid that had been, he began swinging the gun back in Hunter's direction just as Hunter made his move.

To McCoy it all unfolded in slow motion, as such situations always did for him. He'd first became aware of his capacity to slow things down when he was just a schoolboy. This unique phenomenon only seemed to occur in situations in which Hunter's safety, or that of someone close to him, was threatened. It had protected him many times over the years, but never more so than in his former work as an agent for the Defense Intelligence Agency.

This time, as before, when the guard resumed his stance and brought his gun around—seemingly in slow motion to Hunter—he had plenty of time to assess the situation and react. Dropping and planting both palms on the floor, he pivoted as fast as he could, lashing out with his right leg to sweep the feet out from under the man. As the guard began to fall, Hunter reversed the move and kicked the gun out of the guard's hand with his left foot. Then, with the man momentarily stunned, he drove a fist into his chin that sent him to the floor, unconscious.

He carried the unconscious man to the janitor's closet, where he found what he needed to tie him up and duct-tape his mouth. Then he returned to the records room and removed one of the scans taken on June 6th before the implants and all three taken on the 13th showing the strange implants in place. He put the folder back, hoping when they searched the room the next day, as they no doubt would, they wouldn't immediately know which file the intruder had been looking at.

Before leaving the building he looked for the hidden camera he knew he must have missed earlier. He found nothing in the record room, the hallway, or the custodial closet. It wasn't until he stepped outside that he saw the camouflaged night camera on the lamppost outside the wooden door.

As he made his way back through the campus and woods to his car, parked on a narrow street in the residential area above the Institute, he saw what he'd completely missed earlier: cameras attached to strategically placed lampposts, disguised as decorative ornaments on the ornately fashioned poles. He should have seen them anyway. Clearly he'd gotten a little rusty, he thought.

Once back in the car he drove out of camera range and cleaned his face of the night black. Then exchanging his black clothes for a more traditional set, he drove the fifteen miles to his hotel, the Amalfi in Pompeii, where he'd taken a room earlier. Back in his hotel room, he showered and turned in, immediately falling into a deep sleep.

Chapter 25

THE BRIGHT SUNSHINE STREAMING through his office window in Building E of the Caravaggio Neurological Institute did nothing to brighten the rapidly souring mood of Giovanni Phillippi as he listened to the guard tell his story of last night's intrusion. Carlo Mansi, the Institute's security chief, was questioning him.

"Come on, man, quite stammering. What did he look like?"

"I'm, I'm sorry, sir, it all happened so fast. He was all in black. Face black too. I—I don't know."

Mansi didn't suffer fools gladly. "Tell me, do you need this job? Do you want to keep this job? At this point you don't have a job. You'd better start remembering, and fast."

The guard just looked dumfounded.

Shaking his head and rolling his eyes, the security chief demanded, "Was he big, small, young, old? Anything."

Rubbing his aching jaw with his aching wrists from his hours tied up on the hard floor before he was rescued by his daytime replacement that morning, the guard shifted from foot to foot in front of his seated and seething superior. "I'd say big. Don't know how old. Probably young, he moved so fast. Yes, probably young."

"Was he Italian? Did he speak Italian?"

"He didn't speak at all. Not once."

"What was he doing?"

"Looking in the file cabinet."

"Which one? Which one was he looking in?"

Scratching his head he thought about it for a minute. "I think he opened that one." He pointed at the second of the two file cabinets.

"Did you see him take anything?"

"No, sir."

The security chief dismissed the man.

Phillippi wondered what the intruder was after. And who he was? He spent the next half hour going through the file cabinets, trying to see if anything was missing. But not knowing what he was looking for, it was virtually impossible to determine. The files were almost exclusively patient records. The vast majority were routine cases of tumor treatment or vascular repair that had caused the patient to stroke. Why would anyone break in to look at those? Something wasn't right. What was the guy after?

An hour later, still in the security chief's office, Dr. Phillippi sat examining video camera footage from the night before that Mansi had asked him to view.

"What am I looking for?" he asked.

"We have the man on camera from the time he entered the stroke campus," Mansi told him. "He obviously didn't see our camouflaged night cameras. You'll notice he spent considerable time trying to stay in the shadows. Tell me if you see anything that looks familiar about him."

Phillippi watched the video on a large monitor. It was impossible. All he saw was a black figure darting in and out of the trees, obviously trying to stay hidden. He couldn't see the face at all. Even the man's height was impossible to determine. He looked fit.

The man had started in the administration building, entering through the side door and emerging thirteen minutes later. He wasn't carrying anything when he left. Next he went around the front of the building and then seemed to make a circle of the campus, passing in front of buildings B,

C, and D before entering Building E to be surprised by the watchman.

"Why didn't the guard intercept him in building A?" Phillippi demanded.

"He was on a different campus," said Mansi. "He didn't see the intruder right away."

"And why don't we have any film of the man in the buildings?" Phillippi asked in disgust. "Don't we have cameras inside?"

"No, Doctor," Mansi said with an accusatory tone, "The medical staff wouldn't let my department install them. As I recall, all of you felt your privacy would be invaded, and you wanted no part of it."

"Humpff," grunted Phillippi as he reluctantly acknowledged the accuracy of the statement.

"So," challenged Mansi, "does he remind you of anyone you know?"

Phillippi racked his brain. "No," he told the security chief.

Mansi called to his assistant. "Rocco, bring us some coffee. Dr. Phillippi will be here for a while."

"What are you talking about? I've got important things to do."

"More important than finding out who and why someone broke into your office and rifled through your files?" demand the security chief.

Calming down a little, Phillippi asked, "What do you have in mind?"

"Your man may have been on the campus earlier in the day, checking out the grounds. He didn't just walk in dressed like a cat burglar last night for the first time. I want you to look at the video for the stroke campus taken during the day. We might get lucky."

Phillippi grudgingly took his coffee and sat down in front of a monitor while Mansi programed the computer to fast-forward through scenes with familiar faces, but slow down when someone new appeared.

After viewing for over an hour, Phillippi said, "There's nothing. I don't recognize anyone who doesn't belong."

Mansi excused Phillippi who returned to his office. Next, the security chief called Gino Gallo, another neurosurgeon at the Institute. "Dr. Gallo, I want you to come over to my office to view some security videos. We might have a problem, and I want to start with you before I bring Caravaggio in."

An hour later, after learning that Phillippi's office had been broken into and his files rifled, Gallo said, "Whoever did this has to be stopped right away. There's too much at stake to risk letting him continue to snoop."

He viewed the videos. Something about the intruder's attitude in the way he carried himself seemed familiar but nothing came to him. He couldn't put his finger on it. It was probably nothing. Next Mansi showed him the same long daytime videos that Phillippi had seen earlier. A half an hour into it Gallo shouted, "Stop, back up. Stop right there. That man. I know that man."

Mansi and Gallo watched Mrs. Lombardi showing a man around the campus. "Now I recognize him. He was at the Final Care facility at the Miami airport. He was working for Lahti's widow. What was the guy's name…?"

He turned to Mansi, "Call Miami and talk to the manager there. His name is Dyson; He can give you the name. Also, talk to Mrs. Lombardi. See what name he gave and if there's anything else she can tell you."

"Good work, Dr. Gallo. We'll get right on it."

THE PALATIAL HOME IN THE HILLS ABOVE the Caravaggio Institute had almost as spectacular a view of the Bay of Naples as the oceanfront house in Miami had of the Atlantic. Unlike the Florida home, Rache actually owned this one.

He told Traveler to wait outside. The assassin had just given his report on McCoy, and Rache needed time to think.

McCoy knows about the bodies being shipped to Miami. He's linked Final Care to the Institute. He's connected with Donckers and his daughter, and now he undoubtedly knows about the implants in Lahti's brain. He can't have figured anything out yet and certainly knows nothing of the plan. I need to know more about him?

Chapter 26

WHEN HUNTER OPENED HIS EYES, glaring bright red numerals were staring back at him from the hotel nightstand's all-purpose radio and alarm clock. 8:30. He stretched his big frame and climbed out of bed, showered, shaved, dressed, and went down to the Amalfi's breakfast room, where he devoured a huge omelet and three breakfast rolls with marmalade. The morning paper listed another big jewelry heist, this time in Paris, again no clues.

Whoever is doing this is making a clean getaway. Still, if they keep it up, they'll make a mistake somewhere and get caught.

Refocusing, he reviewed his own escapade from the previous night. He couldn't believe he'd missed the security cameras on the light posts. Maybe he *was* losing a step or two. He'd be more vigilant going forward.

Knowing he had to discover what the strange objects in Charlie's MRI scans were, he thought he'd drive back to Naples and find a neurologist who might be able to tell him. Of course he could confront Phillippi directly, but that would tip his hand and let them know he suspected something was going on. He didn't want them suspicious at this point. He didn't even want them knowing he was here. He was sure the security guard wouldn't be able to give a clear description, nor would the cameras actually identify him.

Two hours later he was in the office of Dr. Lisa Marino. In almost flawless English, the sixtyish matronly neurologist asked Hunter, "Where did you get these images?"

Using the prepared story he'd thought up during the thirty-minute drive back to Naples from Pompeii, Hunter decided to stick to as much of the truth as he could. He explained he was a physiologist in the Medical School at the University of Virginia. His own specialty was vascular physiology but earlier he'd studied neurology. He'd come across the images in the course of his investigation on behalf of a friend whose scans he wished to show her.

Fortunately for him, she was more interested in the images and extending professional courtesy than in pressing him on how precisely he got them, so she put one up on a lightbox on the wall next to her desk and examined it.

"The image shows a coronal section through the brain just anterior to the central sulcus. You can see the stereotactic coordinates printed below right after the letters SRE. I don't know what the letters mean."

"Doctor, would you agree the objects are placed in the cortex, the outermost portion of the brain?" Hunter asked.

"Absolutely. In fact with these coordinates, I'd say they've been deliberately placed in the primary motor cortex, or Brodmann's areas 3, 1, and 2."

Hunter knew this, having worked it out for himself, so he proceeded to the real question to which he had no answer. "Doctor Marino, do you have any idea what they are?"

Leaning back, clasping her hands behind her head, and closing her eyes in thought, she slowly shook her head. "I have no idea. I've never seen anything like it."

Hunter continued, "The man suffered a unilateral stroke while on vacation in Italy, last month. He was undergoing therapy at the Caravaggio Institute for three weeks when a second stroke killed him. Do you know of any surgical procedure for the treatment of stroke that would indicate the kind of intervention seen in this image?"

Doctor Marino answered immediately. "No, none. And even if there were, why would they be bilaterally placed, when you said he'd suffered a unilateral stroke?"

Hunter agreed. "Exactly."

"Why don't you just drive over to the Institute and ask this Doctor Phillippi yourself? Why come to me?"

"I believe I'll do that, Doctor. Thank you very much for your help."

As Hunter got up to leave, Marino extended her hand and smiled. "Be sure you return the professional courtesy when you get your answer and let me know what you find out."

IN HIS SECOND-FLOOR OFFICE in the main administration building, Dr. Nero Caravaggio sat at his desk, sorting through a stack of files and fretting over a fundraising project that was bogged down, when his secretary told him Dr. Eugenio Gallo wished to see him today. Nero was inclined to put the man off until tomorrow. He just had too much to do.

He knew if he'd only give up trying to micro-manage the place, he'd be free to enjoy the pure science that was really his first love. And he could do it too. He had people, very capable people, to handle all the rest of it. He'd have to start letting go of the day-to-day stuff.

As he thought of the joy of pure research, his mind returned to Gino Gallo. In the four years since he'd recruited the neurosurgeon, their success rate with stroke patients and others had improved considerably. The man was good, no question about it. Nevertheless, the business with Lahti was really out of line; in fact, it was really out of character for the neurosurgeon. When Nero had found out Gallo had allowed Lahti's body to be sent to Final Care before they'd taken the necessary steps, he was furious. What the hell did he think he was doing? The Institute could get in major trouble, and their special program seriously threatened, by too close a scrutiny if the authorities discovered it.

It especially troubled him that Lahti had been their first attempt with a patient who'd actually had a legitimate stroke, and the early results had been phenomenal. The man was proof that their secret protocol of SRE could promote new growth and rewiring in a brain that had suffered stroke every bit as well as in a healthy brain.

Tired of looking at finances, and feeling the onset of a headache, he picked up his phone. "Anna, call Dr. Gallo and send him over now."

When the neurosurgeon arrived, Caravaggio indicted a chair by small coffee table, and as the two men sat, asked him, "What's up, Gino?"

"I don't know, but last night someone broke into Phillippi's office in Building E of the stroke campus and rifled through his files."

Nero looked up sharply. "What?"

"The intruder tied up that fool of a night watchman in the janitor's closet after he'd caught him in Phillippi's office. He got away.

Getting up and pacing to the large panoramic window overlooking the bay in the distance, Nero put his hands up in supplication. "Is anything missing?"

"I'm afraid so. He took a normal image and all three MRI images showing the implants in place. The watchman must have interrupted him before he could take anything else, but I don't like it. I've identified him from security camera footage. It's the same guy who was looking for Lahti at the Final Care facility in Miami when I was there."

This was too much for Nero who fixed the neurosurgeon with a furious glare. "Dammit, man, what have you done? Is this foul-up of yours ever going to be over? What's he doing here? You said he bought your story about the ID tag."

Nervous under Caravaggio's withering stare, Gallo only had a weak answer. "I thought he did." Then, looking sheepish, he added, "There's more. Yesterday he introduced himself as Harry Ashworth from Ohio. He told the front desk his aunt was considering coming to the Stroke facility and asked to check it out first. It was a phony name. His real name is Hunter McCoy; he's a professor of physiology at the University of Virginia School of Medicine in the States."

"Oh, great. This just keeps getting better and better. What's a professor doing checking on a misplaced body?"

Recovering a little from his earlier embarrassment, Gallo said, "Whatever he's after, he's still out there and we've got to stop him."

Nero walked back to his desk and sat down, churning through the implications. Abruptly he looked up. "McCoy thinks you're Phillippi so we can't let him see you—or Phillippi come to that. I'll call the IT department and have them take your pictures off the staff listing on the Institute website. Then I'll insist Phillippi go off on that vacation he's been wanting. Don't let McCoy see you while we deal with this. I'll call Carlo Mansi and have him beef up security today. Now get out of here and let me think."

When the neurosurgeon left, Nero Caravaggio got up and poured a small limoncello from his side bar, took it to the window overlooking the Bay of Naples, and sipped slowly as he contemplated the foul-up. Returning to his desk and the work he had piled there, he wondered if the break-in at Phillippi's office was just about the Lahti body mix-up, or did it go beyond that? Was this Hunter McCoy looking into other things—things Nero desperately wanted to keep secret?

He punched his secretary's number. "Anna, get Carlo Mansi in here, now.

Chapter 27

DESPITE THE CONFIRMATION FROM Dr. Marino that the objects in Charlie's brain made no medical sense to her, Hunter wasn't yet ready to confront Phillippi directly.

Over a sandwich and beer in the dining room at the Amalfi, trying to figure out his next move, he wondered about Kat's mother. Had she also been at the stroke campus and treated by Phillippi? Did she have something inserted in her brain as well? Was that what had caused her second stroke? Was that what had caused Charlie's second stroke?

He figured another breaking-and-entering at the Institute might be too risky, convinced they'd surely have beefed up their security system by now. Instead, he decided to return to Belgium and have another meeting with Kat and her father. Maybe they'd have some answers.

IN THE SKIES OVER THE ITALIAN ALPS, Hunter thought about Phillippi's lame explanation of why a neurosurgeon had to fly all the way from Italy to Miami simply to remove an adhesive patch from the wrist. He was now convinced Phillippi came to Miami to remove the surgically implanted items. It was the only explanation that made any sense. He couldn't take the risk of anyone finding them even though there was little chance of that since Charlie would have been buried almost immediately and any secret device concealed in his brain would have been buried with him.

After renting a car at the airport, he checked in again at the Royal Windsor a little after 6:00 p.m. He had no way to contact Kat. She hadn't given him a phone number or an address. But she had been staying with her father while she was in town. He'd have to contact Johannes Donckers. Just as he was about to use his smart phone to find his number, he noticed he had an email from Henry that came in during his flight.

> *Hunter, I don't know where you are. Ed just told me you were in Europe somewhere, working on the case. He thought you said Belgium. Is that right?*
>
> *Anyway, your dad's about the same. I told him he'd been acting strange lately, kind of distant and forgetful, and maybe he should see a doctor. He said, "No need for that. I was just imagining things. If something was wrong with me, Hunter would have mentioned it, and he didn't."*
>
> *I'll keep an eye on him, but it looks like you'll have to talk with him when you get a chance.*
>
> *Henry*

Hunter sat back in the hotel chair next to his bed and stared at the ceiling. *Henry's probably right; he'll only listen to me. At least Henry's there and hopefully can keep him out of trouble until I get back.* He emailed Henry an acknowledgment.

There were three Johannes Donckers in the phone book, and he got the right one on the first try.

"Mr. Donckers, this is Hunter McCoy. I talked with you in your office a few days ago."

After a long pause, during which Hunter imagined the man was weighing his options, Donckers finally answered, "Yes, I remember."

Hunter was sure the man thought he was going to turn him over to Ms. Janssen after all. "It's nothing, Mr. Donckers, I just wanted to speak with your daughter Kat, and she'd told me she was staying with you. Is she there?"

He could hear the relief in the man's response. "Oh, I see. No. I mean no she's not here. She's gone away on business—Munich, I think—for a few days, but she told me she'd be back tomorrow. Would you like me to have her call you?"

"Yes, if you would. I'm staying at the Royal Windsor. Um—Mr. Donckers?"

"Yes?"

"I wonder if I could talk with you briefly about another matter altogether. It has nothing to do with Final Care or embalming. It's about the Caravaggio Institute."

"The Caravaggio Institute?" the man asked, sounding confused.

"Yes. If you have time now I could come to your house. It shouldn't take too long. Would that be all right?"

Again, Hunter could imagine the man thinking through all the ramifications of meeting with him again.

"I don't know what I can tell you," he finally replied, "but yes, you can come over now."

After getting the address, Hunter called a cab, which took him on an enjoyable forty-five-minute drive to his destination. Johannes Donckers lived in a large home in Woluwe St. Pierre, a Brussels district of beautiful homes amid commercial centers with shops, restaurants, hairdressers, and banks. Hunter also noted the district wasn't far from the city's embassies. He assumed the evident luxury was due to the earnings of the embalmer's late wife, the internationally known concert pianist. Surely the man's earnings alone would not have been sufficient to afford such a place.

Donckers met him at the door and invited him in. The home was nicely but not excessively furnished, except for the magnificent grand piano in the living room. "Would you like a drink, Mr. McCoy? I was just going to fix myself one." Donckers gestured to a well-stocked bar behind the piano. The walls on either side of the bar were filled with framed photographs of Irena Rousseau's performances and programs.

"Fine, whatever you're having," Hunter answered, moving to the piano to examine several framed photographs sitting on its broad back. He picked up one showing a striking woman with beautiful red hair in a long black gown, seated at a piano in front of an orchestra.

"Your wife, Mr. Donckers?" inquired Hunter as the man handed him a snifter of cognac.

Taking the picture from Hunter, he looked at it dreamily, "Yes. She was performing here with Sir Neville Mariner and the Academy of St. Martin in the Fields. She was a beautiful woman, Mr. McCoy, both inside and out. Do you know she performed more times for charity than any other concert pianist before — or since? Your *TIME* magazine even featured her once on its cover." He pointed to the framed *TIME* cover on the wall showing her seated at a piano, surrounded by packages of food and clothing.

Hunter nodded appreciatively and took a sip of the cognac Donckers had handed him. "She must have been a remarkable woman. As I told Kat, I have several of her recordings at my place in Virginia."

Leading Hunter to a seating area in the large room, the two men sat, and Johannes asked, "So what can I do for you, Mr. McCoy?"

Hunter decided to tell him about the similarity between Charlie's stroke and Irena's. He described how he'd been suspicious of Dr. Phillippi's story about removing the patch in Miami. Then he admitted he'd broken into the Caravaggio

Institute and told him about the brain scans showing the implants he'd found in the imaging center. He explained that a neurologist in Naples said there was no known treatment for stroke that involved such surgery. He also told Donckers he was a medical scientist himself and had no idea what they were.

"The widow of the late Mr. Lahti insists he had no surgery while at the stroke campus," he concluded. "Yet he clearly did, since Charlie's name was on the dated scans showing his brain both before and after the work was done."

Donckers thought for a long time before responding to this news. "Now I see why you're here. Kat must have told you about her mother's experience at the Institute."

"Right, I believe Phillippi went to Miami to remove the devices, so there'd be no evidence he'd done something to Charlie when he was recovering at the Institute."

"You suspect if they were up to something with Mr. Lahti at the Institute, they may have done something to my wife as well, since her story is similar?"

"I don't know, Mr. Donckers. All I can tell you is I'm going to find out what happened to Charlie Lahti, and while I'm doing that I may learn something about your wife's treatment as well. I just wanted to let you know ahead of time. Do you know if she had surgery at the Institute?"

"No, she didn't. I would have known, since I was there with her almost all the time. Final Care was very generous and gave me all the time I needed to care for her after the stroke. She lived in the residence building and I had a room in town. I saw her every day."

"Every day?"

"Well—except for two days about a week after she was admitted when I had to fly back to Brussels to straighten out a paperwork error at Final Care. It turned out there was no error; the accountant just read my notes incorrectly. He apologized for the inconvenience and I flew right back to Sorrento."

Hunter nodded respectfully. "I know this is indelicate, but was an autopsy done on your wife after she died?"

"No, Irena and I both agreed we wanted cremation when the time came, and that's what happened. She was cremated."

"Did you ever have anything to do with the neurosurgeon, Dr. Phillippi?" Hunter asked.

"No, I'd never heard of him until you just mentioned his name. I only met the physicians and therapists who worked with Irena. I never met any surgeons."

They were both quiet for a moment and sipped their drinks. Donckers got up and walked to the piano. Picking up a photo of his wife, he turned to Hunter. "McCoy, if you do find out something is going on there that's not right, you'll tell me, won't you?"

Hunter finished his drink, stood up, and shook Johannes's hand. "Call me Hunter. I have a feeling you'll be hearing from me, and yes, I'll tell you anything I learn about your late wife."

Chapter 28

HUNTER'S FATHER, ED MCCOY, had fallen off the fifty-foot cliff to the rocks below Anue. He was alive but barely able to move. He was banging on a log with a piece of driftwood, trying to get someone's attention. He needed help and was fading fast. Hunter could hear him but was unable to move. What was wrong? Why couldn't he help? The banging continued, and suddenly Hunter opened his eyes. Covered in sweat, he realized he'd been dreaming.

The banging continued. Someone was knocking repeatedly on his hotel room door. A glance at his clock said it was 6:45.

What the hell?

His first thought was the maid. No, it was too early. When the knocking continued, he went to the door and looked out the peephole. *Kat? What the—?*

Rubbing his eyes, and naked, he opened the door slightly. "Kat?"

She pushed the door open and rushed past him into the room.

"McCoy, you're still here. Good. Have you had breakfast yet?"

Aware he was standing there completely nude, he quickly searched for something to cover himself and stammered, "What—wait," then grabbing a pillow to do the job, said, "Go down to the breakfast room. I'll meet you there after I've cleaned up."

Then, fully aware of what she'd done, she managed a, "Sorry, that'd be great." She twisted back before closing the door, gave him an appraising look and smiled, in contrast to the astonished look on his face.

Showered, shaved, and dressed, he joined her at a small table in the dining room and immediately sensed her seriousness. "Always happy to see you Kat, even when I'm naked and still half asleep," he remarked.

"I had to see you before you'd left for wherever you're going next."

"Well you certainly saw me."

He wasn't sure, but she may have blushed a little at that.

"We have to talk about my mother."

Hunter had suspected as much. The potential bomb he'd dropped on her father the night before was sure to resonate equally with the daughter.

"I got in late last night and my father told me what you'd learned through your breaking-and-entering skills." She put her hand on his and the flirting smile was back. "Nice work. Have you thought of starting a career as a second-story man?"

"Not likely, since my former career was putting criminals behind bars."

Kat jerked her hand back, lost her smile and froze. Then recovering, she stammered, "I—I don't understand. What do you mean?"

"Before the physiology thing, I was with military intelligence and worked with Interpol."

This seemed to leave Kat speechless for a moment. She regarded him as if she was working something out in her head and then met his eyes, appraising him anew. "I didn't think cops broke into offices and stole brain scans," she said.

Hunter laughed, his mood beginning to lift now that he had a cup of coffee, had to agree. "Not often, that's for sure," he agreed. "So, to what do I owe this early morning visit?"

Kat turned serious as she answered. "What you've discovered about the Institute tells me something is going on there, something wrong and probably illegal. I want to know if any of it involved my mother."

"When exactly was your mother there?"

"I looked up the dates, last night, just to be sure I got them right. She had her first stroke following a performance with the London Philharmonic Orchestra on January fifth this year. She was admitted to the Caravaggio Institute on January ninth. Her second stroke occurred a little over three weeks later, on February second, the day she died. So that puts her there about six months earlier than Mr. Lahti."

While Hunter was thinking about this, she continued. "I'm going to help you find out what's going on. I owe it to my mother and my father. And before you tell me you're going to do it on your own, let's be clear. You're not."

Hunter hadn't counted on that. He knew she'd want to know whatever he learned. He was prepared for that. But he didn't need a partner, even a very attractive one like Kat. "Do you have a computer with Internet access?" he finally asked.

"Of course."

"Maybe you could help by getting background information for me." He hoped she'd settle for that.

"Look, McCoy, I don't think you understand what I'm saying here. I'm going with you. I'm not an assistant filing papers, I'm part of this investigation, whether you want me or not. My interest is solely in finding out if something was done to my mother. I'm going to investigate that no matter what you say, but we'll be less likely to get in each other's way if we coordinate our activities and work together."

Recognizing he really had no choice if he didn't want interference, Hunter knew he had to agree. He hadn't told

Kat anything about the murder of Willard Bremmer. He knew he might have to at some point, but for now he kept it to himself.

"All right, but it's going to be dangerous," was all he said.

"I'd expect nothing less."

"Then you should know something I didn't tell your father. I was interrupted by a security guard who I had to tie up and gag in order to give me time to get the scans and get out of there. I hadn't noticed the night cameras and they've probably got me on tape, even though I'm sure they can't make an identification."

"They got you on video? How could you miss the security cameras on the lampposts?"

Startled, he paused and thought about what she'd just said. "How do you know about the security cameras?" he asked slowly, fully aware he hadn't told her about them.

"I saw them when I visited my mother during her treatment."

Hunter thought it was pretty bad that he, a trained agent, had missed them, while this woman, this gemologist with no police background, had spotted them. "What made you notice them? Why'd you even look?"

Pausing before answering, she twisted the gold ring on her finger which had a variety of small gems embedded in the band, "I'm not sure," she answered lightly. "I might have read about them somewhere, that kind of camera, I mean. That's probably it, must be." She waved a hand. "Anyway, we need to plan our next move."

"Our next move," he said, "Is to confront Phillippi."

Chapter 29

THE FOUR-HOUR FLIGHT BACK TO NAPLES was filled with questions from Kat about his background. She seemed particularly interested in his work with Interpol. He'd kept his answers as general as possible and downplayed it as much as he could, saying he was now only occasionally reactivated by either DIA or Interpol when his investigations overlapped with theirs. He assured her that breaking and entering wasn't a regular activity. He *was* just a professor who occasionally helped others find and correct things, as he was doing for Jenny Lahti in this case.

Figuring the Amalfi Hotel in Pompeii was a good staging area with almost equal access to Naples and Sorrento, they pulled up in their rental car, a black Beamer, to the front entrance and checked into two adjoining rooms.

There were several newspapers at the front desk and Hunter noticed that an English edition of one of them featured the latest European jewelry heist. It had just happened in Munich. The thieves had gotten away clean leaving the authorities with no apparent leads.

"Have you been following this? One of these days they're going to make a mistake," Hunter said, "They can't get away with it forever."

Kat nodded and said nothing.

Hunter suggested they go to her room and do a computer search since she'd brought her laptop with her. Kat sighed. "Okay."

Kat linked her computer to the hotel's Wi Fi system and began to search for everything she could on Giovanni Phillippi, M.D. Reading aloud to Hunter when she found anything of interest. Like most physicians, Phillippi was all over the web. Most were dead-end sites just asking the viewer to evaluate the listed physicians. Some were legitimate though. Phillippi's bio in the Caravaggio Neurological Institute website was complete and professional. He was a graduate of Saint Louis University Medical School in the United States and did his residency in Neurosurgery at The Johns Hopkins in Baltimore. Nero Caravaggio recruited him to the Institute after he'd read Phillippi's scholarly papers on chronic indwelling release tubes.

"Check this out," Kat called. "Chronic indwelling release tubes." Do you suppose that's what you saw in the brain scans?"

Hunter read the reference and told her to move over and let him have a go at it. In the old days, published research papers had to be accessed physically by going to a medical library, finding the bound or unbound journal, and looking up the article you wanted. The problem with that was most articles weren't what you were looking for. Of course you didn't know that until you'd done all the work of looking it up and reading it.

Today, as with practically everything else, the Internet made it infinitely easier. All he had to do was type "chronic indwelling release tubes" into Google and up came all kinds of things. In this case, the "hits" included titles of papers in which the phrase appeared. Several papers listed Giovanni Phillippi as the principal author. He clicked on one entitled *Dopamine Replacement using Chronic Indwelling Release Tubes in Parkinson-Induced Rats.*

Hunter read the abstract and then scanned the entire paper. It seemed that Phillippi was trying to develop a way to deliver dopamine to that part of the brain that fails to produce it in patients with Parkinson's disease. Dopamine-filled tubes were implanted in the basal ganglia of the brain on both sides, slowly releasing the drug in an attempt to mimic the normal state. Hunter thought it was brilliant if it worked. He continued to read.

Apparently, because the dopamine was released directly into the depleted tissue, only a tiny amount measured in nanoliters was required. Much more of the drug was required when a patient took a pill because it was diluted in the bloodstream. So Phillippi estimated each tube could hold enough dopamine solution for up to two years. Moreover, as Hunter saw when he read the conclusion, that's exactly what happened. The rats lived for about two years with no other source of dopamine than the two implanted tubes. During this time they demonstrated no signs of Parkinson's disease.

He scanned a few more papers in which Phillippi's technique was used on other animal models. None of the papers involved human patients. Apparently they weren't up to human trials yet. Hunter scratched his head.

So what were they doing with Charlie?

"This is a pretty remarkable technique he's developing," he told Kat. "If it works it could have tremendous beneficial applications for many chronic disease states."

"When can they try this on people? I mean, who approves it?" she asked, pacing back and forth.

"I don't know how it works in Italy, but in the United States the process is pretty rigorous. Any new treatment, such as a drug, a medical device, or a biologic—like a vaccine, blood product, or gene therapy—needs to be studied in laboratory animals first to determine potential toxicity before it can be tried on people. If the treatment is shown to be safe and demonstrates promise, the Food and Drug Administration can approved it for clinical trials on volunteer patients. Italy probably has a similar system."

Kat stopped him. "So either the comparable group in Italy approved clinical trials and Charlie volunteered, or they've jumped the gun and are conducting their own trials without approval or volunteers."

Hunter nodded, "Neither Charlie nor his wife approved any surgery to implant anything."

It was getting late and they hadn't eaten so they found a quiet bistro not far from the hotel and had dinner and a bottle of wine. Afterward they stopped at her door.

"I'm glad you're here, McCoy. Between the two of us we'll find out what's going on. She took his face in both of her hands and kissed him. It was a long kiss. It was an invitation. Hunter would have to be stone dead not to recognize it as such. After a silent interval, she smiled and said goodnight, squeezed his hand, opened her door and went inside.

Something kept him from following her, something he couldn't articulate. He couldn't determine if it was related to her or to him. When no answer came forth, he went to his room.

RACHE STARED AT TRAVELER for a long moment and the man just waited. If he weren't so valuable an asset he'd have him killed for that insubordination. Continuing his withering stare, Rache determined his unspoken threat had been successfully delivered when Traveler finally lowered his eyes. "I'm sorry sir, I was out of line."

Traveler, who had been following McCoy, trying to determine what he knew and who he was working with, had just finished giving his report. He'd crossed the line when he'd told Rache what he should do next—momentarily forgetting that his role was to uncover information, and not to tell Rache how to use it. No one told Rache how to do anything.

McCoy is more resourceful than I'd thought. He knows about the implants. He broke into that idiot Phillippi's office and took the images. He brought them to a local neurologist, no doubt to determine what they were. Now it appears he's teamed up with Kat, that spawn of the devil.

He smiled as he thought of the conflicted state that would put her in, working with a man who could have her arrested. *Enjoy the agony, my dear. I know I will. Oh, yes, I'll enjoy it very much.*

Then, remembering Traveler was still standing there, he told the man to continue following them, learning all he can, but not to harm him—not yet. Then he dismissed him.

Chapter 30

THE NEXT MORNING OVER BREAKFAST, Kat said, "I've got an idea. I'll go to the administration building at the stroke campus and ask to see my mother's record. It probably won't help you with your case, but they might show whether or not Phillippi had anything to do with my mother. We know she had no authorized surgery. I can see if his name is in there or not."

"It's worth a try. I'll go along as your husband. Maybe I can learn something."

Kat shot him that enigmatic challenging smile again, then nodded assent. She called to make an appointment and was told to come right over and they'd be happy to help her with any questions she had.

An hour later they arrived at Building A of the stroke campus and were ushered into the office of the assistant director, a stern-faced man in his mid-forties with Buddy Holly glasses and a business suit that looked as if he'd worn it for years. In spite of his visage, he proved to be friendly and quite helpful.

"Of course I remember your mother, a lovely lady. We were honored to have her with us and everyone found her to be charming. No theatrical airs for her. She was working so hard to recover, and we were all greatly saddened by her death."

As Kat glanced at him, Hunter could see she was moved by his comments.

"I understand you have some questions for me, Ms. Donckers. What exactly would you like to know?"

Having talked this through with Hunter earlier, Kat was ready. "It's a little convoluted, but here's the thing. My father told me my mother made reference to members of your staff who'd helped her during her convalescence. She'd expressed a desire to reward them, but didn't mention any names, only what they did for her. I thought if I could look through her file I'd be able to identify them by what she told my father and how she described them to him."

The man brightened at this, no doubt thinking he might be one of them. As he mulled over Kat's proposal, Hunter could almost see the silent debate he was having concerning the ethics of showing her file to a family member versus the potential reward. As it often does, greed won out.

"Of course it's highly irregular to divulge the contents of a patient's personal file to anyone but the medical staff, but in this case, with your mother gone and all, and you being her daughter, I don't see that as a problem. If you'll just wait a moment I'll get it."

When the man left the room, Hunter turned to Kat with an appreciative grin. "Nice work."

"After love and hate," Kat asserted, "greed has to be the next most common human trait, don't you think?"

"It's definitely in the top ten."

A few minutes later the man returned with a large folder filled with papers. The name ROUSSEAU, IRENA was printed on the tab. "I'm afraid the law prevents me from allowing you to photocopy anything, but you're free to read through the files and make a note of any names you'd like."

Indicating a sofa and chair at the side of the room, he added, "Perhaps you'd be more comfortable over here, while you read. Would you like something to drink, water, coffee, perhaps tea?"

"No thank you," they both said, happy to leave the straight-backed chairs they'd been sitting in for the more comfortable furnishings. While Kat sat down to read, Hunter asked if there was a men's room he could use.

"Of course, sir, just down the hall on the left."

Hunter walked down the hall knowing exactly where the bathroom was, as he'd seen it the night he'd broken in. It was right next to the record room; the same room the assistant director had presumably just gone to for Irena's file. He noticed the key lock on the door had been changed to a more secure combination lock with push buttons, although even this wouldn't stop him if he had to get in again.

After using the bathroom, he returned to the assistant director's office and found Kat still reading. He could see she was moving through the files very quickly. Either she was a fast reader or was just skimming them. With the folder open on the desk, she'd take a sheet from one pile, scan it and then set it in a second pile. At the rate she was going she'd be done in a few minutes. There had to be close to one hundred sheets in there. Obviously, Hunter thought, they had a pretty thorough file on her mother. It was much fatter than Charlie's had been.

Finally she was done and handed the folder back to the assistant director. "Thank you. I believe I've found the names I'm looking for and I noticed yours is among them."

The assistant director beamed and modestly bowed his head. "It was a pleasure to work with your mother. She was a wonderful woman. Would you like a notepad to write the names on?"

Kat briefly glanced at Hunter, and then turning to the assistant director said, "Why yes, that would be very kind."

On the way back to the car, walking side by side, Hunter casually said, "You didn't really need that notepad, did you?"

"No."

"Because you had them memorized already, right?"

"Yes."

"What about the rest of the material?"

"That too. I've got it all."

"All of it? There had to be a hundred or more sheets in that folder."

"It wouldn't have made any difference if there were five hundred sheets. I'd remember it all. The technical name is eidetic memory. I've known it since childhood."

"So you can recall anything you've read."

"Anything I've read, seen, heard, smelled, touched, and tasted. Eidetic memory isn't just the ability to recall visual events, but all of the sensory characteristics of the event as well."

Spotting a bench up ahead, Hunter needed to know what she'd found. "Let's have a seat and you can tell me what you've learned."

They sat in the shade of a cluster of tall umbrella pines common to that part of Italy. Hunter wondered what that must be like, total recall of everything you'd ever experienced. He supposed in a way he could imagine it. After all, he could never get the events of his brother Gary's death in Pakistan out of his mind. The nightmares had pretty much gone away now, but the images remained, horrible and unchanging—the sound of the explosion, the smell, everything.

"So what did you learn from your mother's file?"

"Most of it was pretty innocuous stuff, physical and occupational therapy reports on her progress, medical exams, lab work, two reports on her mental state from a staff psychologist. There were weekly reports from the team of physicians who handled her case. Everything showed she was making good progress and would likely be back to full capability as a touring pianist again. There wasn't a negative report in the file."

"What about the surgery building, or the imaging building—was she ever there? Or did Phillippi's name show up at all?" Hunter asked.

"Phillippi wasn't mentioned and her timeline didn't include the surgery building. Her records show she was admitted on January ninth and died on February second, three weeks later."

Just like Charlie, Hunter thought.

"She was housed in Building B, the residence building, the whole time. There was no mention of surgery. She did make one trip to the imaging building on January sixteenth for an MRI but returned to the residence building the same day. The only mention of Dr. Phillippi referred to the possibility of calling him if necessary, but there were no records showing that happened."

Hunter thought there had to be something. "Were there papers referring to the second stroke and your mother's death?"

"Yes. The second stroke occurred at three a.m. on February second. She was pronounced dead and they took her body to the morgue. She was then transferred to Donnelli's funeral home in Sorrento, where she was cremated the next afternoon."

Hunter thought about this. "Doesn't that seem a little quick? How did they know that was her wish? Did she have a living will in the papers?"

Kat again scanned the invisible screen of her memory. "No, her file contained no living will. In fact, I don't know if she even had one. Probably they just called my father and asked him what to do."

"Did he see the body?"

"I believe so. I don't know."

"Call him. Call him now and ask him how that happened. Have him give you the timeline from the time of your mother's death to the cremation. I've got a funny feeling about this."

Not sure why, Kat nevertheless called her father and asked him if her mother had a living will and whether it included cremation. When exactly had he learned of the death and where was he at the time? Did he see the body? Did he give permission for the cremation and what time was that? She listened while her father searched his memory and answered all of this.

While Hunter waited, Kat interrupted her father a few times for clarification. Finally, they said goodbye and she hung up staring straight ahead for a moment. Then she turned to Hunter. "He saw my mother's body briefly and then met with a representative of Final Care who said my father could fly home to Brussels and rest assured they'd take care of everything. He didn't give permission directly and she had no living will. Nevertheless, she and my father had talked about cremation but hadn't done anything to formalize it."

Hunter started to speak, "But then, how could—"

"They told my father she had signed a paper to that effect when she was admitted, but there was no such paper in the file I just saw. He was too broken up at the time to question it."

"Looks like we both have a mystery here, Kat. I suggest we pay a visit to Donnelli's Funeral Home. This doesn't smell right."

FEDERICO DONNELLI, A TALL MAN in his late fifties, ushered Hunter and Kat into his office assuming they wished to arrange for services on behalf of a loved one. Unctuous and overflowing with care and concern, he offered them two comfortable seats and took a chair behind his large, ornate antique desk. Leaning forward, he clasped his hands and asked, "How may Donnelli's be of help to you?"

Kat took the lead. "You can help by giving me some answers about the cremation of my mother, Irena Rousseau, in February."

Confused, Donnelli sat back. "Answers? I don't understand. Your mother was Irena Rousseau?"

"Yes; she was cremated here on February second of this year. I'd like you to find her file and tell me who authorized it."

"I see," offered Donnelli, clearly not seeing. "One moment." Stepping to a long and low cabinet against one wall, he opened it, and after a brief search, removed a folder and returned to his desk. He thumbed through it until he found what he was looking for.

"Yes, here it is. Time of death, three a.m. February second, massive cerebral hemorrhage." Then, looking guilty for having said that out loud, he put his fingers to his mouth and added, "Sorry." Continuing, he recited, "We picked up the body from the Caravaggio Institute at nine-thirty a.m. and transferred it here, where the cremation took place at one-forty-five p.m. the next day. As per instructions, we shipped the cremains to Johannes Donckers in Brussels."

Looking up at Kat, he asked, "Is that your father?"

"Yes, and he did receive her cremains which were buried with a proper funeral. What I want to know is who authorized the cremation?"

"Yes, yes, of course. Let me see now. Here it is, a Giovanni Phillippi, M.D."

Hunter and Kat looked at each other, both contemplating the significance of this revelation.

"Mr. Donnelli," Kat asked, "does your file contain a copy of an authorization signed by my mother, in which she asked to be cremated in the event of her death?"

"No, I assume that would have been kept at the Institute in their files. That's the usual case in these situations." Clearly becoming uncomfortable with the direction and implications of her questions, Donnelli asked, "Do you think cremation wasn't you mother's wish?"

"That, Mr. Donnelli, is what we are going to find out."

Chapter 31

HUNTER ADJUSTED THE AIR CONDITIONING to a comfortable level as they drove back to Pompeii. The car was hot and stuffy after sitting in the direct sun at Donnelli's.

"Phillippi's got some explaining to do," Hunter said. "We've got brain scans taken from his own files that show surgical implants on Charlie Lahti done by Phillippi himself, scans that neither Charlie nor his wife knew about, and the neurosurgeon denies having done. He claimed he was sent to the Final Care facility in Miami to remove an identification patch from Charlie's body because he was the man's principal physician, yet nowhere in his files is Phillippi even listed on Charlie's medical team."

They rode in silence for a while.

"Right," agreed Kat, picking up where they left off, "and then when the assistant director showed me my mother's file, there was no mention of Dr. Phillippi being on her medical team either, yet he's the one who signed off on her cremation."

"Your father says he never authorized it," Hunter continued, "but the Institute said she'd signed a paper stating her wish to be cremated in the event of her death, a paper that was not in her files and that Donnelli never saw."

"So Phillippi is the unexplained common denominator in both my mother's death and Charlie Lahti's," mused Kat.

They resumed thoughtful silence until Hunter turned to Kat. "I think it's time for another unauthorized visit to the imaging building. This time I know about the lamppost cameras, and I'll work my way around any additional security they might have installed."

Kat took a deep breath as if contemplating her response. "When we get back to the Amalfi we'll plan this out— together. I have some ideas."

Back at the hotel they decided on coffee in the lounge and found it empty when they arrived. Hunter didn't like the idea of Kat going with him. It was too dangerous now that the Institute's security people were alerted. He'd been trained in this kind of thing, and Kat would just be in the way. He had to talk her out of it.

"Listen, Kat, I'll be on the lookout for information on your mother every bit as much as I'll be looking for information on Charlie. There's really no need for two of us to break in. It'll only add to the danger and increase the likelihood of getting caught. I've been in there and know my way around. The best thing for you to do is to let me go in alone."

"You listen, Mr. Agent Man, Mr. Interpol Man. If you're so damned good at this, how did you miss the cameras I saw when I visited my mother here? How did you miss the big panoramic camera on the flagpole over the gazebo? How did you miss the nighttime sound detection system installed in each of the buildings on the campus?"

Her defiant stare as she squared her shoulders and jutted out her chin, told Hunter she wasn't buying it. Actually, he was a little impressed. Clearly there was more to this woman than he thought. "I did see the gazebo camera, and I didn't miss the sound-detection system. Care to tell me how *you* know about such things?"

"I told you, I read a lot. I must have read about the system somewhere and how to determine if one is in place."

Now Hunter wasn't buying it. "All right, lady, let's stop this. I've told you who I am and what my background is. It's time for you to do the same. You don't pick this stuff up by reading it in a magazine. It takes training and practice. We both know that, don't we? If we're going to work together you need to be honest with me. Now let's have it. Who the hell are you, Kat?"

"None of your damned business, you—" She got up and turned away from him, fists clenched. After several minutes in which Hunter imagined she was searching her soul deciding what to tell him, she opened her fists and faced him. Wiping a tear from her eye, she began.

"When I was young, about sixteen, I met a man—a boy really, he was twenty-three. He was a thief, a very skilled thief. He'd break into homes at night and steal things. He never got caught because he was so good at it. He'd identify a property, then find a way to legitimately enter the house during the day and examine it.

"His favorite technique was to claim to be an insect-control expert who could offer them complete one-hundred-percent protection from all pests for a very reasonable price. He'd tell them his evaluation was free. All he had to do was to look through the entire house and he'd give them a free estimate with no obligation to accept service.

"He was charming, and the housewives he'd typically encounter during the day when he made his visits were more than happy to have his company while he made his 'evaluations.' Of course this took him to every corner of the house —every window, every opening where insects could enter, and of course he would observe and carefully note every security device as well.

"I was young and thought I loved him. Maybe I did. Anyway, he taught me everything he knew. I thought it was exciting. I learned how to detect and disarm all forms of entry security systems. I learned how to open safes. I learned all the tricks of a second-story man. I learned all this from him." Kat sighed wistfully with a thousand-mile-stare.

"Then one night I decided to go with him on a job. It was stupid, I know, but I did it. It was a large estate just north of the city on a huge lot with no nearby neighbors and dense woods surrounding the main house.

"He'd done all his preplanning and thoroughly examined the house the day before, using his pest-control scheme. We'd successfully gotten in and were on the second floor, going into the master bedroom where the wall safe was hidden behind a painting. He was just ready to remove the painting when I saw it. It was no thicker than a fine hair, but it was there. If he'd lifted the picture the alarm would have gone off.

"He didn't see it, McCoy, I did. He was the expert, but I saw it. We were able to disarm the alarm and breach the system. We got away with a lot of cash they'd kept in the safe.

"He took all the money. I wanted no part of it. It didn't really hit me until then that the excitement and the precision of planning the operation was what really attracted me. It wasn't even him as much as it was the intellectual effort and finesse of the execution that appealed to me. Only when we got away with the money did I understand for the first time that what we were *really* doing was stealing. I know that may seem hard to believe, but it's true.

"I told him I was done with him after that. A year later I read in the papers that he'd been shot and killed breaking into a home in Antwerp."

She looked at Hunter, her stare no longer challenging, but not submissive either. "I'm not proud of this. It was wrong, and stupid, and dangerous. Had I been caught I can only imagine the damage the scandal would have caused my father as well as the negative effect on my mother's career. Understand this: I was very good. I could have made a career of it but didn't. Now I have the opportunity to use these skills for a good purpose, maybe even to avenge my mother, if that proves to be the case. So make no mistake about it, we're in this together."

Hunter spent several minutes weighing the pros and cons of working with her. Something was gnawing at the back of his mind, just a sense of something wrong, maybe something related to what she'd just told him, he didn't know what. Finally, unable to discern what it was, he made up his mind, exhaled an audible sigh, and said, "Okay, you're in. Let's get to work."

Chapter 32

LATER THAT NIGHT HUNTER AND KAT stealthily approached the campus through the woods in the hills behind the Institute. With two pairs of eyes instead of one, they identified all the cameras and stayed in the shadows so that not even their black-clad figures would be detected on film. They felt they were succeeding, but knew the real danger would occur the closer they got to the imaging building. Once they had to move out of the shadows they'd be seen, and no doubt someone was now monitoring those cameras continually around the clock, even if they hadn't been before.

Fortunately, the moon was not out and the sky was overcast, so their shadows weren't distinct but more like gray splotches without clear borders of light and dark. They hoped to make use of that.

"You're right," whispered Kat, "the side entrance with the wooden door you used before is too bright, even in this stuff."

As planned, they worked their way around, still staying well back in the shadows, until they had a clear view of the main door at the back of the building facing the courtyard and gazebo. It was completely in the dark except for the light mounted on the wall to the left of the door. If they could put it out, as their plan called for, the entrance would be as black as coal. As they'd hoped, it appeared to be a standard outdoor halogen light. They planned to approach from the side where it was completely dark, and disable it.

Kat, being the smaller of the two, was going to help here but they had to work fast.

The light was mounted on the wall about nine feet up with a housing that made it extremely directional. The door was completely illuminated while it was completely dark beside it. Kat moved to a position behind the light and turned to McCoy.

"Lift me up so I can examine the light."

Hunter lifted Kat so she stood on his shoulders while he held her steady by the ankles. She examined the light from the dark side.

"There's no motion detector and it doesn't appear to have a tamper-proof guard," she whispered.

Using a small Phillips screwdriver from her pack, she deftly removed the back plate and examined the wiring inside.

"This is standard stuff. No tamper loop. Easy." She disconnected the wires and the lamp went black. With the door now completely in the dark and Kat still high on his shoulders Hunter carefully stepped over to it. Using her red LED light, Kat swiftly determined the door had a security lead. "The idiots actually wired it on the outside, above the doorjamb."

It was a simple magnetic trip system she easily overcame. After scanning the rest of the door from her high perch, she indicated to Hunter to let her down.

"It's clean up there now," she whispered.

Hunter nodded. "Good, I see nothing down here. Let's go."

Hunter picked the door lock and they were inside.

"That's speedy," Kat said with professional admiration. "If they teach you that stuff, I wonder why more cops aren't burglars?"

Ignoring her, Hunter signaled for her to be on the lookout for any additional security beyond what he'd already told her about, then led them directly to Philippi's office.

Within ninety seconds they were in the office in front of the file cabinet. Hunter checked it and could see no additional security. He indicated for Kat to do the same. She shook her head. Nothing new.

They carefully opened it and waited. Nothing. They looked for but found no file on Kat's mother, neither under the name Irena Rousseau or Irena Donckers. She wasn't in there at all. It was a two-drawer file cabinet, and Hunter only had time to look through one drawer the last time. This time he opened the lower drawer: more patients, but still nothing on Kat's mother.

Finally, Hunter withdrew Charlie's folder and looked through it again. Nothing appeared to have changed. Maybe no one had noticed the images he'd removed earlier. They briefly looked at each other, shrugged, and closed the drawer. They saw nothing of interest in the rest of the room.

Just as Hunter was ready to leave, Kat tapped him on the shoulder. He turned and saw she was pointing at a framed diagram of the brain on the wall behind Philippi's desk. She approached and carefully examined the edges. No trip wires. Nothing. It was okay. The frame was on a hinge. She swung it open, revealing a wall safe.

The safe had a combination lock and a good one. It took Kat almost four minutes to open it. They were running out of time and knew it. If the darkened doorway hadn't already been noticed by whoever was monitoring the cameras, it would be soon.

Hunter reached in and removed the safe's contents. It held several travel brochures for cruises in the Baltic area as well as personal security papers for stocks, insurance policies for their house and cars, modest life insurance policies for both Phillippi and his wife, and a small black notebook.

Hunter thumbed through the notebook that mostly contained budgetary items for Phillippi's surgery, then paused at something very interesting: a list of names including Kat's mother, Irena Rousseau.

Name—Irena Maria Rousseau
Skill—Pianist
Demand—High
Contributions—(See Phoenix)

Name—Wilhelm L. Linz
Skill—Juggler
Demand—Low
Contribution—(See Phoenix)

Name—Kirk Jean Perot
Skill—Guitarist
Demand—Medium
Contribution—(See Phoenix)

Name—Larry Steven Masternink
Skill—Golfer
Demand—Estimated High
Contribution—(See Phoenix)

Name—Simona Marie Tavolacci
Skill—Memory
Demand—Unknown
Contribution—(See Phoenix)

Hunter handed the notebook to Kat so she could memorize the entries. In a few moments she tapped her head.

"Put it back in the safe and close it," she whispered.

Hunter did, and she swung the picture back into place and they left. Outside they reconnected the door light and left the campus undetected, they hoped.

Chapter 33

BACK IN THE CAR ON THE WAY to Pompeii and the Amalfi hotel, Kat was unusually quiet. Hunter knew she was working things over in her mind. He decided not to push her, but to wait until she was ready. Finally as they swung down from the hills behind Sorrento and reached the highway running along the Bay of Naples, she spoke.

"My mother—"

The crash sent the car over the edge of the road, and down through a field. It bumped and flipped and rolled several times before coming to a stop upside-down against a pole at the bottom of the hill. It was 3:20 a.m. The only noise was the sound of the back wheels slowly spinning to a stop, followed by complete silence.

Slowly opening his eyes, Hunter found himself hanging upside-down from his seat belt. Kat, also hanging from her belt, wasn't moving. Gaining focus as he slowly came around, he found his latch, unfastened it, and dropped with a thump.

Taking stock, he determined he was bruised but nothing was broken. He unfastened Kat, gently lowered her down, and laid her on her side. She was breathing. Trying his door he found it jammed, but reaching over Kat he was able to open hers a little. Good, they had just enough room to get out. He crawled over her and out, and then reached back to pull her out of the car as well. She was slowly beginning to recover.

"Kat, can you hear me? Wake up. We've got to get out of here."

Putting her hands to her head, she shook it as if trying to clear her mind. She gazed at Hunter imploringly. "What happened?"

"Are you all right? Are you hurt anywhere?"

As if the thought hadn't occurred to her before, she moved her arms and legs to check on their integrity and slowly began to stand up. "I'm okay. What happened?"

Wrapping his arm around her waist to support her, he walked her about twenty feet from the car and looked back at it, mangled and dented. "I'm not sure. I think we were run off the road. I remember a bang and the steering wheel jerked out of my hands." As he tried to clear his mind, it slowly came back to him. "Yeah, I'm sure of it. We were forced off the road. This was no accident. Can you walk?"

Kat answered with a surprising degree of strength, given what they'd just been through. "Yes, let's get out of here."

With no other choice, they called the police and reported the accident. The rental car company would demand a police report. Hunter was glad he'd taken out the full insurance package on the rental. When a Breathalyzer test showed no alcohol in their blood, the police were cooperative, but insisted they be checked out at the emergency room of the hospital.

Finally, at 8:30 a.m. the police drove them to the rental car company where they filled out paperwork for another two hours before they were able to drive away with their new rental and a misplaced stern warning to be more careful with this one. Totally exhausted, Hunter drove them to the Amalfi, where they both collapsed for much needed sleep in their adjoining rooms.

HUNTER FELT A MOVEMENT ON HIS BED. He opened his eyes to see Kat sitting on the edge staring down at him. She was still wearing the nightie she'd apparently slept in, which—unlike the black and white she normally wore was a pale blue that accented her red hair. Hunter couldn't help but notice that she wore nothing under it. Then realizing he was staring directly at this enticingly obvious fact, he quickly lifted his eyes to hers.

"Hi there. How're you doing?" he asked.

Not unaware of her affect on him, she answered. "I've been better. How about you?"

"The same." He slowly sat up and ran his hand over his face and through his short hair. "I've definitely been better."

"McCoy, let's get cleaned up. It's seven-thirty p.m. We haven't eaten in twenty-four hours or more. I'm starved and I have something to tell you about my mother."

AN HOUR LATER THEY WERE SITTING at a table in a cozy trattoria on a side street only two blocks from the Amalfi. It was the first time Hunter had eaten anywhere in Pompeii other than the hotel's dining room. It was charming and a welcome relief from the hectic events of the past twenty-four hours.

They both ordered the house lasagna along with large salads and rolls. They ate silently, drinking the local red wine the waiter said would perfectly accent their meal. Hunter couldn't get the image of her near naked body out of his mind.

Come on, man, concentrate.

Finally, over coffee and a delicious tiramisu, Kat was ready to talk.

"Something happened with my mother. I don't know what, but I'm going to find out. Her piano skills were listed as if they were a commodity."

"A commodity? What do you mean?" asked Hunter.

"The reference with my mother's name said:

Name—Irena Maria Rousseau
Skill—Pianist
Demand—High
Contributions—(See Phoenix)."

Kat scowled. "Why would a clinic that treats stroke need information on how high the demand was for her piano skill, and what the hell does contributions mean, and what is Phoenix?"

Hunter thought for a moment but came up with nothing. "What about the other names? Did any of them mean anything to you?"

Kat shook her head. "Not really. They were all listed the same way, with different skills and an estimate of demand. Under contributions they all said 'See Phoenix.'"

"I only recall seeing Golfer. What were the others?"

"One was a juggler, one a guitarist, and one said memory."

"A juggler? Jenny Lahti said her husband had become quite a juggler before the second stroke killed him."

Kat frowned in puzzlement.

"There's one thing we do know," Hunter said, "last night's car crash was no accident. We've stirred up a hornet's nest, and one name figures large—Giovanni Phillippi."

"It's time to meet him."

RACHE FUMED. "THE FOOL." Why was he following McCoy? On whose orders?" Traveler had just reported on the near death of McCoy and Kat Donckers. "He was acting on his own, sir. I questioned the man. Caravaggio and Gallo were afraid of what McCoy might learn and the security chief took that as a license to eliminate him. Obviously he couldn't even do that properly. I told him to leave them to me. He got the picture loud and clear."

Chapter 34

KRIS HANSON WAS INCREASINGLY CONCERNED about the headaches. Her husband, Carl, kept trying to convince her to see a neurologist. They both feared the cause was somehow related to her head injury in Italy.

They'd started about four months ago, right about the time she noticed her piano playing deteriorating from the incredible level she'd shown at her concert performance. She couldn't make her fingers perform the smooth runs and crossovers as well as before. She had no trouble using her hands and fingers to perform routine tasks around the house; it was only when playing the piano that her lack of coordination and loss of fingering skills was noticeable.

The headaches had only been annoying at first, but over time they began to occur more often and lasted longer. At first aspirin helped, but now the almost daily headaches failed to respond to any medication. She'd become increasingly depressed.

Kris, who'd been reading in the living room, heard Carl call from his study. "Kris? Can you come in here for a minute? We need to talk."

Joining him, she asked, "About what?"

"You know 'about what,' your headaches. I think you should see Dr. Mallard now. I know you said your next checkup isn't for another six weeks, but we need to see if he can get you in earlier. Let me give his office a call."

They'd had this discussion before, but now Kris couldn't disagree. Something was definitely wrong.

She sighed and nodded an affirmation. "I suppose you're right."

"HOW LONG HAVE YOU HAD THE HEADACHES, Kris?" Dr. Mallard asked as he examined her eyes with clinical precision. His specialty was internal medicine, and he was performing a rudimentary neurological exam.

"About two months. They've gotten more frequent and more intense."

Dr. Mallard did a thorough job, saying he saw no signs of tremor, choreoathetotic movements, fasciculations, muscle rigidity, restlessness, dystonia, or early signs of tardive dyskinesia. She showed no signs of mental loss, speech disorders, or sensorimotor loss, and her reflexes and gait were sound.

"I'd like to order a CT scan of your brain to rule out tumors, bleeding, or blood clots, just to be on the safe side. Also, I want you to see Dr. Nesbitt, a neurologist in our practice. He can read the scans and interpret them for us. Your pattern of headaches has me concerned and, I'd feel better with input from Dr. Nesbitt."

As her regular physician, Dr. Mallard was aware of the head injury she'd had in Italy and the subsequent surgery to correct it at the Caravaggio Institute.

THE CT SCAN WAS DONE THAT AFTERNOON. Dr. Mallard told Kris and Carl to wait while he and Dr. Nesbitt reviewed the images and conferred. Approximately forty-five minutes later, the nurse called a nervous Kris into Dr. Mallard's office. When she and Carl entered, Dr. Mallard introduced Dr. Nesbitt, the neurologist, and asked them to take a chair.

"Kris," Dr. Mallard began, "the CT scan clearly shows you have another subdural hematoma—two of them, actually. Small pockets of blood are collecting on the surface of each side of your brain. We're fairly sure these are causing your headaches, and the good news is we can do something about it.

However, we see something else in the scans we don't understand. There appear to be two small-unidentified objects on the surface of your brain, immediately under each hematoma. They're very likely the cause of the pooling blood. We don't know what they are."

Alarmed, Kris put her hand to her mouth, in fear.

Dr. Nesbitt took over. "Mrs. Hanson, the two objects are perfectly symmetrical, and while I've never seen anything like it, they appear to have been implanted. Do you know what they are?"

Husband and wife looked at each other questioningly.

"Implanted? No," she answered with her voice quivering. "I don't."

"The pressing issue here—the first thing to deal with are the hematomas," said Dr. Mallard. "We'll need a neurosurgeon."

Dr. Nesbitt the neurologist agreed and made several phone calls to neurosurgeons he had confidence in and set it up. "The earliest we can schedule you is four days away and the surgeon said he'd want more scans to properly identify the objects and their precise location in relation to the hematomas."

Kris bit her lip, tears in her eyes. *My god, what's happened to me?*

Chapter 35

HUNTER AND KAT STRODE TO THE RECEPTIONIST'S DESK at the administration building.

"I'm Doctor McCoy. I need to see Doctor Phillippi immediately. It's very important." Hunter had decided to use his "doctor" credential. Sometimes it was enough to get past the guardian at the gate. Not this time.

"I'm sorry, doctor, but Doctor Phillippi is leaving on a three-week holiday. Is there anyone else you could see?"

"He's leaving? Where is he going?"

"I'm sorry, sir, I don't know. And even if I did, I wouldn't be at liberty to tell you." She seemed genuinely sorry she couldn't help.

"Has he left yet?"

"I believe so, doctor," she answered.

HUNTER DECIDED IT WAS TIME FOR SOME OUTSIDE HELP. He called a special number in Lyon, France, at the headquarters of Interpol, the International Police Organization. A moment later Eduard Gautier came on the line. Hunter put the call on speakerphone so Kat could hear.

"Do I actually have the pleasure of talking with Hunter McCoy himself?"

"Afraid so. Hi, Eduard, how are you?"

"Busy, man, very busy. I'm sure you read the papers and keep up with the news. Homegrown terrorists are everywhere. Any young man with an Islamic background and nothing else to do seems to think joining the jihad is cool."

Hunter knew all about it.

"Say, I just saw your name come up on the temporarily reactivated list. I thought you'd retired to academia. What's the matter? Couldn't stay away from the cloak-and-dagger stuff?"

"Apparently not," Hunter said, "but since I'm official again, could you check on a few things for me? I've got five names for you. I need to know if they have anything in common. I'm not sure what I'm looking for, but they may be associated with something called Phoenix. The case—if there is one—may be linked to some kind of international medical fraud. I'm still in the early investigative stage here."

Eduard Gautier had worked with Hunter many times in the past and knew that, while he often operated outside strict protocol, he'd always done great work. He'd almost single-handedly been responsible for solving a case of killings and sabotage at CERN's Large Hadron Collider the previous year. So, with an exaggerated sigh, he said, "Okay, give me the names and I'll see what I can find out."

Hunter read them off, still finding it hard to believe that not only did Kat remember all five of the names, but she could spell them as well. He also told Eduard that associated with each name was a skill they apparently possessed, along with an estimate of the demand for that skill.

Name—Irena Maria Rousseau
Skill—Pianist
Name—Wilhelm L. Linz
Skill—Juggler
Name—Kirk Jean Perot
Skill—Guitarist
Name—Larry Steven Masternink

Skill—Golfer
Name—Simona Marie Tavolacci
Skill—Memory

"Give me until tomorrow and call back. I'll give you what I have then."

"Thanks, Eduard, I'll owe you."

"Yes, you will, and don't forget it." He chuckled and hung up.

Kat was strangely quiet over the next hour as they tried to figure out what to do while they waited for Gautier's report. Hunter suggested several possibilities and all he got out of her was an occasional, "That sounds okay to me," or "sure, that's fine."

Frustrated, Hunter finally said, "Look, are you staying with this or not. You seem preoccupied."

"Right, yes, I'm okay. Just wondering what Phoenix might be. Why would they be looking at my mother and the others as commodities rather than stroke patients?"

Hunter nodded, not convinced she was leveling with him. "Let's hope we learn more when we hear from Gautier."

"So, how do you know him — this Gautier?" she asked tentatively.

"Eduard and I have a long history. He came to Interpol about the same time I started collaborating with them through the DIA. We worked several cases together. The really odd thing is we've never met, not in person. All our work has been over the phone. However, I trust him completely, and I think he feels the same. There's something about a man's voice and mannerisms; after a while, they're as much a 'tell' as looking into his face, and Eduard is very thorough. If there's any link between those names, he'll find it."

Kat mulled this over. "So, Mr. Agent Man, what's our next move?"

Happy to see she was recovering some of her sass, Hunter said, "I think it's time to beard the lion in his den. Maybe he hasn't left on holiday yet. Let's go to his house."

AN HOUR LATER THEY WERE PARKED in front of a large home in Sorrento, having found the address by nothing more complicated than checking *white pages* on his smart phone. The house was like the others in the neighborhood, upscale as befitting a surgeon, with a well-kept lawn and expertly manicured hedges.

At the front door they pressed the buzzer and waited. A young woman wearing an apron opened the door, and when they asked for Dr. Phillippi, she answered in broken English, "The dottore is on holiday. He not here." After she refused to say where he was or when he'd be back, they left.

Back in the car Kat said, "Is it just me, or are we learning more by breaking and entering than we are by trying to actually talk to people?"

Hunter had to agree, they weren't making much progress this way.

As they were driving away, He caught site of a car entering a garage behind the house. Suspicious, he drove around the corner so he could see the garage from the back. It was separate from the house. Whoever was in the car would have to walk to the house to get in. They waited, concealed behind a hedge. Soon the door at the back of the garage opened and two adults stepped out, walked to the house, and entered.

Hunter parked the car and locked it. "Come on. I'm going to try something, but let me do the talking, okay?"

Kat shrugged and joined him. "All right."

Again at the front door, Hunter banged the elaborate knocker. When the young woman with the apron again opened the door, Hunter was ready, holding up his credentials. "Interpol. I'm Agent Hunter McCoy and this is my assistant. Tell Dr. Phillippi I want to see him now. Official business, and don't tell me he's not here. I just saw him enter through the garage out back."

Seemingly terrified, the young woman was about to speak when a well-dressed middle-aged man with thinning, very dark hair combed straight back stepped into the doorway.

"What's going on here?"

"I'm Agent Hunter McCoy with Interpol," Hunter said holding up his credentials. "I'm here on official business to see Dr. Giovanni Phillippi. Would you get him please?"

The man scrutinized Hunter's badge, then asked nervously, "What's this about?"

"My questions are for Dr. Phillippi."

Looking confused, the dark haired man held up his hands in supplication. "I'm Dr. Phillippi. I don't understand. What's this about?"

Hunter froze and just stared at him, stunned. This was not the man he'd met in Miami.

Chapter 36

THE PERSON WHO CALLED HIMSELF PHILLIPPI in Miami had been much larger and hairier than this man. Come to think of it, he never did see any ID, Hunter realized. *Was that guy an imposter?*

"Would you show me some identification, sir?" he asked a little less authoritatively.

The man reached into his pocket, took out his wallet, and showed his driver's license to Hunter. The picture on the license matched this man and the name was Giovanni Phillippi.

What the hell's going on here?

"May we come in, sir? I have a few questions for you."

"Who's there, Giovanni?" a feminine voice called from inside. A moment later a pretty women in her late forties joined them at the door. "Oh, hello," she said, seeing Hunter and Kat. She extended her hand. "I'm Gina Phillippi."

"Gina, they're from Interpol," Phillippi said, confusion obvious in his tone.

Hunter introduced himself and Kat saying, "I have a few official questions. Thank you for seeing us."

Frowning with concern, Phillippi ushered them into a large room at the front of the house. Gina Phillippi, excused herself to go upstairs to pack while the three of them took seats around an ornate table Hunter recognized as a good copy of a Florentine design from the fourteenth century. On the walls of the room hung copies—at least he assumed they were copies — of several early Renaissance paintings of Italian landscapes.

"What do you want? We're just getting ready to go on holiday, and we don't have much time?" said the man claiming to be Phillippi.

"Were you Mr. Charlie Lahti's principal physician when he was at the Institute?"

"Charlie Lahti?

"He died of a stroke at your facility."

"Yes, he did. That's what this is about?"

"For starters, sir, were you his principal physician?"

"No, of course not. There are no principal physicians on the stroke campus. Every patient is treated by a team."

"Were you a part of that team?"

"Yes."

"What exactly did you treat him for?"

"He'd had a cerebral blood clot that resulted in a stroke. We dissolved the clot and instituted physical therapy to overcome the temporary loss of motor control."

"Did you ever perform surgery on Mr. Lahti?"

"Surgery? Certainly not."

"Did you ever take MRIs of his brain?"

"We took a few MRIs to establish the size and location of the clot, yes."

"Just a few MRIs?"

"Yes."

"Did you do them all at the same time?"

"Of course. What's this about?"

"You didn't take multiple MRIs on two different days?"

"I told you, we did them in one setting. Now look, just exactly what are you after? Where are you going with this?"

Hunter reached into his satchel and extracted the envelope containing Charlie's MRIs. "I removed these images from your files earlier. Can you explain them, please?"

Without picking them up Phillippi exploded. "You— you're the man who broke into my office? Why should I cooperate with a man who broke into my office and rifled my files?"

Hunter put his palms up as if to hold off the man. "You'll find that was also authorized by Interpol," he replied knowing no such thing was true.

"What do you want? Why did you break into my office?"

"Let's get something straight, doctor; I'm asking the questions here. Your job is to answer them correctly and honestly."

He picked up the scan taken June 6 before the implants and handed it to Phillippi. "Do you recognize this?"

Phillippi examined it carefully, "Yes, this is one of the scans I told you about, Look, here you can see the clot."

Hunter looked. Sure enough he could see the clot. He hadn't noticed it before because his eye had been immediately drawn to the bigger difference between the scans—the insertion of the tubes in the other images. On the bottom of the MRI was the date, June 6, the date Charlie was admitted to the Institute. Also listed was the name of the ordering physician, Dr. Giovanni Phillippi.

Hunter removed the other scans, the ones showing the implants and handed them to Phillippi. "Can you explain these scans, doctor?"

Phillippi examined them. "What the hell? What is this? Those are my tubes. Where did you get these?"

Hunter had to admit that Phillippi looked genuinely shocked and surprised. "Have you ever seen these images before?"

"Of course not," Phillippi shouted, "You can't put those in a human brain. Who did this?"

"Check the name on the bottom, doctor." Hunter tapped the bottom left corner of the scan.

Date: June 13
Patient: Lahti, Charles
Odered by; Giovanni Phillippi, MD
Surgeon: Giovanni Phillippi, MD

"Goddammit, what is this? I never ordered this scan and never did any such surgery. There are no authorized human trials using my tubes. I'm going to find out who the hell did this. If these MRIs aren't doctored, someone used my tubes and did this. Jesus."

"How do you explain the fact that I took both of these scans from your files?"

"Of course not. I've never seen that second scan before in my life."

"What do the letters SRE mean?"

"How the hell do I know?"

Hunter thought the man was either a terrific liar or he was telling the truth. He temporarily switched gears.

"Why did you sign off on the cremation order for Irena Rousseau?"

"What? Who?"

"Irena Rousseau, the pianist who also died while being treated at the stroke campus."

The man claiming to be Phillippi looked totally confused at the sudden change in topic. Then, slowly recovering, he said, "Irena Rousseau…yes, now I remember her. She was rather famous, wasn't she?"

"Yes, quite famous," Hunter agreed, anxious to hear his answer to this one. "Were you her principal physician, too?"

"I told you we have no principal physicians, and no, I never treated her at all."

"Then why did you sign off on her cremation order with the Donnelli Funeral Home here in Sorrento?"

Phillippi looked mystified for a moment as if he, too, were wondering the same thing. "Did I?" he asked tentatively, stroking his chin and looking up as if trying to remember.

"Yes, you did, and you implied the Institute had an order for cremation in the event of death signed by Mrs. Rousseau."

"If I signed it, I did it as the 'Officer of the Day.' We—by that I mean the physicians—take turns signing such paperwork when the need arises. Central Administration would only ask me to sign a cremation order if they had the properly signed clearance form on file. That must be it. Why are you interested in Mrs. Rousseau?"

Hunter nodded at Kat. "Let me introduce you to my assistant, Kat Donckers. Irena Rousseau was her mother."

Phillippi's radar ratcheted up a notch. He raised an eyebrow and studied them both as if for the first time.

"Did you ever perform surgery on Mrs. Rousseau?"

"Never. Certainly not."

"No unofficial insertion of tiny tubes."

"I told you, no."

"What is Phoenix?"

This stopped Phillippi cold. He caught his breath and seemed to hold it, unable to exhale. He got up and started pacing. Finally, he called to the maid. "Maria, bring us some tea."

Then, turning to Hunter and Kat, he sighed deeply, "This may take a while."

Chapter 37

"PHOENIX. WHERE DID YOU GET THAT NAME?" Phillippi asked, licking his lips as if they'd gone dry.

"I found it in your wall safe in a notebook. The notebook described five people including Irena Rousseau. Each was accompanied by a skill, the relative demand for that skill, and the term 'contribution' with the phrase 'see Phoenix.' So, what is Phoenix?"

Phillippi puffed out his cheeks and exhaled, shaking his head. "It's nothing, just a game, a mental exercise—two people talking and speculating, that's all. It was nothing."

Hunter and Kat looked at each other, eyebrows raised in disbelief.

Kat spoke first. "Would you explain that?"

Phillippi sighed deeply and reached for his tea, taking a long slow sip. Setting it down he began. "One day, maybe two years ago, Nero Caravaggio and I were in the research lab discussing the results of one of our experiments with lab rats. You wouldn't know this, but Nero discovered a unique protein that appears in peripheral motor neurons— the ones that control your muscles — when they're damaged. I'm afraid this might be a little too technical."

"Go on, doctor. I'm also a physiologist."

Phillippi shook his head in apparent disbelief. "Good God, an Interpol agent who's also a physiologist. Now I've heard everything."

Hunter nodded. "Go on with your story."

"This protein, called PRNP, activates two genes that allow the neurons to self-repair the damage. This PRNP doesn't appear in damaged primary motor neurons—the ones in your brain. That's why damaged brain cells can't repair themselves. The studies we were doing together were designed to deliver PRNP to these damaged primary motor neurons in the rat brain in an attempt to get them working again—the idea being that this might one day lead to the possibility of regenerating damaged primary motor neurons in humans with brain disease.

"We were having some success, but not much. In any case, we were just thinking out loud, the way you do in the research lab, when he began speculating. We imagined if we could get it to work and were able to affect cures in paralyzed humans caused by brain damage in the primary motor cortex, what might be the next possible step or use for the technique? That's what scientists do, they speculate."

He's right there. Hunter nodded. "Please go on."

"Then we thought, if we could get damaged motor neurons in the primary motor cortex of the brain to repair themselves and regenerate and help paralytics, maybe someday we could mirror the marvelous connections that must exist in the brains of highly skilled people. Possibly, down the road, we could duplicate them in someone else, allowing them to become, for example—nodding at Kat—a great pianist like your mother. Nero's PRNP protein might possibly be used that way as well." Phillippi looked at Kat apologetically as he said this.

"For our flight of fancy, if you will, we considered several people with extraordinary skills, adding our speculations on how in demand their particular skills might be. In any case, it was just speculation. I'd forgotten those notes were even in there until you reminded me just now."

Hunter thought this over. As much as he didn't want to believe the man, he had to admit, it made sense. He certainly knew about speculating in the lab. He'd done it often enough with his own post-docs—the M.D.s and Ph.Ds. who worked with him in his vascular smooth-muscle research laboratory at the medical school. There wasn't a scientist out there who didn't enjoy this pursuit.

"So you never followed up on any of this with humans?" he asked.

Phillippi waved a hand, scoffing. "Of course not. Like I said, these were just speculations. There'd have to be years of preliminary work before such a thing would be possible. Even then, the ethics of such work would have to be thoroughly discussed long beforehand. I doubt it would ever be considered ethical, much less possible."

Hunter believed the man was telling the truth. Everything he'd said was plausible. He and Kat needed to talk, alone.

"Doctor, before we go, could you show me your passport? You must have it with you since you're getting ready to travel."

Phillippi got up and returned shortly with his and his wife's passports. Hunter examined them and handed them back. Clearly this man was Giovanni Phillippi.

Then who did I meet in Miami?

"Dr. Phillippi, if you're telling the truth and you didn't do this surgery on Charlie Lahti, then someone else did. That same someone else flew to the Final Care facility at Miami International Airport and claimed to be you. He probably removed those tubes you saw from Charlie Lahti's brain after he was shipped to Florida for burial. He was probably also the person who inserted them. Do you have any idea who might do that?"

"Good God, no. I'm still struggling with the idea someone jumped the gun and tried this on a human, on poor Mr. Lahti."

The man who claimed he was you in Miami was huskier than you, and younger—maybe thirty-five—and very hairy.

Does that ring a bell? Do you know anyone that fits that description?"

Hunter watched Phillippi's face and was sure he saw recognition.

Finally, Phillippi whispered, "Gallo? Dr. Gallo? Gino? No, it couldn't be. It wouldn't be."

"Who's Dr. Gallo?" Hunter asked.

"He's one of our neurosurgeons," Phillippi responded. "But why would he do that." Then, as if the thought just now occurred to him, he asked "Wait, who put this image in my files? It doesn't make any sense." Suddenly alarmed anew, he asked, "What's going on here McCoy?"

"That's what we're going to find out, doctor."

Standing up, Hunter thanked Dr. Phillippi for his cooperation but told him he should probably cancel his holiday plans and stay available while he tried to figure this out, at least for the next week or so. To Hunter's complete surprise, Phillippi immediately agreed and even seemed relieved at the request.

"One more request," Hunter added. "This is going to be hard but I'll have to ask you to keep this to yourself for now. Don't contact Dr. Gallo or anyone else at the Institute—or let on that anything is wrong—until we learn more."

"HE'S EITHER THE BEST LIAR IN THE WORLD or he's telling the truth," Kat said during the drive back to their new hotel, the Capri, this one in Sorrento itself. Not knowing who'd run them off the road but convinced it was related to their investigation, Hunter told her they had to keep on the move.

"I agree," said Hunter. "And if what he said about being the 'officer of the day' involves signing off on such things as cremation orders, that explains why he did it. I think we should check on that, though. Find out if there really is such a policy."

Kat gave a thumbs-up to that. "Exactly. And there's something else we should check on before we let him off the hook."

"What's that?"

"Does central administration have a cremation order signed by my mother?"

"Right," agreed Hunter. "And it's time to look up Dr. Gallo."

BACK AT THE NEW HOTEL—THE HOTEL CAPRI—over dinner in a quiet corner of the dining room, Kat was continuing the discussion with Hunter when his phone rang. While Hunter was busy with his caller, Kat grew increasingly anxious. Ever since she'd learned about Hunter's background, she wasn't sure what was more threatening, the fact that someone was trying to kill them, or that she had recruited an active law enforcement agent to help her find out what happened to her mother.

She was seriously conflicted. If he found out what she'd been doing, he'd never understand. On the other hand, she knew Hunter's credentials could open doors and avenues of investigation that would be closed to her. Like it or not, he was her best chance to find out what happened to her mother at the Institute. She'd seen the way he'd looked at her sitting on his bed, maybe getting closer to him was the best way to keep him from looking too closely into her other activity. While she was contemplating the irony and potential pleasure of that thought, she heard Hunter speaking.

"Thanks, Eduard. I got it."

"That was your Interpol guy wasn't it?" Kat surmised.

"Yeah. He got back to me on that list of five names we found including your mother's. You'd never heard of any of the others before, right?"

Kat wrinkled her forehead in thought as she ran the names through her mind. "No, none of them. Why?"

"For one thing, your mother was the only one who was a patient at the Institute undergoing therapy for a stroke."

"Are the others alive?" she asked.

"Yes. All of them."

Kat felt a pang of grief, thinking of her mother, as Hunter continued. "You remember how each of the names on that list was associated with a skill? Your mother, of course, was an excellent pianist, but it turns out the others are also near the top of their game at whatever they do. Wilhelm Linz isn't just any juggler he's the current champion of the World Juggling Association. And the guitarist, Kirk Jean Perot, is considered by most of his peers to be among the finest classical guitarists in the world. Larry Masternink is a star of the European Ryder Cup golf team. Are you sure you never heard of the last name on the list, Simona Marie Tavolacci?"

"No, why would I?"

"Well, unlike the others on the list, her skill isn't physical but mental. She's a grand master and the winner of the 19th World Memory Championships."

With a slow disbelieving shake of the head, Kat said, "I didn't even know there was such a thing."

"Neither did I," Hunter agreed.

After a pause, Kat said, "Do any of them have any link to the Institute besides my mother?"

"Nope, none."

"Hunter?"

"Yeah?"

Kat leaned across their small dinner table and taking his face in her hands kissed him gently on the lips.

"Again, thank you for helping me."

BACK IN HIS HOTEL ROOM, Hunter thought a long time about the kiss. It was more than a thank-you. It was clearly an invitation, he was sure. He could have acted on it, he knew. He had no doubt about its implication for more, a "more" he would have enjoyed for sure. Kat was a beautiful and highly intelligent woman. Just the type Hunter found attractive. She was dedicated too. He knew that nothing would stop her from finding out what happened to her mother. He admired that and knew he'd help her do it.

Still, something held him back. It was something nagging in the back of his mind, something about her, something he couldn't put a name to. Or was it something else? Was it Genevieve? What they'd had was real. He knew it. But the long distance thing was always an obstacle. She was in Paris and he was in the States. Still, he knew his feelings for her were strong and genuine. Maybe it was something about Kat herself. She was holding something back, he was sure of it even though he didn't know what. He fell asleep trying to figure it out.

Hunter felt a movement on his bed: no—*in* his bed. He opened his eyes and was startled to see Kat sleeping next to him, naked and lying on top of the sheet. Apparently, she slept *au naturel* just as he did. When had she come into his room?

Not wanting to wake her and thoroughly enjoying the sight of her beautiful body in its languorous pose on his bed, he had no choice but to continue to stare.

Now tell me again McCoy, why you're holding back from this?

Just then she moaned a little, turned, and opened her eyes. Propping herself up on one elbow she smiled and seemed completely comfortable with her nudity.

"I'm sorry, McCoy, I woke up several hours ago and was suddenly afraid to be alone. The adjoining door wasn't locked and so I just—."

Then sitting up and giving him a spectacular view of her naked breasts, she smiled and murmured, "I hope you don't mind."

At that moment they both noticed the rising sheet over Hunter's lap. She laughed. "Well, at least I can see that *"he"* doesn't mind.

Then realizing they were both staring directly at his growing erection, he slowly scanned up her body—pausing again at her breasts—and then reluctantly up to her eyes. Then, just as his reticence was rapidly disintegrating, she completely surprised him by jumping out of his bed and stood facing him.

"McCoy, I'm starved. Let's go out for breakfast. Then she turned on her heels and went through the adjoining door into her room.

Completely confused and, he had to admit, more than a little disappointed at the sudden end of what might have been an enjoyable experience in bed, Hunter took a cool shower and wondered anew about Kat Donckers, and his confused feelings about her.

DURING BREAKFAST THE SUBJECT OF HER NAKEDNESS came up only once.

"I'm sure you haven't forgotten, McCoy, that I busted in on you in the nude first."

"Yes. That's true. You did."

"So, now we're even then," she said smiling.

"Not quite. You've busted in on me twice, once with me naked and once with you naked."

Kat nodded. "That's true."

"So it would seem that I'm still two 'busting-ins' short."

They both quietly mulled over the implications of that throughout the rest of the breakfast.

Afterward, Hunter accompanied Kat to the Institute where officials showed her the signed permission form for cremation in the event her mother died while she was there. Kat said the signature was clearly her mother's. It appeared to be authentic and was dated the day after she was admitted.

They were also able to verify the 'officer of the day' policy was real and that Dr. Phillippi was indeed designated as such on the day he signed the order for Irena Rousseau's cremation.

Running out of options on what to do next, they decided to call on Phillippi once more. The man was cooperative and invited them over.

"That speculation you and Dr. Caravaggio were doing—about transferring skills from one person to another—was Dr. Gallo in the lab as you two were discussing this?" Hunter asked.

"No, just Nero and me, and that's all there was to it, that initial brainstorming and me writing down the few notes you saw. That was the end of it. We never discussed it again."

"What about Caravaggio?"

"What about him?"

"Do you think he ever pursued it?"

"What do you mean, 'pursued it'? There was nothing to pursue."

Hunter wasn't sure where he was going with this, but forged on anyway. "Did he ever propose any animal studies along those lines?"

"You mean transferring skills?"

"Yes."

"No, the only animal studies he did, at least with me, involved stimulating motor neurons to replace damaged cells in rats, using my indwelling release tubes. Those experiments never showed much promise, though, and there hasn't been much incentive to continue—at least I wasn't too enthusiastic. He and his two research assistants are still doing studies along those lines, but I'm no longer interested or involved. He certainly never proposed any real studies involving transfer of motor skills from one animal to another. And, since I'm on the Animal Care and Use

Committee for the Institute, any such proposals would have come to our committee's attention."

Hunter scratched his chin. "So his lab is continuing animal studies on nerve growth but not on skill transfer."

"Yes."

"What about human studies; would you know about those?"

Phillippi looked exasperated. "There *were* no human studies. Any project like that would have to have the appropriate animal studies already in place and completed, showing the procedure was safe. Only then could you make a request for human trials. Besides, any study that important would certainly have surfaced, and we'd all be talking about it. No, there have been no human studies."

"Does the Institute have a committee for evaluating proposed human studies?" Hunter was sure they did since all hospitals and research facilities in the United States had such committees, usually made up of medical people, ethicists, and ordinary citizens.

"Yes, we have such a committee; of course." Then, as if something had just dawned on him, Phillippi looked sharply at Hunter. "Dr. Gallo is the current chairman of that committee."

Chapter 38

HUNTER SEARCHED THE INSTITUTE'S WEBSITE for photos of the medical staff. Most of the doctors had pictures linked to their brief bios but several didn't—including Phillippi and Gallo. A search of the Internet showed lots of research but no photos.

Hunter went to the main administration building where Gallo had his office. In contrast, Phillippi's office was on the stroke campus.

"I need to see Dr. Gallo, Please."

The receptionist asked Hunter who he was and did he have an appointment.

"Dr. Hunter McCoy, and no, I don't. Just need to see him for a few minutes."

The woman opened the center drawer to her desk and looked down. It looked to Hunter like she was checking something. He was sure of it when she looked up sharply and swallowed. I'm sorry, Dr. McCoy, Dr. Gallo isn't in. In fact he's out of the country right now and won't be back for at least a month." Then she smiled, "If you'd tell me where you're staying while you're visiting here and give me a number where I could reach you, I'll have him contact you if he returns early."

Hunter stared hard at the woman. "What makes you think I'm visiting? Did your desk drawer tell you to ask for my address and phone number once you verified my name and picture?"

She clasped one hand over her mouth and the other on the front of the now closed desk drawer, as if to keep Hunter from opening it. Then she recovered. "No, not at all. I'm sorry, doctor, he's gone for a month. Now if you'll excuse me I have work to do."

"One more question, if you don't mind. Can you tell me if Dr. Gallo has been out of the country in the past month, perhaps to Florida?"

"I really can't give you that information. Now if you'll—"

"Can't or won't?"

"Sir, I'll call security if you don't leave."

"Thanks so much. You've been a great help." Hunter gave her his best smile and left.

"EDUARD. HOW ARE THINGS IN LYON?"

"It's been slow. You know how it is. Mostly I just sit here sipping coffee and reading the newspaper praying someone will ask me to check on something."

"Well, good. As it happens, I'm just your man."

Eduard groaned. "Somehow I knew it. Okay what is it?"

"I need you to check if Dr. Eugenio Gallo of the Caravaggio Institute in Sorrento, Italy was on a flight to Miami, Florida on a particular day a few weeks ago."

"That's too easy. Give me the day. I'll get it for you and be back sipping coffee again in no time. Might even take a nap after that."

Hunter gave him the date. Ten minutes later Hunter got Gautier's return call.

"Dr. Eugenio Gallo, Italian citizen, flew out of Naples on Alitalia at five p.m. and arrived in Miami at a little after seven the next morning. He returned to Naples the next day using the rest of his round trip ticket."

"Thanks, Eduard. Pour yourself a cup on me."

"Thanks, big spender. I'll do that."

HUNTER TOLD KAT HE WAS NOW SURE that Gallo was the Phillippi imposter in Miami and that he and Caravaggio were definitely up to something.

They decided they needed to get into Caravaggio's office and see what they could find, knowing they were pushing the envelope of their luck.

If it wasn't Phillippi, someone had to be involved with the implanted release tubes in Charlie's brain; it seemed unlikely Nero Caravaggio was doing it on his own. The man, for all his brilliance, wasn't a neurosurgeon—But Gallo was. They'd break into his office, too. Clearly, something inappropriate was going on at the Institute, and it was likely it involved Kat's mother as well as Charlie Lahti.

Chapter 39

THEY ENTERED THE BUILDING just before the scheduled closing time at 7:00 p.m., and then sequestered themselves in a janitor's closet on the same floor as Caravaggio's office. Not knowing when the janitor might appear, they waited until 6:30, poked their heads out, and locating what appeared to be a larger storeroom down the hall from the receptionist's desk, they stowed away there. They stayed there for another hour to play it safe before making their way to Caravaggio's door behind the reception desk. Kat opened the locked door faster than Hunter would have imagined, and not for the first time he thought what a great team they'd make if they actually were thieves.

Fortunately, it was a clear night and the moon—about three-quarters full—illuminated the room in pale blue light through the vast wall of glass. Looking for nothing specific, just anything that might indicate a crime was being committed, Hunter took the man's desk and Kat went to work on the small credenza that served as a four-drawer hanging file cabinet. The desk revealed nothing of interest, and no secrets were taped under or behind any of the doors.

"I'm coming up empty here. Have you found anything?" Hunter asked.

"Not really; mostly personal files on research projects dating back fifteen to twenty years. Maybe you should look through these. I don't understand them at all."

"Okay, I'll do that while you check out the rest of the room."

As Hunter went through the files, he could see the progression of Caravaggio's work and thinking. The earliest papers described projects designed to learn about the capabilities of central nervous system neurons in general. Following this were many collaborative works with international scientists focusing on the potential for stimulating damaged CNS neurons to regenerate new processes.

Later still his work focused on attempts to get the newly formed processes from motor neurons to innervate — actually form synapses with and control muscle cells. On three of the papers, Caravaggio collaborated with Phillippi, inserting tubes to deliver nerve growth stimulants to damaged motor neurons in rats. The last of these was almost three years old. Since then, the animal study papers — exploring the same themes — were written by Caravaggio and two research assistants. It looked like this really was a dead end, just as Phillippi had implied.

"McCoy?"

Startled, he looked up and Kat was waving him over to the back wall. He was done with the file cabinet anyway.

"What've you got?" he asked, as he approached one of the many paintings he'd noticed on the their earlier visit.

"There's something odd about these paintings."

Hunter strolled up and down, looking at them—ten of them. "They all look like they were done by the same artist," he said.

"Exactly. But there are none of those little brass plates you usually see with the artist's name and the painting's date and title."

Hunter didn't find this particularly unusual. "No doubt Caravaggio knows who painted them and doesn't need a plaque. Most people don't have little signs up next to the paintings in their homes. Only museums do that, I think."

Kat shrugged. "I suppose so. Did you find anything in the files?" she asked hopefully.

"Nothing stood out, just a chronology of his research career."

"Nothing strange at all?"

"Nope. Nothing."

They both scanned the room for any more potential sources of information. "I wonder if any of these paintings covers a safe?" Hunter mused.

Kat carefully checked the first one. "No trip wire." She did the same for the other nine—nothing there either. Finally she tried lifting one from the wall and found nothing behind it or behind any of the other nine.

Hunter used his phone camera to take pictures of the entire office, including Caravaggio's desk, credenza, and each of the paintings. He even took general photos of all the walls, floor, and ceiling, in case they had to review anything later.

"Looks like we're out of luck," Kat said reluctantly.

They were just about to leave when Hunter noticed a small pedestal at the far end of the room where the enormous curved windows ended. He immediately recognized the marble bust sitting on it: Camillo Golgi. He knew that Golgi, a nineteenth-century Italian scientist, together with Santiago Ramon y Cajal, had received the Nobel Prize in Physiology and Medicine in 1906 for his studies of the structure of the nervous system.

"This guy won a Nobel Prize. Caravaggio must keep him around as an inspiration."

"So what?" Kat muttered in frustration.

Squatting securely, Hunter lifted the heavy bust.

"What are you doing?"

"Let's see if this old boy has any secrets."

He held it up so Kat could see the bottom.

"There's a card here, "she said excitedly. She read aloud:

"FENICE Michelangelo MdC

CES—GALEICII
NAR—HCOIOREC
EMM—GAFILO
LUC—OERIF
SBU—TATURF"

"Have you got it, Kat?" Hunter asked, figuring her memory could handle this with no problem.

"Of course; put it back."

"Use my cell phone to take a picture of it just the same, while I hold it up."

She did as he'd asked just as they heard a door closing somewhere.

"Time to get out of here, Kat. Let's go."

Peeking out the door to Caravaggio's office, they saw no one and quickly retraced their route, leaving the building unnoticed, they hoped.

While Hunter drove away, Kat reproduced on a piece of notepaper the cryptic words and letters they'd found under the Golgi bust. Hunter hadn't had time to really look at it.

"Does it make any sense?" he asked. "Do you recognize anything?"

Kat shook her head. "No sense at all. And why should it be hidden under the bust? Did Michelangelo ever do a painting or sculpture called FENICE?"

"Beats me," said Hunter. "What else does it say?"

Kat studied what she'd written. "There are five lines of letter groupings. Each line has three letters followed by a space line and another group of letters."

Hunter drove quietly for several minutes, thinking it over, trying to imagine what it meant.

"What about the second group, how many letters?"

"That varies. The first grouping always has three while the second grouping varies from five to eight letters. It must be some kind of code."

BACK AT THE HOTEL IN HUNTER'S ROOM, Kat used his laptop to search the Internet to see if Michelangelo was associated with anything called FENICE. After fifteen minutes of trying she had her answer—nothing. Michelangelo and the term FENICE were not linked in any way. They tried working on the cryptic letter arrangements next. After thirty minutes, Hunter told Kat he was going to call someone who might be able to shed some light on this. Puzzled, she watched as he made a call on his cell phone.

"Genevieve? It's Hunter, I need your help."

Chapter 40

"HUNTER? WHERE ARE YOU?"

"Believe it or not, I'm in Sorrento, Italy, working on a case."

After a long pause in which Hunter wondered if she'd heard him, she asked, "Sorrento? That's not far from Naples, is it?"

Hunter wondered at this then answered, "No, it's less than an hour away. Why?"

Genevieve laughed and laughed.

"Okay, what's so funny?"

Genevieve spoke with delight in her voice. "Don't you see? You called me on my cell phone, but you don't really know where I am, do you? I mean I could be at my job at the National Library in Paris, or with my parents in Oxford, or even less than an hour away—say in Naples."

She laughed again. "And you need my help, too, is that right?"

Hunter was totally confused. "Yes—all of that's true, and I do need your help, your professional help as a Renaissance scholar. But first, I give up. Where are you?"

"You're not going to believe this, but at this very moment I'm in Naples at an International Conference on Medieval and Renaissance History. I just presented a paper two hours ago. I'm beat, and about ready to go to bed."

He couldn't believe his luck. Genevieve was here, or at least almost here. "Look, will you still be there tomorrow?"

"Yes, I'll be here two more days attending meetings before I fly back to Paris. It would be great to see you, Hunter, I've missed you."

"I know Genevieve, me too." Hunter meant it. During the Michael Servetus affair the previous summer, they'd faced enough life-threatening dangers together to bring them emotionally close in a way both of them wished could have continued. But his work in Virginia and hers in Paris just wouldn't allow it. Now here she was, just an hour away. Hunter longed to see her.

"The case we're working on has just coughed up a coded clue, with Michelangelo's name on it. It's just begging for your expertise to help decode it. We can be there tomorrow morning."

"We?"

"Yes, there'll be two of us. I'll explain when we get there. Where should we meet you?"

"I'm staying at the Mercure Hotel in the historic district not far from the Convention Center where the meetings are being held. Let's meet there for lunch at noon....Hunter?"

"Yes?"

"Give me a hint. What's the puzzle?"

"In involves some words linked together, Michelangelo, and some scrambled letters. We'd like you to—"

"Tell you what it means," she finished.

Hunter laughed, remembering how she always finished his sentences for him. "Now I know it's really you, Genevieve. See you tomorrow. And thanks."

Kat narrowed her eyes, "Who was that?"

"Her name is Genevieve Swift. She's a Renaissance expert at the National Library in Paris."

"So how do you know her, and how is that going to help anyway?" Kat asked coldly.

"Last summer she helped me find a lost book dating from the Inquisition. She's also very good at codes. Her mother is French, her father English, and both are professors at Cambridge. The father's field is medieval history and the mother's is astrophysics. Genevieve's own Ph.D., from the Sorbonne, is in Renaissance History."

"Were you two—you know—close?"

Sighing and staring upward, looking at nothing, he didn't answer right away.

Were we close? Her quick reaction in Villanueva de Segna in the foothills of the Pyrenees saved me from a sniper's round. I rescued her from a bomb-loaded rowboat triggered by a sadistic assassin. Together we stopped a madman from blowing up the Large Hadron Collider operated by CERN, the European Nuclear Research Agency. She understood my nightmares over Gary's death. She was courageous, smart, and beautiful—and we became lovers.

"Yes, we were close," he finally answered.

Kat nodded curtly and headed for her room. "I'll leave the clues with you," she said coldly. "See you in the morning."

Hunter watched her go, but his thoughts remained with Genevieve, and she filled his dreams all that night.

AND THEN THERE SHE WAS. She was sitting at a table in the rooftop restaurant under the shade of an umbrella, sipping coffee and staring out at the ancient city of Naples, when Hunter and Kat approached.

She looked up, smiled, and rose to greet him just as Hunter swept her up in a close embrace. Neither spoke; they just breathed each other in while Kat stood there and stared. Finally breaking off, Genevieve said, "It's so good to see you again, Hunter," then reaching out her hand to Kat, "Hi, I'm Genevieve."

Hunter recovered enough to introduce them. "Genevieve, this is Kat Donckers. She and I both have a vested interest in whatever help you can give us."

The two women shook hands, appraising each other. While Kat, with her red hair and green eyes was attractive, she didn't compare to Genevieve. Genevieve was flat-out beautiful. Before the reflective pause could continue too long, Hunter suggested they sit down and he'd bring Genevieve up to speed on the situation.

Just then, a middle-aged tall man wearing dark trousers, a light shirt, and tan jacket carrying several books walked by and apparently tripped on something. The books flew out of his hands and landed near their table. He quickly apologized in Italian, got on his hands and knees, and began to pick them up including one directly under their table. Hunter collected two of them that landed directly on the table and gave them to the man who apologized again for his clumsiness. The man was completely bald, not even eyebrow or lashes.

When the man left, Hunter continued. He told Genevieve about Charlie Lahti's missing body and how he'd become involved. He explained about the mix-up, Kat's connection to Final Care through her father, and how both Charlie's and Kat's mother's experience at the Caravaggio Institute strongly suggested something irregular, possibly criminal, was going on there.

"I'm sorry about your mother, Kat, I'm familiar with her music," Genevieve offered with sympathy. "My father has a collection of classical piano performances, and I remember hearing your mother playing Mendelssohn many times at his home."

"Thank you," Kat said coolly.

When the waiter had taken their orders for lunch, Kat reluctantly handed Genevieve the notepaper with the cryptic message.

"Let's eat first," Genevieve said, placing the note in her purse, "and we'll look at it later."

Their orders arrived. Hunter had mussels Neapolitan ala marinara served with Italian bread, orange slices, and basil.

Kat's choice was ravioli Capresi, while Genevieve had crocchè di patate, which turned out to be fried mashed potatoes with herbs, cheese, and salami mixed in, lightly coated in breadcrumbs, and fried. She confessed this was the third time she'd ordered them—they were so good.

Traveler could hear them clearly through the bug he'd placed under the table when he'd retrieved his books. It was bad enough that Rousseau's daughter had teamed-up with McCoy but now this Genevieve Swift—whoever she was—was going to poke her nose into things too.

He heard Genevieve say they should go to her room after lunch to decipher it. He didn't know what that meant but she did mention the room number. He gave this number to the harried desk clerk and asked for a new room keycard, saying he'd locked himself out. Traveler couldn't believe it when the idiot actually complied and made him one.

He searched the room thoroughly looking for any evidence of who she was. He found a program for a conference at the convention center, something to do with the Renaissance. The room had a safe but he had no way to get into it. In one of the dresser drawers, under some of her clothes, he found a laptop computer. Thinking it might tell him something about her, he took it to examine later.

Through the receiver in his ear bud, he heard the Swift woman say they should go to her room now. Traveler knew it was time to leave.

When the trio reached Genevieve's room she opened the dresser drawer to retrieve her computer, and furrowed her brows. "It's not here."

Confused, Genevieve looked again and tried the other two drawers, in case she had put it in one of them instead, although she was sure she hadn't.

"It's gone. My computer's gone. I put in in this drawer before I left to go to meet you."

A thorough search of the room and bathroom turned up nothing.

"Let's check with the desk and ask if anyone's been in here," Hunter said. "Clearly the maid hasn't made up the room," seeing the unmade bed.

The embarrassed desk clerk admitted he'd given a new card to a man who said he'd locked himself out.

Genevieve fixed the man with a cold stare. "You gave a key to my room to a man when the room is clearly registered to me—a woman?

"What did he show you for identification?" Hunter demanded.

The clerk, clearly terrified now, admitted he hadn't asked him to show anything.

"He gave you her room number?" Hunter asked.

"Yes he—"

Beginning to get an idea, Hunter said, "What did he look like?"

"I think he was wearing a light colored jacket," the clerk said trying now to be helpful as if that would erase his earlier stupidity. "And he was bald, with funny eyes—no brows.

"The man with the books," Kat said.

"Exactly," replied Hunter.

Hunter nodded to Genevieve and Kat, "Come with me."

He led them back to the table where they'd had lunch and the man had earlier dropped his books. Hunter got down, looked under the table surface, and saw what he expected— a voice-activated transmitter.

Chapter 41

GENEVIEVE REGISTERED A FORMAL COMPLAINT with the management of the hotel over the loss of her computer. Hunter drove them to an Internet cafe where they could access the Internet and try to solve the mystery of the code. Both his and Kat's laptops were back at their hotel.

Hunter noticed that Genevieve was unusually silent, staring out the side window.

"Are you all right? Hunter asked.

She paused before answering. "No, not really."

"What is it?"

She turned from the car window and looked at them both. "That laptop contained all my notes for a book I've been writing on the legacy of the Inquisition today. None of that material is backed up, and I've already written a large part of it. There's a year's worth of writing on it. I have to get it back."

As a scholar himself, Hunter couldn't imagine losing that much work.

Genevieve continued. "Who do you think that man was? Is he linked to this stuff your investigating at that Institute?"

"I do."

"What have you gotten me into? What do you think is going on at that place?"

Hunter exhaled a large sigh and shook his head. "We really don't know. You'd think we would by now, but we don't. Maybe if you can help us decipher the code, or whatever it is, we can find out."

Genevieve sighed and nodded in acknowledgement, her lips still tight with anger at the loss of all her work. She removed the cryptic note from her purse and looked at it for the first time.

FENICE Michelangelo MdC

CES—GALEICII
NAR—HCOIOREC
EMM—GAFILO
LUC—OERIF
SPE—TATURF

Hunter tapped the note with his finger. "We believe the director and founder of the Institute, Nero Caravaggio, might be involved in the irregularities we've found. This message was taped to the bottom of a bust of Camillo Golgi in his office. We don't know what it means or even if there is anything shady about it. We haven't been able to make anything out of it at all, but since it has Michelangelo's name, we thought maybe you could—"

"Tell you what it means. What did you say the name of the Institute was?"

"The Caravaggio Neurological Institute," replied Hunter. "Why?"

"Perhaps this Michelangelo MdC isn't the Michelangelo you think it is."

Hunter knit his brows, "What other Michelangelo is there?"

"My guess is, Michelangelo Merisi da Caravaggio, an Italian artist active in Rome, Naples, Malta, and Sicily between 1593 and 1610."

"Caravaggio?" Kat and Hunter said together.

"What about FENICE? Does that name connect to Caravaggio?" Hunter asked.

"Not that I'm aware of," Genevieve responded. "It's Italian for phoenix. I'm not familiar with all of his work, but it—"

"Phoenix?" cried Kat. "Hunter, that's—"

Hunter nodded, excited now. "Genevieve, this could be important. The name Phoenix might refer to a project we thought was only imaginary. We have to figure out what the rest of this means."

Genevieve used the cafe's computer to look up the painter Caravaggio. When one of his paintings appeared on the screen, Hunter stopped her.

"Hold it. I think that's one of the paintings Nero Caravaggio had on his wall. I have a picture of it here on the cell phone." He quickly found it. "Here, look at that. It's the same. Genevieve, see if these others he had on his wall are also Caravaggios."

Hunter brought them up one at a time. Some Genevieve recognized instantly as Caravaggios; others she had to look up on the computer. In the end, she identified all ten paintings hanging in Nero Caravaggio's office as reproductions of original Caravaggios.

Genevieve said, "He must be fascinated with his namesake."

Instantly, Hunter had an idea. "Genevieve, do these paintings have names or titles?"

"Probably. Let's look them up." She gave them the titles as she found them.

> *Boy With a Basket of Fruit*
> *Boy Bitten by a Lizard*
> *Boy Peeling Fruit*
> *The Calling of St. Matthew*
> *The Fortune Teller*
> *Narcissus*

Saint Matthew and the Angel
Supper at Emmaus
Young Sick Bacchus
The Musicians

All three of them scrutinized the titles, trying to see any relationships to the cryptic letters.

"Wait, here's something," Hunter said, pointing to NAR on the sheet. Maybe NAR is short for Narcissus. Maybe he's referring—"

"To the painting," Genevieve finished. "Let's look at the other three-letter groupings."

CES
NAR
EMM
LUC
SPE

"Maybe EMM stands for *Supper at Emmaus*," Kat said, reluctantly getting into the idea although it was plain to Hunter she was not happy to have Genevieve here.

All three eagerly looked at the remaining titles.

After a few minutes, Kat sighed dejectedly. "Maybe the first two were just a coincidence."

Hunter stroked his chin. "Genevieve, correct me if I'm wrong, but aren't Narcissus and Emmaus proper names?"

"Yes," she answered, "Narcissus was a boy who fell in love with his own image in a pond in Greek mythology. Emmaus was an ancient town near Jerusalem where Jesus supposedly appeared to two of his followers after his resurrection."

"So they would be spelled the same way in English and Italian, correct?"

Genevieve nodded. "Yes."

"Then wouldn't—"

"The titles *also* be in Italian?" Genevieve finished. "Right, good thinking. We should be looking for Italian words reduced to the first three letters," Genevieve clapped her hands in excitement. "Hunter, I know your Italian's not too good. What about you, Kat?"

"Not really, no."

"Okay, let me see what I can do." She stared at the titles they'd written down for a few minutes. "Okay, I have one. *Boy Bitten by a Lizard*. The Italian word for lizard is *lucertola*, LUC. So now we have:

CES
NAR   *Narcissus*
EMM   *Emmaus*
LUC   *Lucertola*
SPE

"Good work. Just two more to go," said Hunter.

"Here it is, *Basket of Fruit*," said Genevieve. "*Cestello* is basket in Italian, CES."

"How about the last one, SPE?" Kat asked.

Genevieve looked at the list of titles they'd written and translated each into Italian. Then she had it. "*Spellato*. It means peel or peeling. It has to be *Boy Peeling Fruit*, SPE. There we have them all."

CES   *Cestello*
NAR   *Narcissus*
EMM   *Emmaus*
LUC   *Lucertola*
SPE   *Spellato*

All three of them stared at the list for a moment before Genevieve asked. "So why would he have a code referring to only five of his ten Caravaggio paintings? It seems the more we learn, the more confusing it gets. What are the other letters all about? They're certainly not Italian words." Hunter wrote what they had so far on a notepad.

CES (*Cestello*) GALEICII	*Boy With a Basket of Fruit*
NAR (*Narcissus*) HCOIOREC	*Narcissus*
EMM (*Emmaus*) GAFILO	*Supper at Emmaus*
LUC (*Lucertola*) OERIF	*Boy Bitten by a Lizard*
SPE (*Spellato*) TATURF	*Boy Peeling Fruit*

The trio stared at the remaining puzzle, the groups of letters. Were they words or just groups of letters?

Finally, Kat rose from her perch on the edge of the bed and paced in the small room. "Let's try something. Take the first one, *Boy With a Basket of Fruit*. Can you bring that painting up on your computer screen?"

Genevieve nodded. "Sure, hold on."

Caravaggio's painting soon filled her screen, and they all stared at it. It pictured a young boy with dark curly hair holding a wicker basket filled with apples, peaches, pears, grapes, and cherries.

Kat asked Genevieve to give the Italian names for the fruits.

"Well, let's see, apple would be *mela*, peach is *pesca*, pear is *pera*, grape is *uva*, and cherry is *ciliegia*.

"M, P, P, U, C," Kat murmured.

Suddenly, Genevieve shouted. "Hey, there it is—cherry!"

Hunter and Kat squinted at the photo, confused. "What do you mean?" he asked.

"Cherry, *ciliegia*. It's an anagram. Rearrange the letters and GALEICII becomes *CILIEGIA*."

Hunter and Kat quickly saw she was right. "That's got to be it, Genevieve." Hunter squeezed her shoulder. "What about the others?"

Since Genevieve was the only one with a good grasp of Italian, she told them to leave her alone for a bit while she tried to figure it out. While she worked through the possibilities on Hunter's notepad, he and Kat retreated to a corner of the small room.

"McCoy, where do you think this is going? What's Caravaggio up to? It can't be a coincidence that the name Phoenix is on that list."

"I agree. Either this is Caravaggio's notes on his meeting with Phillippi in which they were just speculating, or it's gone beyond that."

"You think they might actually be trying something along the lines Phillippi suggested?"

"Perhaps, though it doesn't seem as if the two are working together anymore. Maybe Caravaggio's taken their speculations to the next level. Either Phillippi isn't involved or he's a world-class liar."

Kat thought for a moment. "This code, or whatever, is beginning to feel like more than just speculation. Why the link to the paintings? Something has to be going on there."

Genevieve called them over. "Okay, I have it. Look at this. As you saw GALEICII becomes CILIEGIA, the Italian word for cherry. The others are also anagrams of the Italian names for ear, leaf, flower, and fruit."

HCOIOREC	*ORECCHIO* (ear)
GAFILO	*FOGLIA* (leaf)
OERIF	*FIORE* (flower)

TATURF *FRUTTA* (fruit)

"Genevieve, you're a genius," said Hunter, giving her a hug, while Kat looked on unsmiling. "Let's look at the first of the five entries on the list under the bust. Apparently, CES is short for *cestello*, which is Italian for basket. This suggests the painting on Caravaggio's wall, *Boy With a Basket of Fruit*. And Genevieve, since you've solved the anagrams, we know this painting is also linked to the specific fruit, cherry."

"Are there cherries in the basket of fruit?" Kat asked, getting back into it.

Genevieve pulled the painting up on the computer. "Yup, there are cherries in the basket along with some other fruits."

"Let's complete the others," Genevieve said. "Hunter, you write them down. After a few minutes they had it.

Boy With a Basket of Fruit—cherry
Narcissus—ear
Supper at Emmaus—leaf
Boy Bitten by a Lizard—flower
Boy Peeling Fruit—fruit

Within a minute they'd checked them all. "Bingo," Hunter said. "Each painting has the anagrammed word as part of the image."

All three were quiet for a time, trying to imagine what it meant. After several minutes, Kat finally spoke up. "McCoy, show me the painting of *Boy Bitten by a Lizard* again. The one on your cell phone."

"Why do you want to see it again?" he asked, while already starting to find it on his phone.

"I'm not sure; just let me see it again."

When he had it on his phone's small screen, he handed it to Kat, who stared at it for a long time. Occasionally she'd look away as if staring at something else, and then she'd come back to it.

Unable to contain himself, Hunter finally asked, "What do you see?"

"Something's not right with this painting."

"What do you mean?" Genevieve asked.

"Just a minute, I'm bringing it up."

Hunter and Genevieve watched impatiently as Kat seemed to be looking at something—'out there.'

Suddenly she shouted, "I've got. It's the flower behind his ear."

"Huh?" asked Hunter.

"The flower. Look at your picture, McCoy. See? He has a flower over his right ear and one over the left."

"Yeah, so what?"

"I'm sure there is only one flower in the original we saw earlier on the computer screen. And, it was over the right ear."

Genevieve was amazed. "You remembered that? You've only seen the original once, for less than a minute. How could you possibly know that? I'm not even sure it's true."

"Believe me, it's true," Kat said.

"She has an eidetic memory, Genevieve. She remembers anything she sees, hears, smells, whatever. She never forgets it. It's always here." He tapped his temple.

"That's incredible, Kat, I've never heard of such a thing."

Then Genevieve turned her attention back to the computer. "I'm going to pull up Caravaggio's painting of *Boy Bitten by a Lizard.*" When she'd found it, she expanded it to fill the screen so the three of them could see it.

"There it is. Kat's right." She pointed to a flower in the boy's hair. "There's only one flower and it's over his right ear."

Hunter compared it to the photo of the painting in Caravaggio's office on his cell phone. It had a second flower over the left ear, a flower clearly not in the original. "But why? Why would that be?" Genevieve wondered aloud. "Flower was the anagrammed word for this painting. What about the anagrammed words for the other paintings?" Hunter leaned over Genevieve's shoulder. "Pull up the other four paintings and see if there are any other irregularities."

Genevieve brought up *Boy With a Basket of Fruit* next. While she did this Hunter brought up the same painting on his phone. "Cherry" was the anagrammed word. All three of them stared at both pictures.

Kat saw it first. "Look, McCoy's picture has one more cherry than the original, twenty-five instead of twenty-four."

Sure enough, the painting in the office had been doctored to add one more cherry to the basket. Excited and sure they were on to something now, they worked their way through the remaining three paintings and confirmed the pattern. All five of the paintings in Caravaggio's office had been doctored. There was one extra leaf on the table in *Supper at Emmaus*, an extra fruit on the table in *Boy Peeling Fruit*, and Narcissus had an earring in his ear that wasn't in the original painting.

Just then Kat's cell phone rang. She checked the screen for caller ID and excused herself to take the call. While she stepped outside Genevieve asked Hunter what he was going to do now that they'd apparently explained what was on the card.

"I'm going back to Sorrento to have one more look at those paintings up close. Those extra items have to mean something. But I'm fully convinced of one thing now — Phoenix is more than just a mind game, and I'm sure it involved Charlie Lahti and Kat's mother."

Hesitantly, Genevieve asked, "Hunter, are you and Kat—you know—"

"No, we're not. It isn't like that at all. She's on a mission to find out what happened to her mother, just like I am for Charlie. There's nothing between us."

"Well, she certainly thinks there is or wants there to be."

Hunter nodded. "You might be right, but there's still nothing between us."

As Hunter was saying this he could see Kat outside through the window, obviously arguing with whomever had called her. He could tell she was getting as much grief as she was giving.

As he and Genevieve continued to speculate about what the decoded message might mean, Hunter continued to watch Kat.

Her evolving body language as the call went on suggested she was reluctantly agreeing to whatever her caller was telling her. When she hung up she just stood there for a few minutes, staring into space, presumably assimilating whatever the call was about, her free hand in a fist. Finally, she rejoined them inside.

They waited for an explanation.

Kat gave a long, exasperated sigh. "I have to go to Prague for a few days. One of my clients insists I assess a huge amount of estate jewelry that's suddenly come available and is about to be auctioned. He wants to make a bid."

Interested, Genevieve asked her, "What do you do, Kat? Are you a jeweler?"

"No, I'm an appraiser. I have my own business, with clients all over the continent. Unfortunately, when they want me I pretty much have to go. This is one of those times." Turning to Hunter she added, "I've got to leave right away, but I'll be back in a day or two and we can continue."

Hunter didn't comment right away. He knew Kat didn't want to miss any part of the investigation, but he couldn't afford to wait. He needed to get back into Caravaggio's office.

Genevieve turned to Hunter. "If this guy, the one who bugged our table and stole my computer, is linked to your investigation, he'll probably be heading back to Sorrento, won't he?"

Not knowing where she was going with this, he answered, "I suppose so. He's going to go through your laptop to see what he can find out about you."

"Exactly," Genevieve said. "And that's why we're going to Sorrento today."

Simultaneously, Hunter and Kat both said, "What?"

"That man has my laptop with a year's worth of research on it. I'm getting it back. You might remember, Hunter, I don't like being pushed around and I don't like thieves. I'm going with you."

"But—"

"No buts, I'm going.

Hunter had to smile inwardly, remembering all the times in their last adventure when he'd told her it was too dangerous and she should go back to Paris, and she'd responded the same way. He knew there'd be no talking her out of it. Still he had to try.

"Genevieve, you can't do it. There's already been an attempt on our lives. I can't let you take the risk."

Genevieve squared her shoulders, and fixed Hunter with a level stare. "Can't? You can't *let* me do it? Maybe you'd like to rethink that?"

"Really, Genevieve, I'd—"

"It's no good, Hunter, I'm coming."

"I'm not going to be able to talk you out of this, am I?"

"Nope."

Hunter sighed and put up his hands in defeat, inwardly smiling to himself. "Okay."

THE THREE OF THEM DROVE TO SORRENTO, where Kat checked out of the adjoining room at the Capri but not before noticing that Hunter checked Genevieve into his room. The two women looked at each other and said nothing. Kat took a cab to the airport for her flight to Prague.

"Tonight, I've got to get back into Caravaggio's office and see what gives with the paintings," Hunter said.

"I'm going with you."

Hunter had been expecting this.

"Look, I know you have a good reason to help, but the break-in—I'll do that myself. Here's what I really need. You stay here, with your cell phone on. I'll get in and examine the paintings. If I need your expertise, I'll text you. If I need you to see something, I can flash it on your phone. That way you can supply what I can't, but you'll be safe. We'll be considerably less likely to be discovered if it's just me going in. Okay?"

Genevieve frowned. "But didn't both you and Kat go in before? You didn't get discovered then."

Hunter nodded. "Let me tell you about Kat. She's an expert at breaking and entering. She can handle any lock, any safe, and any security system. If she chose a life of crime instead of the path she's on, she'd be a major international criminal. She's probably better at it than I am. She may choose to tell you about her past, I don't know, but if she does, you'll understand. In any case, this is the best and safest way for you to help. Okay?"

He paused as Genevieve digested his little speech.

While she did, Hunter had a sudden revelation—a moment of certainty. All at once, the ideas that had been stewing just below the surface, the unfocussed things about

Kat that had been moving around but not linking in any recognizable way, all came together. *Why didn't I see this before? Kat's a skilled burglar with extraordinary breaking-and-entering skills. She can disable security systems and open safes. She's an expert jewelry appraiser who frequently travels all over the continent. I'll have to check but I bet her time in Paris and Munich will overlap perfectly with the heists reported in the papers.*

Genevieve said, "Okay."

"What?" Hunter snapped back to the present.

"Okay. You go in alone and I'll be your resource back here."

Chapter 42

WITH ONE MORE DAY TO WAIT before the surgery to correct the hematoma and remove the strange unknown objects from her brain, Kris became more agitated.

"Carl, I want to call Dr. Gallo in Sorrento and find out what he knows about those things in my head and what they are."

Carl agreed and she made the call.

"Dr. Gallo, this is Kris Hanson. You did surgery on me six months ago."

"Yes, Mrs. Hanson, I remember. How are you? How's the piano playing?"

"Not good actually. I've lost all my piano ability. It's all gone. I'm back to where I was before. Only now I've been having severe and frequent headaches."

"Your piano skills are gone? Completely?"

"Yes. Like I said, I'm back to where I was before."

"Mrs. Hanson, would you give me a minute, I need to check something."

"Sure."

After a pause of about eight minutes, Gallo was back.

"Mrs. Hanson, could you fly here to Sorrento immediately so that Dr. Caravaggio and I could examine you. There will be no charge, of course, but we are probably in the best position to help you."

"I don't think so. I had a CAT scan done here and they found two more hematomas. I'm scheduled to have a neurosurgeon here drain them next week."

"What?"

"Yes. In fact the other reason for my call is related to what else they saw on the scan; two unidentified objects. Do you know what they are?"

After a long pause, Gallo came back. "When is your surgery?"

"Tomorrow."

"Mrs. Hanson, I'll call you back." Then Gallo hung up.

THAT NIGHT THE HEADACHE WAS the most severe ever. Kris took the maximum dose of painkiller the doctors had prescribed for her to relieve the headaches until the surgery. Carl kissed her goodnight and fell fast asleep. Kris lay awake for an hour, unable to think about anything but the pain, which didn't seem to be responding to the medication the way it had before. Even though the lights were off in the bedroom, she could see the doorway to the hall and the bathroom beyond. Suddenly the image blurred as a shooting pain knifed through her head, and the total oblivion that followed stopped her agonized scream before it got started.

Carl found her dead beside him in the morning.

Chapter 43

THE OVERCAST SKY WIPED OUT the moonlight that had been so helpful on Hunter's last trip to Caravaggio's office. That time he and Kat had been able to see their way around without using any artificial light, the enormous window in the room bathing everything in pale moonlight. Unfortunately that wasn't the case tonight.

Getting into Caravaggio's office wasn't as easy this time either. Clearly they were beefing up security. His office lock had been upgraded to a digital model that took Hunter thirty-five minutes to breach. Apparently they were now aware of his earlier break-ins. He'd have to be careful.

He quickly went to the paintings. While there were ten in all, the five they were interested in were right next to each other, starting from the left, in the same order as on the cryptic card under the bust of Camillo Golgi.

Does the order mean something?

Using the light from his cell phone, he stepped over to the first painting, *The Boy With a Basket of Fruit,* and found the extra cherry they'd seen earlier. The addition was skillful. If he hadn't seen the original, there'd be no reason to give it a second look.

Since this was an oil painting, or at least a good copy, it wasn't covered with glass. Carefully he ran his fingers over the cherries. He didn't feel anything unusual until he pressed a little.

Is it my imagination, or did it give a little over the extra cherry?

He pressed directly on the extra cherry.

It does depress.

He tried all the other cherries and nothing happened. Clearly this extra cherry was different; he could push it like a button. He moved to the next painting, the *Narcissus*. The anagram for this painting meant ear, but when they'd compared it to the original they saw that in this one, Narcissus wore an earring that wasn't on the original.

He tried pressing the earring. Sure enough, it depressed. Nowhere else on the painting could he get any area to depress. He moved to the next three paintings and found that in each case, the added element—a leaf, a flower, and a fruit—could be depressed like a button.

What's going on here? Is this some kind of combination lock? If I press the buttons in some order, will something happen, will something open?

Taking stock of his situation, he listened carefully for any sign of anyone being about. He'd taken pains this time to schedule his break-in for later, just in case the janitor had a routine and always cleaned this office at the same time each night. He didn't want to run into him like they almost had on the last trip. He heard nothing.

I'll give it a try.

He pressed the buttons in sequential order from left to right: cherry, earring, leaf, flower, and fruit. He waited. He heard nothing. He moved to the desk and file cabinet. Nothing opened or unlocked. Nothing else had noticeably changed in the room. He decided to try it in reverse, fruit, flower, leaf, earring, and cherry. Again nothing. Not having any other ideas, he knew it was time for Genevieve. He texted her:

> *Cherry, earring, leaf, flower, fruit are buttons. Any idea on the order to push them?*
> *Right to left or vice versa doesn't work.*

She responded: *Give me a minute.*

A few minutes later she replied: *Try alphabetical order in Italian: Cherry, flower, leaf, fruit, and earring*

Hunter tried it, nothing. He even tried alphabetical order in English. He texted her back: *No luck.*

She responded: *Hold on, have an idea*

He waited several minutes. Finally: *Try chronological order Caravaggio did paintings Fruit, cherry, flower, earring, leaf*

Hunter punched in the order Genevieve gave him. Immediately he heard it. The paneled wall at the side of the room began to open. It revealed a metal stairway leading downward into the darkness. He stepped in and using the flashlight app from his phone, scanned the immediate area. It illuminated a button on the stairway. Thinking it might close the wall again he pushed it. Sure enough, the wall slid back to its original closed state, leaving him standing on the stairwell in complete darkness.

Having nowhere to go but down, he shined his phone light on the stairs and began the descent. He quickly discovered that the stairway kept switching back after dropping for a while, like a fire escape on the outside of an old building. After a descent of what he imagined was about thirty feet he reached the bottom.

He found a wall switch and flipped it on. Momentarily stunned by the bright light after being dark-adapted for the last twenty minutes or so, he recovered to see he was in a laboratory of some kind—a completely modern facility.

What does he do here?

Across the room he spotted a workstation with a wall rack of files.

Just then he heard a noise. It was coming from above. He quickly returned to the light switch and flipped it off, returning the room to complete darkness. He listened and waited.

Someone is definitely up there in the office.

He continued to listen. It sounded like someone just walking around, nothing rushed. He waited for another five minutes and then heard a door close. After that, he heard nothing.

He waited another fifteen minutes, and when he heard nothing more, he turned the light back on.

Returning to the wall rack, he took out its single file and began to examine it: Kris Hanson. It listed her age as sixty-five, her address, and several pages of clinical information. Toward the back of the file, it stated Kris Hanson was healthy and a viable candidate for Phoenix.

Phoenix? There it is again. Caravaggio is definitely doing something with this, but what? The answer has to be here somewhere.

On the last page he saw that Hanson had been scheduled for, and received Source Reversal Enhancement—SRE on January 22 this year.

SRE: source reversal enhancement. So that's what the SRE meant on Charlie's brain scans, Hunter realized. What is it?

She'd been scheduled for and received SRE January 22 this year. Then Hunter read who the donor was and almost stopped breathing. The donor was Irena Rousseau.

SRE donor—Irena Rousseau?

He checked the date. It was just before Kat's mother died. Apparently she'd donated something to Kris Hanson on January 22nd and then died of a stroke eleven days later on February 2nd. Hunter photographed the entire file.

What about Charlie Lahti? Should Charlie's folder have been here? Has it been removed? But there was no folder for Irena Rousseau, either just the reference to her being a donor. Maybe Charlie was also a donor.

He looked around the workstation to see if he could find any more information. He was about ready to give up and get out of there when he saw a metal fold-over clipboard hanging on a hook on the side of the station.

The clipboard held a single sheet identical to the last page in Kris Hanson's file. The name at the top was Tony Pompa, age thirty-four.

That name sounds familiar.

He was scheduled for SRE the day after tomorrow. But it was the next notation that really startled him.

The scheduled donor was Irena Rousseau.

Chapter 44

HUNTER GOT BACK TO THE HOTEL CLOSE TO 1:00 A.M. and found Genevieve a nervous wreck. The moment he entered their room she wrapped him in a tight embrace and buried her head in his neck, so glad he was safe. Then she pulled away and pounded on his chest with both fists.

"You scared me to death, you know. You never texted you were all right, and that was almost three hours ago." Realizing what she was doing, she retreated, opened her fists to palms, and gently replaced them back on his chest. "Sorry."

Knowing what she was doing and silently thanking her for it, he took her in his arms again and only then understood how much he'd missed this woman. "You're right, I should have, and I'll tell you all about it in the morning. But, Genevieve?"

"Yes?"

"I seem to recall you and I did our best work together after—"

"Yes?"

"Well, after—"

"Hunter?"

"Yes?"

"Why don't you take a shower and meet me under the covers. You can try to explain it then."

STILL IN BED TOGETHER THE NEXT MORNING, neither wanting to get up, Genevieve said, "Okay, now tell me everything about last night."

Hunter grinned, "Well, I took this beautiful woman to bed. We got under the covers and—"

She poked him in the ribs. "Not that part, dummy, before that."

"Oh, okay, before that. I don't remember much before that."

"Hunter, I swear, if you don't—"

"Okay, okay."

He told her the chronological order of the paintings was the correct sequence to open the wall that led to the underground surgical suite. He explained about the files and how Caravaggio was doing something called Source Reversal Enhancement or SRE, using donors in some way. "But most surprising of all," he concluded, "is that tomorrow a man named Tony Pompa, age thirty-four is scheduled for an SRE and the donor is to be—" He paused dramatically. "Irena Rousseau"

"Kat's mother? How can that be? She's dead, isn't she?"

"Dead and cremated. And I've never heard of Source Reversal Enhancement. But maybe the source is the donor, and if so, and Irena Rousseau is the source in Source Reversal Enhancement, it would be highly unethical without letting her family know about it. Besides, why would they do it anyway?"

Hunter jumped out of bed. "Let's go down to breakfast. Are you hungry?"

As he stood there naked, Genevieve eyed him appreciatively. "Hungry? Yes. Get back in here."

Hunter sighed and slipped back under the covers. "With you it's just work, work, work."

A little over an hour later they were having breakfast downstairs. Both were famished.

"I've got to find out when the procedure, whatever it is, is scheduled for tomorrow," said Hunter, slathering butter on a fresh-baked roll. "I'm sure it's going to happen in Caravaggio's secret lab and he's somehow a part of it. If it involves surgery, he'll need help. He's not a surgeon. If it isn't Phillippi, it must be Gallo."

"Maybe you could try to schedule an appointment to see Caravaggio tomorrow. That way you might get a hint of his schedule—even get a look at his appointment book."

Hunter remembered Genevieve had proved to be a good detective with great instincts when they'd worked together the previous summer. "I'll do that, and I plan to be there when this SRE thing—whatever it is—happens."

"I'M AFRAID DR. CARAVAGGIO is completely unavailable tomorrow, but I'm sure he could give you some time next week. Would that work for you?" The bubbly receptionist batted her lashes at Hunter.

"Not really, I just need to see him for a few minutes. Couldn't he squeeze in some time somewhere?"

"I'm afraid not. He meets with the board from nine until noon. Then he has a luncheon scheduled with one of our volunteer groups until one-thirty, and then he has something scheduled in his lab until three. Immediately after that he goes to the airport to catch a flight to a conference in Rome. He specifically told me he was unavailable for anything else tomorrow."

Hunter mulled this over. "Do you know where his laboratory is?"

"Of course. It's in the lower level with all the other labs."

Other labs?

"Maybe I could see him for a few minutes in his lab tomorrow."

"Oh no. That would never do. He is completely unavailable when he's in the lab."

Hunter left, certain that whatever SRE was, it was going to happen the next day from 1:30 to 3:00 p.m. in Caravaggio's secret lab. He'd have to find a way to be there. Thanks to the talkative receptionist, he knew the man would be out of his office from noon until 1:30, due to his luncheon meeting with the volunteer group. He'd have to distract her or get her away from her desk long enough for him to slip into Caravaggio's office, sequence the painting code, and get downstairs to the lab.

Back at the hotel Hunter used his laptop to search for any information on Source Reversal Enhancement. Nothing came up.

What is it?

THE NEXT DAY, HE WAS READY. The night before he'd gone over everything with Genevieve so she'd know exactly what his plans were. He'd installed an app on her cell phone that used GPS coordinates so she'd know where he was at all times. He'd signal her with a one-word text— OK—after each step was completed. That way she'd know the plan was proceeding without complications. It seemed a little excessive to him, but he understood her anxiety and need to be in the loop.

"FLOWERS FOR ME, AT THE FRONT DESK downstairs? I don't understand. Okay, I'll be right down." The receptionist, unsure why, but still pleased someone had sent her flowers, hung up the phone on her desk and went to the elevator. Once she was on her way down, Hunter stepped out from around the corner, passed by the unoccupied receptionist desk, and slipped into Caravaggio's office after entering the digital code.

He quickly activated the painting code. The wall separated. He stepped onto the stairway and was shocked to find the lights were already on below. Closing the door, he waited silently for a full five minutes and heard nothing below. If anyone was down there they hadn't moved.

Why were the lights on? *Maybe he's already got things set up for later and just left them on.*

He crept down the stairway, making as little noise as possible. At the bottom he immediately saw the room had been changed. In the center was the oddest instrument he'd ever seen in a scientific laboratory—a grand piano. Next to the piano bench was a workstation of hardware, including an EEG electrode harness that was connected through a shielded cable and plugged into some kind of rack-mounted box. There were no dials or digital readouts of any kind. Emerging from the back of this box, another large cable went up to the ceiling.

Hunter followed it with his eyes across the ceiling, where it disappeared through the wall. He crossed over to the wall and stepped up to a small freestanding bookcase that was the only piece of furniture against it. When he tried to slide the bookcase away, he found that rather than slide, it opened, hinged on one side revealing a second room.

What he saw was even more confusing: another grand piano. Beside it was a setup similar to the one he'd just seen in the first room, and the same kind of electrode harness system. The shielded cable from this one, however, entered a rack-mounted box that shared space with several interconnected sophisticated electronic components and computers. The cable from the first room passed through near the ceiling, looped down, and connected to one of the rack-mounted components.

He scanned the rest of the room, noting a biohazard suit on a table against one wall.

What's that for?

The room had three other doors, in addition to the book-case door he'd come through from the first room. He tried one and found it led to a relatively large storage room.

A second door apparently led out of the lab because printed on it with large red letters was an admonition.

THIS DOOR MUST REMAIN LOCKED FROM
THE OUTER HALLWAY AT ALL TIMES
DR. NERO CARAVAGGIO

So, there must be another way in and out of here.

Given how far down the stairs he had to walk from Nero's office on the second floor to this level, he assumed he was on the lower level, one floor below the surface. The outer hallway referred to on the door must also be on the lower level.

I wonder what else is out there. Maybe the other labs the receptionist referred to?

Suddenly he heard someone enter the first large room with the piano. They must have come down the stairway. He closed the storage room door and hid inside.

Good thing I pulled the bookcase back into place. It must be Caravaggio. He's here early—it's only 12:45. He must have cut his luncheon short.

He texted Genevieve an "OK" hoping it wasn't premature.

Chapter 45

HUNTER HEARD ANOTHER DOOR OPEN, this one much closer. Which one was it? It had to be the third door, the one he hadn't gotten to yet. It must be an entrance from somewhere else, not a third storeroom. He listened and waited.

He heard nothing for a few minutes; then a voice came over a speaker system. "Gino, are you set up?"

"In a minute, Nero, I just have to power up the rack. Hold on."

Gino? That must be Gallo, the other neurosurgeon Phillippi had told him about, the chairman of the Institute's Committee for Evaluating Human Studies.

"Okay," the man called Gino said, "we're up and running over here. How about you?"

"Everything's in place. I'll call PT and tell Tony to get over here now."

PT? Physical Therapy? Tony must be Pompa.

"All right, Irena's just outside. I'll bring her in and get her set up."

Irena? Just outside? Irena Rousseau? Is she actually alive?

Hunter carefully cracked the door just enough to give him a view of the room. He'd had to take the chance "Gino" wouldn't notice. Luckily he didn't. But what he saw confirmed what they suspected.

It was Phillippi. Not the real Phillippi, but the man who'd said he was Phillippi in Miami at the Final Care facility. His face and the large hairy frame were unmistakable. This was Gallo.

Hunter watched as the man began to don the biohazard suit. What's that all about? He examined the storage room and saw several large boxes he could duck behind if for some reason Gallo approached the storage room. Now fully suited, the hairy doctor went out through the third door and returned within a few minutes with *Irena Rousseau*.

Her garb was a striking contrast to the evening gowns he'd seen her wear in photographs. Now she was wearing a loose-fitting white jumpsuit that reminded him of a surgical scrub suit, though not blue or green like most scrubs. It was snow white. It was cinched around her wrists and ankles and neck, but didn't appear to be uncomfortable. He could see she had white stockings coming through the cinched ankles of the jumpsuit and she wore white soft slippers. Her red hair was cut very short in a pixie style unlike the shoulder-length fashion he remembered from pictures he'd seen of her. Nevertheless, this was definitely she.

Gallo led her to the piano bench and asked gently, "How are you feeling today, Irena?"

"Okay, I guess," she answered in a voice so soft and mournful Hunter couldn't help but detect a sense of depression. "Am I really getting better, Dr. Gallo?" she asked, almost pleadingly. "The sores are almost all gone."

My God it's true. That is Irena Rousseau. She really is alive. She didn't die of a stroke. She wasn't cremated. She's here—alive—and about to donate something.

"Yes, of course, my dear, you're getting better all the time, thanks to the treatment and the care you're getting here. You do understand these treatments are the key to your full recovery, and they require your very best effort."

"Yes, although I still don't understand how it works."

"Well, that's okay. The important thing is it does work."

"I suppose. Then let's get on with it."

Hunter silently put his cell phone camera on video and began filming through the slightly opened door.

Gallo carefully applied the electrodes from the harness to selected areas of her head after parting the hair with his gloved fingers. Once they were in place he walked over to the rack-mounted instrument panel, made some adjustments, and seemed to be checking readouts on the digital displays. When he was satisfied, Hunter heard him say, "Nero, are you ready over there?"

"All set," came the amplified answer from the other room, "Irena, are you ready?" Caravaggio asked.

"Yes, doctor, I'm ready."

"Very good. You can begin when I've counted back from five. All right, here we go. Five—four—three—two—one—zero."

Irena began to play. It was spectacular. Hunter immediately recognized the piece as Liszt, one he had in his collection. She played it beautifully. During the performance, Gallo would periodically check the instrument panel as if they were in a recording studio and he was a sound technician. When the piece finally ended, Hunter longed to applaud, but of course he didn't.

"That was wonderful, my dear," Gallo told her as he began to remove the electrodes. "Dr. Caravaggio and I think you will only need two more treatments to complete the cure."

Complete the cure? What cure? What's he talking about?

"And then I can see my family, my Johannes and my daughter Kat? I'll no longer be a threat to them?"

"We believe so, but of course we will have to do a final examination before we take that risk. You understand, I'm sure."

Risk? Is that what the biohazard suit is all about?

"Yes, of course, but I do so miss them." With that, she got up, and Gallo led her from the room.

A FEW MINUTES LATER, Hunter saw the door from the first room open, the one he'd come through behind the bookcase, and Caravaggio entered with a fit-looking man in his thirties with very short cropped hair Hunter had never seen before.

"You remember this room, Tony. It looks a little different than when you were here before."

Gallo re-entered the room, already shed of his biohazard suit.

Maybe Pompa is not supposed to see it.

"Hi, Dr. Gallo," Tony said. The two men shook hands.

Pompa walked over to the piano Irena had just vacated, sat on the bench, and picked up the electrode harness she'd worn during the performance. "So the other piano player sits here and plays with this electrode get-up on, just like mine."

"That's correct," Caravaggio said. "Just like you did when you juggled and wore the electrodes in this room and Lahti was learning to juggle back there."

Pompa nodded, apparently recalling the incident.

That's where I heard that name before. Jenny said that Tony Pompa was the physical therapist that helped Charlie learn to juggle. Charlie must have been a recipient.

Caravaggio continued. "The player in this room plays the piece, and you hear it in the other room. You play it on your piano at the same time. As you know, though, your piano makes no sound. You only hear the piano sounds from the player in this room. So while you make all the finger movements as best you can, the sound you hear is the perfectly played performance coming from the piano in this room."

"Yeah, I get that," said Pompa. "It's weird; it's almost as if I'm playing it and making the beautiful sounds myself. But even though you went through it with me before, I still don't fully understand the electrode thing and how that will make me a better player, or even how that made Lahti a juggler."

Caravaggio said, "I know. It's even a little mysterious to us, and we invented the process. But let me try to explain it again." He walked around to the back of the piano and looked across at Pompa sitting on the bench.

"One of the differences between you and the master pianist you just heard is what is sometimes incorrectly called muscle memory. It means you learn through repetition to consolidate a specific motor task into memory. The more you practice something, the better you get at it. Eventually you can perform it expertly without even much conscious effort. The same is true for all motor tasks; the more you practice the better you get, like riding a bike, hitting a golf ball, typing on a keyboard, juggling balls, and in this case, playing the piano."

"So why is it incorrect to call it muscle memory?" Pompa asked.

"Well, you see, the memory isn't in your muscle as such, it's really in your brain. Unlike you, the person who just played the piece you simultaneously attempted really had to learn it the hard way, through many years of repetition. During the long repeated practice sessions, the nerve cells in the motor cortex of his brain gradually formed incredibly complex circuits called motor programs that enabled him to play with perfect fingering and timing, virtually making no mistakes. Of course, as you know by our agreement, the real pianist will remain anonymous."

"I understand. But don't I have those same neurons in my brain?"

"Yes, you do, and you even have the motor programs to play the piano, but—and this is important—your nerve cells haven't formed motor programs as complex as his, because you haven't put in the time to form them. Hence, you don't play as well, you can't make your fingers go as fast, and their timing and placement on the keys is off."

"It still doesn't seem possible that I'll be able to get that highly sophisticated motor program without all the years of practice? I don't see how that happens."

"This is where we come in," Caravaggio said, extending his hand to include Dr. Gallo. Gallo bowed slightly and picked up the narrative.

"When you're learning a motor skill—like playing the piano—and you practice it over and over, it isn't just you who wants to get it perfect, your brain does too. There are thousands of nerve cells in the motor cortex of your brain directing the activity.

"Initially, these nerve cells aren't connected to each other in the most optimal way to perform the motor skill, because they've never had to direct it before. But when you practice the skill over and over again, they 'figure out' they could do it better if they begin to sprout branches and form more optimal connections with each other. With enough practice, these connections — we call them synapses — develop and become as efficient as they can get. Now these optimally interconnected nerve cells begin to fire in perfectly timed sequences, allowing you to play without error."

"Okay, I see that," Pompa said, running a hand over his bald head, "but I'm still a little confused about the whole brain thing—the different kinds of surgery and wearing the electrode harness during the practice sessions. I mean, how does that help me get this optimal alignment?"

Caravaggio took over here. "My entire professional career as a neuroscientist has been to learn to control nerve growth. I've discovered how to promote nerve sprouting in brain cells. Well, to be fair, I didn't discover this myself, but I did learn how to maximize it and speed it up. By applying a combination of nerve growth factors and other stimulants I call *'Enhancement II'* directly to nerve cells in your motor cortex, we can speed up their rate of sprouting a hundredfold. It's remarkable, really.

"A key ingredient in this mixture was taken from the other pianist's brain earlier through a simple procedure. You recall we used the same procedure to take a small sample from your brain earlier to make the *Enhancement II* we used in the tubes in Charlie Lahti's brain during his juggling training. That time, you were the donor because—as it happened—you're a very good juggler. This time you're the recipient for piano skills. Again, you're an amateur pianist, but not an expert—yet.

"As you know, based on our agreement, Dr. Gallo here inserted a permanent micro-tube filled with *Enhancement II* into the motor cortex in each hemisphere of your brain. Part of what happened this afternoon was that during the piano session, we released—by remote control—a small amount of *Enhancement II* over the motor cortex on each side of your brain."

"I get it, so I'd begin to sprout more optimal connections while I was playing."

"Well, sort of," agreed Caravaggio. "It's actually a little more complicated than that. Moreover, that's where the electrodes come in. I've discovered the sprouting connections can be speeded up not only by the use of *Enhancement II*, but also by supplying them with a little guidance as to where to go. It turns out the new sprouts are drawn to areas of maximal nerve activity in the brain much the same way moths are drawn to a flame. Of course we want them specifically to connect to neurons that are active during the playing of complex piano pieces." So we have to tell your brain where these areas are. What better way to do it than to show it the neural activity in the brain of an accomplished pianist during the playing of the same complex piece?

Pompa nodded, but still looked puzzled.

"Surprisingly, the electroencephalogram, or EEG, does just that," Caravaggio explained. "We pick up the EEG from the surface of the brain of the pianist in this room as he plays the piece, and then, through the electrical equipment you see over there on the rack, simultaneously transfer it to the electrodes on your head while playing the same piece."

"Now of course the signals picked up from the donor pianist are just small voltages and need to be converted into small stimuli that mirror the voltages in time and space. I know it's a little complicated, but it works. As you play and move your fingers, which starts the sprouting process, we release *Enhancement II* to speed it up, while at the same time the active nerve cells in the donor pianist's brain stimulate your brain, through the reversal process, directing the sprouts to their proper connections."

"If I hadn't seen this work with Charlie Lahti," Pompa said, "I wouldn't believe it.

"It does, and in a few days you'll already see significant improvement in your playing. After two more sessions like today, you'll be able to play as well as the donor. Of course, reading the music and supplying appropriate expression and feeling for the music will be up to you, but you'll be able to physically do it. You'll be amazed. In two weeks with us you'll be as good as if you'd practiced for years."

So that's what they've been doing. This whole thing must be what he referred to in his notes as Source Reversal Enhancement. The source is the donor—Irena in this case—and the reversal is reversing the pickup voltages from her brainwaves to identical stimulus signals in the recipient's brain, coupled with the Enhancement cocktail.

But can they really do that—transfer the motor skills of one person to another? And what's this talk about a cure? Does she have some disease? She mentioned sores.

Hunter felt as if he'd just had brain surgery, himself. This was science fiction, complete with mad scientists.

Chapter 46

KAT RETURNED TO BRUSSELS AS SOON as she'd gotten the call from Willie. *Damn him*, she thought. Her Father's cousin had been making their lives miserable for as long as she could remember. Terrified and out of her mind with worry, she knew she had to see her dad as soon as possible. He was at work, but when she told him what it was about, they'd met in his office.

"He said you'd gone to the police, that we're on our own now, that whatever happens we have only ourselves to blame. What's Willie talking about, Dad? What did he mean? Have you gone to the police?"

Johannes was never surprised when Kat showed up suddenly and unannounced. She never told him where she was going since her work took her all over the continent. He also wasn't surprised to hear she'd been with Hunter McCoy trying to find out if something was going on at the Institute.

"Of course I haven't gone to the police. He knows we can't do that. He's got to be talking about McCoy," Johannes said.

"How could he know about McCoy?" asked Kat. "Anyway, McCoy isn't investigating anything about the jewels. He believes your story about the reason some bodies went to Miami. All he's trying to do is find out if anything unusual happened to Mom and Charlie Lahti while they were at the Institute. Why—do you think McCoy's actually investigating us?"

Johannes shook his head. "No, I'm sure he's not. And you're right, how would Willie even know about McCoy?" Then, thinking about his own question for a moment, he jerked his head up. "Wait a minute. It must have been Miami. Didn't McCoy say he'd gone to Final Care at the airport to find Lahti's body? Maybe Willie heard about that and thought he was investigating the jewel business, when all he was doing was checking on why the bodies were going there in the first place. That has to be it. He just assumed McCoy knew something about the jewel smuggling."

Seeing the logic of this, Kat nodded, "Yes, and he assumed we told him. That has to be it."

They sat quietly for a few minutes while they thought it through.

"What exactly did Willie say to you," Johannes asked. "The threat part. What were his exact words?"

"He said, 'It's too late now, you shouldn't have brought in the police. I've set the endgame in motion. Everything happens by the clock from this point on. You're dead.'"

"You're dead? He said you're dead?" Johannes shook his head, incredulous. "The man's crazy. I think he always has been. Your mother knew it too. She always thought there was something fundamentally wrong with Willie. She sensed it when they were first dating. I think it wasn't so much that she liked me better as much as it was she knew something wasn't right in the head with him."

Kat still grew angry, recalling the painful story her dad had been forced to tell her.

HER FATHER'S COUSIN, WILLIE HOFMANN, had met a beautiful piano student named Irena Rousseau while he and Johannes were in mortuary science school together. She and Willie had dated several times, and it seemed to Johannes they were getting serious about their relationship.

Then one day, Irena asked to see Johannes alone. She'd

said she wanted to ask him something—something about Willie. Unsure what this meant, Johannes agreed, and the two met for coffee at a city cafe far from anyplace the three of them normally frequented. This distant location was Irena's idea.

"Thank you for meeting me, Johannes. I know this is a little unusual, but I didn't know who else to turn to." Irena clutched her purse, looked around fearfully, and frowned.

Johannes had no idea what she wanted, but it was obviously something serious; her manner left no doubt about that. "What is it? What's wrong?"

With that, she burst into tears and sobbed for a full two minutes before she got herself back under control and could continue. Nervously playing with her teaspoon she said, "I don't know how to put this, and I have no real proof. It's more of a feeling than anything else, yet I'm sure of it."

"Sure of what?" Johannes asked, completely confused now.

"There's something wrong with Willie," she finally got out. "I'm afraid of him."

"Afraid of Willie? That's crazy, why would you be afraid of Willie?"

"Johannes, there's something about your cousin you don't know. I'm convinced he's psychotic or something— and he's dangerous. Let me tell you what I know."

Willie's psychotic and dangerous? Johannes thought, taken aback. What the hell is she talking about? "Maybe you'd better tell me what you think you know," he allowed, convinced Irena was imagining something. Maybe it was one of those female things he knew so little about.

"Johannes, listen to me; he's dangerous, I know it. About four weeks ago we were in the coffee shop near the art school, you know the one—you've been there with us. One time, the owner, Mr. Van Acker, stopped by the table and complimented me on some sketches I'd done for a drawing class I'd been taking. They were cityscapes of Brussels, and

I'd laid them out on the table. I thanked him for the compliment."

"After he'd passed by, Willie was so upset he insisted we leave immediately. I was shocked, but not as shocked as I was to find that the next day, Mr. Van Acker's shop was closed down temporarily because of hundreds of cockroaches running rampant through the store."

"I remember that," Johannes added. "It made the papers."

"I'm convinced Willie did it."

"What? Why would he do that?"

"Because he's crazy jealous, that's why. Let me tell you some more stories, and then you can judge for yourself. I can't remember if you've met Louis, my friend Anna's boyfriend. Well, one day about three weeks ago, the four of us were out on a double date, and Louis put his arms around both Anna and me and hugged us close, saying to Willie, 'We sure have two beautiful girls here, don't you agree, Willie?' Anna kissed him on one cheek and I kissed him on the other, and we all laughed. That is all except Willie. He smoldered and was a grouch the rest of the night.

"The next night Louis was attacked in an alley near his apartment and beaten nearly to death by someone with a lead pipe. The pipe was found next to his unconscious body with no fingerprints on it, none at all. Later, when I told this to Willie, you know what he did? He smiled. The bastard smiled."

"Surely you don't think that Willie—"

"I'm not done yet," Irena interrupted. "There's more. After the episode with Louis, I told Willie I thought we should see less of each other—that I wasn't ready to get serious at this point, as my piano career had to come first. I told him I needed more space and time to practice and grow musically."

"What did he say to that?"

"It was horrible. He stood up and stared down on me

with the most menacing look I've ever seen. He became someone I didn't know at all. He said, 'Listen carefully, Irena. Don't ever even think of leaving me. You belong to me and you always will. If I even get a hint of unfaithfulness, you'll pay and he'll pay.' Then he smiled, the most evil smile I've ever seen. And then, as if nothing had happened, he said, 'Would you like to catch a movie?'" Johannes was shocked. What the hell was wrong with the guy? You couldn't behave like that, not to anyone, much less a lovely woman like Irena.

Two weeks later Johannes and Willie both graduated from the mortuary science program. Johannes accepted a position as an embalmer with a funeral home in Antwerp and began work immediately after moving out of Willie's apartment. The two hadn't spoken since Johannes brought up the topic of his behavior with Irena. After exploding at Johannes for seeing Irena behind his back, he had said Johannes was "dead" to him from then on, and the two hadn't spoken since.

As far as he knew Irena and Willie were through, at least as far as Irena was concerned. In spite of Willie, Irena and Johannes met for a few minutes one afternoon in the park before Johannes left for his new job in Antwerp.

"I'm still afraid of him, Johannes, and now I'm afraid for you, too. He's crazy, I mean really crazy, like insane crazy. I haven't seen him in two weeks, but I feel he's out there looking and plotting something, maybe following me, I don't know."

Johannes took her hands in his and asked as kindly as he could, "What are you going to do?"

This was the first time the two had actually touched, and it triggered a response both had probably been trying subconsciously to suppress. She wrapped her arms around him and buried her face in his neck. "I'm leaving Brussels too," she whispered. "Can I call you if I need you?"

Not wanting to break the embrace, he whispered back "Of course, Irena, of course."

WITH A CONVICTION SHE DIDN'T FEEL, Kat declared, "He won't get away with it."

Slamming her fist on his desk, she stood up. "All I know is this.— Whatever that shit has planned, he won't get away with it."

Chapter 47

HUNTER WAITED WHILE POMPA LEFT through the door with the KEEP IT LOCKED warning, leaving Gallo and Caravaggio alone. They began shutting down the racked equipment and generally tidying up the room. Hunter waited for them to leave so he could figure out a way to get out of here himself.

"That went well, Gino; what do you think?"

"I'd say it went very well. I agree with Pompa, it still amazes me this actually works. Two more sessions and the man will be a piano genius."

"I know," Caravaggio mused. "It's a shame we can't tell the world about it yet.

Gallo nodded. "I'm amazed we were able to talk Pompa into being a part of this."

Caravaggio agreed. "Certainly the money Rache paid him didn't hurt any. You know, I've been thinking. Neither of us has any doubts SRE actually works. It does just what we thought it would do. I think when we get two more sessions out of Irena we should call it quits and shift our efforts to designing and running some animal studies to set the stage for a human trials request.

Gallo gave him a thumbs-up. "You're right. I sure won't object to quitting this charade with the biohazard suit and fake disease. I never enjoyed treating Irena with that salve that actually caused her sores to develop."

The bastards, Hunter thought, still listening.

"I know, it bothered me too, but at least we've been 'curing' her by putting less and less of the skin irritant in the salve. We still have the problem of the loss of skill with Kris Hanson though and her headaches and death."

Kris Hanson? Right, she was the earlier recipient for Irena's piano skills that I saw in the notebook at the workstation.

Gallo frowned. "Do you really trust Rache to take care of removing any evidence that could link her death to us?"

"We have to, Gino. What else can we do?"

Gallo wasn't convinced, but continued. "We still have an even bigger problem, Nero. You and I both know what it is. How do we deal with that? We still haven't figured it out. We can't just explain it to her and ask her to be quiet."

Nero sighed heavily and paced. "I know, I know. And we don't have much time left to come up with a solution."

With that, Gallo followed Caravaggio out through the bookcase door. He heard them climb the stairs to Caravaggio's office.

HUNTER WAITED FOR FIFTEEN MINUTES to make sure they weren't coming back. Then he carefully emerged from his hiding place and used his cell phone to photograph everything: the piano, the headgear, the biohazard suit, and the instrument rack. After checking it was empty, he returned to the first room and photographed everything there. Then seeing the door with the warning to keep it locked from the hallway side, the one Pompa exited through, he wanted to know what was on the other side.

Taking a chance he opened it slightly and looked out. It opened onto a busy hallway with several doors leading to several well-marked labs and a physical therapy wing. Turning to look at the hallway side of the door he was holding slightly open, he saw it had no markings of any kind. He quickly closed it and heard it lock in place.

Hunter called Kat's cell phone. She answered on the third ring.

"McCoy?"

Keeping his voice just above a whisper, he said, "You need to get back here as soon as possible."

"Why, what have you learned? Why are you whispering?"

"It's about your mother."

"What about her, what have you found out?"

"Kat, get ready for a shock. She's alive."

"Oh my God. She's alive? No, she was cremated."

"Believe me, Kat, she's alive, I just saw her. But she's in danger."

"You saw her? I don't understand."

"Listen, Kat, I can't talk now. I'm going to bring in Interpol. We have enough evidence now to charge Caravaggio and a surgeon named Gallo with kidnapping at the very least, but I'm going to have to act fast before they destroy any evidence."

"And my mother would be evidence, wouldn't she?"

"I'm afraid so."

After a pause, while he assumed she was digesting this information, Kat came back. "Listen, McCoy. My dad and I will be on a flight out of Brussels within the hour."

"Brussels?" *Not Prague?*

"I'll explain when I get there. And McCoy?"

"Yeah?"

"Don't call Interpol until we talk with you. There's something we need to tell you. Something you need to know first."

Before he had time to imagine what she meant by that he heard a noise.

Time to get out of here.

"Okay," he whispered, and hung up.

Exiting through Caravaggio's office—the way he came in—wouldn't be safe; the man might still be working in there. Thinking that exiting into the hallway might be equally dangerous, he decided to try the other door, the one Irena and Gallo had come through.

The door opened into a small, darkened room about twelve by twelve feet. A single bulb light mounted on one wall gave just enough light to reveal a remarkable sight. He was apparently standing on a small railway platform. A car about the size of a minivan sat on a track that led away into a tunnel, which curved away in a slow gentle turn to the right and disappeared.

Hunter saw no other doors into or out of the platform room. This little station had to be the way Irena got here, but from where? Where did the tracks go?

Suddenly bright overhead lights came on, almost blinding him. Two large men in security uniforms with guns drawn came out of the lab onto the platform. Hunter was armed but had no time to draw his Beretta.

They must have come from the hallway. Opening that door must have triggered a silent alarm.

"Hands up. Get down on your knees. Lay flat on the floor with your hands stretched out in front of you," the larger of the two ordered.

Hunter had no choice but to cooperate. The second man expertly frisked him, taking his gun and his wallet but missing the cell phone tucked under his belt. He then used a plastic tie to bind Hunter's hands behind his back. They strong-armed him to the rail car and got in with him. The man in charge worked some controls, and the car gave a jolt, then left the station and entered the tunnel.

Hunter studied the driver. He was a muscular man, around six feet. He was dark, probably Italian.

"You just couldn't leave things alone, could you, McCoy? You had to keep coming back." The big man shook his head at the stupidity of it. "That's right, we've known who you were from the beginning. You and your friends could have left any time, but not anymore. Now you've gone one step too far."

From the beginning? What's he talking about?

"And just who are you?" Hunter asked.

Neither man answered.

Hunter had no idea where they were going, but the ride lasted maybe five minutes. He asked several questions during the ride but was met with silence. When the car finally stopped he found himself in a platform room much like the one he'd just left.

The big man led him off the platform, and while pushing Hunter in the lower back felt something hard—Hunter's cell phone. He retrieved it and cursed his assistant while grinding the phone into a useless mass of metal and plastic under his boot.

Damn, that was going to get me out of here.

He was brought to what was apparently once a fruit cellar, dark and heavily oak-beamed. The man pushed him in, and he heard the door locked from the outside by the huge padlock he'd glimpsed as he'd entered.

The room smelled musty and unused. After a few minutes his eyes adjusted to the darkness and he was able make out several large workbenches with pots and baskets and two or three wooden stools.

He waited and listened, but the men were apparently gone. The only light in the cellar came from a small slit window about four-inches high by a foot wide, set up near the ceiling, probably at the level of the ground outside.

Hunter looked around for something to cut the plastic straps holding his arms behind him. He saw a small workbench with drawers. He backed into it and pulled the top drawer open. Much to his surprise, it contained small garden tools. He selected a small pair of trimmers and quickly sliced through the strap. His hands were free.

He tried the door, which of course was solidly locked. Obviously they hadn't intended to use this room for a jail, or the tools would have been removed. No doubt they would be back soon. He had to assume his discovery of

Caravaggio's lab was not something they'd anticipated. Now that they had him, they were likely scrambling to figure out what to do with him.

He spent the next twenty minutes or so scrutinizing his surroundings. Three of the walls were stone, and were apparently built right up against the earth outside. The fourth wall that contained the door was solid wood.

With no other doors and a window way too small to crawl through, it seemed he was here to stay until they came back for him.

GALLO AND CARAVAGGIO PACED the large expanse of Nero's office. Carlo Mansi, the muscular security chief who'd captured Hunter, sat and waited.

"He saw it all. Damn him, the man saw it all," Nero shouted. "What are we supposed to do with him now? We can't just let him go, he knows everything." He continued to pace, nervously patting down his prematurely gray hair. "And on top of everything else, he's with Interpol and he's some kind of American intelligence agent." He brandished Hunter's wallet.

"Did you see those credentials? What does that mean? Do they know about us? Is there an investigation going on?" He spun on Mansi. "How did you miss this, Carlo? How did you let it get this far? For that matter, how did he get in the lab?"

Gallo spoke for the first time. "It's obvious we can't let him go. Right now Interpol knows nothing. They'll only know what McCoy tells them. He's the only one with the knowledge. We silence him and the investigation—if there is one—is over."

Gallo and Caravaggio looked at each other, silently, knowing what had to be done.

Mansi interrupted the silence. "I've been following McCoy since you identified him on the video," Mansi said, nodding to Gallo. "He's teamed up with a woman."

"What woman?" demanded Nero.

"Her name is Kat Donckers—Irena Rousseau's daughter."

"Irena's daughter?' Where the hell is she?" an exasperated Caravaggio yelled.

"She flew to Brussels yesterday, probably to see her father," Mansi said.

Trying to calm himself down, Caravaggio thought for a minute and then said, "So, even if she knew McCoy was going to break in today, she can't know what he learned. There's no way she can know her mother's alive. We can watch her, but I don't think she's a threat."

A silent gloom settled over the room. They all knew McCoy had to be silenced permanently, but the two medical men, trying to hold on to a shred of decency so they could carry on with their self-delusion that they were actually doing good for society, couldn't bring themselves to say it out loud.

Caravaggio, whose international reputation was legitimately based on excellent, top-quality research, firmly believed what they were accomplishing with SRE would be an incredible gift to humankind. In his mind, holding Irena Rousseau under the false pretense of a deadly skin disorder wasn't so much imprisonment as it was "treatment" for those potential thousands who'd stand to benefit from the wonderful gift her sacrifice could pave the way for. He even envisioned a day when he'd explain it all to her, she'd understand, and he'd let her go. It was fantasy, of course, but he needed to hold on to the possibility.

He knew Gallo's motives were more monetary; nevertheless, Gino was still a physician, and the thought of intentionally doing harm to someone was a difficult pill to swallow.

"Carlo," Caravaggio said, addressing Mansi, "the greater good here has to be served. Make this problem go away. Do you understand?"

Mansi hadn't told them about his earlier attempt to kill McCoy and the woman by running their car off the road.

He certainly hadn't forgotten the threat by Traveler. Mansi knew all about the unique skills of Rache's personal assassin, and the knowledge chilled him to the bone. He'd been told to leave McCoy and the woman alone. He knew that Caravaggio and Gallo had never met the man or they wouldn't be so brave.

Caravaggio waited for an answer.

Mansi slowly nodded his head, convinced he'd just given himself a death sentence.

Chapter 48

GENEVIEVE WAITED AT THE HOTEL as long as she could. Hunter should have been back by now. Something must have happened. The only "OK" she'd received from him was shortly after noon at 12:45, indicating he'd successfully gotten back into the lab. The GPS indicated he'd been in the lab until just before 3:00 p.m.

He should have sent the next OK when he successfully left the building. He hadn't, even though the GPS locater showed he'd obviously gone somewhere else. Then the signal abruptly stopped and she got a system message saying his phone had been turned off. He wouldn't do that, she knew. He had specifically said he'd keep it on so she could track him. Something was definitely wrong.

Using the GPS coordinates on her phone for Hunter's last position, she entered them into Google Earth on his laptop. The globe spun, found Sorrento, Italy, and zoomed in on a large wooded estate behind the Institute that appeared to be occupied by a large modern home and several smaller houses. *What's he doing there?*

HUNTER HEARD PIANO MUSIC, DISTANT but soothing. Where was it coming from? Was it a recording? Maybe this was where they keep Irena? Was she in this building somewhere, and was that her playing the piano now? Then the music stopped, and he turned his attention back to his immediate dilemma.

It was obvious Caravaggio and Gallo had never expected anyone to see what they were doing in the lab and didn't know exactly what to do with him. That would probably change for the worse once they found the credentials in his wallet. They'd figure he knew too much to let him go. He'd been in the cellar for several hours by now and was sure they'd have decided on a plan to get rid of him. He couldn't have much time left to get out of here.

The door hinges were on the outside, so nothing to work with there. He'd found a trowel and wooden mallet in the third drawer and had been working on the stone surrounding the small window for several hours. He hoped he could chip away at enough mortar between the stones below the window to remove a few and dig through the dirt outside.

GENEVIEVE WAS IN A STATE OF NEAR PANIC. It had now been almost twenty hours since Hunter had texted her from the lab. She knew something had to be wrong. In spite of his telling her to stay put until he got back, she had to do something. Using the Google Earth map she'd printed out on the hotel's equipment, she drove Hunter's rental toward the last GPS location sent from his cell phone. "Turn right in zero-point-three miles," intoned the car's GPS system.

Suddenly, a large black van raced past her and turned into the driveway of the property she was looking for. Only then did she see the van had barreled through a security gate that had opened in a tall metal fence surrounding what looked like a compound.

Peering through the fence and the trees, she could see the black van parked in front of the large house she'd seen on the Google Earth view. Two large men got out and opened a small door on the side of the van.

Genevieve pulled over, cut the engine, and watched the scene that unfolded in front of her. One man stayed with the van while the other entered the building. Within minutes the first man reappeared, leading Hunter to the van and holding a gun on him.

Relief flooded through Genevieve. *He's alive.* Then she said to herself, *I've got to get him out of this,* silently acknowledging what she'd known for a quite a long time—she loved this man.

Chapter 49

NERO CARAVAGGIO WAS SITTING ALONE in his office, confident that Mansi would deal with McCoy, the only real threat to his Source Reversal procedure and his plans for researching it legitimately. He didn't think Irena's daughter was a threat, but he knew deep down, Mansi did. When he'd told the security chief to "take care of it," on one level Nero meant McCoy, but he knew Mansi would also include Irena's daughter.

As it often did, his reverie turned to Rache and he cursed the day he'd met him. Rache had read about Caravaggio's work with neuroplasticity in a newspaper article following an international conference on Neuroscience where Nero was the featured speaker. The presentation was a summary of the groundbreaking work he'd done up to that point.

As is often the case with notable scientists, he ended his speech by describing several *potential* future applications for his work. One of these was the possibility of someday transferring highly skilled motor performance from one person to another. This and several other possibilities he mentioned were only speculation and not really taken seriously by anyone at the time—except for Rache.

Rache was an incredibly wealthy man with—with, at least as far as Nero could learn, no apparent explanation for his wealth. Caravaggio had tried tracing him on the Internet, but nothing came up. The man was a mystery. Nero didn't even know his first name—if he had one.

Nevertheless, when Rache had made an appointment to meet with Caravaggio and explained he would be willing to completely fund his research on transferring motor skills, Nero couldn't help but be intrigued.

Nero explained to Rache that they'd be able to do animal studies, but that human trials were out of the question. Rache had told him to forget the animal studies, that he wanted Nero to do the human work right away. Of course Nero told him that was impossible. But Rache said he'd build him a complete laboratory dedicated to the project, would fund all of the experiments, and would also give him forty-nine percent ownership of a highly successful privately held international mortuary system called Final Care, Nero had to stop and think. Why would the man do that?

When he asked Rache this very question, his answer chilled Nero to the bone.

"Let's just say, Dr. Caravaggio, my complete knowledge of your life during the two years of your neurology residency, and the circumstances of your own sudden wealth following that time, allow me to ask this of you without giving you any explanation at all. Moreover, lest you doubt the extent of my knowledge, I ask you to read something. When you are finished, I'm sure you'll want to dispose of it as soon as possible. You can take some comfort in the knowledge the only other copy is safe with me."

With that Rache handed Caravaggio an envelope that he slowly and reluctantly opened and read. While he was reading, Nero blanched a pasty white, the room started to turn in circles and he slumped into his chair, weeping.

With no choice but to comply, even though they hadn't gone through the appropriate steps leading to human trials, Nero was sure it would work—and amazingly, it had. He and Gallo had tried SRE on Kris Hanson, a so-so pianist, and turned her into a concert-level performer. They'd even tried it on a man who'd suffered a real stroke, Charlie Lahti, and he'd developed some remarkable juggling skills, although he died before they could see how much he'd really be able to improve. Now, with Tony Pompa, they were well on their way toward a third trial.

Nero knew international recognition for his Source Reversal Enhancement technique would only be possible if he went through the proper steps, seeking permission for human trials and so on. This is why he and Gallo had to keep anyone from discovering what they'd already done with Kris Hanson, and Charlie Lahti. They were both dead and couldn't tell. Maybe Tony Pompa would have to be silenced, too, once they succeeded with him. He didn't want to think of them as lab rats—but they were. Of course there was still the issue of Irena Rousseau to be resolved. She would be different, and that troubled him.

He'd begin designing the necessary animal studies as soon as possible. When those were completed and reported, he and Gallo could begin preparing the paperwork for controlled human trials with the Italian medical authorities, trials that they already knew would be successful. Only by going this route could this triumph be added to his already impressive list of neuroscientific achievements.

As Nero thought it through, he was more and more convinced that sacrificing them, however unpleasant, was a small price to pay for the greater good.

Chapter 50

MCCOY KNEW HE DIDN'T HAVE MUCH TIME. They'd hand-cuffed him by his right wrist to the grab bar above the passenger seat door. "Who the hell are you?" he asked.

"My name makes no difference," Mansi answered.

"Let me guess. You're the head security guy. Is that it?"

"Just shut up, will you."

"So, mister no-name, did you run me off the road a few days back?"

"I told you to shut up." With that he backhanded Hunter across the face with the gun he held in his right hand.

Blood ran down out of his mouth and from the cut on Hunter's face, staining his shirt. He could taste it with his tongue.

The man in the back seat slugged Hunter again and he slumped forward barely conscious, hanging there tethered to the grab bar in the roof above the passenger door.

THREE CARS BACK GENEVIEVE TRIED to stay out of sight but still keep the black van with Hunter in view. The rear window was tinted so she couldn't see Hunter inside.

The road turned into a two-lane paved road heading east, away from the city. Traffic had fallen off and there were fewer and fewer houses as the route became more rural. Unable to hide in the traffic, the man with the gun must have noticed Genevieve's car following him, and he'd accelerated to over eighty-miles-per-hour.

"Damn, I can't risk an accident at this speed," Genevieve muttered, increasing her own speed to keep up with the van ahead.

Don't lose him.

Genevieve could see up ahead, beyond the black van, that the road veered sharply to the right. Neither vehicle could navigate the turn at this speed. As she began to slow down, the van surprised her by accelerating even more. *What's he doing?* She thought. *They'll all be killed.* Then, at the turn, the van left the road and plowed into the trees beyond.

"Oh, my God," Genevieve shouted. "Oh, my God."

As she approached the turn, scanning for the wreckage, she saw not a car wreck, but a dirt road, a straight extension of the highway heading back into the woods that couldn't be seen earlier.

Unnerved, she plowed on, following the cloud of dust kicked up by the speeding vehicle ahead. Every pothole was like hitting a speed bump and the car rebelled at this mistreatment. Genevieve had to slow down or she'd have no car at all.

He won't get away. I can follow the dust.

She was proven instantly wrong as the dust trail disappeared and she came to a three-way fork in the road, bringing her to a complete stop. All three dirt roads had tire tracks on them. Which one had he taken?

In the end she lost him. The first trail she tried ended up in an olive grove. A second dead-ended up against a dirt berm after a ten-minute drive. On neither road did she see any houses or any side roads the van might have taken. The third trail, no doubt the route Hunter's captor had taken, eventually came back out onto the highway. She'd lost him.

SLOWLY OPENING HIS EYES, HUNTER saw the leather seat of the van. His head hurt like hell, his shoulder ached and he was hanging by his right wrist from the "Oh Jesus handle" over the passenger door. He remembered instantly where he was. He didn't move. There were two of them, the guy driving who had pistol-whipped him in the face and the one in the back seat who must have hammered him from behind. He had to be ready when he got the chance.

They drove on for another ten minutes or so and then began to slow down. Hunter felt the road get bumpy, as if they'd left the pavement and were on a dirt road.

Get ready.

The vehicle stopped.

"All right," the driver said. "Unhook him and drag him over here."

You're only going to get one chance.

The man in the backseat released the handcuff attached to the bar, leaving Hunter with one cuff on his right wrist and the other now hanging free. Still slumping down as if he were still out cold, Hunter opened his eyes slightly, trying to get a sense of the layout as the goon pulled his dead weight forward by the right wrist. Hunter could see the driver was standing just two feet away, no doubt with a gun out and ready. The goon grabbed him under the armpits to haul him out of the car.

This is it you've got to do it now.

As the man dropped him, Hunter thrust out his right arm, grabbed the ankle of the driver and pulled as hard as he could. Taken by surprise, the man lost his balance and fell. Hunter slapped the gun out of his hand, sprang to his feet, and whipped around with the loose handcuff catching the goon, who hadn't yet realized what had happened, square in the side of the head. As the man yowled and started to fall, Hunter and the driver both grabbed for the gun. The driver got there first, but before he could bring it up, Hunter kicked him square in the balls.

The man cried out in an ungodly groan and dropped the gun again. This time Hunter got it first, but not before the security guy, recovering now, brought up his own gun and fired at Hunter. The shot missed but Hunter's return fire didn't, catching the man square in the center of the chest.

As Hunter turned with the gun now aimed at the groaning driver, the man surprised him by producing a second weapon. Before he could fire, Hunter put a nine-millimeter round just above his nose.

Hunter staggered back against the car and dropped his arms in exhaustion. Only then did he look around to see where he was—an empty field on a dirt road. He checked the men. They were both dead. Where was he?

He dragged the bodies into some nearby brush and left them there. He checked their wallets. As he'd suspected, the driver was Carlo Mansi, security chief. He pocketed the man's cell phone.

Hunter fired up the van, thankful the keys were still in the ignition, and watched the GPS screen came alive on the dash. He had to get to the house where they'd kept him and get Irena out. He was convinced it was her he'd heard playing the piano while they held him in the room downstairs. He knew he had to get there fast. Caravaggio and Gallo were obviously trying to get rid of all the evidence they could, and Irena was definitely evidence.

Chapter 51

USING THE VAN'S GPS, HE FOUND his way back out of the killing field to the highway. It had now been almost twenty-four hours since Hunter had entered the secret lab and had seen the entire procedure of Source Reversal Enhancement. It seemed like a lifetime. He was exhausted and hungry.

He called Genevieve using Mansi's cell phone.

"Hunter? Oh my god. Where are you? Are you okay?" she asked, joy and relief evident in her voice.

"I'm all right. Now listen, you've—"

"How did you get away from those men? Are they still after you? They had guns."

"Whoa, slow down. How do you know about men with guns?"

"I tailed the black van when they took you away from the house. I tried to follow, but lost the trail in the woods."

"Where are you now?" he asked.

"I'm driving your rental and heading back to the Capri. Kat and Johannes are there. They got in earlier from Brussels."

"Good. I'll meet you there. I'm driving the same black van you were chasing earlier. And Genevieve?"

"Yes?"

"This time I'll be alone."

WHEN HUNTER GOT TO THE HOTEL, EVERYONE—Genevieve, Kat, and Johannes—was already gathered in his room. Genevieve rushed up to him, crushing him in her embrace.

Kat instantly demanded, "Where did you see my mother, McCoy?"

Hunter uncoupled himself from Genevieve's hug. "She was brought into Caravaggio's secret laboratory two floors below his office by Dr. Eugenio Gallo, a neurosurgeon at the Institute."

"That's the guy Phillippi told us about," she said

"Right. Anyway, your mother appeared to be healthy and well."

"McCoy, are you sure it was my Irena you saw?" Johannes pleaded.

"Yes, sir. It was. No question about it."

He described what he'd seen in the lab, and the SRE process as explained by Caravaggio and Gallo, to physical therapist, Tony Pompa. He told her Irena played beautifully and she'd been transferring these skills to Pompa. It didn't sound as if any harm was being done to her.

"I overheard them later saying they're keeping Irena contented by telling her she had some terrible communicative skin condition and needed to be kept isolated while they treated her for it. Caravaggio told her she'd only need two more treatments to complete the cure. I didn't know what they meant by that at the time. Gallo was wearing a biohazard suit in the presence of your mother."

"A biohazard suit?"

"Right, only it's all a mirage. She has no disease. When Caravaggio told her he thought she'd only need the two more treatments, she said, 'and then can I see my family, my Johannes and my daughter, Kat?' He told her he thought so, but they'd have to do a final examination before he could take that risk. She even gets fake emails from you and your dad."

Kat listened with tears in her eyes. Johannes covered his mouth fighting back tears as well.

Over the next half hour, Hunter told them how he'd been captured by Mansi and his goon and taken to the house in the hills behind the Institute and imprisoned. He told them how he'd escaped, killing them both. He told them that one of the men was Carlo Mansi, the institute's security chief.

Genevieve explained how she'd tracked him to the house behind the Institute using the GPS coordinates on her phone. "When you didn't check in as scheduled and you turned your phone off, I went after you."

"I didn't turn it off, they smashed it."

Genevieve described what she'd seen of the compound with the big house behind the institute and gave a thorough description of the security fence around it and the armed guard stations.

"Where is she, McCoy? Kat demanded.

"I think she's in the same house where they kept me locked in a cellar there. I was able to hear a piano playing. It was the same piece I'd seen her playing in the lab."

"Let's go. We've got to get her out of there."

"Whoa, Kat. It's not going to be so easy."

Chapter 52

WHEN HUNTER HAD FINISHED TELLING THEM everything he knew, he said, "It's time for Interpol. I'm calling them in."

"McCoy—Hunter?"

"Yeah?"

She's never called me Hunter before.

"There's something I need to tell you," Kat said, "something I need to tell all of you. It's about my dad and me, and it's something you should know before Interpol gets involved."

Johannes hung his head, apparently knowing where she was going with this. Genevieve and Hunter waited.

"This is hard and I hope you understand," Kat gazed solemnly at Hunter and Genevieve. "We had no choice. My father and I did what we had to do."

Recognizing immediately this was going to be serious and beginning to suspect what it was about, Hunter leaned against the windowsill. Genevieve sat on the bed as if bracing herself for something very unpleasant.

Kat told them everything. She explained about the blackmail, about Johannes's real name, and the reason he fled Germany after killing the mayor to protect his sister. She told them how Willie Hofmann had hated her mother for leaving him for Johannes. He saw this as an unforgivable insult.

"Apparently his hatred for my father and mother smoldered for years, in spite of the fact my father had gotten him the job with Final Care in Miami.

"A little over a year ago he decided on his revenge, saying if we didn't do exactly what he wanted he'd tell the German authorities where my father was. We knew this would lead to Papa's extradition to Germany because there's no statute of limitations on murder. He'd be convicted and sent to prison."

"Tell me about the jewel business," Hunter said.

"He said I had to steal jewelry—only expensive pieces, because I had the knowledge and the opportunity to do it. I'd dismantle them and put the single gems in a tube my father would then insert into a space below the femoral artery on a cadaver to be shipped to the United States. There's not enough room under the carotid artery."

That explains the femoral route for embalming for the bodies shipped to Miami.

"These bodies would always be shipped to the Miami Airport facility where Willie would remove the stones and fence them. He'd keep ninety percent and send ten percent to us. His theory was that by accepting our ten percent, we'd be just as guilty as he was and our silence would be insured."

"He was right about that," Hunter offered with a shake of his head. "Your only way out of that might have been to put that money away, along with a dated notarized letter stating you were being blackmailed and had no intent to profit from your activities."

Kat plopped down on the bed next to her father and hugged him closely. "Hunter, thank you for saying that."

That's the second time she called me Hunter.

"Because that's exactly what we did. We have an affidavit signed by an attorney dated the day he saw us put a letter in an envelope, seal it, and turn it over to him for continual safekeeping. He'll swear that it has never been out of his care. Of course he doesn't know what's in the letter.

"So even after you thought your mother was dead, you had to continue because he still threatened to expose Johannes," said Genevieve.

"Exactly."

"Let me guess," Hunter said. "Charlie Lahti was one of your carrier bodies, but he got accidentally sent to Tampa instead of Miami. That's the real reason his body had to be shipped from Tampa *back* to Miami, Willie Hofmann had to extract the jewel tube from the space below the femoral artery before he could be sent on to Venice."

"Yes," Kat admitted, eyes blazing with anger. "The bastard."

Hunter assimilated all this and marveled how his seemingly simple search for a man's missing body had morphed into such a large and far-reaching operation. He knew Johannes and Kat's only chance at redemption was to confront the blackmailer, but they'd still have to be careful not to let Johannes be handed over to the German authorities.

"Have you two thoroughly examined the deportation laws between European Union countries?"

Johannes answered for them. "Yes, we have. Unfortunately, since 2004, when the European Union introduced the European Arrest Warrant, it's become even easier to extradite people accused of serious crime. If a court in Germany issued an EAW to get me extradited to Germany for murder, Belgium would have to comply."

"I see," Hunter said. "And of course your involvement in this jewelry heist and smuggling scheme won't look good in your defense."

"Isn't there something you can do, Hunter? Explain it to the police or something?" Genevieve asked.

"At the very least," Hunter said, "You're both going to need very good legal advice. I'd suggest you hire someone right away. You need to retrieve and give him your notarized statements and all the information you have on the blackmail and the burglaries. He needs to start preparing your defense for these crimes.

"But you have an even greater problem with the extradition issue," Hunter continued. "If you are extradited, do you have any evidence or proof of your innocence? Can your sister testify on your behalf that you came to her rescue? She may not have been the first victim of the mayor. You'll probably need a private detective to dig up whatever he can on the man. Is the mayor still alive? Maybe he's committed similar crimes since and been caught. You need to start gathering lots and lots of information."

"McCoy?" Kat said. "There's something else you should know."

"You're going to tell me why you went to Brussels instead of Prague, right?"

Somewhat surprised, Kat said, "Yes. How did you know?"

"Let's have it," he said.

"That phone call I got when we were at the Internet cafe near Genevieve's hotel in Naples trying to figure out the painting code…?"

"I remember."

"It wasn't from a client, it was from Willie Hofmann. He claimed we'd gone to the police and said he'd started the clock ticking on the endgame. He said it was all over now and we'd be dead."

"What did he mean by the endgame?" Hunter asked.

"He didn't say; he just repeated that we were dead now and hung up. That's why I went to Brussels—to protect my father."

Chapter 53

HUNTER EXCUSED HIMSELF, telling Genevieve, Kat, and Johannes that he had phone calls to make and they should all stay in the room until he returned. First he called Gautier and asked to be put through to the Director. A few minutes later, Gerard Pelletier, Director of Interpol came on the line.

"McCoy, I remember you from the Collider incident last year. I never had a chance to tell you, nice work."

"Thank you, sir."

"Gautier tells me you've stumbled on something else, this time in Italy. What is it?"

Hunter explained about the operation Caravaggio was conducting at the Institute, how Irena Rousseau was alive, about the deception with the phony disease, and the unethical medical procedure that was undoubtedly not authorized and certainly illegal. He told him it extended internationally and it was time for the authorities to intervene before Caravaggio had a chance to dispose of any and all evidence of his crime.

"I see," said Pelletier. "Where are you, McCoy?"

Hunter told him and Pelletier asked him to stay put; he'd call him back with instructions within the hour.

Hunter returned to the room. While they waited for the Interpol Director's call, Kat and her father talked quietly in one corner and Genevieve took Hunter's hand in hers and smiled.

"You know, one day," she whispered, "we're going to have to have a real date. You know what I mean. One where it's just us having a nice time together without all the extra trimmings that usually seem to mess them up—like deranged scientists trying to blow up the world's largest particle accelerator, religious zealots trying to kill us because of the fear of an old book, psychopathic assassins stalking us, and security chiefs for deranged medical men trying to run you off the road. You know what I mean, Hunter? A real date, with flowers and dinner and wine, and music and—well, you know."

Hunter smiled back, "When you're right you're right. I suggest we—"

The phone rang. Hunter listened for five minutes, then hung up.

"That was the director of Interpol," he said, addressing everyone. "They've contacted the local police department. I'm to cooperate with the local Chief Inspector, one Claudio Mariucci. He'll get the appropriate warrants and make the arrests that are needed. I'm supposed to meet with him now and give him all the information I can.

"But I have to tell you, I have a bad feeling about this already. I've seen local authorities hesitate to move quickly on local notables, and I'm sure Caravaggio fits that category. But, who knows? Maybe I'll get lucky this time and this chief will be different."

WISHFUL THINKING. THE CHIEF WASN'T DIFFERENT. Two hours later Hunter was shown into the office of Chief Inspector Claudio Mariucci. His opening question told Hunter all he needed to know about his attitude.

"McCoy, what exactly are you? Are you an American police officer? Apparently you have some connection to Interpol, but I haven't been told what it is. All I've been told is to cooperate with you in an investigation of Dr. Caravaggio."

"I'm an intelligence agent of the DIA of the United States Department of Defense and a consultant detective with the Charlottesville, Virginia Police Department seconded to Interpol."

Hunter showed Mariucci his credentials; thankful he'd retrieved them from Mansi's body. He had to thank Deacon for securing the position with the Charlottesville police, a requirement for cooperation with Interpol.

Inspector Mariucci examined his creds, and sighed in resignation, signaling he'd have to cooperate, unfortunately. "So, what's this craziness about the Institute? You can't be serious with these charges against Dr. Caravaggio. The man and his Institute have brought nothing but prosperity and pride to Sorrento."

Hunter knew it was going to be an uphill battle with this man. Mariucci was going to protect the local celebrity no matter what, especially from an American lawman, no matter how many credentials he had.

Hunter laid out the full evidence against Caravaggio and Gallo. The charges included kidnapping, conspiracy to commit murder, conducting human medical trials without authorization, and possible fraud. He explained about the secret lab, the experiment he'd observed involving Irena Rousseau and Tony Gallo, the phony disease story, the biohazard suit, the house where Irena was kept, the underground railcar system, and the files he had seen in the underground lab.

When he'd finished, Mariucci swore under his breath. "*Merda!* I can't believe it. My wife and I've had dinner with the man. Are you sure of all this, McCoy?"

Hunter was about to say he had the photos to prove it but then remembered they were on the phone Mansi had stomped on. Then he seemed to recall it was actually harder to crush a chip than one might think. He told Mariucci about the crushed phone. "If the chip is still good I've got pictures."

Next he told Marucci where the bodies of Mansi and his man were and suggested he should send a team out to recover them. He told the inspector he should send teams to the Institute to secure the lab and files with all their evidence and to do the same at the house where Irena was kept. Also he should bring in Caravaggio, Gallo, and Tony Pompa for questioning.

Mariucci stared at him. "Listen, McCoy, I don't know how things are done where you come from, but here we gather the evidence first and then we move. I'll have to present enough evidence to a judge to get search warrants for the Institute and the house you claim exists before I can send men into either place. Or, before I even think about bringing an important man like Dr. Caravaggio in for questioning. Is that clear? And, one more thing; this is my jurisdiction and I'll call the shots. I'll cooperate with you as Interpol asked, but don't for a minute forget I'm in charge here."

Hunter assumed Sorrento, a small town of barely sixteen thousand residents wasn't a hot spot of criminal activity and the inspector probably had very little experience, if any, with a major crime of the magnitude this was shaping up to be. Still, he had to work with him.

"Look, Inspector, I'll get you your evidence," he said evenly. "But at least put someone outside the house and the Institute to make sure nothing is removed in the meantime."

Hunter wasn't sure if Mariucci's head nod was a signal of agreement or a nonverbal version of "I'll take it under advisement."

Chapter 54

WHEN HUNTER GOT BACK TO THE HOTEL, Johannes, Kat, and Genevieve were eager to hear what he'd learned from Mariucci. He told them and said he wasn't surprised at the man's response. Then he explained his own plan, a plan that had a role for all four of them.

That evening Hunter and Kat broke into Caravaggio's office again, but not without a delay. The code on the door lock had been changed in what they hoped was a routine switch. When they finally entered, Hunter immediately activated the painting-based wall code, and the two of them descended into the lab. He switched on the lights. Everything looked as it had before—the piano, the headgear; all of it was exactly as he'd seen it earlier.

"Where is she, McCoy?" Kat asked, anxious to get on with it.

Heading toward the back door, he said, "Come with me, I'll show you."

Together, they approached the door to the rail platform. This was where they'd need a bit of luck. They'd have to walk through the tunnel to the house if the railcar wasn't there. Hunter guessed if there were any letdown in security around the compound it would be here, through this tunnel, since the only way into it was through the secret wall and Caravaggio's lab or the door to the hallway that was kept locked from the outside. The other advantage of this route from Hunter's point of view was that they might be able to recover his smashed phone with all of its recorded evidence.

When they opened the door to the platform, the railcar was there, waiting. He got a better look at it this time. It was about twenty-feet long, with a flatbed accounting for ten feet and with the other ten feet being an enclosed cab with seats. Seeing no one around, Hunter said, "Let's get in and see if we can get this thing going."

They got in and took two seats opposite each other, Kat looking doubtful. "Do you know how to work this thing?"

He reached above his seat to a panel with a red and green button. Taking a chance, Hunter pushed the green button, and the car began to move forward.

"It's not far," Hunter said. "It takes a few minutes. At the other end is a platform, much like the one we just left."

He hoped no one was waiting at the other end when they arrived. Hunter was armed this time, while Kat wasn't.

"Will this thing stop on its own, or do you have to push the other button?" Kat asked apprehensively.

"Not sure."

"So how do we find out?"

"How about if I push the red button when we get close?"

As it happened, they didn't have to do anything. The car began to slow down on its own, just as they rounded a turn and saw the platform in the basement of the house come into view.

"Is that it, McCoy?"

"That's it. That's where they took me. We got off on this platform and Mansi found my cell phone. It should be right over—there it is." He spotted it lying right where Mansi had crushed it under his shoe. It hadn't been moved. Apparently they hadn't used this route since transporting him. That was good. He pocketed the phone, hoping it would yield the evidence they needed.

Hunter led Kat back across the planked wooden railcar platform to an open doorway through a stone foundation wall. Inside, the floor became concrete and it was obvious they were in a basement below ground level.

"Over there," Hunter said, keeping his voice low. "That door leads to the cellar where they kept me."

They surveyed the basement and found a stairway, presumably leading into the house. Suddenly both of their heads snapped up. Flowing out of the house and beautifully interrupting their quiet stealth was the glorious sound of an expertly played Mendelssohn sonata. They listened for a moment; then Kat grabbed Hunters arm; "That's her. I know it, McCoy, that's her playing. She always played Mendelssohn in the evening at home. She's in there."

"We'll get her, Kat. Follow the plan, and we'll get her."

Carefully they climbed the stairs to the closed door at the top and listened for anyone on the other side. Hearing nothing but the piano, Hunter gently cracked the door just enough to see in. The door opened to a small room completely dark except for light coming through a small window in the opposite wall. As his eyes adjusted to the dark Hunter saw the only piece of furniture in the entire room, a stool below the small window. Gently he opened the door and they stepped into the room.

The music appeared to be coming from behind the wall with the lone window. Next to the window was a phone. Hunter presumed it was part of the plot to convince Irena of the necessity to be isolated, and that she used it to communicate with her attendants. He doubted it was active beyond the confines of the house. That was a lucky break and meant the really difficult part of the plan could be abandoned.

Kat got to the window first and looked through. She sucked in a gasp and raised her hands to her face and mouth. "It's her, my God, it's momma. She's really alive." She grabbed his arm. "McCoy, she's alive!"

"Shush, keep it down, remember the plan."

Reluctantly she did. Then Hunter looked through the small viewing window. Irena was seated at the piano, playing. They had a perfect side view of her. Her biohazard suit was sitting on a chair to the left of the viewing window. Then he noticed two other structures in the room. They appeared to be the size of small closets attached to the wall that separated them from Irena, one six feet to the left of the window and one six feet to the right. He saw each had a door into this room.

"McCoy, what's that noise?"

Immediately on alert, McCoy put his hand to his gun.

"No, I mean that humming noise," Kat said.

Hunter had heard it earlier but hadn't paid much attention, as he was focusing on human noises. "It sounds like blowers of some kind."

As Irena continued to play he determined it was coming from the closet on the right. It appeared to be the source of the mechanical sound they'd heard when they first entered the building.

He opened the door to the closet and saw exactly what he expected. Two small circulating air pumps sat on the floor, each connected to two circular flexible venting pipes. One pipe from each pump emptied into a system of smaller pipes that vented air from the room where Irena was playing.

Presumably these represented the controlled air system from the room so no contaminants or deadly skin material from Irena could infect others. If that were the case, this air would have been fed to a scrubbing system of some kind. Instead, it was obvious the air removed from the room was simply vented outside. *So much for contamination control*, he thought. He could see similar pipes going to the closet on the left.

He assumed Irena had been told this was the equivalent of an airlock so nothing in the room's air could escape to the outside and of course nothing could enter either.

He also saw a stairway leading up to what he presumed were her living quarters. Whispering now, in case they could be heard inside the room, Hunter said to Kat, "I'm convinced it's safe in there. This phony system proves it."

Just as they were getting ready to enter the room and take Irena, the lights came on and two men with automatic weapons burst in behind Hunter and Kat.

"Hands in the air, now," one of them commanded.

Before McCoy could get to his weapon, he and Kat were forced to the floor, their wrists tied together with cable ties within seconds. Next they were expertly frisked and Hunter's Beretta was taken, along with the extra magazine he carried. Neither of them carried any identification.

Unlike Mansi and his goon, these guys were professionals, Hunter thought.

Chapter 55

"WE SHOULD HAVE HEARD FROM MANSI by now. It's been over twenty-four hours. Where is the damned man?" Nero Caravaggio was beside himself with anxiety.

Gino Gallo tried to calm him down. "Mansi's good. He'll clean up the problem. Don't forget, he's highly motivated. He's as heavily involved in this as we are."

Not mollified, Nero continued to pace his office. The gathering clouds suggesting afternoon rain reflected his darkening mood. "Rache is taking no chances. He's going to strip the labs bare."

Gallo nodded in agreement. "That's good. We can't be sure if McCoy had a chance to report what he suspected to Interpol, but if he did and they come around looking, it's better if they find nothing."

Both men then went silent, acknowledging the reality of something else, something neither wanted to bring up, but knew they couldn't avoid. Gallo strolled over to one of the paintings, not one that was part of Nero's code, and stared at it as if he were really interested. As if turning his attention to art would allow him to forget, even momentarily, they still had a huge issue to deal with before the authorities came, if they did.

Gallo brought it up first. "What about her?"

Caravaggio knew exactly whom he meant by "her."
"Rache said to forget about her. She is not to be harmed.
He'll take care of her."

"What the hell does that mean? I never did understand
this thing. Why did he insist we use her, anyway?" Gallo
shook his head.

"I don't know, but we have to admit, she's been a
great donor."

INSPECTOR MARIUCCI'S MEN WENT TO THE location Hunter
had given them and found the two bodies, just as he'd
described. They were about to call for the coroner when
they heard a cell phone ring. It was coming from one of the
dead men. Without thinking, the younger of the two police
officers answered the phone. "Who is this?"

The voice on the other end responded, "Who is this?"

"This is Officer Cobo of the State Police. Who are
you?"

Nero Caravaggio ended the call and collapsed into his
chair.

HUNTER AND KAT WERE LOCKED in the same cellar he'd
been held in earlier. One of the two men, who appeared to
be the leader, ordered the other to stand guard outside the
cellar until he got back. Almost immediately, Hunter and
Kat heard noises associated with a lot of activity and the
voices of several men. It was obvious something big was
going on.

Hunter found the same clippers he'd used earlier and freed
them from the ties binding their wrists. But, as before, there
was no way out of the cellar. Hours passed with no letup in
the level of noisy activity. Neither of them had a watch, since
they'd been taken, along with Hunter's gun and his crushed
cell phone. Their only sense of time was the light coming

through the small window he'd noted on his earlier incarceration.

Eventually the activity outside began to slow down, and the sun had already set. After what must have been another three hours, the noisy activity finally stopped completely. Fifteen minutes later they heard the door to the cellar being unlocked.

They heard one of the two men shout, "Back against the far wall. Face that wall with your backs to this door."

Hunter knew what this was about. They wanted to verify they were still bound by the ties. When they discovered they'd gotten free, they were roughly retied with their hands behind their backs.

With more roughness than necessary, Hunter and Kat were shoved out of the room. The men duct-taped their mouths and placed hoods over their heads. A few minutes later they were seated in the back of a van of some kind and were being driven away, no doubt to their deaths.

Damn. I just went through this.

Being careful not to make too much upper body movement and alert the gunmen, Hunter moved his bound hands toward Kat and nudged her butt. She did the same and their fingers touched. Almost as if they had spoken, the interaction successfully conveyed what needed to be done.

She tried working with Hunter's cable tie but got nowhere. She had no idea how to get him loose. Hunter did. He tapped on her hand as if to get her attention. She stopped working on him. He felt his way to the binding lock part of the cable tie.

Most people didn't know it, but there was a way to loosen one of these. When the ribbed tie goes through the lock, a tongue in the lock catches on the rib and prevents it from being pulled out again. In normal use, when someone wanted to remove the locked cable tie, they simply cut it with a scissors or knife. However, it could be done without cutting it as well. Hunter twisted the tie about forty-five degrees where it entered the lock, bending the tongue down just a little so it no longer caught the ribs, and slid the tie back out. He had to do it fast, or the tongue would go back to its original position within a few seconds. He hoped she was paying attention.

Careful not to make any unnecessary movements, in less than a minute Hunter had loosened Kat's tie enough to allow her hands to slip it off.

Next, keeping her hands behind her as if they were still bound, she went to work on Hunter's tie. Not knowing what she was trying to do exactly, she wasn't getting anywhere. Frustrated, she tried harder and her movements caught the attention of one of the men, who shouted something in Italian and slapped her.

After a minute or two she started again, with delicate patience. A minute later Hunter was free.

Good girl.

Now they just had to wait for the right moment. He hoped Kat would wait for his cue. They didn't have to wait long, as the van began slowing down from highway speed a few minutes later. Eventually the van came to a stop and they were hustled out. Hunter exaggerated his stumbling "accidentally" bumping into Kat, until one of the captors said something in Italian to the other. Immediately their hoods were removed.

Hunter saw they were on a pier, being marched to a warehouse about forty yards ahead of them. It was moonless night, and a lone bulb over the door to the warehouse offered the only light. Hunter knew that inside the warehouse, they'd be killed. He'd have to take both men down with nothing more than surprise and his own skills.

The little procession marched single file toward the door, one man in front and one behind. Hunter was behind Kat.

I'd better come up with something fast.

The first man reached the door, opened it, and walked in. At that instant Hunter brought his arms out from behind himself, grabbed Kat by the shoulders, tossed her aside, and spun around, landing a high karate kick to the head of the man behind him. The guard went down, dropping his gun. Hunter grabbed it as the first man turned back in the doorway. Hunter shot him before he had a chance to bring his weapon up. The man behind him, recovering remarkably fast, kicked out with his leg and swept Hunter off his feet.

Knowing he had to end this quickly before others showed up, Hunter jumped to his feet and pumped a short burst into the man as he was tensing for another kick at Hunter. The whole episode hadn't taken thirty seconds. Kat was just getting up from being tossed by Hunter.

"My God, McCoy, you're scary. How did you do that? Are they dead?"

"They're dead."

Hunter motioned Kat aside and searched the warehouse. No one else was around. He returned to the dead men and searched them for identification. They carried none. Thankfully, he was able to retrieve his smashed cell phone and his Beretta from the pocket of the first man. Then he noticed a tattoo of a griffin, a mythical beast with the body of a lion and the head and wings of an eagle, on the inside of the man's right wrist. Oddly, this griffin had the tail of a shark. When he examined the other body he found the same tattoo on the inside of the right wrist.

What did that mean?

Chapter 56

HUNTER DROVE THE VAN BACK to the Hotel Capri to an anxious Genevieve and Johannes. Kat assured her father that the woman McCoy had seen before their capture and escape was really her mother and she was alive. Genevieve embraced Hunter, and Kat hugged her father.

Johannes said in an uncharacteristically strong voice, "We have to get her out of there, now. She's not safe."

"You're right," agreed Hunter.

He called Mariucci. "Inspector, this is Hunter McCoy. Listen, I've just been to the house your men are supposedly watching. Irena Rousseau is alive and being held captive in that house, she's in danger. You've got to bring more men in now and get her out of there."

"McCoy, you still haven't shown me any real evidence. All I have is your say so."

Hunter paused for several seconds before responding, his voice now a cold threat as a sudden realization dawned on him. "Inspector, you haven't placed your men anywhere, have you? Not at the house and not at the Institute."

"I told you. You bring me the evidence first."

Fuming, Hunter said, "Now listen to me, Mariucci, stay by your phone. You're going to get the most important call of your life in a few minutes, and I strongly suggest you answer it."

Hunter ended the call and immediately called Gerard Pelletier, Director of Interpol. He explained what he had learned in excruciating detail, making sure the man got the full picture. Then he told him about the lack of cooperation he'd been getting from Inspector Mariucci and what he'd asked the man to do.

The director told Hunter to wait for a return call from him.

Ten minutes later, Hunter got the call from Pelletier. "Mariucci and his men are converging on the house now. Get over there and see if you like what's happening." Then he chuckled. "Don't expect to see the inspector sitting down, though."

"Why not?' Hunter asked, confused.

"I've heard it can be very painful."

"What?"

"Being ripped a new one."

"I UNDERSTAND. WE'LL BE READY." Nero put his cell phone away and stared out his immense window at the Bay of Naples thankful it was all coming to an end. Rache's men had removed all the equipment and files from the lab downstairs and sealed off the doorway to the railcar platform on both ends of the track. There was no visible evidence at all of what the lab had been like or that the rail system even existed. He had to admit, Rache's men had been thorough and fast, and this call was meant to tie up any remaining loose ends.

Caravaggio called Gallo and told him to come to his office immediately, and to bring any records, either on paper or on computers, related to the SRE work. While he waited for Gallo, Nero did the same, assembling all his records related to the SREs.

Gallo arrived with the asked-for material and demanded to know what was going on.

"Rache wants nothing left that points to the work we've been doing in case the authorities show up. I think he's right."

"But we'll need the records for our own use later. We can't destroy them all."

"Don't worry, we're not destroying them. They'll just be stored somewhere safe a long way from here."

"How do you know this?"

"I just got off the phone with Rache. He's having the house scrubbed as well, so there won't be any evidence of Irena or how we used it either."

"But where will the records be?"

"Look, Gino, he's sending a man over now to take both of us and the records to him. He said he has it all worked out and he'll tell us where the hiding place is when we get there."

"I don't like it. I don't trust him, Nero."

"We have no choice. We have to trust him."

An hour later, they were loading boxes of files and laptops into the trunk of the large Fiat sedan Rache had sent over. When both men were settled into the back seat, the driver asked if they were comfortable.

"Cut the small talk," Gallo said. "Where are we going?"

"Why, you're going to meet with Mr. Rache, of course," said the driver, smiling.

"So who are you?" Nero asked.

"My name is Traveler."

THE DADE COUNTY, FLORIDA water police found the boat pretty much where the alarmed citizen in the multimillion-dollar condo on the beach said he'd heard and seen an explosion on the water. The Coast Guard showed up on the scene at almost the same time.

The larger Coast Guard ship began spraying fire retardant immediately over the hull of the thirty-six-foot cabin cruiser. Within minutes they'd put the fire out and stood by while the police sent two men aboard to search for survivors. The blast had been directed upward and outward blowing out windows and starting the fire. Had it gone downward the boat would have sunk.

They found one body, male, dead, his face unrecognizable. Apparently he'd been making meth and things exploded. There were remnants of brake fluid, drain cleaner, fertilizer, beakers, and burners.

"Jesus," Officer Fred Barkley said to his partner, Sam Christianson, "this stuff is dangerous enough to make on solid ground. What kind of idiot would try it on a rocking boat?"

"Obviously this guy qualified."

"Check him for ID while I look around the cabin."

"Sure, give me the dirty work," Christianson said as he stared at the grisly corpse and gingerly started going through his burned pants pockets, not enjoying the task.

"Hey, would you believe it, Fred? This guy is carrying a wallet. Let's see, we have a Florida driver's license here. Our dummy is a Willem A. Hofmann of 53 West 6th Street, Hialeah, Florida."

"Anything else?" Barkley asked.

"Yeah, here's a business card. Looks like he was an embalmer at Benson's Funeral Home."

"All right, let's give what we have to the Coast Guard, and see if they can pull this wreck in."

TRAVELER DROVE CARAVAGGIO AND GALLO to the marina. There, they helped him load all the files and computers onto a twenty-five-foot Sea Ray. He told them he was taking the materials to Rache, who had a yacht offshore where they'd be kept safe until the two men needed them again.

"Mr. Rache, instructed me to tell you to take the Fiat back to the Institute. I'll pick it up later."

Nero watched as the boat drove off in a roar of foam, noticing the image of a griffin on the transom. Still griping about turning all their records over, but having little choice, Gallo got behind the wheel and Nero took the passenger seat as they left the dock and headed back to the Institute.

"What do you really think, Nero, is Rache going to return those records to us later? I don't trust him. He may look harmless, but there's something about him that just chills me. I can't put my finger on it, but it's there all the same."

"I know what you mean. He never explained why we had to use Irena Rousseau for the experiment. We had other candidates just as good, but for some reason he was fixated on her."

"Right, what's with that?"

Nero shook his head. "I once asked him, and he just stared at me with those cold eyes, and I have to tell you, I shivered. Then, in a voice with no inflection, but carrying a meaning that was loud and clear, he said—'Just do it.' Frankly, I find the man terrifying."

OFFSHORE, USING BINOCULARS TO TRACK the Fiat, Traveler waited until the sedan approached a cliffside curve on the climb up to the Institute. At just the right moment he pressed a key on his cell phone. At that instant the accelerator pedal went to the floor, and the Fiat sedan roared through the flimsy guardrail out into space and started its two-hundred-foot drop to the rocks below.

Chapter 57

HUNTER HAD A HARD TIME CONVINCING HER, but Kat reluctantly agreed to stay with her father while he and Genevieve took the rental car over to the house behind the Caravaggio institute. In the end she had to admit Hofmann's threat about the endgame and his statement that "You're dead," directed at both her and Johannes, meant they had to stay together for safety.

When they arrived at the compound Hunter counted at least six police cars with flashing lights at the front gate. He parked, and they walked up to the main entrance, where a security man was having a losing argument with a policeman. Mariucci's men were already in the house.

Hunter showed his Interpol credentials, and the man reluctantly let them pass.

"Come on," he told Genevieve, "we're going to the room with the viewing window where I saw Irena."

It was more difficult to find now, because he didn't know where to begin. From the basement there was only one way to go, up the stairs to the room with the window, the stool, and the two phony closets.

Inside the front door they ran into Mariucci. He wasn't happy.

"There's nothing here, McCoy. My men have found nothing—no pianist, no piano, no anything."

"Have they been downstairs into the basement? There's a railcar platform and an old fruit cellar."

"Hey, Pugliano, what did you find in the basement?"

"Nothing, sir, just an old cellar."

"What? No railroad tracks, no first-class high-speed train to Lake Como, no ticket office?" Mariucci's sarcasm was palpable.

"Ah, no sir, nothing like that, just an empty basement."

Unwilling to accept this, Hunter told the man to take him there. The three of them followed Pugliano through the house.

"Down here, sir," Pugliano said to the Inspector.

Hunter was beginning to get a bad feeling about this as they descended into the damp basement. At the bottom of the stairs, Hunter saw the door to the cellar where he'd been kept, but now the platform was gone. A new wall stood in its place.

"Stand back," Hunter cautioned them and kicked the wall with his heel. His foot went right through the drywall.

"What are you doing?" shouted Inspector Mariucci, "That's private property."

Ripping at the torn drywall with his hands, he pulled away enough so they could see beyond into complete darkness.

"Ask your man to shine his flashlight in there, Inspector and tell you what he sees."

Mariucci grabbed the light from Pugliano and looked through the torn wall himself.

"Shit! Goddammit! Pugliano, get some men down here and tear this fucking wall down."

"Inspector, you should have your men do the same thing in the room upstairs. They'll find another phony wall."

Frustrated and angry, Inspector Mariucci narrowed his eyes at Hunter and sighed. "All right. What else are we going to find in this goddamn house, McCoy?"

TWO HOURS LATER MARIUCCI'S MEN had torn down the wall in the basement and found the railcar. They'd torn down the wall upstairs and revealed the piano room where Irena had played, as well as her living quarters upstairs. The only access to either of these was through the phony airlock Hunter had seen earlier. The piano was gone, along with any of Irena's personal effects. There was no sign of Irena anywhere.

At least Mariucci was now treating the house as a crime scene and significantly ratcheted up the level of both security and inspection. He also sent a team over to the Institute to detain Nero Caravaggio and Eugenio Gallo for questioning.

"There's nothing left, McCoy. If someone lived here they've removed all evidence in a remarkably short time. There's not a stick of furniture, no clothes, nothing in any of the cabinets, not even a smidge of toothpaste in the medicine cabinet."

"I don't know if anyone else lived here, Inspector, but Irena Rousseau was here yesterday. If no one else was here —just her—and she only had access to the piano room and the small living quarters upstairs, it's not unthinkable they could remove all traces of her that quickly."

Hunter now understood the meaning of the noisy activity outside the cellar when he and Kat were there. They'd been removing the evidence and walling-up the tracks.

"Inspector, we need you for a moment upstairs," one of Mariucci's men interrupted. "We may have found something."

As Mariucci went off with his man, Hunter said to Genevieve, "Let's go downstairs to the platform again."

"Why?"

"Two things, really. I'll show you."

Retracing their steps through the large house, they descended stairs to the basement.

"First I want to see if the cellar is open. There should be evidence of my trying to dig out."

The cellar was unlocked, and Hunter used the flashlight feature of Genevieve's phone to light up the dark space.

"Over there, by the window. See? I used a trowel from the workbench and tried to separate the stones around that window up there. Look, you can see the pile of dirt I made, and there's the trowel. Whoever did this 'shut-down' of the house didn't come in here."

"I'll get some pictures with my phone."

Her comment reminded Hunter he still had to try to retrieve the images on his crushed phone.

After Genevieve took her pictures, Hunter called her over to the platform.

"Be careful stepping over the drywall and two-by-fours."

The railcar was there, waiting for its next trip back to the lab.

"Let's take the car back to the lab and see if they've walled it up over there," Hunter said. He helped her into the dark cab.

As they settled into the bench seats, Genevieve said "Ow. Something's poking me in the butt." She reached back and found a partially hidden pink rectangular compact.

Hunter quickly took it from her. "This could be hers."

"It could have her DNA," Genevieve said.

"It could; let's look inside."

It was just what it looked like, a compact with a mirror, brush, and powder.

"This could establish she was here."

Hunter pressed the green button and the railcar began to move into the pitch-dark tunnel.

"It won't take long, maybe five minutes to reach the other platform."

After about two minutes, the car came to a complete stop after hitting something in the tracks.

What the hell?

Hunter checked his gun and carefully got out. Genevieve followed with the flashlight phone and she pointed it at the obstruction.

"Well this is definitely a first, wouldn't you say?" Hunter asked Genevieve. "A train colliding with a grand piano?"

They crawled behind the piano and saw the rest of what had to be Irena's stuff. He recognized furniture, clothes, shoes, the white jumpsuit he'd seen her wear, bedding, a coffeepot, toiletries, a bedframe with mattress and box spring, and two biohazard suits. Carefully stepping over this, Genevieve saw something on the track that was very large, but she couldn't make it out.

"Hunter, look down there. What's that?"

Without seeing it Hunter had an idea what she was looking at. They crawled past Irena's stuff, and when Genevieve's light reached the unknown objects Hunter knew he'd guessed right: All the equipment from Caravaggio's lab—the rack-mounts, the electrode harnesses, two more pianos, everything.

Genevieve shook her head. "What's all this stuff doing here?"

Hunter had to smile. "It's pretty clever, really. The fact they were able to completely eliminate all traces of the lab and Irena's presence in the house so quickly means they had this all planned out from the start."

"You're right," agreed Genevieve. "All it took was some manpower. They'd use the railcar to haul the equipment to the center of the tunnel from both ends, then seal up the entrances with new walls. No one would ever know about the tunnel's existence and there'd be no reason to suspect the walls covered anything."

Hunter nodded. "There was only one thing they didn't count on."

"What's that?"

"Me. I have to be the only one outside their group who knew the tunnel existed. But they figured with me dead, their secret would still be safe." He gestured to the detritus, which reminded him of King Tut's tomb.

"Take pictures of everything."

On the railcar ride back to the house, Genevieve snuggled close to Hunter and he put his arm around her.

"Life is never dull with you, Hunter. I like that. You know, we make a pretty good team."

"Yes, we do." the kiss lasted all the way back to the house.

BACK AT THE PLATFORM THEY WORKED their way through the torn-down wall, ascended the stairs and looked for Inspector Mariucci. They were told he was outside, behind the house.

When they found him he was on the phone, clearly agitated. From his facial expressions and eye rolling, they could tell something was up. Finally, he ended the call and stared at Hunter and Genevieve. "You're not going to believe this, McCoy."

"What? What's happened?"

"Nero Caravaggio and Eugenio Gallo."

"What about them, have they confessed?"

Mariucci shook his head. "No, and they won't either. They're dead, both of them, car accident."

"How?"

"About three hours ago. Their car went through a guardrail at the highest point of the cliffside road. They had a two-hundred-foot drop to the rocks below. Killed them instantly."

The Inspector massaged his temples and swore in Italian.

"There's something else, McCoy, something that doesn't add up. My men searched Caravaggio's office. There were no records of any kind there—no computers, no laptops, no notebooks, nothing. They also followed your instructions on how to open the wall using the painting code to get down to the lab. Nothing there either, just as you'd said, no equipment, no records, *niente.*"

"What about the platform. Was it walled off, like the one here in the house?"

"Yes, exactly the same. When you went through the door out of the second lab to where the platform was, all you saw now was another closet. If you hadn't been down there, we'd never know any of that existed. Good work, McCoy. I should have listened to you."

Hunter nodded. "You better check on the physical therapist, Pompa. I have a feeling you'll find he's dead too."

"I'll have my men check on it now."

"That leaves one very important mystery left."

"What's that?" the inspector asked.

"Where is Irena Rousseau?"

Chapter 58

IRENA FELT GENTLE ROCKING AS SHE slowly awakened. She was surprised to find herself in a luxurious bed, under satin covers, in a room she'd never seen before. A dream, that's what this was, it had to be. It certainly wasn't the meager room she normally slept in. Then she noticed she was wearing a satin nightie that felt glorious against her skin.

Her skin. She jolted up. This was no dream this was real. She was actually here in this bed. She looked around, rose, went to the window, and brushed aside the curtains. Water. She was on a boat.

A boat? How could this be? Where was her biohazard suit? Just as her confusion ratcheted up another notch, a phone rang—the telephone on the nightstand next to the bed. Hesitantly, she picked it up.

"Madame Rousseau, I'm so glad you're up. Senor Griffin would like to offer you breakfast with him on the back deck. You will find clothes in the closet opposite the window. Please select what you'd like to wear and someone will fetch you in forty-five minutes." The pleasant female voice hung up.

Irena replaced the receiver and sat back down on the bed. What was going on? Who was that? Who was Senor Griffin? How could she meet with anyone? What about her skin condition? Thinking this still had to be a dream, but knowing it wasn't, she stood up and found the closet and a bathroom.

Forty minutes later, showered and wearing white slacks, a blue blouse, and matching blue sandals, all in her size, she opened the door to a lovely young woman who said, "Welcome aboard, Madame Rousseau. Please follow me."

Alarmed, Irena stopped her. "But don't we need biohazard suits?"

"Trust me, they aren't necessary. Senor Griffin will explain everything."

Irena followed her, completely confused. Where was she? One thing was obvious, she was on a ship or a boat that was very large and ornate, with teak paneling and gold fixtures everywhere. Even the clothes she was wearing were expensive. She passed what must have been other staterooms, but saw no one.

At the end of the hallway, they took an elevator up one deck and emerged into bright sunlight in what must be the main salon. Toward the stern of the boat she could see in the distance a table set for breakfast, a waiter standing by, and a man — presumably Senor Griffin — seated at the table waiting for her.

As they approached the table, the man stood up and greeted her. "Irena, let me welcome you aboard my yacht. I know you have many questions, and I will do my best to answer them all. But first let's sit down and have a bite."

Irena had never seen the man before, but when the waiter brought plates of fresh cut fruit and a delicious Greek omelet with toast and jam, she ate it all, completely surprised at how hungry she'd been. When she finished, the waiter took the plates away and refilled their coffee cups.

"That will be all, Arturo; you can leave us alone now."

When the waiter left, the man stood. "First, let me introduce myself, Irena. I am Constantine Griffin, and you are aboard my yacht, the *Sea Griffin*. To begin, there are several things you should know, things about what's happened to you, things you are not aware of, nor could you have been."

Irena was sure she'd never met this man before, but something about his voice seemed familiar. No, she must be imagining it; she didn't know him.

"First of all, you have no skin disease. You never did. No nurses died in treating you. It was all a fabrication. The story was concocted by Doctors Caravaggio and Gallo to keep you indefinitely so they could use you as a donor."

Irena jumped up. "What? What are you saying? Of course I had a skin disease. That's why I was separated from everyone and had to undergo the treatment and wear the biohazard suit."

Waving his outstretched hand, Griffin said, "Look around you, Irena. Do I or any of my staff look concerned in the least about being here with you?"

Irena saw the waiter casually working at his bar and a woman who must have been a housekeeper busy tidying up the main salon. All were completely oblivious to any threat she might pose to them.

"But you *are* at risk, you *must* be."

"Believe me, we are not. Here, let me hold your hand." With that he took her hand in his and then let it go. "See, no danger."

Irena felt a wave of caution and distrust. "So, tell me who you are again?"

"As I said, my name is Constantine Griffin. But of course what you're really asking is how do I know all this and what do I have to do with it?"

"Yes, that's right." Irena sat back in her chair, full of questions.

"What do you have to do with this?" she demanded. "And for that matter, how did I get here? I don't remember anything about it. In fact, the last thing I do remember is getting back to my room at the house after my piano-playing treatment at the Institute with Dr. Caravaggio and Dr. Gallo."

"Get ready for another shock, my dear," said Senor Griffin. "Playing the piano had nothing to do with a treatment for you. Instead, you were functioning as a donor at the time."

"There, that's the second time you said that—donor. What do you mean?"

Griffin took a long drink of his coffee and indicated for Arturo to come to the table and refill their cups. When the waiter had and retreated to his workstation, Griffin continued. "What exactly did they tell you about your treatment?"

Irena took a moment before answering while she tried to remember their explanation. "They said I had to be quarantined because my skin cells had become lethally toxic to anyone who touched me directly, and even if my dried skin cells sloughed off and became airborne they could harm others."

He took her hand again and said, "So this would surely kill me?"

Still afraid she might do it, she quickly withdrew her hand. "Yes."

"And what did they tell you about the electrodes attached to your head while playing the piano?"

"How do you know about that?"

"All in good time, my dear. I will explain everything. But first, what did they tell you?"

"They told me the active ingredients in the salve I had to apply would be most effective when I was in a relaxed state. They'd tried to figure out when this would be for me and initially tried many different situations—sleeping, reading, napping, walking, piano playing, and others. The way they could tell, they said, was to record my brainwaves with an electroencephalograph. The one they used was very thorough and used several electrodes placed over a specific part of my head on each side. I would have thought sleeping or napping would be the best, but as it turned out dreams upset the process, and I dream a lot. They finally concluded my brain was most relaxed when I was playing the piano. I guess that's not surprising; I do love to play."

Griffin stroked his chin and stared out at the blue Mediterranean. "I see. Now let me tell you what was really going on."

Griffin accurately described the procedure involving an amateur player in the other room who wore a similar electrode arrangement and was trying to learn from her brain how to play as well as she did. He explained how Dr. Gallo had inserted drug release tubes into the other player's motor cortex that—under direction from Dr. Caravaggio—would release a cocktail of nerve growth factors to promote development of the same wonderful and efficient nerve connections she had in her brain.

He explained the electrodes in her headgear would pick up signals from her brain during her playing that would be converted to stimulus signals that would instantly be delivered to the other person's brain. Caravaggio had discovered that if the nerve growth cocktail were released into the other person's brain at that precise time, it would effectively rewire the other person's brain.

Irena sat stunned, unable to speak, unable even to think.

"There's more," Griffin went on. "It seems the initial cocktail Caravaggio put together was not quite up to the job. Something was missing; but he finally figured it out."

"What was it?"

"Why, a little bit of your own brain tissue, my dear."

"What? What are you talking about?"

"Do you recall that day you spent in the imaging center on the stroke campus of the Institute? They warned you not to move even a little during the sixty minutes you were in the imaging machine or the images would be distorted, and they'd have to do it again."

"Yes, that's right," she said. "They told me I'd be more relaxed if I was sedated, and I wouldn't remember a thing about it later."

"Exactly. And you didn't. During that time they did a needle biopsy of each side of your brain in the motor cortex and removed a small amount of tissue. From this they extracted a glial cell-fraction unique to you that was essential for developing the wonderful neuron connection patterns that allow you to play so beautifully. When Caravaggio added this to his cocktail mix, the results were remarkable."

Irena sat, numbed by the revelation.

"So you see, my dear, you truly were a donor of your amazing talents."

"Are you saying each of my 'treatments' was really a training session for some other pianist?"

"Yes, and it worked. Just a few months ago one of your 'trainees' made her triumphant debut as a soloist playing with a symphony orchestra in Indiana. And the next one was almost finished, though I'm afraid I've brought that one to a stop."

Suddenly angry beyond belief, Irena pushed back from the table and started pacing. "Well, we've got to stop them. We have to call the police. They need to be arrested now. They—"

"Now, now, it's been taken care of. Please sit down and I'll explain."

"And you still haven't told me how you know all this."

"Patience, please."

Irena was becoming annoyed with the man, sensing he was playing with her. Before she could go on, he continued.

"I'm afraid—quite accidently—Dr. Caravaggio and Dr. Gallo have both already paid for their sins. I was informed a few hours ago that their car went off a cliff in Sorrento and they were both killed immediately."

Shocked by this news, Irena couldn't be sure, but it seemed as if the man had smiled slightly as he said this.

Could it be true? She no longer knew what—or whom—to believe.

"Why did they do it?" she wailed. "Why did they hold me captive like that, tell me I had a disease when I didn't, tell me I couldn't see my husband and my—Oh my God, Johannes and Kat, I have to call them, now. Give me a phone."

Griffin put his hands out to calm her down. "Now, now, you'll see them soon, I promise. I've already arranged it."

"You have? Oh, how can I ever thank you? When will I see them?" Irena pleaded.

"Very soon. I've arranged for the three of you to meet at my villa, where you can have your reunion and be my guests."

Overcome with joy, Irena asked where his villa was.

"We're sailing there now, my dear. It will take some time, but my yacht is very well equipped and you'll have every comfort at your disposal."

Irena sat back and closed her eyes, trying to picture Johannes and Kat. She couldn't hold back the tears, and she wept for joy. In a few minutes, a little embarrassed by her display, she apologized to Senor Griffin and then remembered there was one thing he hadn't yet answered.

"I still don't understand how you know all this."

Before he answered, Constantine Griffin smiled broadly. "Why it's simple, my dear. I personally arranged it."

Chapter 59

HUNTER AND GENEVIEVE LEFT THE HOUSE and headed back to the hotel, planning to tell Kat and Johannes what they'd learned and that Irena was missing. On the ride back Genevieve was thoughtful.

"You know, Hunter, something's missing here, and I don't mean Kat's mother."

"What do you mean?"

"Consider this," she went on. "You have two suspects in this case; Caravaggio and Gallo, and they're both dead. They didn't move all that equipment and wall up those entrances to the train tunnel by themselves. They wouldn't have had enough time to do it, even if they could."

"You're right, they had help, no question about it. They clearly had some muscle working for them. But even there, something isn't right."

"That's what I'm saying, and I think I know what it is."

"You do?"

"I think there's another player here—another major player here—directing things, or at least working equally with Caravaggio and Gallo. Someone you haven't told me about or someone you don't know."

Hunter furrowed his brow. "There was one player we had our eyes on in the beginning, a Dr. Phillippi. However, Kat and I are convinced Caravaggio and Gallo set him up to take the fall if they got caught, and I still believe our assessment of him was correct. He had nothing to do with any of this."

Genevieve eyed Hunter as he drove. "Any other ideas? Did you come across anyone else who looked suspicious?"

Just then Hunter's cell phone rang and the screen showed it was Eduard Gautier from Interpol headquarters. He pulled over and put the phone on speaker so Genevieve could hear.

"Eduard, what's up?"

"I've been doing some research on your man Caravaggio. It seems a few years back he suddenly came into possession of forty-nine percent of Final Care, the international mortuary firm."

"I know," Hunter said. "Johannes Donckers's daughter told me he owned the company."

"Yes, but did she tell you how he got it?" Hunter could hear the mischievous challenge in his voice.

"No."

"Well, in spite of being a world-famous scientist and director of his own Institute, he wasn't really a wealthy man as important men go. He owned his house, a car, and had maybe a half-million euros in his bank account, but that was it. His forty-nine percent share in Final Care was worth about two-hundred-million euros when he acquired it."

Still not getting it, Hunter asked, "So how did he leverage that?"

"Well, that's the strange part. There was no loan. The company just turned over forty-nine-percent ownership. I can't find any quid pro quo, nothing. It seems someone just gifted him half their company."

"Why would someone give a two-hundred-million euro gift to Caravaggio?"

"That's the question, isn't it?"

"You know what you have to do now, Eduard, don't you?"

"I'm already doing it, my friend, and it's proving to be equally confusing. Who owned Final Care at the time, and does he have any kind of relationship to Nero Caravaggio?"

"Eduard, you are amazing. And now you're going to amaze me even more by telling me what you've found, aren't you?"

"That's just it, Hunter. The ownership of Final Care, except for Caravaggio's forty-nine percent, is a complete mystery. I'm working on it, but I've got nothing so far. I'll tell you this, though; your man Caravaggio owed someone a very big favor. I'll keep working on it and call you when I get something."

With a questioning look to Genevieve, Hunter pulled back on the road heading for the hotel.

"Is it just me, Hunter, or did Eduard just confirm our suspicions?"

"He did, and if Eduard can identify him, we might just be looking at this elusive third major player in the scheme."

Back at the hotel they took the elevator to their room on the second floor and Hunter rang Kat's room to tell her they were back. After five rings and no answer, it was apparent no one was there.

"It's close to dinnertime. Let's head down to the dining room; they're probably there."

Five couples were already seated, but Kat and Johannes weren't among them.

"Maybe they went out to eat," offered Genevieve.

"Maybe, but given the threat from Uncle Willie, you'd think they'd stay here. Let's check with the front desk and see if they left a message."

"No sir, there are no messages for you," the desk clerk informed them.

Walking out of hearing by the clerk, Hunter said, "I don't like this. Let's go to their room."

Their room was also on the second floor four doors down from the one Hunter and Genevieve were sharing. They found the DO NOT DISTURB sign was hanging on the door handle. Hunter knocked and they waited. Nothing.

Hunter reached into his pocket and said, "Let's go in and have a look."

"Do you have a key?"

Hunter rolled his eyes.

"Oh, right, how could I forget? Nothing as petty as a locked door is going to stop you, is it?" Genevieve said with a sly smile.

Within ten seconds the door opened and they entered.

"Hello? Kat? Johannes?"

No answer. Something was definitely wrong. The suitcases were gone, and there were no clothes in the closet or drawers or personal toiletries in the bathroom. They were just ready to go down to the desk to see if they'd checked out when Hunter saw something on the wooden floor between the twin beds. He got down on his knees to examine it—blood, still damp.

Then he saw something else, wedged between the nightstand and one of the beds. He reached in and pulled it out: a shoulder patch, like the ones the military wore to indicate their unit. It appeared to have been ripped off, maybe in a struggle. Hunter stood up and unfolded it. He and Genevieve found themselves looking at the emblem of a griffin with a shark's tail.

"What does it mean?" she asked.

"They've been taken. This is the same symbol worn by the two men who tried to kill Kat and me yesterday at the dock. They must have struggled with Kat and Johannes, and one of them ripped off this patch. I don't think it was an accident it was stuffed away between the bed and the nightstand. It was meant to be a message for us."

Genevieve pointed to the empty closet. "They must not be planning to kill them. Otherwise why would they take all their clothes and personal things?"

Right, Hunter thought, nodding at Genevieve. "Could this be linked to Willie Hofmann's threat to Kat and Johannes? Part of what he referred to as the 'endgame?' " He wasn't convinced. "It just doesn't seem possible Willie would have an army of professional fighters to do his bidding. He's an embalmer, for crying out loud. We're definitely missing something here."

TWO HOURS LATER, AT THE STATE POLICE Forensic Crime Lab in Naples, Hunter turned over his crushed cell phone to the technicians to see if they could salvage the images that would serve as evidence of Caravaggio's activities. The young expert assured him that if there were images on the phone, he'd get them.

Hunter called Mariucci to see if he'd learned anything new.

"No, not really," the inspector said. "What I don't understand is how they could have marshaled enough manpower to empty out a house and a lab and bring everything to the middle of the tunnel, and build two walls to hide it in such a short time."

"They must have arranged it ahead of time so if they needed to hide it all, they could do it quickly and efficiently. The question now is where is Irena Rousseau?"

As soon as he'd said it, Hunter realized Mariucci didn't know about Kat and Johannes or any of the other finds he'd made. "Inspector, we need to talk. I've got more information for you."

An hour later in Inspector Mariucci's office, Hunter introduced Genevieve as a colleague and working with him on the case. Mariucci accepted this without even asking her for any credentials, now convinced Hunter was, if not in charge, at least to be believed.

Hunter began the briefing. He told Mariucci about Kat and her father, only pointing out their relationship to Irena Rousseau. He told him nothing about the jewel business or the threat from Willie Hofmann. He also said Kat had been working with him, and both she and her father were now missing. He mentioned the blood they'd found in their hotel room.

Hunter told him he and Kat had barely escaped with their lives when two men had tried to kill them on the dock yesterday. He showed the patch to the inspector. It matched the tattoos on the two men he'd killed.

"Have you ever seen this symbol before?"

Mariucci shook his head no, then remarked. "McCoy, you're a very dangerous man. From what you've told me so far, you've been taken somewhere twice to be killed by two men—two men you instead killed each time. In twenty-three years on the force I've never even been in a gunfight, much less killed a man."

Facing Genevieve, he added, "I'm not sure it's safe for you to even be around him."

"You may be right, Inspector," she replied. "Nevertheless, we've now got three missing persons connected with all of this, and if they're not already dead, they may soon be."

Hunter told him they suspected there might be another player out there as well. "Did your men find anything to indicate someone other than Gallo might have worked closely with Caravaggio?" he asked.

"No, like I told you, Caravaggio's office was empty. The woman at the desk in his outer office did say he sometimes took work home, though."

Not wanting to give Mariucci a direct order, but making sure he got the point, Hunter said, "I'm sure you're ahead of me on this, Inspector, and have probably already ordered it, but we need to search his house."

Recovering quickly, but not without Hunter noticing, Mariucci said, "Of course, we're on top of it. My men will be—are—on their way over there now."

Hunter's cell rang. It was Gautier. "Excuse me, Inspector, it's Interpol. What do you have Eduard?"

"I've got a name for you—Rache. At least I think it's a name. I've found paperwork that shows the transfer of forty-nine percent of Final Care to Nero Caravaggio. Records of the transaction were filed in the Federal Court in Antwerp. Signing for the company was someone by the name of Rache. No first name, just Rache."

"Did you have any luck tracking the person down? Does he live in Antwerp?"

"That's just it. There is no one with that name anywhere in Belgium. It's a dead end. So I followed up by finding out what I could about the company. It was founded in 1987 in Brussels, starting out as the Flanders Funeral Home. From there it grew into a giant. The name Rache first appeared in 2008, when the company began to grow exponentially."

"So do you have any names before Rache, say from 1987 to 2008?"

"Yes, one. The company founder and original owner was one Willem Hofmann."

Chapter 60

WILLEM HOFMANN? UNCLE WILLIE? COULD IT BE?

Hunter sat back, stunned. The same guy who had been blackmailing Johannes and Kat?

"Eduard, listen, this could be very important. I need all the information you can get on this Willem Hofmann: where he was born, where he went to school, where he lives, what relationship he has to this Rache—everything."

"Got it."

"And Eduard?"

"I know. You need it yesterday."

"Right."

Hunter relayed what he'd learned from Eduard Gautier to Inspector Mariucci, who then left to direct his men in the search at Caravaggio's home.

Hunter and Genevieve left police headquarters and ate a late dinner not far from the hotel.

"So," Hunter said. "Someone named Rache gave forty-nine percent of Final Care to Caravaggio in 2009. Willem Hofmann formed the company in 1987. This could be Willie Hofmann, the man who's been blackmailing Johannes and Kat. I've asked him to find out all he can about him. We'll know more later."

Genevieve considered this. "If it *is* him, then he's linked to Final Care, and potentially to Caravaggio and the Institute."

Suddenly Hunter remembered something. "Wait, when I first met Johannes Donckers in his office, I asked him when he'd been hired by Final Care. I think he said 2010 and the top man at Final Care had specifically wanted him. Johannes was working in Antwerp at the time, and the man said he'd double his salary if he came to work for him at Final Care in Brussels."

"So who was the top man?" Genevieve asked. "Willem Hofmann or this Rache?"

"Or," said Hunter just getting an idea, "are they one and the same?"

Genevieve frowned. "But if they're the same man, why the name change?"

"And," Hunter added, "If they're the same man, why would he hire Johannes, the man whom he said is 'dead to him', and double his salary at that?"

JOHANNES DONCKERS HAD NEVER BEEN so afraid in his life. Two heavily armed men had burst into their room in an explosion of noise. Kat was just coming out of the bathroom when the first one in the door slammed her in the face bouncing her head off the wall. Johannes remembered the sound of her head hitting the wall as she slid to the floor in a daze. He'd been sitting in the lounge chair next to the desk and jumped up, rushing to Kat just as the second man slammed him in the chest with the butt of his rifle. Johannes fell back and hit his head on the nightstand, opening a wound that bled on the carpet. He remembered clutching at the man and something came off in his hand. When he saw what it was he stuffed it between the bed and the nightstand.

Kat and Johannes were instructed to get all their gear together and pack their suitcases. Johannes did as he was told but Kat had apparently been hurt badly by the first man, was slow to get up, and even then seemed confused so Johannes pretty much packed for her. The two men marched them down a back staircase and into a van where a third man was waiting to drive them away.

Forty minutes later, handcuffed together, they were hustled onto a motor launch that zoomed away from the pier in Sorrento. The boat was large enough to have a cabin below deck, where Johannes cradled Kat's head in his hand and spoke softly to her. The two men who'd burst into their room sat opposite them in the cabin, unsmiling, with small, evil-looking weapons constantly aimed at them.

"Who are you? What do you want?" Johannes begged. "My daughter's been injured and she needs help.

"She'll get help soon enough."

In spite of his own injuries, Johannes comforted Kat as best he could.

"Sit and be quiet, old man, we've got a ride ahead of us."

After a while, the two gunmen went above and left them alone in the cabin.

"Kat, can you hear me?" Johannes pleaded, hoping for some sign she was recovering. Her nose was bleeding. He hoped it wasn't broken.

Kat tried to open her eyes, and Johannes saw they were flicking back and forth.

"Everything is spinning. I can't focus my eyes," she managed to mumble.

"You're going to be all right, Kat. I don't know how, but you are. I promise. We're going to find Irena."

Kat began to come around and slowly garnered a little strength. "Oh my God, those men. Dad, are you okay?"

"I'm fine, honey, it's you I'm worried about."

"When they come back try to see—when you get a chance—if they have those tattoos on their wrists," Kat said, keeping her voice low. "Do you have any idea where we're going?"

Johannes shook his head. "It's the same guys who attacked us earlier. They didn't say where we're going, just said it would be a long ride."

Kat tried sitting up but saying she felt nauseous, she lay back down and fell asleep instantly.

A few hours later, with Kat still sleeping, Johannes felt the boat beginning to slow down. He couldn't see where they were as the handcuff to Kat's wrist prevented him from standing tall enough to look out the port hole. The sun had set though, and it was getting dark.

Voices from above and the banging of the boat told him they were docking somewhere; if they were docking, why was the boat moving up and down so much? His answer came soon enough when the two gunmen returned below to get them.

Grabbing Johannes by the arm, one of them shouted, "Get her up and come with us now."

Kat, still groggy, followed Johannes to the upper deck, where an incredible sight greeted them.

They were tied up next to one of the largest yachts either of them had ever seen. It was clearly an ocean-going vessel and could have been used as a small cruise ship. They were hurried across a gangplank through an open boarding door. Ascending via an elevator, they were taken to a middle-level deck and escorted to two adjoining cabins with an open connecting door. Their handcuffs were removed and they were locked in.

Kat still seemed groggy but set about checking out the cabin. Each had one bed, a bathroom with shower, a window that was quite large, and a small built-in dresser. Their luggage and personal things had been delivered to the rooms as well.

"Dad," Kat said, her voice stronger, "I've got to clean up and use the bathroom. When I'm done, we need to talk."

He nodded. "I'll do the same."

TWO DECKS UP IN HIS OPULENT CABIN, Constantine Griffin had just received word that Johannes and Kat were on board. When the messenger left, Griffin sat back and smiled. The endgame was unfolding just as he'd planned. Soon everything would be in place.

The *Sea Griffin*, capable of a comfortable twenty-eight knots, would sail for another three days before she reached her destination. During that time, Irena, Johannes, and Kat would be his special guests.

IRENA RESTED IN A WELL-APPOINTED CABIN of her own—equally a prisoner. She was completely confused. Who was this man, who told her he'd arranged her false illness and the rest? Why would he do such a monstrous thing?

If he did arrange it all, as he'd said, why was he putting her up with such opulence now? Her room was a gorgeous suite with a large bed, a sitting room, a balcony with sliding glass doors, and a bookcase filled with several current novels and magazines. Her meals were brought to her, and they were exquisite. A room steward changed her sheets, made her bed, and kept the suite in perfect condition. She even had access to a small exercise room by walking out of her cabin and turning left down the hallway. A locked hallway door prevented her from turning right, so she had no access to the rest of the ship. She was definitely a prisoner, though a pampered one.

The only thing that kept her going was that the man had said he'd arranged for Johannes and Kat to join them at his villa. Then there was the other thing. Although she didn't recognize him, there was *something* familiar about him. She just couldn't put her finger on it. Was it his voice? Was it something else? She just didn't know. She hadn't seen him since their breakfast when she first came aboard. All she knew was she had no choice but to wait it out in hopes she would once again see her beloved Johannes and Kat.

AFTER KAT SHOWERED, she tended to the scalp wound on the back of her father's head with the bandages and first aid cream she always carried in her luggage. She'd suffered a deep cut to her own cheek where the first gunman had slammed her with the back of his fist. He must have had a ring on, because the cut was deep and really needed stiches. She didn't think her nose was broken, but it hurt like hell.

"Here, let me help you with that," Johannes said.

He did the best he could with her kit, cleaning the gash, applying first aid cream, and closing the wound by pulling the cut edges close together with tape.

"It's time to find out what's going on, Dad."

She tried the door again; still locked. Whoever put them in here either knew about her lock-picking skills or was lucky in his choice. There was little chance she could crack this particular lock even if she had her tools.

My tools—my God, are they still there? She searched the secret hiding place in her luggage where she kept them. Relieved, she saw they were. *Well, that's a break,* she thought. *Maybe we'll get out of here yet.* She went to work on the door lock.

Chapter 61

FRESHLY SHOWERED, HUNTER HUSTLED Genevieve back into the rental car for another trip to police headquarters. "Inspector Mariucci said they found something that could be important," he explained. "We need to take a look at it before we search for Kat and Johannes."

At the police station, Inspector Mariucci handed Hunter a lab notebook. At least it looked like all the lab notebooks he'd ever used: stiff cardboard cover, spiral bound, about eight-by-ten, maybe a half-inch thick.

"What am I looking for?" he asked, hoping Mariucci actually had something and didn't just want him to decipher scientific notes.

"This is one of twenty-five notebooks Dr. Caravaggio kept in a safe at his house. They contain pretty much all the work he did in the past three years at the Institute."

Right after he stopped working with Phillippi.

He noticed this was number four in the series of twenty-five notebooks. Leafing through it, he saw it contained speculations about the possibility of transferring neuro-muscular skills from one person to another—exactly what they'd eventually done with Irena Rousseau.

The inspector tapped the book, still in Hunter's hands. "Turn to page seventeen, McCoy, and tell me what you make of it."

Confused, Hunter did and read out loud:

Neuroscience Meeting, San Diego,
California
2009

Following my presentation to the
plenary session today, a most extraordinary
thing happened. A man—not a scientist—
came up to me and said he'd like to fund my
research on skill transfer. He wanted to
discuss it with me over dinner. I asked him
why, and he said he'd explain it this
evening. I'd only mentioned this potential
research at the end of my talk, and even then
only as a way to get the group thinking of
future possibilities. The man's name was
Rache. He gave no first name. I was
somewhat intrigued, so I said I'd meet him.

"How does this help us?" Hunter asked.

Enjoying this, the inspector told Hunter to scan page thirty-two. Hunter did and quickly saw what Mariucci was getting at. He read aloud:

Rache. The man is pure evil. I have no
recourse to avoid his blackmail efforts,
none. I've come so far, done so much good. I
can't lose it all. I won't. What I don't
understand is his insistence on using Irena
Rousseau. There are other candidates just
as good, maybe even better. Why her? If
only I could turn the clock back, refuse his
offer of forty-nine percent of Final Care.
God help me, what have I done?

Hunter, Genevieve, and the inspector all looked at each other. Hunter said it first. "There's our third man, Rache, the man whose name started appearing as the head of Final Care in 2008, replacing the founder, Willem Hofmann.

"I've already got Interpol checking on Rache and Hofmann. This is a good find, Inspector. It clearly links Rache to the experiments and kidnapping of Irena Rousseau. Good work."

Inspector Mariucci beamed, clearly enjoying the praise. "Always happy to cooperate with Interpol."

Yeah, right.

Hunter perused the other lab books and one caught his eye. "Inspector, I'd like to take this one with me temporarily; you'll get it back."

"Why? What's in it?"

"Just maybe the answer to another mystery."

BACK IN THE CAR, GENEVIEVE TURNED to Hunter. "I noticed you didn't tell Mariucci about the possibility that Willem Hofmann and Willie Hofmann are the same man. In fact you didn't tell the inspector about Willie Hofmann at all, or about his blackmail scheme or the jewel thefts."

Hunter nodded. "The inspector is a good man and maybe even a good cop, but I don't trust him with that information. He might contact the German authorities on his own out of a sense of duty. He might feel obligated to tell the authorities about the jewel heists throughout the continent. I'd rather get the Donckers family back first and deal with the robberies and smuggling later."

Hunter called Gautier and put the phone on speaker mode so Genevieve could hear.

"We've learned a few things on this end, Eduard. Rache was blackmailing Caravaggio into carrying out his wishes, wishes that included experimenting on Irena Rousseau. We need to find out what the connection is between Willem Hofmann and Rache, and if he and Willie Hofmann are the same person. Are you making any progress?"

"You know, Hunter, I don't think you have a very realistic view of my job. I do have other duties besides tracking things down for you."

Before Hunter could respond Eduard went on, "However, since your stuff is generally more interesting than my usual stuff, I'm happy to comply. That and the fact I'm truly amazing at my job," he said with a chuckle.

Relieved, Hunter waited.

"All right, here's what I have so far. I was almost ready to call you. The Willem Hofmann who founded Final Care in 1987 is most definitely Willie Hofmann who attended mortuary school with Johannes Donckers in Brussels. After graduation, Johannes moved to Antwerp while Willie stayed in Brussels and started Flanders Funeral Home. He was a good business manager, and when he got his first order from the US consulate in Brussels, he began to expand. Through careful planning and timely purchases, his business grew rapidly throughout the continent and beyond. He renamed it Final Care in 1992. He invested his profits carefully and successfully and soon became one of the wealthiest men in Europe.

"In 2008, he changed the name of the CEO of Final Care from Willem Hofmann to Rache. I believe this was just a pseudonym for Hofmann. Then, in 2009, he gave forty-nine percent of his interest in Final Care to Dr. Nero Caravaggio of Sorrento. Willem then moved to Miami, Florida and went to work for a small funeral home called Benson's as a part-time embalmer."

Hunter interrupted at this point. "So we have one of the richest men in Europe give away almost half of a highly successful business and take a job as an embalmer for a small American funeral home? What's that all about?"

"It gets even stranger. In 2010, Willie—using the name Rache—offers a job with Final Care in Brussels to his cousin, Johannes Donckers, who accepts and moves from Antwerp to Brussels. A little later, using the name Johannes would surely recognize—Willie Hofmann—Willie pleads with Johannes to recommend him for an embalming job with Final Care. He tells Johannes he's just learned that Final Care is opening a facility at the Miami International Airport. This is the first time Johannes has heard from his cousin since they were in school together in Brussels."

"And," Hunter added, "Willie would know about this new facility, since he actually owns the company, only Johannes doesn't know that."

"Correct, and Johannes does exactly what he asks and recommends his cousin for the job. So now, one of the richest men in Europe is working part-time for a small funeral home in Miami and doing part-time work as an embalmer for a company he actually owns. Only his cousin thinks Willie is barely getting by and he—Johannes—has done him an enormous favor by getting him the job."

After ending the call with Eduard, Hunter exhaled and Genevieve said "Wow." But before they could even begin to discuss what they'd just learned, Hunter's phone rang. It was Eduard again.

"Hunter, this just came in. Willie Hofmann is dead. Two days ago, he was found dead in a powerboat fire offshore near Miami. Apparently he was cooking up some crystal meth in his boat when it exploded. The body was burned beyond recognition, but they verified it was him by a watch, a ring, and a burned wallet."

"Eduard?"

"Yeah?"

"Does this smell as fishy to you as it does to me, no pun intended?"

"You're the detective, but I agree. Who knows whose body that really was."

"Exactly. I think we've heard the last of Willie Hofmann as a player but his alter identity, Rache, is still going strong."

"Well, that's the other info that just came through."

"There's more?" Hunter mirrored Genevieve's surprised expression.

"Afraid so. As of yesterday, Final Care was sold to an international holding company called EuroMeld that had been in negotiations with Rache at Final Care for six months. Yesterday the deal was completed and the money was transferred to an offshore account in the Cayman Islands. The name Rache seems to have disappeared off the radar simultaneously. We only have one small clue, and it may be nothing."

Hunter was getting a bad feeling about this. "What is it?"

"Well," Eduard continued, "I don't know if it means anything, but the transfer order was signed 'Griffin.'"

After ending the call, Hunter continued driving, pondering what this information meant. Then he turned to Genevieve. "I think it's no coincidence this dead Willie Hofmann met his fate just one day after Uncle Willie Hofmann threatened Kat and told her the endgame had begun. So let's see what we know about the endgame."

Genevieve and Hunter alternated giving answers.

"One, Caravaggio and Gallo die in a car accident, probably murdered," Hunter began.

"Two, Caravaggio's lab and the house where Irena was kept are cleaned out and the holdings stored in the walled-off train tunnel."

"Three, we encounter armed men with Griffin tattoos."

"Four, Irena, Kat, and Johannes all disappear with a clue linking the abductors to Griffin."

"Five, Willie Hofmann conveniently disappears in a very suspicious boat explosion off Miami."

"Six, Rache sells Final Care to EuroMeld."

"Seven, Rache disappears as an entity after the sale."

"Eight, the money is transferred to an offshore account in the Cayman Islands by 'Griffin.'"

Unable to come up with anything else, Hunter said what they'd both been thinking. "So who or what the hell is Griffin, and where are Irena, Kat, and Johannes?"

Chapter 62

IT WAS OBVIOUS TO THOSE ABOARD the *Sea Griffin* that she'd left the Mediterranean and was now in the open Atlantic. They'd sailed past the Pillars of Hercules, the phrase applied in antiquity to the promontories that flank the entrance to the Strait of Gibraltar. Powering through the waves at twenty-eight knots, the ride was nevertheless smooth due to the calming effect of powerful computerized stabilizers.

Constantine Griffin stood on the bridge enjoying the ride. All he'd worked for and planned for over the years was coming to fruition now that all the players were in place for the endgame. He marveled that — barring just a few glitches—all had gone according to plan.

How ironic Johannes had taken the bait and condescended to help him get a job as a part-time embalmer with his own creation, Final Care. The bastard no doubt thought he was doing charity work for his lazy cousin. How Johannes must have regretted that when a few months later he'd told him he and his disgusting daughter had to start stealing and smuggling jewels or he'd turn him in to the German authorities and Irena's career would be ruined.

And then there was Nero Caravaggio. Against all odds, the man had actually been able to do what he'd claimed was theoretically possible, transferring motor skills from one person to another. The combination of funding his research and giving him a large piece of Final Care, coupled with the threat of exposing his medical internship lapses in moral judgment, was all it had taken to get the man to do his bidding.

In fairness, he had to admit to himself that he might not have insisted on using Irena for his experiments had she not gone on that telethon to support a center for abused women. She'd told those lies about him when the interviewer asked if she'd had personal experience with criminally disturbed individuals. Granted, she didn't name him personally, but he knew the filth she was spouting referred to him.

She had no idea how much he'd loved her, a love ultimately turned into an unbearable seething hatred. Now, she, and his miserable cousin, and their spawn would all pay for what they'd done to him.

He was a man of immense wealth, but no real happiness. Like so many people he hadn't actually believed it was possible to be wealthy and unhappy at the same time. In fact it was. The wealthier he got, the more obsessed and unhappy he'd become.

Now that was all about to change. Now they were in the endgame and retribution was at hand.

IRENA ROUSSEAU WAS BECOMING excessively agitated. What was she doing here? She asked the steward where they were going and all he'd tell her was that Mr. Griffin would clear up everything for her when they reached port. What port? She'd pleaded. He only smiled and said she would have to wait for Mr. Griffin.

Who was this man, and why had he done this to her? What had she ever done to him? She couldn't get over the sense there was something about him that was familiar even though she knew she'd never seen him before. What was it? His face, his attitude, his voice? Then suddenly, out of nowhere, she knew. Without a shadow of a doubt, she knew.

It was his voice. Once she put the voice together with a name, all doubt was erased—Willie—it was Willie Hofmann.

He must have had plastic surgery, because she would have recognized him even after all these years. But the voice, you can't change the voice. She had no doubt—it was Willie.

But surely he'd gotten over her after all this time, hadn't he? What sane person would keep her a prisoner and use her for medical experiments? As soon as she thought it she had her answer. He wasn't sane.

That had to be it. Wasn't that why she'd left him in the first place? He had something psychologically wrong in the head. Something evil. He'd scared her right into Johannes's arms.

Johannes. Suddenly, with a cold snap of fear, she remembered Johannes—and Kat. Was he really going to bring them to her? Could he do that? Of course he could. Look what he'd done to her. *Oh my God,* she thought, *what will he do to them?* A great sob took away her breath as she thought of all of them in the hands of this madman.

Could they already be aboard the ship? Sure, she thought, they must be. That's why he'd said he'd already arranged for them to meet her. She had to find them.

Up to this point she hadn't really tried to break out of her small area—the suite and the hallway, including the workout facility. Was there a way? If Johannes and Kat were aboard, she had to find them and warn them that Willie Hofmann was behind all this, and the man was deranged and dangerous.

She'd thoroughly searched her suite. There was no way out except through the single door that led out into the short hallway. She stepped out there now and saw what she'd seen before. She could only go left toward the workout room, as the door to the hallway on the right was locked.

She walked down the hallway, feeling the walls on both sides. There were no other doorways.

In the workout room she began a meticulous examination of the walls and ceiling. There were no windows so she assumed it was an inner room of some kind. Other than a few air ducts, which were clearly too small for her even if she could reach them, there appeared to be no way to exit the room other than back through the door. Frustrated, she sat on a bench and began to cry silently.

KAT PACED HER STATEROOM, FRUSTRATED with her efforts to break out. She and Johannes didn't know if McCoy, Genevieve, and the police had been able to free her mother from the house because the armed men who brought them aboard the boat had stormed into their hotel room about the same time that should have been happening.

She could only hope Irena was finally safe and out of Caravaggio's hands. She and Johannes continued to search for a way to escape, but so far they'd found no chinks in the armor that was their prison on board.

BACK AT THE HOTEL IN SORRENTO, Hunter and Genevieve set to work. All they had to go on was the name Griffin. Had Willie gone from Hofmann, to Rache, to Griffin? It seemed reasonable, since Griffin was the name on the paperwork transferring the funds from the Final Care sale to the bank in the Cayman Islands.

"We're going to need some computer searching," said Genevieve. "Give the name Griffin to your man at Interpol and see what he can come up with."

Hunter nodded. "I've already done it. I'm going to have Mariucci try as well."

DOWN IN THE HOTEL'S COMPUTER ROOM, Genevieve took one computer while Hunter, using his own laptop, began to search the name Griffin. "A griffin is a mythical beast with the body, tail, and back legs of a lion and the head and wings of an eagle, with an eagle's talons as front feet," Genevieve offered after a minute.

"It's used on a lot of coats of arms," was Hunter's initial salvo. Then he continued, "Wait a minute, here's a page with pictures of twenty or so griffins. They're all a little different, depending on how the artist draws them."

Genevieve jumped in. "Its use in heraldry is to signify courage and strength. Also, the erect ears that are often seen signify intelligence."

They continued searching for another hour and were finally interrupted by a phone call on Hunter's new cell. It was Eduard.

"I've got something interesting here, Hunter. Rache was the owner of the house behind the Institute in Sorrento where Irena was kept. I can't find any record of any other house he owns or ever owned. But I did find this, which might be useful. Last year he negotiated for and purchased a mega-yacht from a dealer in Barcelona. Castile Marine in Barcelona refitted the yacht to meet the specifications of the new owner. I've been unable to get a list of those specifications, but you might be interested in the name of the yacht."

"And what would that be?" asked Hunter.

"The *Sea Griffin*. I'm emailing you a picture of her now."

"Great work, Eduard. This could be big."

A few minutes later the email came through. When they looked at the yacht's name and logo on the stern they knew this was it. The griffin depicted was the same seen on the wrists of the men and on the patch they'd found in Kat's room—a Griffin with the tail of a shark.

Gathering up his laptop, Hunter said to Genevieve, "Come on, we're going over to the port authority in Naples. If the yacht's in the area they should be able to locate it."

The drive to Naples seemed to take forever, even though it was only twenty-five minutes. They drove to the dock, found the port authority building, and went to the office of the director. The director, a large man in his sixties, looked as if he'd made his way to the top spot the hard way, maybe starting out as a dockworker. His grip was strong when Hunter shook it.

"Director, I'm Agent Hunter McCoy, with Interpol. I'm investigating a kidnapping, and this is my assistant, Genevieve Swift." He showed the director his credentials.

"What can I do for you, Agent McCoy?"

"We have reason to believe there may be three kidnap victims on board a mega-yacht called the *Sea Griffin*. We don't know where this yacht currently is but hoped you might be able to help us."

"I see. Hanna?" The director called his receptionist into the office. "See that Agent McCoy and Ms. Swift are comfortable while I look up some things for them."

While they waited Genevieve asked Hunter, "Can he really find an individual yacht anywhere in the world?"

"I don't know. Maybe they have tracking devices like cell phones so they can locate it if you lose it."

Genevieve grew pensive. "If Willie Hofmann is behind all of this, and he's really Rache, or Griffin, or whoever, what do you think he has planned? I mean, if he has them aboard his yacht, what is he going to do with them?"

"I've been thinking about that, too. If he just wanted them dead, they'd be dead by now. He'd have made that happen. I think he has something else in mind, something bad, and we've got to stop him before he does it."

The receptionist brought them coffees and they waited.

Forty-five minutes later, the director came back in and took his seat behind his desk. "I believe I have what you're looking for. The *Sea Griffin*, a ninety-two-meter yacht, carrying a Cayman Island registry and currently owned by Constantine Griffin, is currently traveling at approximately twenty-five knots in the Atlantic west of Gibraltar, presumably en route to Madeira.

"I say presumably as that is its most frequent port. The *Sea Griffin* is usually docked in its own private slip in the marina at Funchal, the capital. If that's her destination, she should make port in another nineteen hours, about seven a.m. local time tomorrow."

BACK IN THE CAR HUNTER PHONED EDUARD. "Eduard, get me everything you can on a Constantine Griffin. He's the current owner of the *Sea Griffin*. See if he owns property in Madeira, the Portuguese island in the Atlantic. He is probably scheduled to dock at Funchal about seven a.m. tomorrow. I want Interpol to intercept him there. Can you transfer me to Director Pelletier now?"

Hunter told the director everything they'd learned about Caravaggio, Willie Hofmann, Rache, Final Care and its sale to EuroMeld, Constantine Griffin, the tracking down of the *Sea Griffin*, and the abduction of Irena, Kat, and Johannes.

"Director, I have a request. I'd like you to alert the local Portuguese authorities so we can board the yacht when she docks. If I'm right, she'll be heavily guarded with armed men willing to fight. We'll need all the firepower they can muster to keep things under control."

"Keep your line open; I'll call you back."

Three hours later the plan was in place.

Chapter 63

BOTH COMMERCIALLY SCHEDULED FLIGHTS from Naples to Funchal, Madeira involved two stops and would have taken twelve hours. There were no more flights until the next morning. They'd be too late, so that was out. Instead Hunter convinced Interpol to arrange for a private jet to fly them there in three hours.

During the three-hour flight they finally had a chance to briefly relax. Genevieve had been waiting to ask Hunter something she'd meant to do earlier but never had a chance. "That notebook of Caravaggio's, the one Inspector Mariucci found, the one you took with you. What was that all about?"

"Ah, the notebook. Yes, it was very interesting."

"What do you mean?"

"Remember when I told you how Caravaggio and Gallo accomplished their skill transfer technique—what they called Source Reversal Enhancement? In Irena's case, for example, it involved simultaneous piano-playing between her and Pompa while wearing electrodes that synched their brain activity."

"Yes."

"Well, something's always bothered me about that. It just didn't seem as if the brainwave synchronizing and the addition of Nero's nerve growth factor cocktail would be enough to accomplish the amazing results he got. I thought there had to be something else."

"And was there?"

"Yes, and he described it in the notebook."

"So what was it? Or is the science too complicated for me?"

"Not really. I'll give you a condensed version. I think we'll find Irena had a small sample of glial cells removed from the surface of the motor cortex of her brain. She probably didn't even know they'd done it. Glial cells are brain cells that don't conduct impulses. Caravaggio cultured these cells to grow a large population of them and then separated out a subpopulation called radial glial cells."

"What do they do?"

"When our brains are first developing, these radial glial cells generate new neurons and direct them to the proper locations to form synapses with other neurons. Once this is done, these cells become relatively inactive but still retain the memory and the potential for doing it again if called on."

"So what did he do with these cells?"

"He removed the surface antigens from them so they wouldn't trigger an immune response by the recipient— First Kris Hanson, and most recently, Tony Pompa. Then he added them to his original *Enhancement* cocktail. He called this new version *Enhancement II*. The original one didn't produce much change with the source reversal technique but *Enhancement II* was almost a miracle."

"I get it. So when the SRE was going on and they were squirting this out of the tubes onto Pompa's brain, these cells fired up and started directing new connections in his piano-playing neurons."

"Pretty much, yeah. Oh, and he got the idea when he heard a tour guide at the Pompeii ruins describe how a slave boy running from the eruption tripped and spilled a quiver of arrows. One of them lodged upright on the ground and his master, an expert archer, tripped and fell on it, killing him instantly as it pierced his skull. The master's brother immediately pulled out the arrow and drove it into the slave boy's skull in exactly the same location. But slave boy didn't die; his sister rescued him and they escaped.

"Later, the boy recovered and not only lost his earlier clumsiness, but became an expert archer. Caravaggio correctly determined something had been transferred via the arrowhead from the skilled archer to the slave boy."

"And that something was a pack of these cool glial cells," Genevieve, said.

"Right. Caravaggio even gave the phenomenon a name in his notes. He called it the 'Pompeii Effect.'"

WHEN THEY ARRIVED AT THE AIRPORT in Funchal, it was after 6:00 p.m. local time and Hunter was surprised to be picked up personally by the Judicial Police commander, a "no-nonsense" professional named Fidalgo who drove them directly to police headquarters.

Already present and immediately introduced to Hunter were the commanders of the Public Security Police, the Portuguese Republican National Guard and its Coastal Control Unit, and the Foreign and Border Service. All had been briefed and were ready to cooperate. Most amazing of all, they seemed to accept that Hunter was in charge. This was certainly not what he'd expected, thinking they'd be hesitant to take orders from an outsider.

Genevieve stayed in the background while Hunter took the floor. "Gentlemen, we're going to need all of you to pull this off, and surprise is going to be a large part of it. As you know, we believe three kidnap victims are on board the *Sea Griffin*, due to dock in..." Hunter looked at his watch, "about ten hours. Commander Garcia, I'd like the Coastal Control Unit to surround the yacht to see no one gets on or off via the water. I'll go on board with the Security Police. Commander Fidalgo, do you have the search warrant yet?"

"Yes, we secured it from the judge two hours ago. We have clear and unquestioned authority to board and search the vessel. No one will be allowed to board or disembark without my permission."

"Excellent."

Then addressing Commander Emilio Lima, the head of the Foreign and Border Service, Hunter asked, "Will your men be able to complete a thorough search of the vessel when called on?"

"Yes, sir. My men are expert at finding things on vessels that people try hard to hide. If they're on board, don't worry, we'll find them."

Hunter spent the next hour-and-a-half going over the detailed plans for each unit. He was satisfied the job of boarding and searching would be done thoroughly and professionally.

Later, they checked into the Albergaria Catedral four-star hotel overlooking the harbor, ate a late dinner and retired to their room.

THE NEXT MORNING AT 6:15, WITH THE SUN just beginning to light the marina, the *Sea Griffin* majestically entered the marina at Funchal and proceeded to its familiar dock space. Commander Fidalgo, along with Hunter and Commander Lima of the Foreign and Border Police and ten armed officers, appeared on the dock. At the same time the National Guard moved six boats into the marina and had them take up positions around the vessel.

Once the *Sea Griffin* was secured and a gangplank lowered, Commander Fidalgo and Hunter walked across and showed their credentials to the captain, who had seen the boarding party from his vista on the bridge as they tied up.

"Sir," Commander Fidalgo began, "we have a warrant to search this ship completely for the possible presence of three individuals who may be on board against their will. You are instructed to offer my men any assistance they may need, and neither you nor your crew may interfere in any way. Do you understand?"

The *Sea Griffin's* Captain nodded his head. "I assure you, sir, I have no idea what this is about. We certainly have no one onboard who isn't here by choice. But as you have a warrant, you are free to conduct your search. I'll inform the crew to cooperate."

Hunter addressed the captain. "While the commander's men are doing their search, I'd like you to take me to the owner, Mr. Constantine Griffin."

"That's quite impossible, sir."

"I'm afraid you have no choice in the matter."

"Sir, when I say it's impossible, I mean exactly that. He is not on board for this trip, just myself and my crew."

Hunter was stunned. He hadn't considered this possibility. If Willie really wasn't on board, where were Irena, Kat, and Johannes? Had he made a colossal miscalculation?

"Take me to his quarters, then."

"Certainly, sir. Follow me."

While the Foreign and Border Police began their detailed search of the vessel and Commander Fidalgo's men saw to it no one left the yacht, Hunter followed the *Sea Griffin's* captain.

The yacht was gorgeous. He'd never been on one this large and well appointed. Everything gleamed from paint and polish. The yacht had four full decks, and they'd come aboard on the second. Taking an elevator up one deck, he was escorted to the most lavish stateroom he'd ever seen on any ship anywhere. It pretty much occupied the back third of the entire deck. It had its own master bedroom and bath, as well as a large living room that opened out through floor-to-ceiling glass doors onto its own outside deck with a full complement of furniture.

Hunter noted everything was in mint condition, as if it were waiting for the owner. It didn't appear any of it was currently being used. The thought depressed him. Maybe the man really wasn't on board.

"Captain, where is Mr. Griffin now?"

"I really can't say, sir. He comes and goes as he pleases and contacts me only when he needs the *Sea Griffin*."

"Where does he live? He must have a home somewhere," said Hunter. "Surely you know."

"Oddly enough, I don't. He does stay on Madeira sometimes and contacts me to pick him up here."

"Are you picking him up this time?"

"No, I was just told to bring the *Sea Griffin* here and await further orders."

"You have no idea where he is?"

"That's correct, sir."

Something's going on here.

"How does he contact you, by phone?"

"No, by encrypted email."

"Doesn't that strike you as odd? Why all the secrecy?"

"Agent—McCoy is it?"

"Yes."

"I've captained yachts for several immensely wealthy owners over the years. I've never found one yet who isn't a little odd in some way. Yet one thing they all have in common is a concern for strict secrecy concerning their current location and an equal concern about secure communications. I've learned to live with it."

"So even if you did know his current location, you wouldn't tell me, would you?"

The captain shrugged and produced a weak, confirming smile.

"You do know that this is a criminal investigation and withholding evidence is a crime."

"I don't know where he is, sir."

Frustrated, Hunter began his own thorough search of Griffin's quarters, knowing Commander Lima's men would do an even better job. After opening every drawer and examining everything that might leave a clue as to the man who used these quarters, he came up with nothing.

Two hours later the three commanders and Hunter met on the dock beside the *Sea Griffin*. They'd found nothing and no one had left the yacht. Clearly, Griffin, Irena, Kat, and Johannes weren't on board, nor did it appear they ever had been. Genevieve, who had been waiting at dockside, joined the group as each commander gave his report.

When they were finished and obviously dejected, Hunter spoke up. "Gentlemen? I have an idea. There might just be a simple explanation for finding nothing on board. Try this on for size. Suppose it happened just the way we originally thought: Griffin was on board, as well as Irena, Kat, and Johannes. Then, some distance offshore, probably in the dark, a boat from Funchal or somewhere along the coast goes out to meet the *Sea Griffin*. Let's say the four of them get on board this tender, along with a few of Griffin's bully boys, and they're taken ashore somewhere. Meanwhile on board, the captain and the rest of the crew remove all traces of their presence. The rooms are made up and any materials used to keep the three prisoners locked up are removed and thrown overboard."

No one spoke for almost a minute, but Hunter could almost hear the gears grinding in each of their heads. Finally, Commander Garcia of the Republican National Guard punched in a number on his cell phone. "Milo, check the radar records for last night within ten miles of Funchal Marina. Play it back, identify the *Sea Griffin*, and tell me if she was approached by any vessel, any vessel at all."

Milo was back within minutes. "Sir, an unidentified vessel approached and came alongside the *Sea Griffin* at 2:56 a.m. about twelve miles out. She was alongside approximately twenty minutes and then pulled away. She came ashore at Santa Cruz, about five kilometers up the coast from the Funchal Marina."

Chapter 64

THE COMMANDERS WERE FOLLOWING EVERY lead trying to find the boat that had rendezvoused with the *Sea Griffin*, convinced if they found it they'd find Griffin and the other three. Hunter had a different plan. He had no doubt that Griffin, Rache, or Hofmann, or whatever he called himself, had a property on Madeira. He doubted the slip at the marina was his only nest.

He'd asked the local authorities to find this out and they'd come up with nothing. Either Willie was using yet another name or he was not a property owner. In any case, they were now focusing all their attention on locating the boat.

"Eduard, I have yet another search request," Hunter told his friend at Interpol.

"Really? How novel."

"Sarcasm becomes you."

"I know, but there you are. So what is it this time?"

Hunter took the time to tell him everything so he'd know how his past information had been helpful and gotten them this far. Now he needed a little more.

"The local authorities can't find any property on the island in the name of Hofmann, Rache, or Griffin, but I'm convinced he's taken them somewhere on the island. It's all part of his endgame, and it culminates here on Madeira. He must have a place. I need you to work your magic and find it—soon, before he hurts them."

As he always did, Eduard shifted from joking to professional. "All right, I have a few ideas—some things that came to me when I was searching earlier. I'll check them out and get back to you."

With nothing they could do but wait, Hunter and Genevieve realized they hadn't had breakfast and found a restaurant along the waterfront.

"He's probably got a new name," Hunter said. "It would be in character; he always uses new names to hide his tracks."

"I've been thinking about that," said Genevieve. "No doubt Willie Hofmann is his true and original name, but how did he choose the others—like Rache, for instance? What kind of a name is that?" Taking out her smart phone she started tapping away, ignoring Hunter while he devoured his omelet.

"I Googled *Rache* to see if it has any special meaning. According to Wikipedia, it can refer to an obsolete name for a type of hunting dog used in Britain in the Middle Ages."

Hunter nodded. "That's good; Hofmann's certainly been a hunting dog."

Genevieve went back to her search.

"Now here's something. One of the hits for *Rache* refers to the translation of *rache* in German and guess what? *Rache* is a German word for revenge or vengeance."

"Hey, now that's perfect. Willie Hofmann is German, after all, and would know the meaning."

"Right. So he turns the German word into a proper name that expresses his true intent; revenge and vengeance."

Putting his fork down, Hunter asked Genevieve. "Look up griffin and see if it's ever been used as a symbol for revenge or vengeance."

Genevieve put her phone down on the table. "I know the answer to that one. Remember, medieval history is my field. The griffin usually symbolizes strength and courage. They're thought to combine the speed, ability to fly, and eyesight of an eagle, with the strength and courage of a lion. But not many know about its link to revenge. In Roman art, griffins are often seen pulling the chariot of Nemesis, the goddess of justice and revenge.

"You're on to something here, Gen. I've got to call Eduard back and have him be on the lookout for any name that might signify revenge or vengeance." As he started to do this Genevieve put her hand on his arm and he looked up questioningly.

"Gen?" she said. "You've never called me Gen before."

"Did I?"

"Yes, you did." She smiled with delight. "How about this. I won't call you 'Hunt' and you don't call me 'Gen'?"

Much to the surprise of an elderly couple at an adjacent table, they kissed on it.

Just as Hunter was getting ready to call Eduard, Eduard beat him to it.

"I might have something. As I went back over the transactions of Rache giving forty-nine percent of Final Care to Nero Caravaggio, I discovered he owned the house behind the Institute where Irena had been kept."

"I remember," Hunter acknowledged.

"I came across some other stuff that at the time didn't seem to have any bearing on your case, but maybe it does. As I told you earlier, he was a very wealthy man whose wealth went far beyond the earnings of Final Care alone. He essentially became a venture capitalist who made remarkably wise investments in many ventures throughout the continent, and these became the real source of his incredible wealth.

"One of these was a land holding company called Fim de Jogo Enterprises, which bought and sold properties in the Iberian Peninsula, some in Spain but mostly in Portugal. I know Madeira is Portuguese, so I checked to seen if any of the holdings were on the island—and I found one. I can give you an address, are you ready?"

"Shoot"

Hunter wrote it down, threw some bills on the table, and they raced to the car and plugged the address into the GPS system. The route took them East of Funchal for six kilometers and then headed up into the mountainous central area of the island. They passed through the Madeira Tunnel and were soon on the north side of the island with a spectacular view of the North Atlantic Ocean.

The area they emerged into was not heavily populated. The GPS eventually took them to a side road off the highway and no sooner had they exited than they came upon a guard station manned by a single sentry. A paved turnaround had been built next to the guard station, no doubt for the occasional not-welcome driver who inadvertently happened to get this far.

The sentry approached as Hunter rolled down the driver's side window.

"Can I help you, sir?"

"I'm not sure," Hunter said, wondering what to tell him. "We're looking for a biology camp, for our son. We were told it was in this area. Do you have any idea where it might be?"

"A biology camp? No, sir, there's nothing like that around here that I know of."

Hunter decided to take a chance. "So what have we stumbled on here?"

"This is private property, sir."

"Really? Who owns it?"

In a considerably less friendly tone, the sentry said, "I'm not at liberty to say. Now, if you'll just turn around, you'll find your way back to the highway."

Obviously dismissed, they did just that. Once back on the highway, Genevieve told Hunter to find a place to stop. He did at a petrol station three miles further on.

"That's it, Hunter. That is definitely the place."

"I agree. They're in there."

"No, I mean I *know* that's the place. Eduard said Fim de Jogo Enterprises own the property. I just looked up *Fim de Jogo.* Guess what it means in Portuguese?"

"What?"

"It means Endgame."

Chapter 65

AT FUNCHAL POLICE HEADQUARTERS, Hunter addressed the three commanders again and laid out all he and Genevieve had been able to learn about the property in the hills. He stressed how Interpol had led them to the guarded property and he believed the Donckers family was being held there. For the next hour they worked on a joint plan to get a legal warrant and then enter the property.

Commander Fidalgo convinced a judge they had probable cause and he granted the warrant. He and four of his best men would accompany Hunter and Genevieve to the front gate to present it.

In addition Commander Lima and Commander Talbot would be present. Each of these commanders would be accompanied by two of their best men.

Meanwhile twenty heavily armed Portuguese National Guardsmen would move in and encircle the entire property. These men would approach through the woods and hold-in-place. They would stay in constant radio contact with Commander Talbot and could move in instantly at his command if needed.

The contingent of thirteen arrived at the gate in six public security police cars and stopped at the guardhouse, turning on their flashing-red roof-lights. The lone sentry hesitated for a moment and then stepped up to the lead car with Commander Fidalgo, Hunter, Genevieve, and one of his four men.

Commander Fidalgo rolled down his window, showed his credentials, and said, "I am Commander Fidalgo of the Public Security Police. I have a duly authorized warrant to gain immediate access to and conduct a thorough search of the premises. You will let us in immediately and inform Mr. Constantine Griffin I wish to interview him as well."

This news had an obvious disquieting effect on the sentry. "I—will—ah—have to see if that is—all right with—Mr. Griffin," the man finally stammered out.

"You will do no such thing. You will open this gate immediately to my men and tell—not ask—Mr. Griffin to meet us right away. Is that clear, or do you wish to be arrested right now for interfering with a police operation?"

The man reluctantly returned to the guardhouse, pushed a button, and the gate swung open. The five cars quickly moved through and pulled up to the front of a huge four-story stone-and-brick mansion. All thirteen of them stepped out and followed Fidalgo to the huge double front door.

Commander Fidalgo knocked and waited. When the door opened a tall thin man appeared surprised by the sight of twelve serious-looking men and one woman, eleven of them in uniform. "May I help you?" he asked.

"I'm Commander Fidalgo of the Public Security Police. I have a warrant to search these premises. If you're not Constantine Griffin, would you ask him to come to the door?"

"Please wait here, Commander. I'll inform him." The man disappeared into the house.

Several minutes later, Constantine Griffin appeared at the door. Hunter was surprised to see a man who appeared normal in every way—medium height and weight, hair neatly combed to one side, and wearing a well-tailored business suit. He hadn't known what to expect but this image didn't fit the master manipulator, blackmailer, and killer he knew him to be.

In a calm voice, Griffin asked, "What's this about, Commander?"

"Constantine Griffin, I present you with this warrant to search this house and property." He handed the warrant to Griffin. "You may be present but you are not to interfere with my men in any way."

"Search for what? I do not understand. What are you looking for?"

"We have reason to believe you have brought three hostages into Madeira and are keeping them here against their will."

"Hostages? What are you talking about? There's no one here but myself and my staff."

"Mr. Griffin, this is Commander Lima of the Foreign and Border Police, Commander Talbot of the Portuguese National Guard, and Agent Hunter McCoy of Interpol. Along with me they are directing this operation and you will cooperate fully with them."

Griffin looked at each man as he was introduced but continued to stare at Hunter for a full thirty seconds after he was introduced. Finally, unsmiling, he said, indicating Genevieve, "and who is this?"

"This is Genevieve Swift, who is assisting us."

As he had with Hunter he stared coldly at Genevieve. Finally he said, "Go ahead and search. I have nothing to hide."

"We have some questions for you, Mr. Griffin."

"Let's go to my study. We can talk there."

They followed him into the house.

While the men began their search, Commander Fidalgo, Hunter, and Genevieve followed Griffin to a large room off the hallway that obviously served as both study and library. Both Hunter and Genevieve noted three paintings similar to those on the wall in Nero Caravaggio's office, in that they appeared to be by the painter Caravaggio though not the same images they'd seen at the Institute.

Hunter began. "Mr. Griffin—or should I say Mr. Rache, or even Willie Hofmann? Which do you prefer?"

"Currently I'm Constantine Griffin. As you obviously know, I was born Willem Hofmann and later took the name Rache, and most recently Griffin. Perhaps now you can tell me what this is all about."

"Willie," Hunter said deliberately, "You blackmailed Nero Caravaggio into doing your bidding at the Neurological Institute in Sorrento. A bidding that included holding Irena Rousseau captive while using her for illegal medical experimentation."

"Wait, who did you say?" Hofmann asked with un-feigned surprise in his voice. "Irena Rousseau?" He gasped as if genuinely confused. "Irena Rousseau?"

Hunter wasn't buying it. "Yes, Irena Rousseau. You remember Irena. You gave Caravaggio almost half of Final Care as an incentive—along with the damaging evidence you told him about—evidence he refers to in the diary he conveniently left in a safe at his house."

Hofmann ogled him incredulously. "Are you crazy? Why would I do that?"

"Why? I'll tell you why. Because she threw you over for your cousin Johannes way back when you both were in mortuary science school in Brussels so many years ago. It seems she discovered what a psycho you really were."

Hofmann snorted his disgust at this. "You really have this wrong. She did not throw me over, as you say. I was the one. I told her I wanted to see other people, but she was intent on keeping me all to herself. Anyway, what are you talking about, holding her captive and — for what did you say, medical experimentation?"

"It's no good, Willie, we have all the evidence we need against you for your arrest on kidnapping, black-mail, and murder."

Thank god they were able to retrieve everything from my smashed phone.

"You're out of your mind."

"Try this on for size. We have photo and eyewitness evidence of Irena's presence at your house in Sorrento, a house with an underground railroad to the secret research laboratory of Nero Caravaggio at the Institute. We have photo and eyewitness evidence of the complete procedure that went on with Irena in that lab. We have similar evidence of the bogus skin condition that made her think she had to stay there undergoing a false treatment. We have the evidence of Caravaggio's diary implicating you as blackmailing him into conducting all of this on Irena specifically. We have evidence you had your men kidnap Johannes Donckers and his daughter Kat from their hotel room in Sorrento. We have evidence your men tried to kill Ms. Swift and me at the marina. It won't be long, I'm sure, until we also have evidence you arranged the murder of Nero Caravaggio and Eugenio Gallo by sending their car off a cliff."

Hofmann stared at Hunter with a cold malevolent hate.

"Oh, I almost forgot, one more thing. The Miami police have identified the body that was meant to appear to be you and was found on your boat with the phony meth lab. Surprise, it wasn't you. Here you are, alive and well."

Hofmann stepped back, distancing himself from Fidalgo, Hunter, and Genevieve. Hunter realized too late it was a signal. A man with a very lethal machine pistol held steadily on the trio stepped out from behind a curtain to their left. Hofmann stepped forward and expertly removed the weapons carried by Fidalgo and Hunter. Genevieve was unarmed.

"Cover them, Traveler."

Hunter and Genevieve both recognized Traveler as the man who spilled the books at their table in Naples and placed the bug.

Hofmann then walked over to the three paintings and performed a maneuver similar to what Hunter had done in

Caravaggio's office, pressing each in a specific spot. The bookcases along one wall opened up, revealing an inner corridor that would not have been found by the searching officers.

"Follow me." It was an order to both the gunman and to the others.

Hunter and the police had seen the house plans that had been filed when the place was built. The house appeared to occupy a square around a central courtyard. Rather than featuring hallways, each room opened into the next in much the same manner as European palaces used to do.

Surprisingly the plans showed no entry to the central courtyard anywhere. But now, as they walked through the wall in Hofmann's study, rather than finding the courtyard, they came upon a hallway not shown in the plans, which circled the house just behind the walls of the outer rooms. Central to this hallway were additional rooms that, unlike the outer rooms, could be entered from the circling hallway rather than from each other. Presumably the courtyard was central to these rooms.

As Hofmann's gunman marched them along this hallway they came to a second, smaller hallway that appeared to head deeper into the center of the house. At the end of this hallway, Hofmann opened the door and invited them all into an idyllic courtyard open to the sky above, with decorative trees, a manicured lawn, and a gazebo in the center. Two other armed men were already waiting for the group when they entered.

Hunter's concern, intense before, now tripled. He'd thought he might have a slim chance to overpower the single armed man, but now with three of them, that possibility looked remote.

Chapter 66

"McCoy, Commander, Ms. Swift, come over here, I'd like you to see this," Hofmann said, leaving no room for argument, not that Hunter had much choice anyway. They walked up the three steps to the gazebo, where Hofmann sat down while Hunter and the others remained standing.

"Look around and tell me what you see."

Hunter did and noticed large bay windows on three sides of the square. Looking straight at Hofmann again, Hunter said, "I see an asshole and a madman. What do you see?"

Undaunted, Hofmann said, "I see three windows on this inner courtyard world." Then he pointed to each of them. "Three windows that offer me an ideal view of the world within each."

With growing unease, Hunter began to sense what was to come.

Hofmann continued. "And of course, anyone behind one of those windows would be able to see me sitting here and maybe, just maybe, if they strain a little, get a view of the world behind the other two."

Genevieve spoke for the first time. "You really are a monster, and you are insane. You know that don't you?"

Hofmann shrugged. "Perhaps you're right. But what matters now is what's going to happen next." With that he removed a small black remote control unit from his jacket.

He pressed a button and suddenly the windows, which had been clouded over became clear.

Hunter realized the remote must have opened interior blinds covering the double-paned glass. Soon a figure appeared at each window, and they could see each of them was peering out, as if for the first time. It was Irena, Johannes, and Kat, each in their own quarters.

Hunter found the extent of Hofmann's madness staggering. The man had set up the equivalent of three aquariums, except rather than fish in a tank they were people in prison. Even worse, each could see the two other people they loved most in the world, but trapped beyond reach, and they could see the cause of it all sitting blissfully in the garden, enjoying their agony. The look of astonishment and despair on each of their faces as they saw the other two was heartbreaking.

"So," Hunter said, "you have your three prize fish, each in their own bowl, just for your amusement."

"What a wonderful analogy, and surprisingly apt as well. You see, McCoy, I can end their torment any time I want—slowly, of course." He smirked. "By activating a button on my remote, each of those rooms will actually *become* an aquarium."

As the shock of what that meant played across the faces of the three, Willie smiled again. "I see you understand what I mean. Good. It's only fair, you know, given what they've taken from me. And now that the time has come, I'm sorry to say I won't be around to see it—thanks to you. I'll need to depart to take on my fourth identity, one like the others I've already set up with great planning, precision, and care, I might add.

"Now, I'm afraid, I really must go." Then, indicating the man who held the gun on them, Hofmann added, "This man will tie up loose ends and join me for the next identity. He's utterly reliable, McCoy, and he's been with me through the travels of all three identities. In fact I've named

him based on that: Meet Traveler, McCoy. He'll take care
of final preparations and then join me."

Just then a loud noise, sounding like a wall being
broken through, was followed by two of Fidalgo's men
busting through into the courtyard. They must have seen
what was going on, as they advanced with weapons ready.
As the two gunmen who had been waiting in the courtyard
swung their weapons toward the intruders, the two officers
fired, killing both of them. But before the officers could
turn on the third gunman, the one Hofmann had called
Traveler, pivoted quickly and with two short bursts cut
them both down. Just as quickly he spun back to cover
Hunter, Genevieve, and Fidalgo before they could react.

"Time to go," Traveler said to Hofmann, holding his
weapon steady on the three.

The gazebo where they'd been standing was about twenty
feet in diameter with benches placed so Hofmann could see
all three windows clearly. Hunter was unprepared for what
happened next. Hofmann pushed a button on his remote, and
the wooden floor of the gazebo slid back, revealing a hinged
round metal trapdoor beneath, secured with a locked lever.
Hofmann unlatched the lever, and using considerable effort,
lifted the door open. It was slightly larger than a manhole
cover but appeared to be just as heavy. Hunter and Genevieve
were far enough away that they couldn't see down into the
opening.

With that, Hofmann gave Hunter a shark-like grin and
pushed a button on the remote. The effect was
instantaneous. He could see the expressions on Kat,
Johannes, and Irena as they gasped in response to what
must have been the sight of water rushing into their rooms.

With horror, Genevieve, Fidalgo and Hunter saw the
water beginning to pool around the feet of the three
captives behind the glass. The madman had actually done
it. He was going to drown them. Hunter knew he didn't
have much time. There had to be a way.

Traveler unhooked a canvas pouch he'd worn attached to his waist and tossed it to Hunter, who caught it. "You three," Traveler said, "step off the gazebo and back up ten feet." With little choice, as Traveler's machine pistol never wavered, they did as they were told. Hunter wondered about the pouch—but not for long.

"That pouch contains two pounds of C-4 explosive with a blasting cap controlled by our remote here." Traveler gestured toward the one Hofmann was still holding. "One press of the button and boom. Unless you do exactly as we say, that's what will happen."

"You know what to do; meet me later," Hofmann told Traveler. With that, he handed Traveler the remote, folded his arms, stepped over the opening, and dropped through the floor of the gazebo, disappearing from site.

A second crashing noise told them more officers were on the way. As Traveler briefly glanced toward the noise, Fidalgo rushed him, but never had a chance. Without even turning toward the man, Traveler shot him.

The next few seconds happened in slow motion for Hunter. His old friend in times of peril for those he loved kicked in. The rapid response movements of Traveler slowed down to a crawl in Hunter's mind. He closed the distance between them before Traveler could bring his weapon around. He chopped down on the assassin's wrist and heard the bone break. Astonishingly, the killer instantly produced a knife with his other hand and slashed at Hunter, who was easily able to step back out of range. The two men started circling each other but the advantage was to Hunter who saw the other man's moves almost before he made them. On the next thrust Hunter smashed down on the knife-wielding wrist and again broke bones. Grabbing the dropped knife, Hunter drove it into the killer's neck stifling his scream by severing the carotid artery and ending the threat.

Hunter swiveled toward the windows. The Donckers' plight was worse than he'd feared. The rooms were filling with water, and each of them was now standing in two feet of it as the level steadily continued to rise.

He grabbed the remote from Traveler's body and identified the button for the C-4. He raced to the gazebo. Through the opening in the floor he saw what looked like a long laundry shoot, a tube much like old-time fire escapes he remembered seeing at an orphanage when he was a kid in Marquette. Knowing he had to get the hostages out of their rapidly filling rooms, he took the bag of C-4, tossed it in the tube after Hofmann, closed the iron cover and locked it, waited thirty seconds, and pressed the button. A tremendous explosion erupted below. The iron cover bounced but held.

Hunter tried the other buttons on the remote, searching for the one that controlled the water. Nothing happened. The blinds stayed open, the water kept rising. Apparently once activated, the torture couldn't be stopped. Summoning two officers who'd just showed up, Hunter yelled, "You've got to shoot out those windows, but be careful of the people inside."

Then he found Fidalgo's radio and called Commander Talbot, telling him to get his men in from the perimeter woods.

He beckoned to Genevieve. "Come on, we'll see if we can get to the rooms from the inside." They ran back through the door they'd used to enter the courtyard and through the hallway to where they estimated the rooms with the windows were. Along the way they met Talbot.

"Commander," Hunter said, out of breath, "the three captives are in separate rooms filling with water right now. Your men, when they get here, have to get them out."

"We're on it."

Hunter could see him giving orders through his radio while he and Genevieve desperately looked for an opening to the rooms.

"There has to be an entrance," Genevieve said. "If he was planning to keep them for his own amusement, there has to be a way to get food and supplies in."

"You're right, but it may not be as obvious as a door. Look for anything that could do the job."

One of the National Guardsmen ran up to Hunter. "The glass is bulletproof. We can't shatter it, even at point blank range. The water is waist-deep now. We've got to find another way in."

"Hunter, look, overhead," Genevieve cried.

He and the guardsman did and saw a circular pipe painted the same gray color as the ceiling. They'd almost missed it. It was the size of an air-conditioning duct, which it might actually be. They followed it and saw it branched off at the points where they estimated the three rooms to be.

Hunter told the guardsman to find something they could use to climb up to and cut into the pipe.

The man was back in three minutes with two comrades and a table they could stand on. They quickly got on it and cut through the ductwork with their Ka-Bar tactical knives. The men were all too large to crawl into it, so they hoisted Genevieve up inside.

Genevieve immediately saw a screen grate and light coming from inside one of the rooms. Crawling forward, she reached the grate and pushed hard. It fell into the room. She looked in and saw Kat with water around her chest.

"Kat, up here."

Kat twisted her head and looked up. "Genevieve? Is that you?"

"Yeah. We're going to get you out of here. Come over this way."

The guardsmen miraculously produced a rope.

"Feed it through to Kat and tell her to fasten it under her shoulders so we can pull her up," Hunter called.

Aided by the men behind her, Genevieve hauled on the rope, and when Kat was able to reach the edge of the duct, helped her clamber inside. The two women crawled out to the opening they'd cut in the ductwork.

Kat dropped down on the table and then the floor, gasping. "We've got to get my mom and dad out," she pleaded. "We have to start with her. She's shorter and the water will get to her faster."

The guardsmen moved the table to the duct they assumed was leading to Irena's room and went to work repeating the same procedure of cutting-in and sending Genevieve up first. When they got Irena out she was close to panic.

"Mom," Kat cried as she wrapped her mother in a giant hug.

"Oh my darling daughter," cried Irena as both women wept and hugged.

When they went back after Johannes, the water had already reached his head. By the time they got the rope under him it was over his head and the man was drowning. Once he was out and on the floor, Hunter went to work on him with CPR. As he was compressing the chest and trying to clear the airway, Kat and Irena gazed on with dread. Hunter kept it up, and within a minute Johannes coughed up water and gasped for breath. He kept coughing and his eyes popped open, darting around in panic. Then Irena put her head down to his and met his eyes.

"Johannes, you're back and we're safe, all three of us."

Hunter and Genevieve embraced. "Nice work, Genevieve," he said, "That took a lot of guts."

"Oh sure, now you're saying I'm fat."

Chapter 67

HUNTER, GENEVIEVE, COMMANDER LIMA, and Commander Talbot were in the waiting room in the Hospital Cruz de Carvalho, where Commander Fidalgo was currently in surgery for the gunshot wound suffered at the hands of Traveler. They'd left Kat, Johannes and Irena to a joyous family reunion at the Funchal Old Town Cottages where they'd checked in with the idea of spending one night on the island and then leaving the next day for Brussels and home. Kat was in one cottage and her parents in one next door.

"Whoa, everyone, quiet, I can't hear." Commander Talbot had just taken a phone call. His expression started out with appropriate serious professional concern, then, as he continued to listen, began to soften, and finally became unmistakable chuckles. The others had no idea what he was hearing. After several minutes of "you've got to be kidding," "unbelievable," "that had to be some sight." and "Wow, I wish I'd been there to see that," he hung up.

"Commander?" Hunter asked.

Commander Talbot began to laugh aloud, unable to stop himself. "I'm sorry, give me a minute and I'll tell you." He took a moment to compose himself.

Hunter waved an impatient hand.

"Okay, here's what we know. When Willie dropped through the floor in the gazebo, you have to remember we were almost at the highest point on the island. It seems he dropped into an escape chute and literally slid all the way down the mountain to the coast. Toward the end, the chute begins to level off so a person sliding down it would have a chance to slow down and stop gently at the bottom. The opening at the bottom was hidden from view by long grass and was impossible to distinguish from the field surrounding it. Pretty clever really, and since it was buried no one knew it was there.

"Now it seems this camouflaged opening was near a small harbor populated by commercial fishing boats, and the fishing fleet had just returned with the day's catch and were processing it on their individual boats tied up at the docks.

"Now here's where it gets interesting, McCoy. When you dropped the C-4 into the tube and sealed the iron hatch, you didn't know it, but you'd basically loaded a cannon. And when you pushed the button to detonate the C-4, you fired it."

Hunter and the others were beginning to get the idea of what the commander had been hearing. A slow grin began to crease his face.

"With the iron hatch sealed at the gazebo end and with the tube open at the lower end, Willie—the unwilling human cannonball—was subject to an explosive force that reduced him to tiny bits and pieces that shot out the end of the barrel at supersonic speed."

"Eeeuu, I think I know where you're going with this," Genevieve said. "The fishing fleet, right?"

"Right," confirmed the commander. "One boat captain described it as raining multicolored snow. Another said he thought the explosion was his own boat's motor and the red goo dripping off his wheelhouse windows was exploded fish guts. A third found a finger stuck to the top of an octopus he'd pulled in that was lying on the deck."

They were all silent for a moment contemplating this.

"You know what this means, commander?" asked Hunter, rolling the index finger of both hands to get the man ready for the pun to come.

"What?"

"The griffin symbol he adopted with the head and wings of an eagle, the body of a lion, and the tail of a shark was appropriate."

"How's that?"

"Well, his spectacular finish featured the explosive roar of a lion, followed by his flying like an eagle and becoming bait for the sharks. Not exactly what he had in mind."

Everyone groaned in unison.

The surgeon who'd worked on Commander Fidalgo chose that moment to come out and tell the small group how things had gone in surgery.

"Commander Fidalgo was lucky; the bullet punctured his left lung but missed the heart and any major vessels. We've got a chest tube in and he's sedated, but he'll be all right and should make a full recovery."

BACK AT THE COTTAGES, HUNTER and Genevieve found the Donckers family still catching up with each other. They all agreed to meet for dinner later, and Hunter and Genevieve went to their room at the Albergaria Catedral hotel in the meantime.

"I'm going to call Eduard and tell him how this came out. I also want him to look into something else altogether."

Genevieve nodded, believing she understood what he had in mind.

Hunter made the call and told Eduard how his information was vital to finding the underlying cause of a huge conspiracy. "Always happy to help, Hunter. It might help my yearly bonus if you let the director know how valuable I am as well."

"Have no fear, I've already called him and sung your praises."

"Thanks, Hunter." The man sounded truly appreciative.

"Now, I have one more request for you."

"Ah ha. Here it comes. I knew there'd be a catch," he said good-naturedly.

"Would you find out what you can on the killing of the mayor of Cologne in his home years ago? I'm particularly interested in whether they found any credible evidence his death was a robbery gone bad or if the man had any history of abusing young women or girls. I also want to know where the case stands today and are there any credible suspects."

"That should be easy. Give me a little time and I'll get back to you."

Eduard returned the call within the hour and talked for a full fifteen minutes, with very few interruptions. When he was done, Hunter thanked him and hung up.

"Well?" asked Genevieve. "What do we know?"

"Let's get cleaned up. I'll tell you at dinner, along with the entire Donckers family. But first I have another phone call to make. One I've been putting off because of the unrelenting pace of this 'find-and-correct' operation."

He speed-dialed his cell phone. "Hi, Dad, it's Hunter."

"Hunter. Where have you been, son? Are you okay?"

"I'm fine. It's been some case, but it's almost over now. I should be home with you in Anue in a week or so and I'll tell you all about it."

"That's great. Henry and I've been wondering how you were and when we'd hear from you."

"Has Henry been checking up on you?"

"Good choice of words, son—checking up on me. That's exactly what he's been doing. He even managed to drag me to see Dr. Lepisto in Marquette."

"Good for him. What'd the doctor say?"

"I assume you mean my supposed little memory lapses."

"Yup. What did he say?"

"He said I'm okay, just a little depressed, and we're working on that. I don't have that other thing, you know, Alzheimer's or whatever; at least not yet."

"Dad?"

"Yeah."

"When I get home, we'll work on that depression thing together."

"Right, son. I'm feeling better already."

Chapter 68

RIGHT NOW THE THREE OF THEM, along with Hunter and Genevieve, were seated around a table on Kat's deck overlooking the harbor lined with cruise ships below.

The weather was perfect, the sun had set hours ago, and the brightly lighted cruise ships in the dark harbor provided a magic backdrop. They were sharing a bottle of the island's famous Madeira wine when Hunter decided it was time to tell them about his phone call from Eduard.

"Johannes, I have some news regarding the possibility of extradition to Germany."

Kat immediately put her glass down. "What is it? They can't do it, can they?"

"Let me tell you what I learned from my Interpol contact in Lyon. His name is Eduard Gautier, and he's been supplying us with virtually all the information we've been using to track down Hofmann and find Irena. He's a good man and I trust him completely."

"Tell us, Hunter, what did you learn?" asked Johannes.

"As you know, your sister Lisa's statement that the mayor was attacking her and you'd come to her rescue was treated as a lie by the authorities. The mayor's family said you'd actually killed him during a robbery in which you stole his gold watch and his wallet. You then fled Germany for Belgium and started a new life."

"Believe me, the robbery story was a complete fabrication," said Johannes. "It happened exactly as I told you. The man was ripping off her blouse and forcing her onto the bed when I hit him. The story about the missing watch and wallet must have come from the mayor's family."

"Exactly," agreed Hunter. "You're going to like what Eduard was able to uncover by going through police records. It seems that shortly after the attack on your sister and your coming to her aid, two other young women came forward to say the mayor had also attacked them.

"Your sister didn't know these two girls, nor did she ever learn they'd basically corroborated her story about the mayor's behavior. It was all kept very quiet. When a third girl came forward, the authorities finally began to take the reports seriously. They got a search warrant and found the mayor's watch and wallet in the widow's closet, hidden in a shoebox. The shoebox contained other effects of the mayor's and several newspaper stories about his death, as well as an obituary. Upon questioning, the widow admitted she'd made up the story about the robbery to protect the family's name. Ironically, Willie never had any grounds for his blackmail."

KAT PACED THE BALCONY. "NOW THEY have to believe Dad's version of the events. What about the extradition?"

Hunter shook his head. "Eduard said the authorities would still like to interview Johannes—or Gunter, as they know him—but under the circumstances have no intention of seeking extradition. While the case is still officially open, it's really closed."

Irena rose and gave Hunter a big hug. "Thank you, Hunter. We've been living under that threat for so long, I can hardly believe it's over."

They all expressed relief at the findings and toasted Eduard Gautier for his dedication and thoroughness on their behalf. Still, there was one very dark cloud hanging over their celebration, the elephant in the room, really. Kat finally brought it up.

"What can we do about the jewel robberies, Hunter?" she asked.

"Under the circumstances, the authorities should cut them a break, don't you think, Hunter?" Genevieve asked.

"I've been thinking about that," Hunter said, turning to Kat and Johannes. "As I told you earlier, you need to hire a good attorney and turn everything over to him—all the evidence you carefully had notarized and stored away. When the enormity of the crime perpetrated by Willie Hofmann makes the papers, the public sympathy for your family will be enormous. Any prosecutor will have an uphill battle trying to make you out to be villains. I think you're going to be all right in that regard."

"So that's it then," Genevieve said. "Everything's been resolved."

"Not quite," Hunter said, standing and walking to the ledge overlooking the harbor below. "I read through the rest of Caravaggio's notebooks and got the answer to a question that's been bothering me."

Taking Irena's hand and looking directly at her, Hunter continued. "Irena, you never had a stroke, not a first one, or a second one. Instead, you were personally selected by Willie Hofmann to be a donor. Somewhere you were repeatedly given an injection of a paralytic that mimicked a stroke. Then to make you think you were recovering from it, they simply decreased the dose when it suited them. Of course the whole toxic skin thing was a hoax as well."

Shocked at this new revelation, Irena said, "I didn't have a stroke?"

"No, you didn't," Hunter said. "Caravaggio explained it all in his notes."

Then he addressed Johannes. "After Irena's supposed fatal stroke, Caravaggio heavily sedated her, so you'd believe she was dead when you saw her. There was no reason for you not to believe it. The cremains sent to you were phony. It was all a scam."

Johannes shook his head and said, "The depravity of the man was unbelievable."

Turning to Irena, Hunter continued. "And there were three recipients."

Irena blanched. "Three?"

"Yes. The first was Kris Hanson, who I told you about earlier. She actually did have a head injury while on vacation in Capri, and while Gallo was repairing the damage he secretly inserted the release tubes into her brain. Like you, she was told piano playing was therapy. They explained that her sudden ability to play well was a chance byproduct of her head injury. She died later and the pathologist who did the autopsy found the release tubes that Mrs. Hanson's doctors said had somehow been surgically implanted.

It seems the pathologist was a very curious fellow and with the help of some other experts determined that the real cause of death was due to hemorrhaging triggered by a specific component of the *Enhancement II* released from the tubes. This component, the artificially reawakened cloned glial cells taken from your brain, eventually changed their beneficial role of directing nerve growth to the more lethal activity of seeking and knifing through nearby blood vessels."

"The poor woman," sighed Irena in sympathy.

"So what about Charlie Lahti?" Genevieve asked, "The man whose missing body got you started in all this."

"Ah, yes. Charlie Lahti. He was the only person involved in this whole sad story who actually did have a stroke. Caravaggio and Gallo wanted to see if their technique would work in a truly stroked patient as well as it did in Kris Hanson. They used a similar scam with Charlie as they did with you, Irena. They anesthetized him ostensibly to relax him during an MRI but really performed brain surgery and inserted the release tubes without his or his wife's knowledge."

"Did he learn the piano too?" asked Johannes.

"No, no," Hunter continued. "He was beginning to learn juggling. The donor was his physical therapist, Tony Pompa, an expert amateur juggler. Let me explain. Charlie thought his attempts to juggle using the electrodes was just therapy. His wife, Jenny, said he'd become very proficient at it. According to Caravaggio's notes, they removed a small amount of Pompa's brain tissue to make the *Enhancement II* cocktail for Charlie Lahti's release tubes. Then later, Pompa, who was an amateur pianist, actually agreed to have release tubes inserted in his brain as a way to become an expert pianist without all the hard work. The *Enhancement II* cocktail in his release tubes contained an extract from your brain, Irena. It was taken while you were sedated for an MRI at the Imaging center."

"Yes. I remember. Willie told me that on the yacht."

Hunter nodded. "Willie paid Pompa handsomely to cooperate. Your last session in the lab was actually the first attempt by Pompa to receive your piano skills. Then, when everything started to unravel, Willie apparently had him killed to keep him quiet. Mariucci's men found his body in his apartment."

"So," Kat said, "Charlie Lahti was the only one who actually had an initial stroke followed by a second stroke that killed him."

"Yes."

"Anything else, Hunter?" Kat asked, sure it was now all over.

"There is one thing. I'm going to contact the real Dr. Phillippi, the man who would have been framed for all of this and who was completely innocent. I'm going to suggest to the Institute's board of directors—if they have one—that they owe a considerable debt to him for his help in uncovering the unspeakable evil of Caravaggio and Gallo. Who knows, he might even get a raise and finally take that vacation he wanted.

"Oh, and there is one more thing," Hunter continued, as he got up and went out to the rental car. Confused, everyone waited for him to return. When he did, the look of astonishment and joy that lit up Genevieve's face when he handed her her laptop computer, was priceless.

"They found it in Griffin's study and saw your name on it."

Genevieve quickly opened it and found her work—all there and intact.

She wrapped her arms around Hunter and kissed him long and hard.

Later, the five of them stared at the lights in the harbor, each in their own way quietly thankful the long ordeal was finally over.

Chapter 69

One week later—Venice, Florida

HUNTER AND GENEVIEVE ARRIVED IN TAMPA after a long flight that had intermediate stops in Lisbon and Philadelphia. There were no direct flights from Madeira to the States. Hunter picked up a rental and they'd driven straight to Jenny Lahti's house on the island in Venice. He'd called ahead of time to tell her they'd be coming and that he'd give her a complete report.

She'd said two things that Hunter thought were perfect. One, she'd cook them dinner and they could tell her all about it; and second he and Genevieve could then drive to a second home she owned on Casey Key on the Gulf of Mexico, where they could relax and vacation as long as they liked.

Hunter introduced Genevieve and told Jenny how important she'd been to solving the puzzle of what happened to Charlie. Over the next two hours they gave her the entire story. Jenny, who'd been sitting throughout the telling, got up and walked to the west window overlooking the Gulf and quietly stared out over the blue water for several minutes. Then she spoke.

"I can hardly believe it. Charlie dying was a tragedy to me, and when you found him and brought him back so I could give him a proper burial, I thought the simple mix-up explained it all and that was the end of it—all there was to the story.

"But you, Hunter, you suspected more and how right you were. That poor family and the suffering they endured because of that awful man—those awful men, really. I'm so happy that out of the death of Charlie, you were able to do so much good and stop so much evil. And thank you, my dear, for your intellectual and heroic contribution to solving the puzzle."

"Thank you, Jenny," Genevieve echoed. "I'm only happy to have been able to help."

After they left, and Hunter pocketed the more-than-generous check Jenny wrote out for him, he programmed the rental's GPS for the address on Casey Key. Within an hour they were there.

The moonlight on the Gulf of Mexico when they stepped out onto the balcony off the master bedroom of Jenny's mega-mansion, surrounded by pines, palms, and sea grapes on three sides and no visible neighbors, was spectacular. It was a balmy eighty-four degrees, and they were naked.

She'd reached down and found the long flight hadn't totally exhausted Hunter after all. It didn't take long after that before the moonlit view took second place to a more urgent call to arms, as it were.

Hunter swept her up and they retreated back to the bed. Finally, with the soft blue moonlight playing over their slowly moving bodies, the increasing intensity of the surf as the wind came up proved no match for the intensity of their lovemaking.

EARLY IN THE EVENING THE NEXT DAY, they lounged on beach chairs with a small collapsible table between them that held Genevieve's white wine and Hunter's perfect Canadian Club Manhattan on the rocks with a twist. The sun was an hour from setting, and they were both eagerly awaiting the famous "green flash" the locals had told them was occasionally seen on nights when the sunset was perfect—like tonight.

They both sat back and silently watched the sun drop even lower. Unspoken between them but on both of their minds was, "Where do we go from here?" Hunter's life was in Charlottesville at the medical school. Genevieve's was in Paris at the National Library. Still, the bond between them, strong after the previous summer's search for the lost book, had now amped up to a level they both knew couldn't continue to be ignored.

Genevieve touched his arm. "You know we're going to have to find a way to work this out, Hunter."

Knowing exactly what she meant, he answered, "Yes, and we will."

Neither spoke for the next several minutes as the sun finally disappeared below the watery horizon, accompanied by an unmistakable brilliant green flash both silently read as a sign.

"There it is," Hunter said, "the symbol we've been waiting for—Green for 'Go.'"

Acknowledgements

Writing is paradoxically both hard work and great enjoyment. One of the things that make it so enjoyable is the willingness of others to lend their expertise. I particularly want to thank Carol Gaskin of Editorial Alchemy for her invaluable aid in editing Final Care. As always, her thoughts and suggestions were spot on. Many thanks also go to my readers, Monica Hoover, Carol Kvarnberg, and Barb Stratton. I'd also like to thank Jack Wetherson for line-editing the manuscript, James "Eric" Swope, for his advice on the funeral business, my many friends at the Sarasota Author's Connection, and my invaluable in-house muse and editor, my wife, Pauline.

Also By Don Stratton

A famous historian is brutally murdered with a samurai sword on Florida's Casey Key and Hunter McCoy's dad is arrested for the crime. Searching for the truth, Hunter is drawn deeper into an increasingly elaborate web of deceit.

During WWII, Dr. Li Qiang Chen, a Chinese country doctor is believed to have discovered an extraordinary medicine capable of preventing the development of diabetes.

When Hunter becomes convinced that finding the long dead doctor's missing research notebook is the key to clearing his dad of the murder charge, he teams up with Billie Chen, Dr. Chen's great-granddaughter.

Almost immediately, Hunter finds himself enmeshed in a continuing series of lies and misdirection that only deepens his dad's apparent guilt in the eyes of the law and potentially threatens everything Hunter holds dear.

Available in paperback and Kindle from Amazon.com

Also By Don Stratton

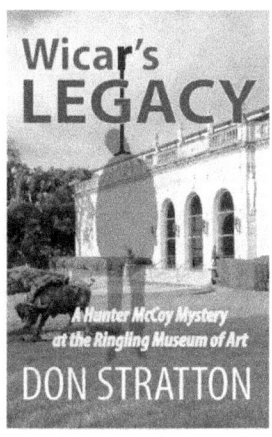

*A Destitute Old Man Leaves a Valuable Painting in a
Gallery at the Ringling Museum of Art and Triggers a
Countdown to Disaster*

A cryptic note left with the painting links it to Genevieve Swift, a
visiting curator from the Louvre, and her father, a professor of
history at Cambridge . . .

In Gallery 3 something unknown is eating the paint on the face of a
small lion in one of the museum's sixteenth-century paintings . . .

A young girl who touches the painting becomes deathly sick . . .

Professor Hunter McCoy investigates the strange events and
uncovers a link to a secretive and deadly group called the Legacy.
As he peels away layer after layer of the Legacy's secrets, McCoy
realizes that a countdown has already begun—a countdown that if
unchecked, could cost countless lives and ruin the Ringling
Museum of Art itself.

Available in paperback and Kindle from Amazon.com

Also By Don Stratton

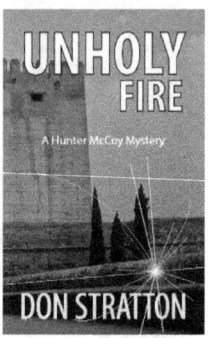

Young scientists scheduled to begin work at the Large Hadron Collider near Geneva are being systematically murdered . . .

Hunter McCoy discovers that their deaths are somehow linked to his search for a lost book—a book written by a Spanish physician who was burned at the stake by the Inquisition in the sixteenth century . . .

A shadowy group with ties to high-energy particle physics has its own compelling and deadly reasons to find the book first . . .

McCoy, trying to stay one step ahead of ruthless unknown adversaries is running out of time as his partner, a beautiful French archivist, is set to become the next victim—unwittingly unleashing a cataclysmic international disaster.

Available in paperback and Kindle from Amazon.com and most major ebook distributors

About The Author

Don Stratton is a biomedical scientist born and raised in Michigan's Upper Peninsula. He was a professor of physiology for many years at Drake University. His research on blood vessel physiology was reported in over thirty-five scientific publications and his textbook Neurophysiology was published by McGraw Hill. Don was granted an endowed chair and named Ellis and Nelle Levitt Distinguished Professor of Physiology and Biology. He now lives as professor emeritus in Venice, Florida with his wife Pauline and dog Gracie where he's writing his next mystery novel.